HeavenSteel

Constantinos T. Hasapis

ISBN 978-0-6152-1517-4

Dedication

For the glory of God through whom all things are possible, the US armed forces, who sacrifice so much and ask for so little, my family who asked "What took so bloody long!", the crazed Scotsman Eddie who designed the cover and provided so much valuable criticism, Jeff who battled alongside me in those dark days of our freshman year and suffered through some terrible Steeler seasons with me and most of all, Michelle, who for some strange reason decided some guy named Haas was her soulmate.

Prologue

"BRIGANDS!!!"

A dozen heads looked up at once from their work in the fields. A dozen pairs of eyes saw the same thing. Prairie dust from many riders approaching from over the horizon. Riders approaching from the wrong direction. Everyone ran at once to the small stone fortress, little more than a collection of large rocks, carrying their tools with them and waving anyone in eyeshot to follow. All across the world, the same scene repeated itself thousands of times every day as civilization teetered on the edge of darkness in the aftermath of the Cataclysmic War.

Men, women and children, young and old, hale and unhealthy, all would band together as best they could. The men would fight from behind the cover their small position provided along with some of the older boys and even some of the women would hurl rocks at the attackers. Everyone else would tend to the wounded and protect the small painfully accumulated stores that would be essential for survival after the bandits had gone. All had a role to play if this small community was to survive yet another bandit raid. The thatched roofed huts would probably burn and most of the fields would be trampled but if the farmers held off the assault, civilization would have a chance to take further root. At least until the next raid.

The village elder looked around to make sure all of his countrymen were within the palisade. Then he saw one person walking *toward* the bridge over the Densk River. Directly into the path of the oncoming brigands.

"Gaking!!!" He shouted. "What in Heaven's name are you doing?! Come here at once!"

"Papa!" A young boy shrieked, hearing his father's name. He slipped out of the elder's grasp and ran across the evacuated field, somehow managing to avoid tripping over the tilled earth.

When he heard the dreaded brigands call, Gaking felt all of his forty-four years catch up to him all at once. He was tired. Very tired. Tired of constantly slaving to meager crops, tired of working to the edge of his strength to keep starvation at arm's length and tired of wondering, every day if he would see another sunrise. Most of all, he was tired of banditry and watching everything he and his fellow villagers had worked to create so senselessly destroyed. Now he was going to do something to change it. Or, he thought, at least I won't have to watch it all destroyed again.

He stopped as his son ran up to him. "Go back and take care of your mother and sisters, boy." Gaking said sternly.

The boy stopped in his tracks and looked up at his father through tear filled eyes. "But Papa..."

"Now!"

The boy threw himself around Gaking in a fierce hug that belied his small size. "Will you come back to us?", he sobbed.

Gaking softened just for a second and looked around at the village, the defensive position its future depended on and then the bandits who were getting closer. He ruffled his son's sandy hair.

"It is as God wills it." he concluded. "Now, be a good boy and take care of your mother and sisters."

The boy nodded and ran back to the villagers.

Gaking nodded in return and walked to the bridge over the river, mentally steeling himself for battle. He spun his hoe so that the sharpened handle pointed in the direction of the enemy. It was a time in history when everything doubled as a weapon. He dispassionately decided to use the stouter staff stuck into the ground next to bridge instead. Gaking pulled it out of the ground and grinned wickedly when he saw its sharp point. It was here for just such an occasion.

Then he stepped onto the small bridge.

It was not much of a bridge but it connected the village to other villages further south and some trade resulted. They did not speak the same language but seemed friendly enough and eager to trade for things they did not have. Unfortunately the bandits used the bridge to cross the river to raid and pillage. Gaking spat in disgust realizing that he could understand most of what the raiders shouted to each other the last time they destroyed his home.

The specks in the distance swelled up to the size of men quickly. There were about thirty of them and their leader rode in the front, leading the charge. He saw Gaking alone on the bridge and strung his bow and notched an arrow in one fluid motion. His horse rode on even without his master holding the reins. It was a well trained animal, the absurd and irrelevant thought rocketed through Gaking's mind.

Gaking could see the brigand's eyes narrow as he aimed. Gaking slowly pointed the staff in his enemy's direction in what only could be a challenge.

The bandits pulled up and slowed to a halt. The leader, with a bemused look on his face, lowered his bow. He was young and arrogant but to Gaking, everyone these days looked young and arrogant. This one, even more so. Especially since he had come to destroy the village.

He remained motionless for a moment, staring at Gaking waiting to see if this foolish man would run or beg for his life. The bandit chief's leather armor with bits of metal sewn in was more than enough protection against an angry farmer on a bridge.

Gaking responded by lowering himself into a crouch, the point of the staff never wavering. He ignored the click in his knee and covered for it with a fierce grunt.

The brigands laughed and their leader took off his floppy hat and handed it off to someone on his right and gave his bow to another one of his men to his left. A short curved sword appeared almost instantly from out of a saddle scabbard. He pointed it at Gaking and said something in his own language. The others laughed again and without preamble, the bandit charged up onto the bridge, his horse's hooves thudding loudly.

Gaking stepped on the back of his staff like he had been trained half a lifetime ago when he had answered the King of Barcova's call to his loyal levy for battle. The brigand charged him head on and swung his sword over and down to dispatch this peasant who had dared to fight him.

Only he wasn't there.

The wily villager stepped to the left and brought up the back of his staff, hitting the surprised attacker right in the chest. The unexpected blow also took the bandit out of his saddle. He hit the bridge planks shoulder first but before the shock could even register, Gaking reversed the staff and brought it down hard, stabbing down through the breast bone with a sharp crack. Bright red blood exploded out of him as Gaking yanked the weapon out with a barbarian yell.

The now leaderless brigands stared for a second unable to believe their leader had been killed by what they thought was a simple, foolish farmer. He was more than he seemed. He was also alone and horribly outnumbered.

En masse, the rest of the bandits swarmed onto the bridge, an angry horde of horse riding demons swinging swords and spears bearing down on one man. Snarling, Gaking charged them, reason drowned in bloodlust.

He ran straight into one horse and swung at its rider as he swung his sword at Gaking. The staff shattered but it blocked the blow. The momentum of the impact however took Gaking, the bandit and the bandit's horse through the railing and right into the river a few feet below.

The whole world turned into a kaleidoscope of spinning colors, green and tan grass, blue sky, brown earth. Gaking could hear the bandits shouting and the horse's terrified shrieks with astounding clarity as he fell toward the river, almost able to sort out individual voices.

Then it was abruptly cut off as he impacted the river and the water closed in on him. Gaking somehow found purchase on the muddy bottom and managed to slog to the bank. His angry enemy exploded out of the water and swung wildly at Gaking but missed as the farmer climbed hurriedly out onto dry land. He wanted to thank God for directing him to the right bank but did not have the time or breath as his lungs threatened to explode. And there were brigands on the bridge and others now on the same riverbank as he. He felt one arrow fly past his head and another sprouted in the spot his foot had been a half second earlier. Gaking ran, ignoring the pain and propelled on by fear. At least he had the sense to run away from the village and pull the bandits after him, he thought. The problem was though a man on foot was not going to outrun thirty or so mounted thieves.

Less one, he thought, a savage grin spreading across his face as he turned to face down the attackers with the only weapon he had left: his fists.

The raiders were not feeling chivalrous. The only reason they had not continued to try to cut the unexpectedly dangerous Gaking down from a distance with arrows, was the fact several of their own were in the way seeking to ride him down themselves.

Then he heard a noise behind him. Not just any noise though. It was the distinctive sound of metal hitting dirt and rock. At first, Gaking thought one of the brigands had managed to get behind him. The part of his mind that never slept, the soldier's part that had stood guard for more than twenty years, told him there was no shadow so it was not an attacker. Still, Gaking was stunned to see a sword there. A good sword, that part of his mind commented as his hand closed on its hilt. Large but surprisingly light. The sun glinted off the sharpest edge he had ever seen. And that was great praise from someone experienced in sharpening a great many things!

Gaking turned and swung his new sword with a strength he did not know he had just as a brigand swung from horseback at him. Gaking's sword not only blocked the blow, but shattered the enemy's blade! And unhorsed the bandit. Or partially. The panicked horse bolted out into the steppes, dragging his rider who had only one foot in a stirrup.

A meaty chop saw another bandit's sword arm fall to the ground and the eyes of a third opened twice their size as this mysterious blade clove his skull in. Gaking nearly lost his grip on the sword with that over hand shot but he remained on balance just as three arrows came for his eyes.

One clipped his ear and the other punched into the bandit still falling out of his saddle but the third was going to hit Gaking right in the throat.

Only it did not.

Later, Gaking would swear on many, many holy relics that the sword moved of its own accord and blocked the deadly shaft. The bandits saw this and decided enough was enough. This raid was now a disaster. They retreated back toward the bridge and suddenly found themselves under attack from outraged villagers. Thrown rocks, scythes and pitch forks do not make the most formidable weapons but the brigands, now panicked and leaderless, could not stand up to the fury behind the assault.

They did not even try to strike back. The bandits broke and rode straight for the bridge and the safety of the other side of the river. They were too fast for the howling mob to catch but two more still fell, dying at the hands of those they had terrorized for so long.

Gaking was on his knees holding his ear and the sword that had appeared from literally nowhere. His family was all ready around him, starting to bandage his ear. His countrymen gathered around him a bit more slowly, looking at him and his new weapon.

"Where did that come from?" The village elder finally asked.

Gaking stood up slowly and shrugged. "I don't know."

"Did you find it out there?" The older man pointed out into the flatlands.

"I found it out there." Gaking said softly, "But I don't think it came from out there. I think it came from Somewhere else." He pointed to the sky.

The crowd gasped almost as one and a few hurriedly crossed themselves. More than a few looked to the heavens.

The village elder stepped forward hesitantly. "May I see it?"

Gaking thought about it for a second and then handed it over hilt first.

"The workmanship is unlike anything I have ever seen." One old soldier said to another. "And still sharp! I do not think a man could make something like this! This is truly great!"

He gave Gaking his blade back and Gaking staggered back to his home, his children wife holding him up. The villagers cheered and chanted his name as he stumbled through his door. Many would bring food and others stopped for a closer look at the blade and the tale of what happened began to spread over the land. Sombody found a couple of nails and the wondrous blade was hung up on Gaking's wall.

"A sword has to have a name.", yet another visitor said. "What will you name it?"

"I will name it for what it is and for the place from which it was sent." Gaking said. "I will call it HeavenSteel".

"A good name." The village priest said. "You must keep it in your family. One day, it may be needed to fight great evil."

Gaking nodded as he sat down. "Yes, one day it will be my son's, and then his son and his son after that. It will always be here, as God wills."

Everyone in the hut cheered.

Gaking was a man of few words, especially after fighting a battle but he would say what needed to be said.

"I am going to rest for an hour or so then go back into the fields. After all, those crops are not going to grow themselves."

Argual
Twin Mountain
Eroik
Talon River
Sea-Faring
Kingdoms
Sevonicus
Torna River
Anker
Mountains
Kielstrock
Northmarch
Barcova
Lans
Northcross
Dunrova
Glossak
Spigiwald
Khaizan
Nyhissia
Kronkus
Lanpha
Blicken River
Drierjan
Chenla
Tornsat
Clotzen
Verrent
Pergus Range
Vostoki
Iphofen
M A S O V I A
Pliken River
Cuxhaven
Regalwood
Frona
Cornsnissh
Rakanic
Keinsen
Barsney
Anelo
Valho
Centola River
Toran City
Toran
Flynein
Asrine
Centola mts.
Rhenia
Kya River
The Transkya
Naur
Herelz
Frontera Range
Theros
Terran
Repris
Saracens
Riverion
Cornsleis
Galeon
Otharnos
Saldis
San Juan
del Sur
N
W
E
S

Chapter 1

It was a bright unusually sunny day in April, the month Spring is about to begin and one hopes Winter is starting to withdraw back into the Far North. The steppe was just thick dark mud covered by melting snow, about two months from turning into the choking dust that tormented travelers crossing the endless prairies. The snow was finally melting loosening, little by little, Winter's frigid, malignant grip on the land, a half year that blanketed everything in white and made the ground as hard as iron.

The midmorning sun rose higher and warmed the earth as best it could. A million tiny rivers and ponds formed as the snow continued to melt and Spring drew just a little closer. In a few weeks, the land would be covered with flowers on a grass carpet that spread out seemingly forever in all directions. The bees, hornets and ants would see to that.

"Spring is not a season!" Densky said aloud to no one. "It is only a truce between Winter and Summer. They divide the year the same way the day is divided at noon."

Densky snickered to himself and patted his horse, Charger, on the side of his sweaty neck. Charger just snorted and continued to walk through the cloud of vapor he had just created. No horse he ever knew was much of a philosopher, he thought. Densky stared down over his large nose at the mud as the horse's hooves sank and studied it for a few seconds as merchants are wont to do at this time of the year.

Corneilus Kejen Densky, who incidentally hated his first name and went by his middle, instead, looked forward to the mud's hardening in order to begin assembling the annual Spring and Summer trade caravans. Every year, he would trade, sell, exchange (some would charge stole...) goods with the Sea-Faring Kingdoms further north and the free nations of Verrent and Nyhissia in the direction of the rising sun. Occasionally Kejen would even venture to, God forbid, Masovia and other places on the bottom of the map and his list of places to visit.

Kejen gauged it would be another month before the caravans went out. Maybe even three weeks if luck smiled on him. The year's first major caravan would set out for Nyhissia and then the capital, Northcross, before heading to Glossak up in the mountains. Business would be good. The gold trade he had become part of would pay off handsome dividends since gold was always in season. The wheat kept in dry storage would be the basis of many good business deals. The Bliben River was starting to overflow with melted snow, effectively delaying large scale farming, so demand, and prices, would be high. Those were most of the thoughts preoccupying the mind of Kejen Densky, who, at the age of twenty-three, was all ready well on his way to becoming a rich man. Of course, there were other thoughts as well.

He closed his eyes and let the horse do the walking. After all, Charger knew the way home probably better than he did. Kejen envisioned what his country would look like in the Spring.

The Northmarch stretched across the northernmost part of the Western world from the mighty Blieben River in the east to the forests of Kielstrock in the west. In between lay countless miles of prairie flowers embedded in the green flatlands that would bronze and tan in the coming Summer months. The north was dominated by the tree covered slopes of the Anker Mountains and to the south; Northmarcher borders not only brushed up on friendly Nyhissia and Verrent but implacably hostile Masovia too.

The task required a lot of imagination even for a well traveled merchant for there was nothing but snow as far as the eye could see. And one had to look over the piled up snow on the side of the road just to see that. Ever the optimist though, Kejen knew rocks and even some plants were starting to poke through Nature's white blanket.

So he decided to look at some of them.

Kejen drew Charger to a sudden stop, and all in one motion, hopped right off and plunged into the first snow bank he saw. Legs churning, he pushed through creating a new path and did not stop until he was about twenty feet off the road standing knee deep in the snowy steppes. Good strong water-proof boots and a sturdy, well made coat kept the cold at bay. One flap of his fur cap had come out from the neck of his coat where it had been securely tucked in but Densky had more important things on his mind. One glove came off and a long arm sank into the frozen moisture, digging, digging, digging until his hand hit the hard ground. Kejen felt around for a bit and found what he was looking for. He stood up and looked at his prize...a clump of moss.

"Look at this!" he shouted, looking at Charger through the canal he just created. "Soon there will be nothing but *green* from one end of the world to the other!"

He shook the moss but the horse just ignored him. Kejen laughed and made his way back to the road. Charger had unearthed some young prairie grass on his own and was cropping it up.

"You found what you were looking for easier than I did." Kejen commented as he climbed into the saddle. "But I enjoyed myself more!"

He spurred the horse on and Charger irritably obeyed. "Don't give me that!" his owner admonished, "You know I have better food waiting for you at home!"

Homeward they trotted, skeletal trees making their appearance, first one at a time and then in groups of two or three before merging into the forest that bordered Kejen's hometown of Sparent. Some of those trees grew over the path, providing welcome shade in warmer times. At the moment, the branches were just creating small shadows even a mouse would have trouble hiding in.

Kejen pulled the other flap of his fur cap out of the coat and shoved it into a pocket. After he ran his hands through his shaggy brown hair, Kejen stood up in the saddle as Charger ambled along and took a good look at the closest branches just over his head. He grinned, spying the first small buds. Another sign of the inevitable march of Spring.

"You would like some apples, wouldn't you?" Kejen shouted at the back of Charger's head.

Charger snorted yet again and walked through another small fog bank. Kejen patted Charger's mane and steered him onto the road leading up the hill that stood before the city's outskirts. Carefully and as quickly as the icy road would allow them, rider and mount made their way past the old battlement and reached the summit.

Kejen jumped off the horse without even bothering to bring it to a halt, landing numbly on his feet stagger stepped. Easier doing that in the snow he opined to himself. A quick whistle brought Charger back to him. Kejen patted the side of the horse's head and, reaching into a bag tied to the saddle, produced an apple.

"A reward for a job well done, eh?" he said, grinning and looking directly into the animal's eyes as he presented his gift.

He took two more apples and scrunched his way down the forward slope of the hill and looked out over Sparent. A few lights were all ready on to greet the fast approaching northern night, which was starting to arrive a little later with every passing day now. Kejen threw an apple over his shoulder in the direction of his horse. A whinny said the apple had landed close enough. He then wandered a few more feet down the slope and looked out past the city until he could see the Densk River. In the Spring and Summer, it was a glittering twisting boundary between the forest and the steppe country. Presently, it was frozen and, on the surface, unmoving. The occasional loud crack and groan however told everyone that under the surface water was moving and with it, the promise of warmer weather.

Kejen shifted his attention to the sky, looking for the aurora borealis. If he could see that, it meant the lakes and rivers elsewhere were thawing out as well. He realized it might not quite be time for that yet as he noticed a figure shambling its way up to him along a path leading out of the city. When the person took off his fur cap and Kejen noticed hair the same color as the steel grey Winter sky, he knew immediately who it was.

Nonetheless, he waited a couple of more minutes until his visitor was closer.

Kejen threw his half eaten apple to him. "Greetings, Kascar. How are you on this fine day?"

Kascar caught the apple and tossed it back. "What makes you think I want this bloody thing? And what are you doing up here on the hill standing about in the cold by yourself?"

"If I were not up here, you would be standing about in the cold by yourself." Kejen retorted. "So why are you out here?"

"Clever lad, clever lad. I thought I would come up here and wonder why I have a new order for weapons not ordinarily carried by merchants. Especially those named after the river." Kascar replied, jerking a thumb over his shoulder. "I do not know of any problems with banditry up here."

"Look at those prices for supplies as of late. If those people are not bandits, I don't know what they are." Kejen snickered.

"Thieves." Kascar snorted and added a contemptuous wave for good measure. "The question, my young friend, still stands. Why do you want your armor reinforced now and why two new shields?"

Kejen bit into his apple and studied his interrogator as he chewed. Kascar was a formidable man and possessed a vigor and vitality of someone much younger. The grey hair and crows feet around his blue eyes announced he would never see fifty again but anyone stupid enough to take that for a sign of weakness was sorely mistaken. Under his great coat were huge biceps and a massive chest. His wide shoulders often stretched the back of his shirts to the breaking point. It was the natural result of years, decades, of carrying metal to be forged into weapons and often bending metal himself with little more than a wooden plank, metal pole and an incredibly strong back. It did not take one long to realize muscled and hale Kascar Trogen was the town armorer.

Kascar was also the local misanthrope. Dour and suspicious of everything, Kascar was not someone with a lot of friends. Or seemingly any friends. He worked almost constantly every waking moment two or three times as much as those in his employ. Some wondered if he slept at all. Kejen, himself an early riser, was occasionally awakened by Kascar moving about in the forge across the street from his home at very odd hours. Then again, Kascar was an odd character to start with. No one could explain how Xavia could stay married to such a strange man either.

"I was over in Gaking's Grove visting my parents. My father and mother send their blessings and greetings I am sure you would like to know."

"I know, I know, Now answer the bleedin' question." Kascar said curtly.

"Can't get the smallest detail past ole Kascar, eh?" Kejen chuckled. "You are obviously quite concerned despite your attempts to cultivate an image of dispassionate aloofness."

"I am not concerned with what you do with your life." Kascar answered. "It's yours to live as you choose. Why should I care what you do? No one made me accountable for your actions."

"Except yourself." Kejen needled. "You are as close as I ever had to an uncle. Don't expect me to believe for a minute that my father does not have you looking out for me even though my grandfather is the Gatekeeper of Sparent. If you are not so worried, why do you bring up this 'mystery order', as you call it, so quickly? And come all the way out here away from the forge to talk about it."

"All right, all right." Kascar admitted. "I am concerned. A little." He held up his hand with a quarter of an inch between a massive thumb and forefinger. "A very little."

They walked back to Charger and Kejen mounted up. "I will take you back to the shop, concerned uncle. Don't worry. He is a strong horse and can carry us both."

Kascar made himself comfortable behind Kejen. If he was worried about Charger, he did not show it. "Uncle not by blood---", he began.

"---But by close association." Kejen finished. "Close enough at any rate."

"Concerned, uncle, but still dispassionate."

"Dispassionate I think not." Kejen parried. "I know that to be untrue."

"And how do you know that?" Kascar inquired, staring intently for reasons known only to himself at someone entering a general store that marked the beginning of the city.

"By simple observation, my dear uncle." Kejen informed him. "You have six children. No one accomplishes such a feat without passion!"

Kascar gave Kejen a mock cuff to the ears. "Watch your dirty mouth. I wonder who you picked that up from?"

"Yes, I wonder." Kejen asked the night sky. "An older gentleman with a description quite similar to yours actually..."

The two Northmarchers rode into the center of the city, trading good natured jabs as the sun sank over the horizon and the night grew cold. Spring may have been close but Winter still ruled the night.

The center of Sparent was dominated by a huge park. Kascar lived next to it and his sole "hobby", other than supervising road cleaning labor gangs, was to lurk about among the trees in the wee hours of the morning. It was the one time, he said, he has the whole park to himself. Kascar did have a point Kejen admitted. Or part of a point he amended just to see the older man glare at him indignantly.

The Centre Park was a popular place for many to stroll about after dinner or to ward off the summer heat sitting under the trees. It was even better for a four in the morning constitutional Kascar asserted as the two finally arrived in front of the older man's home. Arguments with Kascar had a way of drifting into the surreal.

"Well, I guess this is where I leave you." Kejen said as Kascar dismounted.

"We have unfinished business, you and I." Kascar reminded Kejen pointing a large finger in his face. "We still have some talking to do. What sort of nefarious plot do you have unfolding? Are you thinking about raiding Masovia and starting a major war on your own?"

Kejen grinned in what he thought was an engaging manner.

It had no effect on Kascar, not that Kejen thought it would anyway. Kascar would remain Kascar and therefore perpetually suspicious of everyone and everything until Judgement Day. And maybe even beyond that.

"Ride fast and talk about something else. Then dump Old Man Trogen off in front of his house and vanish into the evening." Kascar recapped. "Very clever. I have, if I must say so myself, and I will, taught you well."

"The very master himself." Kejen half bowed in the saddle.

"But not clever enough." Kascar said flatly. "I know you are planning something. Something you do not want to talk about. What is it?" He leaned up against the fence post and tried a different tack. "You can always talk to me, you know. Just like when you were a wee one."

Kejen looked around conspiratorially. If there was one person in the world he could trust, it was Kascar.

"I want to go after my family's old sword." Kejen came right out with it. "You know the one I am talking about. *HeavenSteel*."

"*HeavenSteel* from the legend?" Kascar looked puzzled. "*HeavenSteel* of faerie origin?"

"Yes." Kejen confirmed.

"HAVE YOU LOST YOUR MIND?!" Kascar shouted.

Charger started briefly and even Kejen looked around hoping no one was paying too much attention. Several passer-bys looked at them but anyone living in this part of Sparent knew Kascar shouting was nothing new. Kejen still wished they would look somewhere else.

"Never mind if you don't know where it is or if it even exists," Kascar continued angrily "but that is the biggest violation of Church doctrine anyone could think of!!!"

"What do you mean 'violation of Church doctrine?' "

"You know as well as I do that anything even remotely connected with faerie is anathema!" Kascar said hotly. "Especially after Diln's Crusade! Mess around with that and you'll be excommunicated! See if they don't! What has possessed you to run the razor's edge of Church banishment?"

"My great great grandfather's, ah, adventures have nothing to do with the recovery of an ancient---" Kejen began.

"Don't give me that!" Kascar cut him off. "Will anyone hear that pathetic explanation over the clatter of fallen staves?"

The reference to the infamous excommunication ceremony was not missed on Kejen. His mind filled with the images of hooded monks each carrying a candle mounted on a staff, assembling in two lines with the condemned between them. The Bishop, from atop the dais, looking resplendent in his vestments, would pronounce sentence, rotate the candle representing Kejen's soul and drop in on the marble floor, snuffing it out along with any hope for salvation. Then the monks would follow suit and the sound of fallen staves would echo, drowning out remonstrations.

"I can see it know." Kascar read Kejen's mind. " 'Cornelius Kejen Densky..."---he ignored Kejen's bristling at the mention of his intensely disliked first name---"You are hereby declared excommunicate and deprived of solace from our Mother Church until you are dead and forever after that. May God have mercy on your soul.' What would you say to that, my clever lad?"

"I'd walk right up the stairs, look him in the eyes and tell him to go straight to---"

"You can't say that to an ordained Bishop!" Kascar exclaimed. "Connecting the Densky name to anything faerie is going to draw the notice of the Church! Besides, do you even know where the sword is?"

"Now you are the one changing the subject." Kejen pointed at Kascar, who was irritated by basically any gesture. "If anything, the Church should bless my venture for I have always remained true to my God and Church. Maybe not always by letter but in spirit."

Even Kascar had trouble arguing with that though Kejen could see him turning the argument around in his mind, looking at it from several angles.

"Secondly, yes, I do know where the sword is." Kejen definitely declared.

"Then where is it?" Kascar asked.

"Like I am going to shout that out here in the open." Kejen came back.

Kascar waved him down. "No, no. I mean do you know *exactly* where it is?"

"Nothing in this world is ever *exact*." Kejen said as he dismounted. " And I am quoting you, dear Uncle."

"Then do me the courtesy of quoting me correctly." Kascar growled. "What I said was 'Nothing in this world is ever exact or promised.' *HeavenSteel* is hidden in the Ankers. Everyone knows that but do you have any idea what lives along the way? Not only do you have to look for a sword that may or may not exist but whose *exact* location is unknown. And let us not forget the Church's feelings on this." Kascar was nothing if not stubborn on a monumental scale.

"All sorts of evil lives in the deeper recesses of the mountains. Many, many stories of travelers caught and eaten. *Alive!*" He concluded with a very unKascar-like dramatic gesture.

"Ever hear of a place called Skulka?" Kascar had the bit between his teeth. "Surely in your travels, sir merchant, you have heard of it. Tangled, gnarled trees and unworldly, maybe faerie things, hostile to humanity, have made that place their domain. Dragons, demons and only God, or Satan, knows what else is there. Devil's soldiers and spawn. Then there is the barren wasteland north of the mountains where there are no landmarks. Get lost there and you will never find your way out. End up in the polar regions if the servants of the Argual don't get you first!"

"All Sea-Farer stories, right?" Kejen asked, unimpressed.

"Yes, Kejen." Kascar answered. "And many of them never made it out of the mountains."

"Whatever lives up there have never encountered a Northmarcher or else it would not still live." Kejen shrugged.

Kascar looked at Kejen for a silent awkward moment before exploding.

"HAS ANYTHING I SAID GOTTEN PAST THAT THICK DENSKY SKULL OF YOURS?!!!"

Kejen laughed at the sight of Kascar angrily balling up his fists and quivering in anger. This of course only contributed to Kascar's anger. Kejen wondered briefly if Kascar thought he was possessed or merely insane.

"A tale like that would discourage a trip into the deep Ankers." Kejen said in an attempt to soothe the situation. "The route I had planned would not go into places like that."

"Good" Kascar nodded, leaning back on his fence post. "A small glimmer of reason though probably flickering and fleeting." Kascar, as usual, did not sound convinced.

"Charger here is starting to lose heat from not moving so I will see you tomorrow." Kejen began to take his leave of Kascar. "But promise me, on your honor, that you will not tell anyone of this conversation."

"On my honor," replied Kascar. "But in return, you promise me that you will seriously consider what I have said. You're liable to change your mind five seconds after you leave."

"Done." Kejen agreed. On the contrary, he thought, once I make up my mind, I don't change it. Strange how even your best friends can mistake the practice of keeping your options open to the last minute as flightiness. "Continued good health and happiness to you."

"May good health and happiness follow you too." Kascar returned the traditional good bye.

Kejen led Charger down the street to his home, not far from Kascar. He turned and waved before disappearing around the corner, knowing Kascar was watching him every step of the way.

Kascar stared after his younger charge. Yes, Kejen had youth and vitality on his side and was quite clever but Kascar, never one to dwell on the bright side of anything, knew experience, and a craftiness that came naturally to him, was a great leveler in the game of life.

Kejen hadn't noticed Kascar had his legs crossed at the ankles when he had given his pledge.

Chapter 2

Kejen rode down the center of the street, avoiding most of the milling crowd. The waved to some he knew, some others he thought he knew and a couple of young ladies he would like to know. He snickered and laughed when the first ignored him and the other, to his surprise, actually waved back.. Then she was gone. Kejen shook his head and continued on. He never had much luck with the fairer sex. Part of it was probably his large nose and rather unorthodox looks. The other part, obvious to everyone but himself, was a somewhat loud and unpredictable temperament born out of an adolescence filled with fighting and brawling. Children could be the cruelest of all. For a brief second, Kejen's mind stood on the precipice of understanding. Instead, he dwelled on episodes of childhood combat and the frightening fact he had actually enjoyed it. It was a testament to the strangeness of life that most of the people he had fought with were now his friends. The problem was solved with a warning glance these days. Perhaps it was maturity. Or maybe it was the raw, almost demonic energy one could sometimes feel radiating from young Kejen in almost palpable waves.

Kejen's thoughts marched straight back to what old Kascar had said. Kascar was definitely the type to focus on the negative aspects of, well, anything. It was still worthy of consideration though. A trip into the deep Ankers was fraught with peril. On the other hand, what worth having did not involve risk of some kind?

The silhouette of the Castle of Sparent rose up before him, dark, solid and threatening, a holdover from a time when everything was a risk. Even going out into the fields to till small crops in an all out effort to keep starvation at arm's length. Did *they* ever have someone telling them over and over not to do anything because it was too risky? Back then, over twelve centuries ago, when civilization seemed on the verge of collapse in the aftermath of the Cataclysmic War, Kejen's ancestors would pour into the Castle and fight off the bandits and brigands that terrorized the land. Their view of the world had contracted to the front door. The definition of "risky" was certainly different in that time.

But the definition of suicide has not! Kascar's voice exploded into his mind. Kejen grimaced and continued riding. Home was getting closer with every step. What dour, old Kascar did not understand was that Kejen was tired and bored with the same bloody routine over and over, day after day, year after year. He read and heard the stories of adventures in the old days and yearned for the excitement that must have surely coursed through their veins. That sort of excitement or purpose in life simply did not exist here in Sparent. Yes, it was a good place to live but there was more to the world. And it was calling to him.

Loudly.

Kejen could then hear Kascar again go on about how Kejen the merchant was better traveled than most and still complaining. He dropped the reins and the thought as he entered the stable. Take care of your horse first was an axiom of life in the Northmarch. After riding across the endless prairies for the better part of three days, Kejen could understand that easily enough. Charger had served him well and now Kejen would serve his horse, treating him to a good brush down and drying off.

Kejen tromped through some of the slush over to the small home he shared with his brother, eager to see him and hoping Trif had made some of his legendary liver pudding. If not, Kejen grinned wryly, maybe he could convince him to make some. Actually, Trif's liver pudding was the stuff of neighborhood legend. Kejen would gladly *beg* him to make some.

He opened the door, stamped his feet, and after taking a moment to adjust to the temperature change, he announced. "I have returned!"

"I can see that." Came the reply from the corner of the room. "Now how much of the Winter did you bring with you?"

Kejen stepped forward ceremoniously, grasped the doorknob and with a swing of a long arm, slammed it shut.

"Not much." Kejen answered with a bow.

"You have a way of unburdening my mind." Trif said looking at Kejen from behind a drawing table cluttered with books and papers arranged in some fashion that made sense only to him.

Trif walked out from behind his work and hugged Kejen before relieving his brother of his sleeping bag and hooking it on a peg on the wall.

One would not know it, but Kejen and Trif were in fact twins. Although they were the same size and had the same build, and even moved in the same way as brothers often do, Trif, not possessing the infamous nose, was clearly the most handsome of the two. He had never had problems finding female companionship.

Now only if he knew what to do with it, Kejen chuckled to himself. Kejen knew what *he* would do with it if he were so lucky! Followed by a very long stretch on a work crew cleaning roads in the middle of Winter his mind answered.

Kejen loved his brother fiercely. He was pretty sure Trif felt the same way. It was, on the surface, hard to tell sometimes. Trif was much quieter and soft-spoken (when he spoke at all) as opposed to his much louder (some said crazed) and on occasion, much more obnoxious, brother.

This once led to the mistaken stereotype that Trif was a defenseless introvert. On day in grammar school, two bullies found out the hard way, while losing a couple of teeth, that this was simply not true. The whole time they thought Trif was not fighting back, he was in fact looking for their weaknesses. He found them. And hurt them. For once, it was not Kejen that needed to be dragged out of a fight.

Behind that placid facade there was an active mind that worked faster than any other. If anything, it made him much more dangerous than his brother, who seemed to look forward into wading into trouble. Kejen often suspected the reason he was not thrown out of school was that Trif somehow intervened behind the scenes with the teachers on his behalf. Since he was the best student in school, Trif's word carried some weight. True to form, Trif had never mentioned it to Kejen.

Different people fought their battles in different ways.

"Are Mother and Father enjoying themselves out at the Grove?" Trif asked.

"Very much so." Kejen answered, sitting down to take off his boots. "Not a neighbor for a mile in any direction and alongside the river. What more could you ask? I helped Father fix a couple spots in the roof and the shutters too. I had the feeling he waited for me to show up to do all of that."

Trif grinned and went back behind the desk to scribble some thing down before he forgot what it was. "Quite a difference from living here in the city. I wonder why he moved from Gaking's Grove in the first place."

Kejen put his boots in a bucket so the snow would melt into that and not the floor. Northmarcher homes tended to have floors of rammed earth so anything that melted rarely made it indoors. "I guess he wanted to see something different before spending his life in one place."

Trif looked up from his work. "That sounds very familiar."

Kejen nodded. "How is the history book coming along?"

Trif held up several sheets of paper. "If nothing else, it will be as big as those over there."

Trif pointed to a book self with many, many books on it ranging in subject matter from astronomy to history to geography. Trif knew every page of every book. Kejen did too, a fact that might have surprised a few people. Stereotypes not only closed people's thinking, they were quite often wrong.

"What it means, "Kejen said, "Is that your book will be much better, greater detailed and read longer than any of those."

"I hope so." Trif yawned and slid off his stool. He walked into the small kitchen, calling out behind him. "Are you hungry?"

"Not really."

"I made some liver pudding." Trif pointed out.

"I said 'not really.' I did not say I was stupid!" Kejen laughed. This was turning out to be a good day despite the fact most of it was wasted on the road.

Trif slopped some into a bowl and handed it to Kejen along with a spoon. After got some for himself, he made some room on the table and motioned Kejen to have a seat too.

"How much longer until we send caravans out?" Trif asked. His orderly and quick mind was an invaluable business tool.

"A month at best, six weeks at worst." Kejen projected. "I know you have all ready checked the wagons and horses so I do not really know why I am asking."

"Everything seems all right. There are a couple of wagon axles I took the liberty of repairing." the ever meticulous Trif reported. "I have also spoken with Lepsis about the arrangements you wanted in the event you do decide to take that trip."

That trip Kejen heard the words thud into place. Trif was the only one he had confided in. And of course, Old Man Trogen. Trif, however, was his brother and someone whose trust was absolute. He was hoping Kascar fit into that category too.

"Did you tell Father about looking for *HeavenSteel*?" Trif plunged straight in.

Kejen shook his head. "You know as well as I do he would not understand."

"And why not tell him? If you do follow through on this, he is going to find out. Sooner is better than later." Trif informed him.

"True, very true." Kejen admitted around a mouthful of liver pudding.

"Your manners are in dire need of refinement." Trif said with mock disapproval. He then propped his own feet on the table. Every now and again Trif would climb out of his shell and prove his reputation as an introvert was somewhat exaggerated. "Did you tell our parents we will visit them in the Summer?"

Kejen nodded. "I think they all ready knew since you have not seen them for a while. Plus, that book of yours deals with recent history and our father was part of that. He could tell you all about it. Especially his part!"

Both brothers shared a laugh. Their father galloped off to fight in the Masovian War twenty years earlier. Kejen and Trif grew up with the stories and heard them almost every day of the first two decades of their lives. In all actuality, Father had fought bravely on the Plain of Driergam, living up to the name of the great hero his father had bestowed upon him. Regardless of great men's statures, they are always the same people to their families. Perhaps it is that way to remind them they are human. Kejen's father occasionally forgot that.

Trif asked another question that made Kejen uncomfortable. "Have you told anyone else?"

"Kascar". Kejen answered clearly uncomfortable.

"That was not a wise thing to do, Kejen." Trif frowned. "You know how close he and Father are."

"Yes, I know. After all, he gave us for him to look after." Kejen pointed out.

"Are you positively sure he was not holding a holy relic of some kind?" Trif leaned forward, continuing his interrogation. "He is quite crafty. Very wily. A master in the arts of deception if half the stories are to be believed."

Kascar was also a veteran of the Masonvian War, serving as a scout. One more than one occasion not only did he ride up on the enemy silent as a ghost but penetrated their camp several times. The fact he could speak accentless Masovian helped but the truth of the matter was that Kascar Trogen was a gifted infiltrator. With incredible nerve.

"I am sure he was not holding a holy relic of any kind." Kejen assured his brother.

Kejen got up and walked over to the door, opened it and looked outside, almost expecting to see the older man galloping off in the direction of Gaking's Grove.

"On the other hand, he may have just bloody lied." Kejen admitted.

"Too late to worry about it now." Trif reasoned. "You can always just say it was a thought."

Kejen shut the door and turned around. "Which it still is!"

Trif's silence shouted that he knew Kejen was indeed planning to go in search of the legendary sword.

"That is what I am going to say at any rate." Kejen shrugged.

Trif nodded knowingly and sat down behind his work again.

"I'm going to hop into bed and do some thinking." Kejen announced. "I will probably drift off to sleep so this is good night."

"Good night, Kejen." Trif said as his brother climbed into the top bunk.

The house was soon pitch black save for the candle Trif worked by. The silence was broken only by his scribbling. Kejen stared up at the shadows flickering across the ceiling and his thoughts began their own journey twelve hundred years into the past.

HeavenSteel. It was an ancient name for an ancient sword. It almost sounded like a pagan goddess but the original Gaking had named it the place from which it came. Or from where he thought it came, some might say. Of course, no one could say where it came from in the first place, so why not Heaven? According to legend, it gave its bearer the strength of three men and it handled unlike anything ever seen. A thing like that could only come from one place. The more Kejen thought about it, the more convinced he was it had indeed been made by Someone Else.

The great Gaking had kept the wondrous sword in his village alongside the Densk River. He was determined to keep it, hoping that, God willing, war would never come to his family and village. If it did come though, they had something to protect themselves. What Gaking never counted on was a host of descendents taking the sword and giving battle to others.

Three hundred years after Gaking's time, Roenik Densky, the first of the line to name the family after the river, picked up *HeavenSteel* and sailed down Blieben, further south than any Densky (or perhaps even Northmarcher!) had ever been. There he fought in the mercenary conflicts of the Barsney and other Transkyan barbarian wars. Five years after leaving, Roenik and *HeavenSteel* returned home with treasure, honors and stories of distant lands.

Seven centuries after Gaking emerged bloody, battered but victorious after fighting brigands on the bridge over the Densk, Harkon Densky took up the sword to fight in the Noble's Revolt. Harkon, a noble himself, refused the enticing promises of the treacherous Baron Melas. He remained loyal to his King and fought for nine long years against those who would depose him, marshaling all of his strength, skill and most of all, the sword *HeavenSteel*.

Roenik and Harkon were interesting characters but it was Diln who raised the hair on many people's necks, especially in the Church.

One bright sunny day two and half centuries before the time of Kejen and Trif, Diln picked up the sword and promptly decided to go on a one man crusade against the Masovians. He rode south and killed the first border guards he saw. But it did not end there. Diln's Crusade, as it was later called, became shrouded in villainy as he carved a swath of destruction, destroying and killing all he encountered. A religious man, Diln's hatred for Masovia was probably born of the Masovian Empire's denial and persecution of all religions, decreeing the Emperor was the center of creation. The Masovian definition of persecution included burning churches and killing monks. Diln decided he was going to stop it.

It came to a head at a village called Limbart. Diln plunged into battle and obliterated the village and most of the Masovian cavalry company sent to stop him. Most but not all of it. Diln fell at Limbart but not after taking nearly two hundred souls into the next world. Before the Masovians could take the sword with them however, Diln's brother, Lorac, managed to steal the sword back in a daring raid. He had run after Diln in a vain attempt to stop him but he at least kept *HeavenSteel* from ending up in the Masovian capital of Regalwood. God only knows what the Masovians would have used the power of the sword for! The Northmarch and Masovia were on a collision course for war when the Great Eastern Invasion slammed into Nyhissia from across the Blieben. Nyhissian, Verrentian and Northmarcher soldiers fought bravely at the Three Days' Battle and Lorac carried *HeavenSteel* into the fight, playing a decisive role in turning the tide of war.

After the Easterners had been repulsed, the Church declared that the invasion was punishment from God, brought on by the misuse of *HeavenSteel* by Diln. Therefore, the High Cardinals demanded, Lorac must immediately surrender *HeavenSteel* so that it would not be misused again. Lorac, though a simple soldier, still had a peasant's ingrained stubbornness. He refused. The Church threatened excommunication and finally the King ordered Lorac to give up the wondrous sword.

Lorac said he lost it.

Lorac maintained he lost the sword in the Three Day's Battle. No one could prove he was lying. No one could find the sword either. And to this day, no one had seen it.

Since that time, the Church had preached that faerie was heretical. Anything from that wondrous time before the Cataclysmic War, the Bishops maintained, was inherently evil. The Church and faerie were mutually exclusive and there could be no reconciliation. The subject of the time of faerie, the time of the Elves and Trolls and Dragons and magic, was not something to be taken lightly by the Church. Connecting the name Densky to the legendary weapon *HeavenSteel* was enough to drive a man of the Cloth to the nearest tavern.

In his later years, Lorac Densky traveled quite a lot. He traveled most often to the Sea Faring Kingdoms and spent a lot of time in Nyhissia and Verrent. It was also noted he often avoided more traveled and better maintained roads and trade routes. He had never explained why so the legend that he had hidden *HeavenSteel* grew. Where the sword was remained a mystery and there literally dozens of places it could be. If it even existed. As with most stories, more and more people would doubt it as time went on.

Two and half centuries later, one of Lorac's descendants snored away in his top bunk. Kejen Densky knew the sword *HeavenSteel* existed.

More importantly, he knew where it was.

Chapter 3

The rest of the month flew by. The snow melted, the mud hardened and the days grew longer. The mornings were still a bit chilly but that was nothing new to any Northmarcher, inured to the cold since childhood. Kejen busied himself with the organizing of the Spring caravans and everything was going to plan. Even the last minute problems that always sprung up seemed rather mundane. Kejen's announcement that he was not going on this year's caravan raised some eyebrows. Yes, it meant some extra work but the increased percentages made up for it. Still, they wondered, what was Kejen up to?

The coming of Spring not only saw the revival of long distance commercial traffic but also heralded another faucet of Northmarcher life. Before the caravans went out, it was time to once again contribute to the King's service. In the Winter, almost every able body man helped out with clearing the roads of snow and ice. In the Spring, just before the crops were sown, the men marched off to militia practice.

The Northmarcher Army stood guard over the nation's borders all year, day and night, Spring, Summer, Winter and Fall. The regular army had a job to do and it did it well. In time of war, the regulars would see their numbers swell with the addition of the militias of every city, town, village and backwater hamlet. This, however, was no simple raw mob running wildly over the landscape following the army around with pitchforks and homemade spears. The militia was actually a trained force. Maybe not quite up to the standards of the regular army but still something not to be taken lightly. With the practices and two week training looming, everyone began to assemble their armor and weapons.

"Time to go see if Kascar has finally finished our armor!" Kejen shouted at everyone in market square one fine morning. He was talking to his brother but Kejen being Kejen had basically informed everyone within thirty feet. Trif nodded and continued haggling for things needed for a long distance expedition. Kejen was convinced his brother was the best haggler on the planet. Trif could add, subtract, multiply and divide in his head while talking as easily as he breathed. Many dealers and suppliers simply gave up and gave him what he wanted so they could get on with overcharging someone else.

Kejen tossed a couple of coins to a vender and received some roasted chicken on a skewer for his trouble. He walked the half mile or so to the forge, weaving his way between people and wagons and horses, eating his chicken, before turning down a couple of backstreets with the familiarity of someone born and raised in Sparent. Before long, Kejen found himself in front of a wooden board loudly proclaiming in red ink, TROGEN'S FORGE.

Kascar's eldest son, Ranlo, staggered by under a load of iron a horse would have trouble hauling. Kejen opened the door and sauntered in behind the heavily sweating youth who mumbled some sort of thanks to the kind person he could not see.

Stepping into Trogen's Forge was like descending into Hell itself. The blast of heat Kejen felt walking in and the sudden darkness descending upon him only contributed to the illusion. Kascar was easy to find though. Kejen was fairly certain Satan did not, and could not, bellow any louder in his realm than Kascar did in his.

Kascar was banging away on his anvil, shaping a sword that still glowed orange-hot. Kejen waited until Kascar finished swinging the hammer and dropped the blade into some water. The hissing of the hot metal seemed louder than anything else.

"That better not be mine you're working on!" Kejen shouted above the din. "I paid for it a long, long time ago!"

The scowl on Kascar's face grew deeper when he looked up and saw who had interrupted his work.

"Oh no your Lordship!" Kascar answered back with the usual sarcasm. "Yours was done long before anyone else's! Long, long before anyone else's!!!"

Kejen laughed as Kascar waved him into another room.

"The sword you want was forged a long time ago and is sitting up in the mountains." Kascar said pointedly. "But the one you ordered from me is right here."

Kascar handed the sword to Kejen hilt first. It was a fine piece of work Kejen had to admit. The blade was strong and sharp on both sides. The hilt was reinforced. The cross hilt design was simple but effective. Kejen swung it slightly and felt its perfect balance.

"You have been doing this a long time." Kejen commented.

"Longer than you have been alive, boy." Kascar growled back but with a hint of a smile. "This is definitely some of my best work. Your armor is here too."

Kejen followed Kascar's finger over to a shelf and found what he was looking for.

He picked up the plate mail breast plate and ran his hand over the polished surface. "This looks almost new!", he exclaimed.

"You sound like some little girl getting a new doll for Christmas." Kascar snorted.

Kejen grinned back at him and began putting on his armor. First was the breastplate although it covered his whole upper body, starting at the waist and coming up and over the shoulders like a sleeveless shirt. Next came the shoulder armor, two great pieces of contoured pieces of metal, jointed and flexible, yet strong, strapped on with leather leashes under the armpits. Loosely attached to the edge of the shoulder armor was a smaller piece of metal designed to protect the rest of the biceps from a side blow. It too could be strapped over the muscle it was entrusted to protect but many, including Kejen, let it dangle and swing. He found his forearm greaves next to his feet. They fit perfectly, extending from his wrists along the bottom of the forearm to a point a couple of inches beyond the elbow, allowing for a full span of motion while protecting it.

Kejen held his arm up. "This is how you don't use it."

"Yes, I know." Kascar said with his arms crossed with the usual irritability. "If you try to stop an overhead blow like that, you will just end up breaking your arm. The idea is to knock the shot away."

"Good for bashing someone in the face too." Kejen observed.

"That too." Kascar said with a genuine smile.

"You've done that before, haven't you?" Kejen asked

"Helmet." Kascar said getting back to the business at hand.

Opened faced with two slender cheek pieces, complete with a red and white feathered crest running down the length of it, Northmarcher helmets looked like something Leonidas would have worn at Thermopylae.

"Fits perfectly." Kejen announced. "Of course, I knew it would."

"Quite a feat considering whose head I made it for." Kascar quipped. "Even the crow's beak is perfect."

Kejen touched the nose guard of his helmet. Instead of resting on top of the bridge of the nose, the Northmarchers preferred to have an overhang. After all, a helmet could be used as weapon too so one needed something to hold on while swinging it. In Kejen's case, an overhang was a requirement!

Kejen picked up his sword again and swung it a couple of times. His face told the world he was clearly pleased.

"Despite your many, many other faults, you are a first rate metal forger." Kejen said, jabbing at an imaginary opponent.

"Stop swinging that around in here and go outside with it before you break something." Kascar admonished. He walked through yet another door and Kejen followed him outside into the sunlight.

Kejen heard a crash of metal outside and saw it was Ranlo dropping off some scrap. He waved his sword at the teenager and shouted, "Can you believe your father actually made this?"

"He enjoys playing with it." Kascar retorted. "But does our dear Kejen know how to *use* it?"

Kejen pointed at a post driven into the ground and advanced on it. He delivered an upward stroke that took off the right quarter of the top of the post. Then in the same motion, he reversed the stroke, bringing the blade down and took off the left quarter.

"Not bad." Kascar grudgingly admitted.

Kejen took a step to the right, raised his sword and brought it down hard, splitting the post in half.

Ranlo let out a low whistle and Kascar shifted uncomfortably before crossing his massive arms.

"Perhaps you have learned a few things." Kascar finally said. "A few things perhaps."

"Be a good lad and hand me that bag with my brother's armor in it." Kejen said.

"You have to name your blade." Kascar said. "Surely you do not have a problem with that tradition?"

Kejen swung the burlap bag with Trif's armor over his shoulder. "The sword is light, strong and very sharp." He jerked his head toward the splintered post. "What better name can you think of than '*Wasp*'?"

Kascar brought his hand up to his chin. "Hmmmm. Not the worst name in the world. Maybe the Spring is thawing out your mind somewhat."

Kejen gave Kascar a sardonic salute with his new sword and marched off.

"Are you going to wear your armor home?" Kascar called out after him.

"Yes!" Kejen shouted over his shoulder before disappearing into the crowd. "Easiest way to get used to it I know!"

"Must be pretty strong to walk that fast in it all ready." Kascar said, half to himself, half to his son.

"Do you think I will ever be that strong, Papa?" Ranlo asked his father.

"Pick up those two pieces of iron." Kascar said, his voice rising back to the more familiar bellow. "The ones by the door."

His son's shoulders sagged but he obeyed and picked up both pieces of offending metal. He almost walked through the doorway when he felt his father's massive hand on his shoulder.

"I bet one day you will be twice as strong." Kascar whispered into his ear. Then he shouted again. "Be quick about it. They won't move themselves!"

The next morning found Kejen and Trif out at the practice site beyond the limits of Sparent. Or rather Kejen and Trif found the morning since both were out there before sunrise. Trif's armor was similar to Kejen's though somewhat lighter since he was an archer. Not only an archer but the best archer in all of Sparent. For three straight years, Trif had hit more targets and scored higher in every competition he entered.

"If we go into the Ankers, we won't have to carry too many rations. Your bow and arrow will feed us well enough." Kejen remarked.

"More than likely." Trif agreed in his usual taciturn manner. He probably all ready thought of that a few weeks ago, Kejen thought.

The weather was certainly better now than it had been a month ago. The ground was solid and the breeze blowing through the forests to the south and west of the practice field was most welcome. Spring quite often felt like Summer. To the east and north stretched the seemingly endless steppes. There was plenty of room for all.

Everyone began arriving quickly. In minutes, streams of men began marching through the streets, greeting the rising Sun with the sound of boots hitting the ground, armor clanging against shields. The organized chaos was not synchronized yet but after a couple of weeks, the entire Sparent Brigade would move like one long armored centipede.

Kejen looked over to the hill the Castle of Sparent sat on and saw a group of men riding out from the main gate. Those were the higher ranking officers, battalion commanders and even Namsos the brigade leader himself. Practice was going to commence in a few minutes. Kejen always paused a half second staring at the main gate. That was where he and Trif had reported in for their basic training and initiation into the militia a few years earlier. Training was tough. Training to be an officer was even tougher. But Kejen had done it and was now a cavalry lieutenant. Without the horse today, he thought. Today was the first day, dedicated to awakening muscles that were hibernating all Winter.

"Road clearing work all ready saw to that." Kejen answered his own thought. Trif nodded, reading his brother's mind perfectly.

Kejen looked over at Trif. "Still have not changed your mind about not becoming an officer?"

Trif nodded again. Trif would make an excellent officer, Kejen thought. If anything, Kejen felt that Trif might be better qualified than he but Kejen's brother elected to remain a private in an archer company.

Trif turned the tables on his brother. "Have you considered becoming part of the regular army? You enjoy this sort of thing immensely."

"Who doesn't?" Kejen asked. "You get to ride around, use weapons, travel all over. Other than the weapon part, it is not much different than being a merchant."

Trif agreed in silence. This conversation would have to wait for another time. Kejen's platoon was marching up, led by a wiry man with a mischievous grin on his face.

"Greetings my friends." He called out. "Armored monstrosities though you are!"

Kejen dropped to one knee. "Oh thank you, thank you good sir for the exclusive privilege of being considered your friends...in public no less!--he looked up---*Sergeant* Crinklin."

Crinklin laughed and then halted, giving a proper salute with his sword. "At your service, Lieutenant."

Although he stood below six feet, Crinklin was a skilled and agile fighter and much stronger than his size would indicate. He taught Kejen a lot about hand to hand fighting and Kejen was pretty sure, although Crinklin would never ever admit it, he had taught the wily sergeant a few things too. After all, Kejen spent most of his childhood in hand to hand combat.

Kejen waved to Trif who was all ready jogging in the direction of the archers. He and Crinklin watched the platoon march into its assigned place on its own. That was a sign of a well trained unit. On Crinkiln's watch, it would be.

"All ready set to go, eh?" Kejen asked.

Crinklin took off his helmet and ran a hand through his blonde hair. "You know me, sir. Always set to go! Getting warm all ready or I am just getting old." With that he darted off to the platoon before they started to relax.

Kejen shook his head. Crinklin may have passed his thirtieth birthday but he could still outrun nine of every ten people you saw.

Kejen ran behind him and soon past him. I am number ten he chuckled before coming to a halt in front of his men.

"GOOD MORNING, MEN!!!" He shouted. Kejen had to shout for several other platoons were marching past him. Kejen, of course, would have shouted anyway.

"GOOD MORNING!" His platoon shouted back at him.

"Are you ready to run?!!"

The shouting and stamping feet of more than thirty men said they were ready.

"Are you ready to fight?!!"

An animalistic roar said they were ready to ride off to Regalwood that very moment.

"Are you ready to wreak havoc in the brothels?!"

The men's shouting could be heard throughout the wakening city and probably at the aforementioned establishments as well. Weapons and fists pounded shields and armor. They were ready and in good spirits.

Kejen turned around and signaled the company commander his troops were ready. Kejen looked up and down the assembled soldiery. Everyone was lined up in their places and ready to listen to the brigade commander and whatever general came down from Northcross. This was often called a "tree line assembly". Made sense, Kejen thought, noting the trees behind everyone and the plains stretching out before them.

Before long, everyone was running across the prairies or through obstacle courses some sadist (probably named Crinklin, Kejen added) designed. Trif was right. Trif was always right. He really did *enjoy* this. The armor soon lost its heaviness and began to feel like a second skin. That was the point behind this practice. Plus, it was easy to get used to when you liked this sort of thing.

Before long, the Sun shone directly overhead and the brigade took a half hour off for lunch. Kejen's platoon marched into the forest, singing and shouting (mostly) good natured insults at each other. Discussions of strategy and tactics soon gave way to occasional ribald tales. Even so, the inevitable question soon came up.

"Against whom do you think we could end up fighting against?"

Everyone looked to Kejen since he was the highest ranking man in the platoon. For that reason, everyone seemed to think he had all the answers. Crinklin did not guffaw but the smirk on his face might as well as been one.

"Hard to say." Kejen answered after some thought. "The obvious answer would be Masovia."

The men hooted and cheered. Northmarchers and Masovians had

been enemies for generations and neither bothered to hide their dislike for each other.

"Our fathers fought them twenty years ago and won!" Crinklin broke in.

"You should know! You were there!" Someone made a rude jeer. Someone safely hidden in the massed ranks of Northmarcher soldiery.

Crinklin got up and pretended to look for the culprit with a good dose of mock anger. Relationships between the ranks were a bit more casual in the militia than in the regular army since everyone here was a civilian most of the time.

"Twenty years ago, they supported a pretender to the Verrentian throne and a war broke out." Kejen informed everyone. "Ask my brother about the details. He can tell you about it in his sleep. Ask anyone's father. Chances are, they were there."

"I would not claim any of you as a son!" Crinklin laughed. He was hardly old enough to be any of their fathers but everyone laughed at the joke anyway.

"For some reason, the Masovians have been biting at Rhenia way down south." Leron, the platoon's newest member, broke in. "That's what Father Michael told me after Mass a few days ago."

"Very true." Kejen confirmed. "Though they don't appear to be trying to actually conquer the place. I have no idea why they would go through the trouble."

"Slaves for their mines?" Crinklin suggested.

"Maybe they are just idiots." Kejen concluded.

The whole platoon cheered as did another that was marching by. Bashing the Masovian Empire was a sport everyone liked. It was a shame wars could not be fought with just words Kejen thought but any sign of friendship to anyone Regalwood showed would be the first. Yes, the Masovians had made enemies on all their borders.

A horn sounded signaling the end of lunch and it was time for more practice. Thousands of men marched back out into the sunlit prairies, one of them Kejen Densky, who marched and read a map at the same time.

Verrent and Nyhissia were allies. And the Kielstrokers tended to keep to themselves except for matters of trade. The Sea-Faring Kingdoms, a brawling, rowdy bunch if any ever existed, lived in the far North. Ostensibly farmers, they raided the coast as far south as San Juan de Sur and even had made it into the Southern Sea. And they were enthusiastic Northmarcher allies. Landlocked Northmarcher borders and a shared dislike for Masovia only strengthened the relationship more. The Sea-Farers, divided into many smaller kingdoms that seemed to enjoy fighting among themselves almost as much as with other nations, got a collective thrill from raiding Masovian coastlines and stealing away before any ground forces could strike. With Kielstrock between Masovia and the nearest Sea-Farer kingdom, that particular conflict would only be a war of flea bites.

"How is the new man?" Kejen asked Crinklin.

"Leron is doing well." Crinklin answered. "And it is his birthday tomorrow....his sixteenth", the sergeant added with a wicked wink.

"Oh is it now?" Kejen laughed. "Well then, we must make the lad a real man then!"

The platoon formed up into a circle with the quiet ease of men who had worked together for some time. They called it the bull ring. Young Leron looked somewhat out of place and his nervousness confirmed him as the New Man.

Kejen picked up a staff and walked straight into the center. As the commanding officer, it was his duty to go first.

"Let's see if you trained him as well as you trained me." Kejen whispered to his sergeant, whose grin showed more teeth this time.

Kejen waved the fighting staff and picked someone ostensibly at random. He sought and found who he was looking for. Pointing the staff at him, Kejen shouted, "You, Leron!"

Overjoyed the lieutenant knew his name, Leron ran up to him, enthusiastic and shaking with anticipation.

"First time out, eh?" Kejen asked for some reason.

"Y-Yes, sir!" Leron stammered.

"Let's see what you know." Kejen said and tossed a staff to his newest charge.

Leron caught the staff....and felt a blow to the side of his helmet.

"Always stay on guard!!!" Kejen yelled in his face.

"Yes s----"

Kejen swung at him again and Leron, still seeing stars, blocked the attack with his staff despite nearly dropping it. Kejen swung from the other side and Leron blocked it solidly this time. Kejen attacked again from the same side. Leron prepared to block but Kejen changed direction in mid swing, corkscrewing to the other side. Leron reacted deftly and blocked it...barely. Leron could barely feel his fingers and felt the shock of the blow register up to his elbows. But he held on.

"Not too bad." Kejen admitted as he swung wide again.

Leron saw the wide arc closing in on him and reached out to parry. When Leron blocked the blow, Kejen planted his right foot, pivoted and with his left foot caught the new recruit behind the knee. The newcomer toppled over and a calliope of crashing armor announced he hit the ground.

Kejen helped him up and patted his head. "Not bad for the first time out. Don't overextend yourself and get the enemy to react to you. He will make a mistake."

Kejen picked up Leron's helmet and handed it to him. "You handled the corkscrew very well.--- and you're fast!"

That buoyed Leron's spirits somewhat. "Yes sir." His enthusiasm was a little blunted at the moment but that would soon recover too.

"Crinklin over there did the same thing to me my first time out." Kejen laughed and spied a dozen girls feeding the horses the cavalry would use in the next couple of days. "Keep working on it and soon you might give ole Crinklin there a good hiding."

Crinklin just grinned that vicious grin of his. "Anytime he thinks he is ready!"

"Sergeant!" Kejen called out. "Take over for me for a bit. I need to make sure they are not poisoning my horse."

Crinklin winked knowingly, took command and led the platoon off further into the prairie.

Kejen stood about thirty feet from the girls, studying them. He was particularly interested in a certain dark haired girl he saw about a month ago. He was not sure of her name but if he could just see her...

His eyes flitted from one to another, matching up names and faces but still not finding the one he was looking for. Thankfully, they were too into their own conversations to notice him staring. Look, look, look. Stare, stare, stare. This is getting frustrating he thought, feeling his hands behind his back starting to clench.

There! Maybe...

CLANG!!!

A blinding white pain suddenly materialized behind Kejen's eyes.

Ripping off his helmet, Kejen wheeled around, angrily searching for the culprit in this ill timed sneak attack. He had to look no further than Gusaric, three feet away on horseback, his sword cradled between his elbows and laughing hysterically, just able to maintain his balance.

"What did you do that for?!" Kejen remembered at the last second not to scream.

"Flatblading a pinhead is quite an accomplishment." Gusaric informed him.

Kejen grumbled under his breath as Gusaric dismounted.

"Your soldiers look pretty good for the first day." He said to Kejen who was still rubbing his head. "In a couple of weeks, you can put them next to the regulars and no one will be able to tell the difference."

"That is the whole point." Kejen gave an all encompassing wave. "They have you watching over us?"

Gusaric nodded and took off his helmet. His longish black as night hair tumbled down his neck, along with a good amount of sweat.

"Hot all ready." He grumbled.

"Almost as hot as the day we both showed up at the Castle for training a few years back." Kejen reminisced.

Gusaric nodded. "We were together the first day and here we are together again."

They both laughed.

"You are much smart than I." Gusaric said. "You get to do this a few times a year instead of being the King's slave."

"Hah! You are the finest lieutenant in the regular army! " Kejen slapped his friend's shoulder. "Too bad you can't drink like it!"

Gusaric's blue eyes opened up in shock.

"Are you challenging me?"

Kejen bowed. The pain was now a tolerable throb. "But of course."

Gusaric smiled, took a step back and bowed as well. "First drink is on you."

"Most certainly." Kejen saluted. "When would you like me to pick you up for Leron's birthday party?"

Gusaric returned the salute. "Sundown is good. I can't stay long though. I have the morning patrol."

"Such is life in the regular army." Kejen said. He rubbed his temples. "That was a good shot you gave me."

Before Gusaric could say anything, Kejen lowered his shoulder and drove right into his friend's midsection, lifting him straight up.

"Hah! How do you like that?!" Kejen yelled in Gusaric's ear.

Gusaric wrapped his arms around Kejen's chest. "Not bad! Not bad at all. Almost as fast as Leron!" Then he laughed. "Almost!"

"Give me one reason I shouldn't drop you here!" Kejen said as he paraded around with Gusaric on his shoulder.

"I can give you two." Gusaric informed him with the precision of a regular army officer. "One, I will take you down if you drop me." He tightened his grip to emphasize the point. "Two, most importantly I might add, I will not be able to buy you some ale".

Kejen set Gusaric down on his feet. "Why didn't you say so?" He even brushed his friend off for good measure.

"I believe I did." Gusaric smiled, waved and remounted his horse before darting across the practice field and into the city.

Kejen went back to the work at hand, approaching the ring of Northmarcher soldiery that was his platoon and responsibility.

Bolshin, the platoon's biggest soldier, was in the ring with Crinklin. The wily sergeant was showing off but looked to have picked the greatest challenge he could find for himself as well. The shattered remnants of three practice staves attested to the ferociousness of the battle. Kejen shuddered briefly remembering about what Kascar had told him about the excommunication ceremony.

Troopers from other units had drifted in to watch as well. Kejen wondered if Crinklin had found some way to charge admission. There was an excellent chance many side wagers were being made.

Kejen pushed his way through the crowd, stopping to rap Svaric on the helmet with his knuckles, and imposed himself between the combatants.

"Break it up you two! It's only practice." He yelled. Kejen found himself in Bolshin's shadow but managed to make himself heard. That generally was not a problem.

He held up Crinklin's and Bolshin's arms (or rather the bigger man's elbow) and declared a draw in a great theatrical voice. If there was anything Kejen loved, it was a crowd.

"I, Lord of the River, by the power invested in me, declare this gallant combat a draw!"

"I was winning!" Crinklin nearly shouted. "It was a matter of time!"

Bolshin growled back but Kejen managed to turn him around and get him to walk away.

"Off with you two." Kejen shooed him away. "That was your first cousin? You were fighting like your life depended on it."

"Bolshin has no idea how strong he really is." Crinklin shrugged.

Kejen shook his head. "One more bit of business to take care of."

He drew forth *Wasp* for all to see and walked around the inside of the ring in no particular patter.

"Svaric!" Kejen shouted.

Then he pointed the sword straight at----"Leron!"

Svaric and Leron charged each other from opposite sides of the ring, smashing headlong into each other. Both fought well, wielding the staves impressively. Leron had indeed learned and learned well, holding his own and switching over to the attack. To practice eyes, it was a bit noticeable Svaric was holding back a little but still he made Leron work and strain.. He nearly knocked the younger soldier down but he backed off instead of pressing his advantage. He grinned quickly at Kejen and took an exaggerated swipe at Leron, exposing himself a little more than he normally would. Leron ducked under the blow and came up with his staff, catching Svaric under the arm, nearly lifting him off his feet. Svaric did his part, propelling himself over, completing Leron's victory by landing spread eagled rather than curling up in a ball.

The circle collapsed as the platoon rushed in, lifting its newest and youngest member on Bolshin's shoulders. Nothing like a little subterfuge to help someone's confidence.

"Winning solves everything." Svaric laughed as he got up. He knew this game well. Kejen had done it for him when he first joined the militia.

"And it gives him something to boast about on his birthday to the pretty little maidens." Kejen agreed, adding a little wolfish laughter.

Trif appeared from apparently nowhere, archery practice done for the day.

"Ninety-seven out of a hundred." He answered his brother's question before he could ask. "The last round was the hardest."

Kejen put his arm around his brother's shoulder and walked in the direction of town. "How many people could even dream of matching that? You should be in charge of training archers." He pointed toward a figure in black armor, dressed in a black shirt and black pants walking toward them. "Do you recognize that person?"

"Kuran!" Trif shouted in way of an answer.

Several people turned around, mildly surprised to hear Trif's voice louder than a normal conversation. Trif simply was using the most logical volume for someone to hear him at that distance.

"How are you my friend?!" Kejen shouted at a volume much louder than what was needed for someone to hear him at that distance. Then he stole a phrase from Crinklin. "Armored monstrosity that you are!" Kejen liked how it sounded.

Kejen noticed Trif stopping and saluting.

He then saw why.

"*Captain* Kuran Legvin?"

Kuran tapped the silver marking on his black armor. "Only until someone notices them missing from whoever is supposed to be wearing them."

Kejen saluted his friend solemnly. "No, you earned that, just like you earned the right to be in the elite of the Northmarcher Army."

Trif shook his Kuran's hand. "How are things in Northcross? King and country are in good hands I am sure."

"Is it not a little hot wearing all black in this weather?" Kejen cut in.

Kuran shook his head. "Maybe a little but not as bad as you would think. Besides, it is a small price to pay for intimidating your enemy."

Kejen and Trif found themselves agreeing. Their friend Kuran was a member of the most storied and elite military formation in Northmarcher history. Every unit wore distinctive colors and insignias on their shoulder armor and sometimes helmets. Members of the Sparent brigade painted a small blue and white shield on their shoulder armor. The militia component of the brigade played a small game of one upmanship with their regular army brothers by painting a small blue and white lighting bolt on their helmets. A black and gold shield with a red stripe on the shoulder proclaimed that unit was from the mountain city of Glossak. Kejen thought the plain uniforms of soldiers from the city of Lans were quite distinctive in their own way.

But only one unit and one unit only wore all black armor and black clothes. That group of men, based in Northcross but rarely ever actually there, was the legendary Demon Division. It was the elite of the elite of the Northmarcher Army, tasked with doing things many never heard about. Things that were generally outside the scope of regular militaries. It was said only one of a hundred managed to make it through training. And Kejen's childhood friend Kuran was one of them! Kejen was privy to a few things many did not know of but by and large, Kuran kept Division business to himself. It did not keep Kuran's friend from Sparent from trying though. Kejen constantly tried to find out the exact number of men in the Division and how many were from Sparent. Most of the time, Kuran could satisfy his friend with some detailed reports of what has happening on the borders. Information like that was something any merchant could appreciate.

"Things are fine in Northcross." Kuran answered Trif's question. "The King and Queen are doing well and all is as it should be."

"So what is the big secret then?" Trif asked.

Kuran smiled and Kejen crossed his arms looking at his friend.

"Who said anything was wrong?" Kuran look puzzled.

Trif said nothing.

Kuran shook his head. "You are very hard to trick, my good friend Trif. Even your brother knows something is up."

"Yes." Both brothers said.

"I will assure you our dear homeland is in no danger. I am not totally sure of all the details myself but I cannot get into that, you understand." Kuran declared.

"A secret for a secret." Kejen offered.

"A true merchant at heart." Kuran observed. Nonetheless, he followed Kejen's invitation to come closer so he could hear the whisper. Trif took a step back and looked around to make sure no one was eavesdropping. Two men talking to a Demon Division officer in the open was bound to attract a little attention.

Kejen and Kuran walked out into the prairies. After about thirty yards or so, Kejen finally said, "What would you say if I were to tell you that someone was going to find *HeavenSteel?"*

"The first thing I would ask is if you had been standing in the sun too long." Kuran commented. "Are you making this up to get a free answer from me?"

Kejen raised his hand and continued. "What if I were to tell you that this person all ready knows where it is?"

"So when do you plan on going?" Kuran asked.

"Quick fellow you are." Kejen laughed. "No, I am not making this up and, yes, I do know where it is."

"Sounds like something the Division would go out and look for." Kuran said,

"Are they out looking for it?" Kejen inquired.

Kuran looked at his friend for a few seconds. "No. I am not sure anyone believes it exists."

"Oh it exists." Kejen pointed out. "And I can tell you where it is."

He looked around, nodded to Trif still standing guard, and huddled in close to Kuran. The Demon Division officer took off his helmet and listened closely for about thirty seconds.

He stood up and ran his hands through his blonde hair. Kuran had a look of wonder on his face.

"You have done your homework." He was clearly impressed. "The question now is, 'are you right?' "

" 'Nothing in this world is ever exact or promised' ", Kejen quoted Kascar, correctly this time. Kascar would still find something wrong with it. "I have to admit, there is a possibility it is not there. However, I have researched every source I can get my hands on. And I have done some reaching, believe me. Nine chances out of ten, its there. It HAS to be there."

"Unless someone went there and took it." Kuran shrugged. "It's a long way to go."

"But the only way to find out." Kejen declared.

Kuran's hand came up to his chin. "The place you say it is in is not the first place I would look."

"All the more reason it would be there!" Kejen said adamantly.

"All the more reason we should *look* there." Kuran corrected with the precision of an elite trooper.

"Living in Northcross turn you into a cynic?" Kejen asked

Kuran smiled and laughed. "I have seen a lot of places and a lot of things since the day you, Trif and I began training. It is not cynicism but rather a healthy skepticism. If you are sure it's there--"

"Nine chances out of ten." Kejen pointed out.

"---then I am sure it is there."

Kejen's fists shot up in the air in triumph. Trif took it a sign the conversation was over so he quietly walked over.

"I know, ah, I guess you would call him a wise man." Kuran said. "He lives up in the Ankers. He knows a lot about the deep mountains. He can tell us anything if there is anything to know. I would imagine you are entering the mountains through Glossak."

Kejen nodded. "Best place to go into from. We can pick up supplies and it is in the direction we are going."

"Not bad for a militia officer." Kuran said dryly.

Kejen picked up Kuran put him on his shoulder the same way he did with Gusaric. "I should carry you to Glossak and drop you into the first horse trough I see." he joked.

"Notice he is picking you up in full armor." Trif pointed out to Kuran

"I am aware of that." Kuran answered back as Kejen pretended to walk in the direction of the mountains. "All brawn and no brain. A horse trough here in Sparent would be more efficient. Now put me down".

Kuran turned serious quickly enough once his feet were on the ground. "I know a trapper and a guide there who could be of great use to us. If I am not there, ask for Overdulf at the merchant's guild. I am sure you know where that is."

"Why would you not be there?" Trif asked.

The Demon Division captain rapped on his black armor. "You never know what the King will have us doing."

"True enough" Trif agreed.

"I have to be off." Kuran said quickly and began walking away with a purposeful stride.

Kejen trotted after him. "Don't run away from me quite yet. I gave you a secret, now you give me one."

"Oh yes" Kuran remembered without breaking stride. "Storks do not bring babies."

Kejen slapped his friend on the shoulder. "That's not what I meant!"

Kuran looked at Kejen, smiled and kept walking. "The King is here in Sparent."

"Whatever for?"

"He is meeting with some emissaries from a foreign country."

"What is so strange about that?" Trif trotted along the other side of Kuran. Kejen was consulting his mental map trying to guess which nation. "And why here and not the Royal Castle?"

"All I know is that it is not a country we do not ordinarily talk to that much." Kuran revealed.

Trif and Kejen both looked puzzled.

"So why talk to them here in Sparent?" Kejen asked.

"I must really be going." Kuran said with just a hint of irritation.

Both brothers stopped in their tracks and saluted.

"May good health and happiness follow you." Kejen waved.

Kuran stopped, pivoted and whispered something in Kejen's ear.

Kejen looked surprised. "Really?"

Kuran nodded and darted down the street. He could move pretty fast in his armor too Kejen thought. Then again, Kuran was in the Demon Division.

"Another secret?" Trif asked although he knew the answer.

"A very good one." Kejen announced.

"Maybe we will see her at Leron's birthday party." Trif speculated and walked off.

"How did you know what her name was?" Kejen called after him.

Trif waved and continued walking.

Chapter 4

The work never stopped. The work never went away. The work always had to be done. Kejen enjoyed Leron's birthday party but he knew when to call it a night. It was part of becoming a responsible adult. It still helped to have Trif remind him a couple of times nonetheless.

The caravans were ready to go and last minute negotiations continued over goods, routes, expenses and percentages. Horses were fed and readied and the wagons were checked yet again. And last minute problems still cropped up.

Kejen was dealing with onc of those last minute problems, helping change out a wagon wheel, while Trif shoed a couple of draft horses that were going to be needed to pull that same wagon.

Strange, Trif thought as he held the hammer aloft with a horse's foot between his knees. Kejen walked over, dirt and axle grease on his pants and shirt, and sat down on the hay covered floor of the stable.

"What is it?" He asked his brother. "I saw the pensive look on your face. Putting a shoe on a horse is not something requires a lot of concentration."

Trif quickly finished hammering the small nails into place.

"Have you seen Kascar about lately?"

Kejen rocked back and drew his knees up to his chin. "Now that you mention it. No."

Trif checked his handiwork and dropped the horse's foot. "I saw him at the militia practice, checking armor for cracks and whatnot but since then I have not even heard him shouting. That is unusual."

Kejen stood up. "That is odd."

"I have to take care of one more horse." Trif pointed out. "Why don't you find out where Kascar is?"

"That would be a good idea." Kejen took the suggestion. "Do you think he is all right?"

"I am sure he is very well." Trif said grimly. "Very well indeed. Well enough to do a little riding."

Kejen nodded, spun on his heel and left the stable with long purposeful strides in the direction of Trogen's Forge. He did not like the thoughts that were creeping into his mind but Trif was rarely wrong about anything.

Kejen arrived at the forge quickly. It did seem a bit quiet. Well, not quiet but not as loud as usual. There was no such thing as a quiet metal working establishment. Hammers hit iron and people moved around with a purpose but Kejen did not hear Kascar's loud distinctive voice rise above the din.

He tapped the shoulder of one of Kascar's employee's walking by with an unfinished shield. "Where's Old Man Trogen today?"

The man shrugged and shifted the shield to his other hand. "I don't know. His son is running things today."

Kejen looked through the door for any sight of Ranlo. "He's a bright lad."

"Yes" the man agreed before continuing on his way. "He gets almost as much done as his father but without the yelling."

"Give him time." Kejen laughed. "May good health and happi---oh never mind." The man had all ready gone into the building. Kascar's employees stayed busy even when he was not here. Kejen nodded his head in approval.

He waved at someone he knew riding on a wagon of timber and walked determinedly across the street to Kascar's house. Kejen glared at the fence post in front of the door and was ready to knock. Then he stopped. Yes, he heard Xavia yelling at Kascar's other five children, whose noise rivaled that of the forge, but he should have heard Kascar shouting too. So where was Kascar? The only other possibility (*in Sparent*, Kejen thought darkly) was the Centre Park. Kejen shook his head. No, Kascar would have told everyone at the forge, and everyone else within fifty yards, that he was going there.

Kejen thought of someone who might have actually seen Kascar early this morning. He walked quickly in the direction of the Castle. After ducking through a couple of back alleys, Kejen emerged behind a mounted patrol clip clopping its way toward the old fortification about fifty yards away.

"Gusaric!" Kejen called.

Gusaric turned around in the saddle and saw Kejen.

"How's the head?" Kejen asked, walking up to his friend. He pantomimed someone drinking, complete with his mouth open. "Lots of ale passing that way."

Gusaric waved his command into the Castle, watching it ride across the wooden drawbridge stretching over a twenty foot moat into the bowels of the huge stone fortress. "Wasn't that much!"

Kejen patted him on the knee. "Interesting morning?"

Gusaric shrugged. "Got the patrol together and made our rounds....Slowly I tell you." He patted his helmet.

"No one else out on any early morning rides?" Kejen asked.

"Many people riding around early in the morning."

"Anyone we know?"

"Who are you looking for?" Gusaric asked

"Kascar Trogen." Kejen answered, "Did you see him any place today?"

Gusaric shook his head. "Only thing interesting this morning was someone shouting about a burglar. As you guessed, no burglar. Maybe he is wandering around in the Park. You know he does that sometimes."

Kejen nodded. "Maybe. Good health and happiness to you Gusaric."

"You too, Kejen."

Kejen watched him disappear into the Castle. He thought about asking Gusaric about Castle happenings and try to find out what Kuran was talking about out at the militia practices but at the moment he had other things to worry about. He forgot about those other things when he saw Gusaric return the salute of a rather elderly looking major at the gate.

The old man looked directly at Kejen and waved him over.

"Grandfather!" Kejen smiled and walked over. "I did not know you were on duty today!"

"This is where I have lived for the last twenty years now, Kejen!" His grandfather laughed. "Of course, you are used to seeing me at the other gate."

Leworl was a tall, skinny man with a loose jointed, almost jaunty walk that seemed strange for a man well past the midpoint of his sixties. His long arms and large hands contributed to his rather rangy looks. If "may good health and happiness follow you", applied to anyone, it was Leworl.

"Why are you over here anyway?" Kejen asked.

"King Maridon asked me that same question almost a quarter of a century ago." Leworl laughed. "I thought it was an interesting question to ask considering he was about thirty feet from going over a waterfall."

Kejen heard the story literally hundreds of times but Leworl always found a way to put an interesting angle on it. Exactly a quarter of a century ago, the King of the Northmarch at the time, Maridron, a mountain climbing enthusiast, slipped off a peak and fell into a river. A river that led straight to a waterfall. The King reached out to take hold of a rock thirty feet from the falls but instead found the outstretched hand of Leworl Densky. What Leworl was doing on a rock in the middle of that river was still a mystery. Not even a King could question the business of a man who had just saved his life. A man who seemed a little old to still climb mountains but a live saver nonetheless. The grateful King made Leworl the Gatekeeper of Sparent. It was an honorary position dating back to the days when it was a very real position. Back then in the days of and after the Cataclysmic War, the Gatekeeper was in charge of the Castle guard, always on the walls looking for marauders and ready to close the gate, raise the drawbridge and defend those walls. Now it was occupied by Leworl, who had lived at the Castle since the passing of Kejen's paternal grandmother before either brother was born.

Kejen embraced his grandfather and lifted him up.

"Offf" Leworl said. "Stop that. These old bones are not what they used to be!"

Kejen wagged his finger in the face of the laughing Leworl. "Don't give me that! You will make it to the century mark easily enough. You will still be around when I am *your* age!"

"You and your brother are good boys" Leworl patted Kejen on the head. "You still come by and see me quite often when everyone else has forgotten about me."

"That is because everyone who knew you for a long time has passed on now." Kejen pointed out. "You even outlived the man you saved!"

"He was a good man." Leworl nodded his head. "God is happy to have him in Heaven. Maridon left his son to continue the good work. Too bad you and Fleston are not close as Maridon and I were. I don't think you've even met each other."

Kejen shrugged. "It's nothing personal. You and the old King had a deep personal bond. Saving a life. How much more personal or deeper is that?"

Leworl look sad for just a second. "Everyday I wish your grandmother was here. She would have been so proud of you and Trif." His jauntiness returned quickly enough though. "When I finally go, I will get to see her again."

Kejen put his hand on Leworl's shoulder "Hopefully not for a while."

Kejen followed Leworl to his quarters. He had a few rooms to himself and turned one into a library. There were many, many books there. Mostly history and geography. It looked like the sort of place Trif could spend hours in. Kejen spied a couple of adventure tales as well walking in. However, he liked the maps the best.

Leworl knew that and kept them on the other side of his library. There were many, many scrolls and maps, some open, some on the floor. His grandfather liked maps too. It was times like this Kejen wondered why he seemed to take more after his grandfather than his father.

"I have what you were looking for a few weeks ago." Leworl announced, popping up from behind another table. "I have a correspondence friend in Barcova who was able to find this."

"This" was a detailed map of the Ankers.

Kejen was impressed. But skeptical. "A man you have never met, except through exchange of letters, trusts you enough to send you this to copy?"

Leworl shrugged. "He is an old badger like me."

"If you are looking for a badger in human form, find Kascar Trogen." Kejen laughed and rolled the map on the table.

Leworl grinned. "If there is an advantage to being my age, it's that I can remember when even *he* was your age."

Kejen shook his head trying to imagine Kascar as a young man. "Frightening."

"He was never what you would call a diplomat." Leworl remembered.

"Still isn't."

Kejen looked at the map intently. "Is this where you saved King Maridon?"

"Indeed it is." Leworl answered without looking.

Then he sat down. "Why were you looking at the eastern side of the Ankers when I gave you the map?"

Kejen looked up and smiled. "I am looking for a love potion to entice the pretty girls."

"Things like that bring out the ugly ones too." Leworl said, salt and pepper eyebrows rising for emphasis. "Use character and wit instead."

Kejen touched his nose. "Harder for some than others."

"Don't worry, Kejen. She is out there somewhere." Leworl promised.

Kejen sat down and clasped his grandfather's hands with his own. "What were you doing in the mountains that day, grandfather?" he asked for the thousandth time.

"A man's business is his own." Leworl answered for the thousandth time. Then he let go of Kejen's hands and smiled. "I will make a bargin with you though."

Kejen eagerly agreed.

"If you tell me why you are so interested in the eastern Ankers, your thumb was on the Bleiben River by the way, maybe I will finally reveal to you the mystery of that day."

"Really?" Kejen for once was nonplussed.

"Perhaps I will." Leworl stood up dramatically. "And you do not have to even keep it a secret. Tell everyone! I am too bloody old to care anymore."

Kejen stood up and shook hands with his grandfather.

"Come by for dinner tonight. Even if I decide not to tell you, at least you get a great bit of lamb!" Leworl promised. Like his grandson, he liked to tease people too. Kejen grimaced. He did not like having the tables turned on him.

A soldier Kejen did not know stuck his head in the door and waved at his grandfather.

"I was taking care of the horses and one of my men said there was some sort of parade taking place." The trooper said.

"Parade?" Kejen was confused. "Someone in the stocks again and everyone has a piece of some old bread?"

The soldier shrugged and disappeared into the hallway.

Kejen followed him and Leworl ambled out too.

"Let us have dinner tonight." Leworl easily walked up beside his grandson. "Bring Trif too. I have not had the two of you over for some time It has been too, too long."

Kejen hugged his grandfather with one arm as they made their way out the main gate.

This is where I had one of life's trials Kejen thought as he remembered his basic training here. Little did he know he was about to endure another.

Kejen and Leworl walked over the drawbridge, enjoying the April weather. It was a good day for a parade. It did, however, seem a little early for Easter. Maybe someone was getting a head start on the holiday.

Instead of a parade, he saw Gusaric ride around from behind a corner, shouting for Kejen. Then he saw Kascar trotting on foot behind him. Kejen felt his stomach do a slow lurch. Never one to back down from adverse situations, as this one was promising to develop into, Kejen walked across the drawbridge and stepped out into the middle of the street. Leworl motioned for a couple of the gate guards to follow Kejen. He knew his grandson better than anyone else.

Gusaric reigned in right in front of his friend. "What is this about you going to the Ankers to find that old sword of your forefathers?"

Kascar felt Kejen's gaze cut through him like a knife. Then Kejen lunged at him. A soldier on both sides managed to grab his arms but a third was needed to keep the enraged and shouting Kejen from throttling the town armorer.

"You gave me your word!!!!" Kejen shouted

"I guess it just slipped out." Kascar said with too much sarcasm.

"Just slipped out?!" Kejen shouted again. "Like the way my hand is going to slip out and belt you in the mouth?!"

And it almost happened.

Kejen worked his left arm free and launched a haymaker right at the surprised Kascar's head. It missed the mark by an inch as a fourth soldier helped yanked the Sparent merchant turned berserker back a foot.

A fifth soldier ran past the laughing Leworl to help restrain Kejen just in case. He was wondering if he needed to call in the rest of his squad to hold this demon down.

"What the devil are you laughing at?" the angry Kascar demanded of Leworl.

"You should have seen the look on your face when my grandson's fist almost caved your head in!" Leworl guffawed.

Kascar scowled at Leworl, who just continued to laugh at him. Yet another soldier appeared on the scene, this time taking up a position between the Gatekeeper and Kascar.

Trif once again appeared from nowhere and walked right up to Kascar, standing about six inches from his nose.

"Did you not give my brother your word?"

"This does not concern you." Kascar huffed. Then everyone noticed Trif was carrying a bullwhip.

The sergeant called in the rest of his squad.

"Don't do that, Trif. It'll solve nothing." Leworl decided it was at last time to intervene. "That is enough Kejen. Quit before you end up in the stocks."

Trif looked over at his grandfather, nodded and turn his back on Kascar before walking away a few steps. Kejen angrily complied as well and stopped struggling.

"Enjoying the scene you created?" Leworl asked Kascar. "Do you not get enough entertainment when you are working? Did you not give my grandson your word?"

Kascar snorted and looked up the street at an approaching crowd of people.

"Friends of yours?" Trif asked with a trace of sarcasm. Kascar glared at him, not happy with being on the receiving end of it. The unflappable Trif weathered the return glare with indifferent ease.

Abruptly the crowd halted and split open like a curtain, allowing a man leading a horse to emerge. Smiling, holding one hand in greeting and the other holding the horses reins, was a man named after the great hero. Kejen and Trif's father, Gaking, had arrived.

"Father?" Kejen managed to say. He also saw an older woman on the horse's saddle. "And Mother?".

Leworl did not seem all that surprised. "Looks like old Kascar can still cover quite a bit of distance in no time at all. What brings you to Sparent, my son?"

Gaking ran a large hand through his graying hair. Everyone immediately noticed his resemblance to Trif and compared it to Kejen's wild looks. Kejen noticed what they were doing which only contributed to his anger but he managed to still himself.

Gaking handed the reins to Trif and turned to face Leworl. After a quick bow, his deep voice filled the small street. "I am gladdened to see good health and happiness have found you my father. I have come to Sparent to save my son from chasing relics we'd rather, or shouldn't, know about."

There were murmurs from the crowd and a couple of worried glances at Kejen. A few even hurriedly crossed themselves.

"There is nothing heretical afoot." Kejen announced in his deep and typically loud voice. It had no trouble reaching everyone in the area.

Gusaric quickly came to Kejen's aid, calling on the crowd to disperse. There was nothing heretical afoot and there was nothing more to see.

Kejen watched his grandfather and father embrace and then he followed them dejectedly back into the Castle. Normally he would be overjoyed at his parent's visit but with this *HeavenSteel* quest out in the open now, he began to wish that would have picked another time to visit. Earlier, Kejen had asked his friend Gusaric if it had been an interesting morning. It certainly was.

Kejen's self-pity lasted for about thirty seconds. Even before he crossed the drawbridge leading into the Castle, he almost shouted.

"I am going into the Ankers in search of *HeavenSteel* and that is the end of it!"

The soldiers standing guard there started for a second, surprised by the sheer vehemence of the announcement. Since five of them spend a considerable amount of strength and energy restraining Kejen, they were also a bit alarmed. The energy and anger behind it felt almost solid. Even Gaking looked over his shoulder with a raised eyebrow. They had nothing to fear however. Reri, Kejen's mother, said nothing but she did look back at her offspring. That was more than enough to keep her still seething son in check. Whatever thoughts she had she kept to herself. Trif did likewise and any observant party would have noted that although Trif may have physically resembled his father, he had clearly inherited his personality from his mother.

Kejen's fists balled up and he felt his body girding itself for combat. "Climbing every bleedin' peak in the Ankers is going to be easy compared to the next few minutes" he mumbled to himself.

Three generations of the Densky family shuffled into the map room of Leworl's quarters. Leworl talked to a soldier and secured overnight quarters for Gaking and Reri before inviting everyone to have a seat.

Gaking and Reri sat on one side of the table and Kejen found Trif sitting next to him, hands folded together as usual, on the other side. It was a small but powerful gesture. And typically subtle as Trif was. Kejen quickly reached under the table and squeezed his brother's hand. To his surprise, Trif squeezed it back. And hard!

"You archers *do* have strong hands." he whispered "Is that from *just* archery practice?"

Just a bare hint of a smile flitted across Trif's face.

No one said anything for a full minute.

"One room over" Gaking addressed both of his sons, "Before either one of you were born, I had to carry two dozen heavy stones out across the drawbridge, one at a time, for questioning the orders of my sergeant."

Kejen held out on arm and flexed a large bicep.

"Took **five** soldiers to keep him from tossing your friend Kascar into the moat." Leworl said with a smile.

"It would have never happened if my son did not have such daft notions in his head." Gaking's demeanor suddenly hardened. "He would haul horses out beyond the drawbridge and all the way to Northcross if it were up to me!"

"It's not up to you." Leworl said.

Kejen stood up. "I can speak for myself! And I will!"

"Then do so!" Gaking commanded in a voice straight off the battlefield at Driegam. "Explain yourself!"

"That tone of voice will not solve anything." Leworl cut in.

"He is my son!" Gaking shouted.

"And you are my son." Leworl said flatly but the tone said he would not brook any disagreement.

Kejen had never seen his father brought to heel like that. Leworl had a quiet strength of his own.

Gaking did not look happy but nonetheless continued in a somewhat quieter tone of voice. Like his borderline heretical son, Gaking often did not realize how loud he was. Kejen just thought he was loud.

Gaking's eyebrows came together and his scowl became deeper. "What is this I am told about a quest to retrieve *HeavenSteel?*"

"Exactly that." Kejen answered. "I want to go out and find the sword that belongs to our family. Why are you condemning me for that?"

"No one is condemning you, Kejen." Reri said. "It just seems rash and dangerous."

"Dangerous? Possibly." Kejen replied. "But not at all rash."

He produced a leather bound journal and the map his grandfather gave him before he tried to take Kascar's head off.

Gaking opened it and looked at the meticulous research Kejen had undertaken in ascertaining the sword's location and circumstances of its disappearance. Kejen felt a bit more heartened when he noticed his father looking up from the journal and consulting the map.

At least he is reading it he thought.

Gaking pushed it over to Leworl, who seemed much more interested in Kejen's findings.

"Very well." Gaking said. "You have planned this for quite some time."

After a moment, Kejen nodded.

"And you must know that anything from the time of Faerie is anathema." Gaking spat out.

"There is nothing heretical about *HeavenSteel*. Even the name conjures up nothing but feelings of good and right." Kejen pointed out.

"You could be excommunicated for this!" Gaking's voice rose ominously.

Kejen waved it off. "For retrieving a sword God himself made? I think not."

"Is that why you are against our proposed journey?" Trif spoke for the first time.

"Our?" Gaking and Reri looked at him in shock.

"Do you mean to tell me that you are going on this...this... madness too?!" Gaking exclaimed. His complexion was beginning to turn a shade of red. Leworl looked up from the map and gave his son a warning glance.

Gaking took a moment to compose himself. "My sons...Do you mean to tell me that you are going on some self-proclaimed mission to recover a sword that may or may not exist, whose precise location is unknown and located in a largely unexplored part of the Ankers inhabited by only God knows what?"

"I know it seems that way," Kejen admitted uneasily. Before his father could explode in a fit of titanic rage, Kejen cut him off. "But I know where it is!"

"Where?" Gaking's anger seemed blunted for the moment.

"Rainkin Falls."

Gaking looked unconvinced but Leworl nodded.

"Here." Kejen waved his family to gather around the open journal. "Look at Lorac's very own words.."

I hid the sword in a clearing near Nature's walkway, with a clear view of the falls and the lake which gave it life. The Sun descends behind the upper falls into the river behind. All of this behind the great glacier."

Kejen looked around the room. To him the answer seemed fairly obvious. Unfortunately, every one else, including Trif, looked back at him uncomprehending. Everyone except Leworl.

"Show them." He encouraged his grandson.

"Two waterfalls. One facing south, the other west, forming a ninety degree angle like this." Kejen put his hands together to form the angle. "The Sun is dropping *behind* one. The glacier he is talking about it the Kalagda glacier."

Gaking slowly reached over and looked at the map for a long minute. He looked back at the journal and back at the map again for another long minute.

"I understand what you mean." Gaking finally said. "But are you sure this is the place?" He held the map up. "Lorac was supposed to be visiting the Sea Faring Kingdoms when he was supposed to have hidden the sword. This depository of yours is in the wrong part of the mountains."

"He told everyone he was going to Traiklef." Kejen explained. "It was a white salmon to throw everyone off. If he did lose *HeavenSteel* in the Three Days Battle, why go through this elaborate deception."

"If the sword even exists." Gaking challenged his son.

"If it exists?" Kejen was dumbfounded. "What do you mean if it exists? Of course it exists!"

"No one has seen it in two centuries!" Gaking's voice again rose dangerously.

"That is because it was lost two and half centuries ago." Kejen refused to capitulate. "What sort of daft line of questions is this?"

"Daft?!" Gaking shouted. "Are you calling your father daft?!"

Leworl's fist crashed down on the table. "Enough!"

"Can you read his mind?" Gaking asked his father hotly. "What is it that makes him so? Does he even know what he is talking about?"

"I looked for the sword too." Leworl said evenly.

Now it was Kejen's turn to look shocked. He had always suspected it but now that his grandfather had admitted it, it seemed even more shocking.

Leworl finally broke the stunned silence that permeated the room like an early morning mist.

"Twenty-five years ago. Right after your mother died. " Leworl recalled. "I studied like Kejen here and came to the same conclusion. I even marched right up the bank of the Bleiben. All the way to the glacier. Then the King flipped his boat over and came straight to the rock I was on."

Gaking sat down heavily and shook his head. "It has been one strange day. What can one say about it?"

"That we do not get too many of them." Reri answered him

Another long minute passed. Soon it stretched into another.

"Why?" Gaking asked the question that formed in everyone's mind. "Why did you do that?"

Leworl looked up at the ceiling. "Do you remember the time after your mother died, Gaking?"

Gaking looked down and nodded slowly. It was not a time he wanted to remember. Kejen could not blame him.

"I was lost son." Leworl remembered sadly. "It was as if I had nothing to live for. You remember how I was."

"It was a bad time." Gaking mumbled.

"We named you for the great hero...the man who had found

HeavenSteel." Leworl said. "Do you know why we did that?"

Gaking looked at his father sheepishly. For just a second, Kejen saw the little boy his father was four decades ago. It as astounding! Trif's eyes narrowed a bit. He too was having trouble believing what he was seeing but at the same time, he was etching the moment in his infinite memory.

Gaking finally answered. "Because you and Mother expected great things from me."

"And you did not disappoint!" Leworl bounded up to his feet. "You, Gaking, fought bravely in the war. Then you were the first of our family to leave Gaking's Grove and you became the greatest merchant Sparent has ever seen. You and Reri gave me two splendid grandsons! And you came back to the Grove. You did not forget your roots!"

Gaking looked distinctly uncomfortable amid the praise.

"We all deal with our grief in different ways." Leworl continued. "You immersed yourself in trade. I went to look for *HeavenSteel."*

Leworl sat down and looked down at the table. "You were much more successful than I."

Gaking shook his head. "My father saved the King. My father is part of history. I am only a grain merchant." He grinned at everyone at the table. "A very good one, mind you!"

Everyone chuckled.

"But my father is a greater man than I." Gaking said.

"You are all he ever talks about." Reri added in quietly.

You were *my age* when you went into the mountains looking for that sword. Do you realize what sort of determination that takes?" Gaking asked.

"The same kind your son Kejen shows." Leworl answered. "And do not let Trif fool you. He does not show it as much as Kejen but the fire burns in him too."

They all looked at Trif, who, as usual, said nothing.

"We have an.....interesting family." Gaking began. "All the way back to the original Gaking. We have always lived along the river, as natural as the frogs and reeds and fish. Even Sparent is along the Densk. Kejen and Trif are the first in our family to be born outside the Grove. And it seems they will add more than that to the annuls."

Gaking reached out for Kejen's hand and looked for Trif's as well. Reri held her husband's hand and Kejen's too. Leworl hugged his son and somehow found a way to pat both of his grandsons on the head.

"Leworl the Nimble!" Kejen laughed, "I remember that is what you said they called you as a child! Now I believe it!"

It was a sweet moment that many families never have enough of in any century.

Gaking recovered quickly and bounded up. "Very well my sons. If you are that determined to go, then let me help you get the right supplies and plot out a good route."

Kejen clapped and reached forward to pick up his father. Gaking managed to scurry away toward the door.

"I still have some speed, boy!" he laughed. "Let's get some things together for you."

Gaking opened the door and in tumbled Kascar.

Leworl and Trif quickly stepped in between Kejen and the armorer.

"No need for that." Kejen assured everyone, including Kascar. "Everything is as it should be. He was doing what he thought was right. Who knows? Maybe he was right."

Gaking laughed and helped his old friend up. "The greatest scout the world had ever seen! I don't think even you had much practice in listening through doors!"

Kejen thought he heard Trif mumble something about rats and Kascar's relation to them but decided to let it go especially since he had never seen Kascar hug anyone, even his wife. It was turning out to be quite the day for shocking events.

Kejen walked up to Kascar and solemnly shook his hand.

"So I guess you are going anyway." Kascar said.

"Yes, I am. Tomorrow as a matter of fact."

"Tomorrow?" Gaking stood agape. "We have things to get and maps to study!"

Kejen shook his head. "Very well. Day after tomorrow then."

He felt Trif's hand on his shoulder. "Oh fine! Two days hence and not one moment more!"

Gaking nodded his approval and Kejen offered to take his father's horse to the stable. Gaking was talking merrily to Kascar and waved in the affirmative.

Kejen slipped out of the door, ran across the drawbridge to the hitching post and hopped on his father's horse. It was all ready dark out but Kejen rode down the street at full speed anyway.

He was happy and excited at the same time and the adrenaline was pumping through his system by the gallon.

"It's nighttime and you are galloping around like it is broad daylight!" yelled a women whose dress now had mud kicked up on it from the horse's hooves.

Kejen half waved at her and sped along. He was actually GOING on his quest. All the planning was done and the day to go was only two sunrises away! It was a liberating feeling and he let all of Sparent know about it with a wild whoop. *HeavenSteel* was one day closer to being where it belonged!

Trif walked across the drawbridge and heard a high pitched yell that told him his brother had almost run someone down-again. He could even hear the hoof beats though they quickly diminished. Trif allowed himself the luxury of a rare smile. He felt his hands tremble slightly and knew the same sort of excitement that flooded through Kejen was flowing through him. Leworl was right. Trif was excited by the prospect of adventure too. Maybe not to the same degree as his brother but it did live in him too. He reflected on the irony of that and walked home alone with his thoughts under the flickering light of the *aurora borealis.*

Chapter 5

Kejen was up early. Very early. So early he was not sure he had even slept. Trif, ever practical, had no trouble sleeping. Besides, Trif knew Kejen would load up the horses long before any stable hands, early birds themselves, showed up. Kejen would be ready to go even before the sun was up. And it rose early this far north in the Spring. Nevertheless, Kejen did not have to wake his brother up. Trif knew when it was time to go and he would be ready.

Kejen was in full armor and mounted when Trif rode up.

"Good morning!" Kejen managed to remember at the last second not to shout. At this hour, it was a good bet even Kascar Trogen was still sleeping. Then again, maybe not.

"We are actually going to go and do it!!!"

Trif was fairly certain someone had heard that. Kejen was in high spirits and rapidly crossing the line into exuberance.

"Yes we are going to find *HeavenSteel."* Trif announced. "But the odds would improve considerably if we actually left the stable."

Kejen's laughter pealed off of the surrounding houses. People were certainly awake now. "Yes, that would be a good first step!"

With that, Kejen spurred his mount on into a canter that seemed only a half step removed from a gallop. Trif shook his head and followed. It was going to be a long trip. There was no sense in wearing one's self out before leaving Sparent.

And they would not leave the city quite yet. Kejen saw his mother and father standing in front of his home waiting for them. They were outwardly cheerful but inwardly very worried. Leworl had walked down from the Castle and even Kascar was there, though that was no great surprise given the hour. Kejen was not sure who the other person with his grandfather was.

Kejen stopped and waited for Trif before dismounting to hug his parents and grandfather. Kascar, of course, shunned all but necessary human contact. He sternly shook Kejen's hand.

"Best of luck to you." Kascar said. "Don't do anything stupid."

Kascar was Kascar. Kejen nodded. It was, however, good advice. Then the old armorer surprised him with a bear hug.

"And don't let your guard down!" he growled.

After Kascar had released his iron grip, Kejen walked up to the stranger standing next to his family. He dropped to one knee and took the man's offered hand.

"Good morning Father Michael". Kejen said.

"And good morning to you too Kejen." The priest said. "I wish you nothing but success on your quest." The Keilstroker accent was barely noticeable.

"That means very much to my brother and I." Kejen returned the good intention.

If there was anyone from the largely Asrinian run Church that could win over the trust of Northmarchers, it was Father Michael.

"May I give you the Church's blessing?" Father Michael asked

Kejen nodded, inwardly wondering if Father Michael knew he was looking for something from the time of faerie. Father Michael obviously was not the kind to automatically assume anything unconventional was heresy. In his late twenties, Father Michael was not yet too set in his ways. After all, he had gone well out of this way to learn the language of his flock after he was informed of this new posting in the Northmarch. That endeared him to his congregation more than anything else.

Trif knelt down beside his brother and the priest made the sign of the Cross.

"In the name of the Father, Son and Holy Spirit, I bless your servants Kejen and Trif. May You watch over them and may they return safe."

Both brothers stood up. Kejen shook the priests hand and said "May good health and happiness follow you."

Short, simple and distinctly Northmarcher. Moments like this gave the priest from Kielstrock hope that he might actually fit in one day.

Kejen and Trif mounted up again, waved to everyone and were off. The long promised journey was finally underway. Adventure awaited and now Kejen was determined that he would go out to find it before it came to him.

The stars hung in the predawn darkness and the early morning silence was all but impenetrable. The east began to pinken somewhat but it was still awfully early. Kejen was sure they would not hear any roosters quite yet. Although the brothers were riding in full armor, they traveled light. Kejen had his broadsword strapped secured in the scabbard, which was in turn, strapped to his broad back. Trif kept his bow tied to the saddle. He wore his archer gloves as he rode and the pieces of metal sown between the second and third joints increased his punching power in case something got past his arrows. Or if he ran out of arrows. The ever resourceful brother of

Kejen Densky had another quiver of arrows wrapped up just in case the fifty on his back were not enough.

The dirt road gave way to cobblestones as they approached the Castle. Gusaric was there to meet them and rode with his friends on the way toward the militia training grounds and the prairies beyond. Before long, the cobblestone street ended and they were back on dirt again.

"How long do you think you'll be gone?" Gusaric wondered.

"A day and a half to Northcross." Kejen said. "About three to Glossak and into the mountains. We sell or trade these horses for other supplies and up the river we go."

"I noticed you were not riding Charger." Gusaric pointed out.

"Of course not. I would not leave him in Glossak in a stable he did not know!"

They both laughed and Trif merely nodded. One always looked after your horse. Even these horses, soon to be sold, were fed better and looked after with more care than in any other country. Such was life on the steppes. Your horse quite often came before you.

"Six weeks, eight at the most." Kejen finished.

Gusaric was turned in the saddle looking back at the Castle's menacing silhouette set against the rising sun. It looked like something from a militarist's fantasy. To Gusaric, it was quite comforting.

He turned around. "Six to eight weeks. In that amount of time, you could take a stick and poke every square inch of the riverbank."

"No sense going if we do not look under every rock." Kejen returned.

"In that time, you could look under every rock." Gusaric smiled. "But you are right. If you are going to do it, do it well."

The training grounds appeared and there was Crinklin with the assembled platoon, mounted on their horses, giving a mass salute, presenting arms in the Northmarcher manner, sitting rigidly in the saddle, swords pointed up and angled, hilt held under the chin.

Kejen felt moved by the gesture but before he could express his thanks, the platoon broke into pandemonium riding around, cheering and patting both he and his brother on the back and doing their best to almost knock them out of the saddle. How could you not like people like this?

Kejen, Trif and Gusaric managed to break loose and ride to the edge of the Densk River. Gusaric clasped hands with Trif and then Kejen.

"Take care of yourselves. I don't care if you bring back any sword, just bring yourselves back."

Kejen nodded as he released Gusaric's hand, turned, and rode across the shallows, splashing up water and showering himself and Trif with the river that they were named for and had known all their lives.

He clambered up the bank on the other side and Trif was next to him a second later. They looked back over the city that was beginning to shake off its evening slumber. Kejen could hear ever so faintly, the creaking of wagons beginning to move and the start of the bustling of the streets.

Crinklin led the platoon to the river's edge and led the men in another cheer for their lieutenant and his brother. They jabbed swords and lances in the air and chanted Kejen's name. Kejen returned the favor. He urged his mount into a caracole, the early morning sun glinting off of its sharp steel blade. He felt like what a Masovian would call the perfect picture of barbarian splendor.

"Do you think he is just saying good-bye or challenging the world to try and stop him?" Crinklin yelled over the boisterousness of his soldiers to Gusaric.

"Knowing him, it's a challenge!" Gusaric shouted back. "At least he has Trif with him to try and keep him from plowing into anything head on!"

Crinklin just shook his head. "It just means Trif'll shoot it from fifty yards. It's always the quiet ones you need to be careful of!"

Kejen and Trif turned their horses northward and galloped out into the sprawling plains. At long, long last, their quest was finally underway.

The first day was actually quite boring. Kejen had traveled this very route to Northcross at least a dozen times in his life. He even knew the location of a small forest and the very moment it would appear. Trif shook his head as he watched his brother charge into it head on. Kejen amused himself riding between trees and turning around them at progressively narrower angles. Trif halted his mount and watched the panicked birds fly off in several directions at once. Obviously, they were not amused by the sort of ruckus Kejen was enjoying. Thundering hooves and wild shouting was something even human beings did not really get used too. Kejen burst out of the trees a hundred yards away chasing something that looked like a fox. Well, most human beings, Trif amended silently.

The fox made a sharp left and bolted back into the trees. Kejen smiled wickedly but did not follow it. The flying object hazard created by frightened birds was something even he did not want to brave in the close confines of the woods.

Trif rode up to his brother and lightly punched Kejen's armored shoulder. "You are 'it'!"

Kejen chased after him and the game was on. The unspoken rule was simple. No turning south. You could go left and right but no doubling back. That way they could make progress toward the capital and have a little fun on what so far did not seem all that different from a routine trading mission.

Thus began a game of tag played over several square miles of the vast flatlands. Kejen once got into some serious trouble playing this game. As usual, the problem was his hyperactivity. The object was to touch the other player. Kejen had amplified that to tackling the other the fellow out of the saddle. For some reason, Kejen had reacted rather angrily when the other person threw his helmet at him. A wry grin formed on Trif's face. His brother was much more mature now. Then he decided to tighten the strap on his helmet just in case.

The game lasted well into the late afternoon. The sun dipped toward the west and the shadows grew long. Kejen, much to his brother's surprise, called the game to a halt first. By the conspiratorial smirk on his face, he had a good reason.

"We are going to curve to the northwest a bit." Kejen announced and then urged his mount into a trot in that direction. "For an hour or so until the sun disappears."

Trif rode up beside him. "Why northwest?"

Kejen tapped his dominant facial feature on the side with his finger. "Guess who else is going to Northcross."

Trif shrugged. “You have me at a disadvantage."

"He was coming to Sparent to see us but only after visiting Northcross" Kejen gave another hint.

Trif was puzzled. He spun the problem around in his mind but to no avail.

Kejen leaned forward and said. "*Locklannigh.*"

"*Locklannigh?*" Trif repeated the foreign word. "That is what the Sea-Farers call themselves."

"That they certainly do." Kejen confirmed.

"So Jerik of Warron is going to be in the capital." Trif deduced.

"Indeed he is!" Kejen shouted, taking delight in watching some prairie hens start at the noise. "I received a letter from him a few months ago telling me his plans for the year."

"Every two years he embarks on trading expeditions in Keilstrock and here in the Northmarch." Trif remembered.

"Two places Sea-Farers don't raid." Kejen commented.

"They do hit Keilstrock now and again." Trif corrected his brother. "It depends on which set of Sea-Farers. They don't live in a united kingdom or nation."

"Has anyone every tried to unite all of the Sea-Farer Kingdoms?" Kejen wondered.

"There have been some attempts by one Kingdom to conquer all the rest." Trif brought out some history.

"Let me guess." Kejen rolled his eyes. "The would-be uniters are all dead."

"They crucified one upside down about a century ago."

"Sounds like something Jerik would do if someone tried to take his family's throne." Kejen said.

Trif disagreed. Jerik would want to do something more original. More notable.

Before long, Kejen's ears picked up the faint strains of music wafting out over the land. Kejen pointed and Trif nodded. Their quarry was near. Sea-Farers were never what one would call quiet. Both Northmarchers slowed their horse down to a walk. They did not want to startle anyone on guard with this sound of galloping hooves. While it was true banditry had not been a problem in the Northmarch for centuries, the people Kejen sought out were not from this country. Where they came from, interclan feuds and battles happened frequently inside their own borders.

The sun had all but vanished from the sky and the stars were starting to peek out when the brothers spotted an unmounted man holding a spear, his horned helmet standing out against the orange western sky.

Kejen brought his horse to a halt and remained motionless.

"Good evening!" He shouted.

The sentry started and brought up his spear. He could not see who was out there. The setting sun, after all, was behind him. Just as Kejen intended.

"Over here!" Kejen waved at him.

The outlander shifted his stance to the right and called out something in his own language. It must have been a challenge. Then he mumbled something else.

"That was something like 'friend or foe' " Kejen remarked. "Followed by 'my head hurts.' "

The breeze blew from the direction of the laager, carrying with it the smell of ale and perhaps mead. That explained a lot and also spoke volumes about the Sea-Faring Kingdoms.

"Then I won't speak so greatly...no, loudly." Kejen said in the Warron dialect.

"You still sound loud to me, stranger." The guard said

"Kejen Densky...Sparent." Kejen was still trying to remember where to put the preposition as he waved to the dozen or so other Sea-Farers trotting from the camp.

"Kejen!" One of them shouted. "While I live and breathe! It is all right, Olsen. He is a friend."

Olsen was now using the spear as a crutch. "I am glad to hear that. These two just appeared out of the dark like ghosts. And I am no condition to fight." he hiccupped.

Kejen and Trif hopped off their horses and walked up to the approaching group.

"Sven!" Kejen called out. "How are you on this fine...um, uh..." He could not find the right Sea-Farer word.

Sven found it for him. "Night".

"Thank you. Is Jerik about? And conscience?"

Sven jerked his head in the direction of the largest and grandest wagon. "O'er there. But I am not sure what world he is in right now."

Kejen did not understand every word of what Jerik's second in command had said but he did catch the gist of it and walked toward the wagon indicated.

Jerik, of the family Merkold, Crown Prince of Warron, a minor Sea-Faring Kingdom on the Bay of Halron, was tasked by his royal father with leading trading expeditions to the Northmarch, Verrent and even Nyhissia every two years. The reasoning, Kejen suspected, was to get Jerik used to assuming responsibility for the throne he would one day inherit. The other years, Jerik quite lustily participated in the main Sea-Farer pastimes of raiding and fighting. That was to get him used to commanding men in battle for the throne he would have to one day defend...perhaps from other Sea-Farers. Jerik's travels were even extensive than even Kejen's, his raids taking him well past Masovia to Asrine, Cornsleis and even beyond Galeon. One such excursion even led to a stinging clash with the Thenrosian Navy. Instead of making him wary of rounding San Juan del Sur anytime soon, Jerik vowed to one day return to the Southern Sea empire and spit on the Emperor's shoes.

Kejen climbed up the back of the wagon, peered into the dark cavernous interior and was immediately hit the unholy combination smell of ale and vomit. As his eyes (and nose!) adjusted to the darkness, Kejen could make out the form of Jerik lying face down on the floor, a bottle clutched securely in one huge hand.

Jerik was not the same tall gangly awkward teenager a fourteen year old Kejen had met playing ball in the street in Sparent many years ago. He had become not a large man but a huge one, towering six and half feet tall (when he was standing...) and seemed about as big as one of the wagons he rode. His black as night hair, eyes and beard were as out of place in Warron as his size. That is what made many uneasy about him, prompting less certain souls to clear his path of their presence when he swaggered (or on an occasion like this, staggered...) by. The gigantic Sea-Farer and Kejen had become fast friends that day many years ago, a friendship as strong as the miles between their respective homelands.

Presently, Kejen saw nothing but the Jerik's posterior end facing him. Not wishing to experience first hand the aftereffects of any gastronomical misadventures, he looked for a way around the slumbering behemoth. Kejen could not find any so he simply walked on Jerik's back to the front. After he cleared a place to sit, he jerked his friend's head up by the hair and yelled. "It is good to see you again!"

Jerik's eyes flickered open as Kejen let go of his hair. Jerik managed to hold his head up and gave his tormentor a most baleful look. He propped up himself up uneasily on one elbow and squinted.

"Ah, Kejen!" Jerik slurred. "Or some screaming demon intent on tearing my ears apart. Demon or Densky. Is there a difference?"

"Not much according by some...no...to some." Kejen still was fighting with Sea-Farer prepositions.

Jerik had the presence of mind to switch into Kejen's native tongue. "When did we arrive here in Sparent?"

"You're not in Sparent."

Jerik yawned widely in an attempt to get the dry cotton taste out of his mouth. "Not in Sparent? Where are we?"

"About half a day's ride from Northcross." Kejen told him.

Jerik hit his open hand with his fist. "I told Valk to change direction to Sparent! I was going come there first and surprise you! VALK!!!"

Kejen pulled back a curtain, showing his friend the snoring driver, presumably Valk. "Save your breath. He is in no condition to do anything. Besides, you would have missed us."

Jerik mumbled something in his own language and motioned Kejen outside. Once out of the vile smelling wagon, Kejen felt much better. Wandering to the fire in the middle of wagon circle, Jerik took Kejen's shoulder, partly for support.

The rest of Jerik's men were there and had pressed a mug of ale into Trif's hands. When not whipped up into a blood frenzy, Sea-Farers were a most hospitable folk. Jerik walked over and lifted Trif up on his shoulders. Jerik loudly proclaimed to all around what fine fellows Kejen and Trif were. Everyone cheered the proclamation.

Jerik was the most unaristocratic Crown Prince anyone had ever seen. He seemed more content with feasting, wenching and brawling rather than lording over anyone. His men loved him for it and his retinue was fanatically loyal. He ate what they ate, he worked when they worked, he even took guard shifts to make sure his men were well rested even when he was not. He would occasionally pull rank when it came to wenching but no true Sea-Farer could blame him for that! While his father the king wondered about his son's sanity, his subjects adored him. Jerik had a magnetism that seemed to draw people to him. No one, including Jerik could explain it. Jerik simply did what he did and it all worked out.

Jerik and Kejen found a seat and the festivities continued around them. Trif managed to find a place nearby and listened in.

"What brings you to Northcross?" Jerik asked both Kejen and Trif. Jerik's fluency of the Northmarcher language was better than Kejen's command of anything they spoke in Warron.

"A quest." Kejen answered.

Jerik raised an eyebrow. "A quest? As in high adventure, hurtling into the unknown?"

"Indeed it is!" Kejen confirmed.

"Boldly and recklessly throwing ourselves into the unknown is what we *Locklannaigh* do every day, my good man!" Jerik thumped his massive chest.

"Then you will like this!" Kejen promised.

Kejen told Jerik the whole story of *HeavenSteel* and everything that had happened over the last month. Kejen successfully penetrated the self-induced alcoholic fog Jerik was in earlier.

"This could be something the skalds will sing of forever." The look of wonder on Jerik's face was evident even by firelight. "So this Kuran friend of yours is a good fighter and going with us too?"

"Good?" Kejen felt mildly offended. "He is one of the elite of the Northmarcher Army!"

Jerik threw a massive arm around each brother. "Please forgive me my friends. I have friends in this great land but I am not of this land!"

After they all laughed, Trif had an important question to ask.

"A moment ago you said 'going with *us* too' "

Jerik swallowed a slug of ale a horse would have had trouble with. "Yes, dear Trif, I did. How could I pass up an adventure like that?"

"I said this would appeal to you!" Kejen chimed in. "Granted it's the mountains and not the Sea you speak of so much."

"One day, Kejen, I will take you and Trif to the Sea." Jerik vowed solemnly. Then he laughed loudly. "See the Sea!"

Trif managed to pull him back on track. "What about this caravan your father gave you the responsibility of?"

Jerik gave the world a dismissive wave. "I have done this a good half dozen times. The truth of the matter is that Sven over there snoring can run this better than I can. Besides, I am so tired of doing the same thing and going to the same places over and over and over."

It was Kejen's turn to look amazed.

"I am willing to wager you have said the same thing fairly recently." Jerik correctly surmised. "Trif, you have always been good with numbers. Calculate the odds of losing that wager."

"One in one." Trif said flatly.

Jerik had a far away look in his eyes that had nothing to do with the ale for a change. "I have done all I can do on the Sea. Trying to accomplish something noteworthy on land would be a great challenge. One day soon, I will have to settle my bottom on a throne. That is something I cannot walk away from. So if there is to be a land adventure, the time to do it is now."

Kejen leaned forward. "This might be an opportunity from God Himself."

Jerik, a pagan like the overwhelming majority of his kind, slipped out of Kejen's language to say something uncomplimentary about the Church. Kejen laughed along with everyone too. He was not the kind to let differences of opinion ruin friendships. Trif just helped himself to some more roasted meat.

Jerik stood up and slipped back into the Northmarcher language. "Kejen and Trif. You are my most honored guests. Please spend the night."

Kejen accepted. "I do think it would be a good idea to sleep outside tonight near the fire though. I've seen the inside of your wagon."

Jerik tipped his head back and laughed loudly. "Yes, I think that it an excellent suggestion!"

Kejen was up early the next morning as was his custom. He ran a mile out into the prairies on foot and then ran back. He was a firm believer that it was best to get your exercise in early and then face the day. The thoroughly soaked Kejen jogged back into the circle of wagons as the sun peeked halfway over the horizon. Jerik materialized out of the morning mist, noticeably agitated. Kejen did not need any instinct to know something was wrong. His friend was in full battle armor, topped off by a conical helmet with horns mounted in it in the manner of the Warron Sea-Farers. Jerik, with his usual flair, had them tilted forward somewhat. Most menacingly, he carried a massive double bladed axe, complete with a pointed iron spike mounted on the front. The towering apparition of muscle and armor that was Kejen's friend mumbled something that might have been "good morning." Kejen was not terribly interested in exchanging pleasantries at the moment. He wanted to know what was happening. Jerik slipped between two wagons and walked toward a group of unfriendly looking people.

Trif walked up to Kejen and explained it all in one word.

"Masovians."

"I am getting into my armor."

"Keep Kejen and Trif away from here." Jerik said to Sven. "Who knows what can happen if they confront these people." Jerik knew the history of this part of the world quite well.

Sven ran off to perform his duty, running right past Trif hiding under a wagon. He smiled and rolled out from under it, unobtrusively climbing into Jerik's wagon. Trif wrinkled his nose at the lingering smell and quickly scaled the center pole up to the "crow's nest" Sea-Farers put on their wagons to make it seem more homely while traveling on land. Up there, the archer from Sparent deftly strung his bow and surveyed the scene.

A half dozen Sea-Farers were deployed in a rough arrowhead with Jerik on the point directly facing the mounted Masovian leader, who had two of his soldiers on horseback flanking him. To his irritation, Jerik was tall enough not to be looked down upon by a man on a horse. Nonetheless, his arrogance was still blaringly evident. He wore not armor but instead very clean and rich clothing with the floppy hat Masovians preferred covering his dark hair, which ironically looked much like Jerik's. If the Sea-Farer leader had not been a pagan, the black goatee would have reminded him of Satan. The cavalrymen to his right and left had on breastplates but no shoulder armor. Their helmets looked like something Coronado would have worn looking for the Seven Cites of Cibola.

"I demand to know what you are doing here." The Masovian began without preamble.

"Who are you to demand anything?" Jerik retorted. He took a split second to reflect on the irony that this conversation was in the Northmarcher language.

"Who am I?" The Masovian looked angry. He tugged on his orange shirt so Jerik could see the Charging Bull of Masovia heraldry sown on it.

Jerik had to admit whoever had sewn that had done a very good job. It did not, however seem like a good time to ask how much it was.

"I am Beafalo of the Pugu!" He shouted. "And I have the honor, nay, privilege to serve the Great King Croghen of Masovia!"

Jerik just looked at him and shook his head with undisguised contempt.

"What's a Pugu?" Thirty yards away Sven finally found Trif hiding up in the crow's nest. He all ready saw the futility of trying to get Trif out of a good firing position so he started putting on his own armor just in case.

"Masovians still keep their tribal identities even though they have been welded into an empire." Trif was a teacher at heart. "The Pugu are the dominant tribe at present."

"Kind of like us." The Sea-Farer thought out loud.

"The Sea-Faring Kingdoms do not try to conquer other countries."

Sven shook his yellow beard. "No, much cheaper to raid instead."

Trif looked down the length of the pole at him. "Nor do the Sea-Faring Kingdoms fight with the Northmarch."

"Of course not." Sven looked up at Trif like he had lost his mind. "Do we look stupid to you?"

Beafalo became angry at Jerik's disrespectful silence. "Answer me at once. Why are not making way for us?"

Jerik shrugged. "Ride around us."

"Listen here!" Beafalo was a man used to giving orders. "Make way for us immediately. I am the Duke of Re---"

"A mere duke?!" Jerik laughed. "I am the Crown Prince of Warron. If you want to pull rank my dear *duke*, you will find yourself on the short end of the stick!"

"You lack the refinement of a prince." Beafalo sneered.

"I have draft animals that command more respect than you!" Jerik shot back. "Begone Masovian. Begone and stop wasting my time."

Jerik brought his ax out into full view and his fellow Sea-Farers drew their swords. Beafalo had no idea that Trif was drawing a bead on his head.

"Are you threatening me?" The Masovian lord demanded. "This is a diplomatic mission. How dare you show such disrespect?"

"Then start acting diplomatically." Jerik growled. "Now ride around us and go away to that ramshackle empire of yours while you still can."

"I'd listen if I were you." A voice came forth in grammatically perfect Masovian. This person stressed his vowels a little too much, Beafalo thought.

Jerik heard the hoof falls a few seconds earlier but he kept his face expressionless. A battle was not what he had in mind at this moment. He silently vowed to kick Sven in a part of the anatomy that would not feel pleasant.

Beafalo's eyes became harder and his horse took a couple of steps toward Kejen but only a couple. His guards mirrored his movements and the Sea-Farers took a couple of guarded steps along the Masovian flank. Trif adjusted his aim.

" Northmarcher." Beafalo mutter in obvious disgust. "I complement you on your ability to master our glorious language. It proves animals can indeed learn."

"Its not often I get to talk to pigs." Kejen cheerfully answered.

Beafalo blinked a couple of times. Everyone could see the rage building inside him but Jerik decided enough was enough.

"We have wasted enough time with you!" Jerik roared. "You are outnumbered and outmatched. Somehow I doubt anyone would miss you if you did not return but leave anyway. This is not your land nor mine. I will not be accused of showing disrespect to a banner of truce despite your provocations!"

Beafalo stared daggers at Jerik who returned the stare easily enough.

"We can take this up again at another time if you wish." Jerik offered. "Single combat, just you and I." He hefted his ax to emphasize the point.

Beafalo fumed but complied. He rode off, and around the encampment. He stopped at the last second and turned around.

"I hear that Northmarchers truly love their horses." The Masovian officer yelled at Kejen. Of course it was in Masovian. "You seem like the sort who enjoys bestiality!"

"I would not know." Kejen answered back--in Masovian. His voice had no trouble carrying the distance. "Ask someone who knows. Feel free to ask your mother!"

Trif almost let his arrow fly but Jerik expertly placed the wedge of Sea-Farers between Kejen and Beafalo. Olsen later claimed he could see a ghost of a smile on one of the Masovian soldier's face after Kejen's insult. It was, after all, a good barb!

The offended, and completely outnumbered, Beafalo rode off with his bodyguards, outrage radiating from his upright carriage like an angry cat.

Jerik turned around and looked at Kejen.

Kejen touched the crow's beak of his helmet in a half-salute.

"And good morning to you too!"

Kejen, Trif and Jerik rode into Northcross later that morning. Or rather Kejen and Trif rode and Jerik successfully kept the horse from throwing him out of the saddle. He was an excellent sailor but the Sea-Faring Crown Prince still had a lot to learn about riding on land.

"With a little more practice, you can claim to have the riding skills of someone about ten years old!" Kejen laughed at Jerik in the streets of Northcross.

Jerik good-naturedly gave Kejen an obscene gesture. "Wait until I get you on a ship!"

"In due time, my friend, in due time." Kejen returned the less than polite gesture.

Jerik pointed at the huge iron cross on a hill north of the city. You could see it from anywhere it seemed. "What is the story behind that?"

"That" Trif said, "is the work of St. Elezahn, the only Northmarcher in the Church's panorama of saints. It was erected the Fifth Century of Our Lord---"

"Your Lord," Jerik cut in. "Not mine."

Trif bowed in the saddle. Jerik laughed.

"Seven centuries ago." Trif changed course. "It represents the commitment of the Northmarcher people to the Church."

"Something the Church occasionally forgets." Jerik happily added in.

"That does happen from time to time." Trif found himself compelled to agree. "But on the whole, the Church is a good thing."

"No one wants someone else telling him how to run his kingdom." Jerik summed it up. "Universal personality trait. Tell me some more about this Elezahn."

"He was appointed the 'Bearer of the Message of Christ to the North.' " Trif told him.

"Not far enough north." Jerik added.

"It would seem so." Trif laughed. Jerik had an infectious way about him. Or maybe Trif was laughing at Jerik's struggle with horsemanship. It was hard to tell.

"The conversion process finally culminated it the raising of the Cross. The community you see here started around it and soon took the name 'North Cross'. The space between the words disappeared with the passage of time."

"I did wonder about that."

"The very same year, Northcross became the capital." Kejen added.

"Very good." Trif beamed approval.

"The year was.." Kejen began

"Seven fifty-one!" Jerik surprised both brothers.

"How did you know that?" a puzzled Kejen wondered.

"Your grandfather told me a long time ago." Jerik recalled. "It was the end of the Noble's Revolt."

Trif and Kejen waited for Jerik to tell them more.

"That is all I remember." He said sheepishly.

"By this time next year, I will have a book for you to read." Trif patted Jerik's shoulder.

"We had an ancestor in that fight." Kejen proudly informed his Sea-Farer friend. "He stood by the King when all looked blackest."

"Haaslong, Hadrock..." Jerik tried to find the name.

"Harkon!" Both brothers shouted.

"My apologies!" Jerik bowed in the saddle....and almost fell out.

"Use the stirrups." Kejen suggested.

Jerik looked at Kejen and winked. "Yes! The stirrups!"

"After the Noble's Revolt, the country was finally united and all the nobles gave up their patents of nobility. That way, your loyalty was to the King and him alone." Trif concluded.

Jerik looked oddly thoughtful. "That is why you do not have nobles in this country. If there were, *you* could be living in the Royal Castle. Or the one in Sparent anyway."

Trif shook his head. "Harkon was a minor noble living out at Gaking's Grove."

"History has a way of taking strange twists and turns you can never see coming." Jerik observed. "You probably know that better than I. Nonetheless, I do know one thing you do not know, my good friend. Make that two."

"What are they?" Trif wondered.

"One, you would have made a fine noble. Much better than that Beafalo fool at any rate."

"I am heartened to see you think I am better than some Masovian lordling." Trif brought out his seldom used sense of humor.

Jerik's rumbling laughter filled the busy street.

"What is the second thing?" Trif was genuinely intrigued.

Jerik leaned forward. "That girl selling carpets over there has been watching you since we rode down the street."

Trif turned around in the saddle to look.

"Go chat her up." Jerik commanded. "Go ahead. We will wait here for you."

Trif got down off his horse and walked in her direction. He looked back at Jerik somewhat confused but the big Sea-Farer pointed imperiously in direction of the carpets. He was a Prince and used to giving orders. Trif marched on.

Kejen brought his horse up next to Jerik's. "A lot of girls have been looking at him."

"How else is the lad going to learn?" Jerik chuckled.

The trio rode in the direction of the King's Castle. On more than one occasion, someone in the crowded streets of Northcross stopped to gape at Jerik. Unlike Sparent, Northcross was not close to any border. Since Kejen's hometown was part of a trade route that crossed into different countries, it was not unusual at all to see foreign merchants in Sparent. The markets of Northcross tended to be more domestically oriented. One of those staring at Jerik was a priest. Jerik noticed but he was too busy trying to direct his horse in the right direction to say or shout anything.

"Tell me something, Kejen" Jerik said after making sure his horse was indeed walking in the right direction. "This God of yours....have you ever seen Him?"

"Have you seen what you believe in?" Trif interjected.

"You, my good man, try not to forget that girl's name and where she lives." Jerik laughed to show he was simply in jest. "I am currently berating your brother!"

Trif pretended to give Jerik's horse a swat on the backside.

"No, no, no" Jerik begged. He turned his attention back to Trif's brother. "You do not get off that easy Kejen. Have you seen this God of yours?"

"I have never sat down to eat lunch with Him." Kejen smiled.

"So how do you know He exists?"

"It is called 'faith', my misguided friend." Kejen explained. "The same thing that sustains you on those ocean voyages. How do you know what you believe in exists?"

"Because I can see what the gods do. They reward us with good weather and punish us with the bad. If we do not take care of the sea, it becomes rough and swamps our boats."

"Try sailing in the Summer." Kejen quipped.

"How would you know about sailing?" Jerik barked.

Kejen pointed his finger right at Jerik, "That is what you yourself told me."

Jerik mumbled something to himself in his native language. Kejen was sure he heard the word "outflanked." The merchant from Sparent went on the attack.

"So you are telling me that your gods exist because you have seen what they do."

"Of course." Jerik smugly confirmed.

Kejen gave an all encompassing wave. "Then where did all this come from to start with?"

"Obviously, every god has a small part in it." Jerik used a tone of voice he would use lecturing an eight year old.

"So if every god has a part in this, then one god must be in charge of all of it." Kejen continued.

"And what is your point?"

Kejen stopped his horse cold, leaned over at the approaching Jerik and looked directly into his eyes. "So how do you know your head god and my God are not the same?"

Jerik opened his mouth but found he did not have an answer.

"Castle is this way!" Kejen cheerfully announced.

"I guess he is not just all brawn!" Jerik said to Trif.

Trif shook his head. "I tried to warn you."

Kejen's objective was not the King's Castle. It was the barracks near it. A barracks with two black clad soldiers in full armor guarding it, wicked looking pikes held at a forty five degree angle. Jerik whistled to himself. Anyone trying to ride past them would get himself unhorsed most painfully.

Trying to run past them on foot did not look like a wise option either.

Kejen walked up to them and presented a piece of parchment. A runner appeared as if by magic, took it, and ran into the barracks. All three watched him run across the courtyard. There was all sorts of activity but barracks always hummed with the energy of soldiers doing what they did. To Kejen, that was part of the attraction.

Before long, Kuran appeared, holding a horse's reins in one hand walking towards the open port. His long fluid strides carried him effortlessly past the guards. Kejen could see his friend looking at the gigantic Sea-Farer, trying to figure out who it was. The devil of it was that Jerik did look somewhat familiar.

Kejen and Trif saluted and Jerik just waved. As he had said earlier, it was not his land.

Kuran returned the salute. "Enough of that. This is not a parade ground."

Kejen laughed and motioned Jerik forward.

"You have actually met before, but it was a long time ago."

"Really?" Kuran looked perplexed. Then he snapped his fingers. "Jerik! My God, you've grown huge!"

"I hear that a lot." Jerik said sardonically. "The black makes you look like the Grim Reaper."

"I hear that a lot." Kuran replied.

Jerik rolled his eyes. "I am going to be surrounded by three Northmarchers! I do not fear anything in the mountains. I fear the people going into the mountains!"

Even Trif laughed along. Everyone looked at him. Well, it was genuinely funny.

"I like the odds." Kuran declared. "Kejen here and his brother Trif are tough and resourceful and we have Jerik with us...as large as the Ankers themselves!" His hand clamped down on Jerik's huge upper arm. "Are these arms or tree trunks?"

Jerik had no problem being the center of attention. He held his arms up for people passing by to see.

"Almost like masts on a ship!" Kuran observed.

Jerik turned around. "You have been on a ship?"

Kuran nodded. "Indeed I have. I have been to the Sea. I have even been to the Sea-Faring Kingdom of Warron, if I am reading your heraldry correctly."

"You are!" Jerik was impressed. "Take this for flattery if you wish, but I am very glad you are coming with us."

Kuran pointed at Kejen. "That is the man who brought this together." Then he tilted his head to Trif. "And that man is the best archer I have ever seen. Even better than I."

"Oh, yes. You could not find two other men I would rather have with me on this adventure." Jerik said. "What I meant was that in my experience, most in the service of any King, Warronite, Thenrosian, what have you, tend to be rather stiff necked and narrow minded. Kejen told me you were not like that at all and he is right."

"Of course I'm right!" Kejen cut in.

"If you are looking for stiff necked toy soldiers with no imagination, my friend, then do not bother looking anywhere near the Demon Division!" Kuran said---in Jerik's language.

Jerik stuck out his hand and Kuran shook it firmly.

"I expect we will get along quite well!"

The Demon Division officer swung one leg over his horse and checked the saddle he sat in. "We have someone to meet in Glossak. Let's be on our way!"

The land north of the capital became noticeably hillier and rockier. The forests became thicker and darker as the space between the trees disappeared. Kejen liked to occasionally charge off the road and ride through the prairie grass but soon he was unable to do that. They were beginning to enter the foothills of the Ankers. Kejen wound his way past more rock outcroppings and rode up a small knoll looking east. He could still see a bit of the steppe country from there. It looked a lot like the plains back home in Sparent.

Jerik negotiated his way up the knoll on foot and called out to his friend. "You are not getting homesick all ready, are you?"

Kejen snorted contemptuously. "If you think I am going to be turned around by something like homesickness while we are still in familiar territory, you have gone beyond daft! Going to Glossak is like walking to the stable in the morning."

Jerik reached the summit. "The wind ripples through the high grass like waves on the Sea."

"Now you tell me who is homesick!" Kejen smacked Jerik's shoulder. "I'll race you down the hill!" He spurred his horse on and rode down the side of the hill without much of a problem. Jerik held his ax up, let out a whoop and ran down behind Kejen. The Sea-Farer was amazingly quick for someone his size Kejen thought as Jerik covered the distance between the knoll top and his horse. He still laughed though when Jerik motioned Trif over to help him mount up.

"Look at the bright side." Trif checked the Jerik's stirrups. "Once we get to the mountains, we will be on foot."

"You have a way of making me want to dance with joy." Jerik said dryly but with more than a little relief.

Kuran rode up to Kejen and pointed due north. "Look."

Kejen followed his friend's finger and saw the first few tips of the mountains poking up into the sky. "Getting closer. Looks like it will be uphill soon." Kejen raised his voice and shouted to Jerik and Trif. "The sun is going to up for another hour! Let's see how much ground we can cover!"

The four did cover a lot of ground. Instead of the promised hour, it was closer to three but it carried them ever closer to the mountain city. After winding their way through mazes of rocks, high grass and hills in the failing sunlight, Kejen finally called a halt for the night. They even set up a watch for the night. Would-be bandit's bones had been moldering for centuries but Kuran said it would be good practice. Wolves did live here after all. And the Ankers promised things much more dangerous than ancient bandit's ghosts. Jerik nodded wholeheartedly. Anyone who had lived through the pitched battles Sea-Farer clans fought with each other knew first hand the value of alert sentries.

Kejen was up early as usual and the entire party was moving within minutes. That was a good sign. Even Jerik, a notorious late sleeper, was ready to go albeit with a bit of sleepy hostility in his eyes. The morning chill dissipated and Kejen tromped along the road leading northeast. Before long, they were compelled to dismount and walk up the escarpment that marked the beginning of the mountain range. It was a decision Jerik lent his vociferous support to.

At lunch, Kejen, Trif and Kuran studied the map to find the best and least crowded route into Glossak. The main road was going to be crowded, especially with the advent of the trading season. Kejen and Trif knew that from experience. They elected to go through a place a half mile away called Echo Canyon, where Jerik was currently enjoying himself, yelling into the terrain feature to see if it indeed warranted the name.

An hour later, the expedition descended down into the canyon and crossed into the Anker Mountains proper, surrounded by the huge grayish mountains, covered in green with the occasional bare rocks sticking through. The mountains filled up the sky and for someone who was used to the wide open spaces of the prairies, it felt vaguely claustrophobic. After spending the day traveling through the forests on the mountain sides as well as trying (successfully so far) to keep the horses from crashing down the slopes, the night's chill again made itself felt. Kuran scouted ahead and found a suitable campsite. Jerik took first watch and the night began. Kejen returned from his time on watch and handed the spear off to Kuran, who vanished into the shadows to guard against the wolves one could hear howling every now and again. Kejen saw his brother scribbling in a journal in front of the fire. Kejen wanted to catch a few more hours of sleep but his curiosity was peaked.

"You ought to get some sleep." Kuran called out from somewhere.

"In a little while."

Kejen sat down beside his brother and listened to the scribbling for a few seconds. If Kejen was not Trif's biggest fan and supporter, no one knew who that person was. He felt a small thrill in being the first to see his brother's work. Kejen constantly pestered Trif to let him see what he was doing and even had his own suggestions and ideas from time to time. Many would have been surprised to learn than many of the things Trif wrote about sprang from Kejen's mind.

"What are you writing about today?" Kejen asked after a few minutes. Trif was so into his writing he did not know Kejen was there.

"Every day, I am going to write about what we have done. The things we see. The things we talk about. Impressions and descriptions and such." Trif showed Kejen what he wrote by the firelight.

"Ah, you are writing about the moose we saw today." Kejen read. "Yes, people in Sparent would find that interesting. We don't see that too often there."

"Nor do they get to see or hear about those brave enough to go into largely unexplored regions looking for *HeavenSteel*." Trif said.

"They think we are possessed or insane." Kejen laughed. "Of course, some were convinced of that well before this trip ever happened."

Trif remained silent for a few moments and then closed his journal. "You know, there are some who think being different is a bad thing. It's not. It is a very good thing because the exceptions---" he tapped his brother on the nose with his journal---"are the ones who make history."

That gave Kejen something to think about before sleeping.

The next morning the foursome carefully picked and probed their way down the plateau. After trudging through a mile of unmelted snow that lingered on in the shadow of a mountain, they found a small rock strewn, shrub covered trail that Kuran said would take his fellow travelers into

Glossak in less than an hour. He was better than his word for less than thirty minutes later, all four of them stood on the side of a mountain looking down on the city of Glossak. The city was spread out before them, cupped in the bowl of a valley, surrounded by snow capped mountains on all horizons. The clear mountain air provided alacrity to the view that impressed even Kejen and Trif the plains dwellers, both used to seeing things in great detail from a distance. The rocks and gravel scrunched under their feet as Kejen led Jerik, Trif and Kuran into the city and sauntered onto the main boulevard. Jerik again was the object of some strange looks but they were of curiosity not hostility. Up here in the Ankers, chances were excellent no one had ever seen a Sea-Farer before. I am not surprised, Jerik thought, I am as far from the Sea as one can find himself.

Jerik stopped to read something that looked like a historical marker. He was struggling with the Northmarcher alphabet but making decent progress.

"Glossak-founded in the mid Ninth Century." Trif said as he walked by.

"I would have figured it out!" Jerik claimed.

"I never had a doubt." Trif answered without even looking over his shoulder.

The Queen City of the Mountains was the title proudly attached to the polis, an area set up in the mountains where no one had ever expected a city not only to grow but thrive. It started out as a hamlet owned by a long forgotten man who had lent his name to the new city. The entire area, including smaller towns and villages a peak or two over, based itself on a lucrative fur and salmon trade. Goods from the Queen City found themselves all over the world. The trappers got their fur from the otters, mink and other animals that lived in the wooded mountains and salmon from the Blieben River running through the area. The residents of Glossak were sure to balance the need to not over harvest the sources of their livelihoods nor venture too deep into the Ankers.

No one went too deep into the mountains. For as long as anyone could remember, there had been rumors and stories of "things" living there. Things that were inhuman and hated humanity. Things and black magic from another time and place, there, according to the stories, not only from the time of Faerie but even predating it. Only a few had been to the Bleiben's source but never beyond it or too far off the river. Jerik's kingdom butted up against the Ankers too though far to the west and he had heard similar stories. None seemed to have happy endings.

Kuran left to go find this Overdulf person he mentioned earlier. The rest of the group took the horses to the merchant's square in town. Kejen and Trif had been to Glossak before so they knew the way. Jerik tagged along lest he get himself into some kind of trouble in a city he had never been to. After selling off the horses for more supplies, they walked over to the tavern Kuran had told them to meet.

"I am glad we are walking the rest of the way!" Jerik declared. "I do no know how you people form such attachments to horses!"

"Try walking across the steppes for a few days." Kejen quipped. "Then you will know something no other Sea-Farer knows!"

Soon they entered the tavern and saw Kuran at a table with an older looking man. He looked like a trapper. He looked like a trapper who had seen better days.

Kuran tossed him a small bag that made a metallic thud when it landed on the table top. "Are we in agreement?"

"Indeed we are." the trapper's low voice carried to Kejen who was just sitting down. Trif and Jerik found chairs and Kuran made the introductions.

Overdulf reached over and gently tugged Jerik's beard. "A man who is proud of what God gave him and does not shave it off every morning."

Jerik did not like having his beard pulled but nonetheless stayed on his best behavior, which for a Sea-Farer was quite an accomplishment. Still it slipped out.

"Why is your beard so grey?" Jerik asked without thinking.

There was a moment of embarrassed silence.

Overdulf laughed. "You are a brave one! Brave men wear beards they say. Well, I say at any rate. If you ran after five children and their mother everyday and worked as hard as I did up in the mountains and been through what I have been through, you would look like me after a month, my young friend!" He took another good sized swallow of ale. "This is a present from your friend Kuran to me. We are celebrating my birthday!"

"Is that a birthday present too"? Kejen asked pointing at the bag Kuran had tossed the trapper earlier. Overdulf made it disappear quickly.

"It would have made a nice present!" Overdulf smiled. "After forty-two years in this world, I should get a bag like that every year!"

Everyone laughed but Kuran returned to the subject at hand. "Overdulf here is much more than he seems or that he lets on." Overdulf stood up and bowed to all seated. His tall, rangy form somehow fit behind the table against the wall without a problem. It also said about how much time he spent here. "He is a smart fellow. Smart enough to figure out how to combine chemicals. He has showed us how to make pitch burn hotter and explode."

"But not smart enough to keep away from trapping." Overdulf chuckled. "It is the sort of thing that gets into your blood."

"Overdulf here knows the mountains better than anyone you can find. He has even been into the deep Ankers not once but several times! He could find his way there and back in the dark!" Kuran extolled the trapper's virtues.

"And he has made it back!" Kejen observed. "I am impressed!"

"A bright lad indeed!" Overdulf shouted and waved for another ale.

"When are you going to marry me and take me away?" The tavern girl, twenty years his junior, joked with him.

"About the same time my wife says it's all right. In other words, never." Overdulf laughed back. He did spend a lot of time here.

"We were discussing which routes to take up to Rainkin Falls." Overdulf continued.

"The simplest way to go would be to walk up alongside the Blieben." Kejen said.

"Very true." Overdulf admitted. "But I have been up and down these slopes a hundred times before you were even born. I know someone who can tell us whether or not what you are looking for is even there."

"Sounds like a detour." Kejen was wondering where this was leading. "And many people tell me it is not there so why would I go out of my way to hear another person tell me that?"

"Kuran has told me everything." Overdulf patted Kejen's arm. "*HeavenSteel* is in the Ankers. It might not be where you think it is. It might even be where I want to go first! At any rate, this person I am talking about would know."

"And who is this person?"

"Sevonicus is his name." Overdulf began. "He is a wise man who has lived up in the mountains even longer than I. I know the mountains well but he knows them like the back of his hand."

"Lives in the mountains? Is he even human?" Kejen meant it as a joke but Overdulf slowly shook his head.

"I do not know. I do not know where he came from or even how long he has lived in that castle there."

This was getting stranger. Kuran tended to get involved with some strange things though.

Kejen plunged on. "Show me on the map."

Kejen saw the reluctance on Kuran's face but the elite soldier rolled out the map and pointed it out.

It was in the worst place imaginable. That could not be right but the map refused to rearrange itself to fit his wishes.

"It's right behind that bloody Skulka place!" Kejen exclaimed.

Jerik's eyes seemed to pop out of his head. Even in Warron, The Forests of Skulka was a name synonymous with death and danger. Trif looked down at the map and shook his head. Even his unflappable personality seemed a bit strained at the prospect of traveling through that place.

"I don't suppose you have thought about going up to Rainkin Falls first and then, *if necessary*, come down from the north and skirt Skulka to see this Sevonicus person." Kejen asked.

"Yes, I have." Overdulf told him. "It would take all Summer and into Fall. Remember, up here, snow falls even earlier. The Torna River flows from Sevonicus to Rainkin Falls. Not the other way around."

Overdulf let that sink in for a few moments. " Tell me what would you do if you knew for a fact that *HeavenSteel* were not at Rainkin Falls but with Sevonicus?"

It seemed rather obvious to Kejen. "Leave from Glossak to the northwest, go around the Forests of Skulka and approach from the west."

"That is a good plan." Overdulf clapped. "But there is one problem."

Kejen looked at the map and saw it. "The mountains around the Forests Skulka are impassible?"

Overdulf leaned forward. "I can tell you that from personal experience."

"So you suggest we go to the Sevonicus, sail down the Torna to Rainkin Falls." Kejen recapped. "But how do we get to Sevonicus with the Forests of Skulka sitting between us and him?"

"Go thorough the Forests of Skulka." Overdulf took a quick swig of ale. The look on Kejen's face said the idea was outrageous even by his standards. He demanded an explanation.

"Not right down the middle!" Overdulf said plaintively. "We can clip a corner. Slide along the mountains on the edge."

Kejen looked at the map again. Overdulf's plan made some sense. Only to a point though. Skulka was a big point to deal with. Kejen for the first time felt a bit of doubt creep into his mind. What if *HeavenSteel* was not at Rainkin Falls? The Torna River flowed against them and that would take too long. The river flowed with them from Sevonicus to Rainkin Falls. His mind kept coming back to the Forests of Skulka though.

"Kuran likes the idea." Overdulf pointed out.

Kuran waved Overdulf off. "No, I am not in command of this expedition. Kejen is."

"Lieutenant leading an expedition with a captain in it. That is unusual but then again what do you expect? We are Northmarchers. We never have been conventional people." Overdulf had another swig of ale.

"This whole journey was Kejen's idea." Trif finally spoke.

Overdulf grinned. "I was wondering if you could speak."

Trif was all ready studying the map with his brother. He could not see a way around Skulka either. This was a problem with no easy solution.

"Whatever you elect to do is fine with me, Kejen." Jerik stated simply.

Kejen looked up from the map and at Overdulf. "Will you come with us through the Forests of Skulka?"

Overdulf stood up. Kejen realized for the first time that the rangy looking, grey bearded trapper was almost as tall as Jerik.

"Your friend in black here said this quest was your idea. Going through Skulka is my idea. I served my time in the King's service before any of you were born. I remember what every Northmarcher soldier is told. 'Never tell someone to do something you have not done yourself.' "

Kejen, Trif and Kuran all smiled and loudly agreed. Even Jerik shouted his appreciation of that precept.

Overdulf's hand came down on the map hard. "I will not send someone out into danger when I stay behind."

Kejen stood up and bowed. Then he tossed a few coins on the table. "Enjoy a few more ales my friends. We are going to need it! We leave tomorrow!"

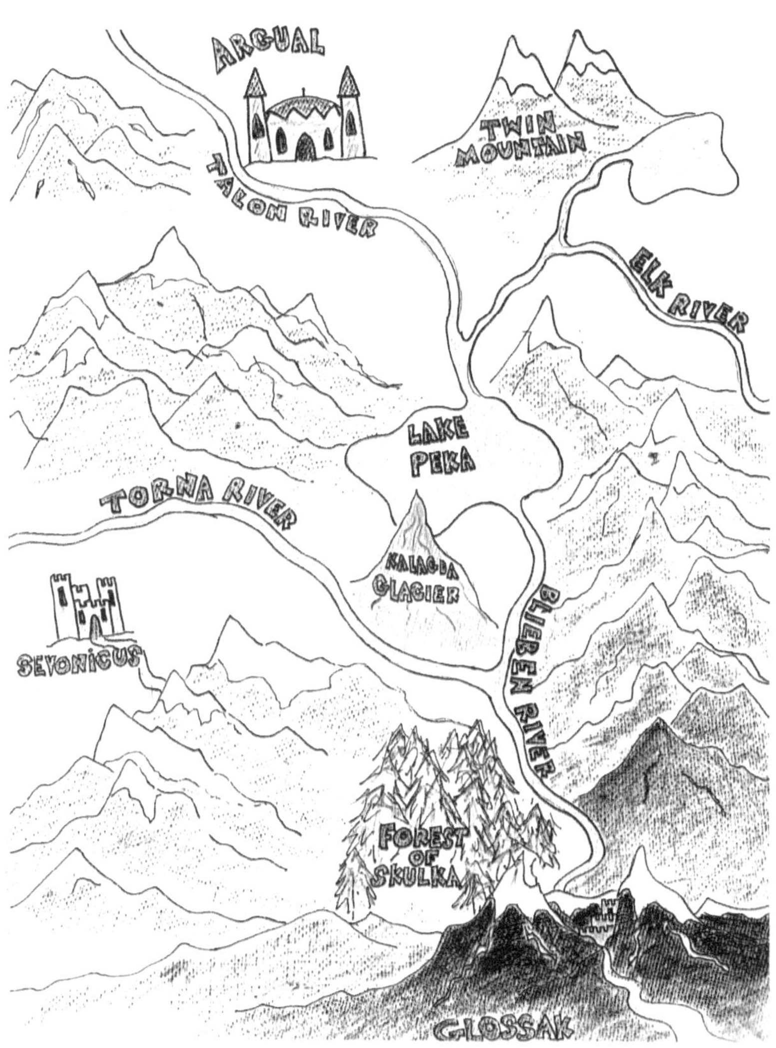
ARGUAL
TWIN MOUNTAIN
TALON RIVER
ELK RIVER
LAKE PEKA
TORNA RIVER
KALAGDA GLACIER
SEVONICUS
BLIEBEN RIVER
FOREST OF SKULKA
GLOSSAK

Chapter 6

They marched out from Glossak early the next morning along the main road leading north along the Blieben. Kejen ran over to the river bank and dumped a cupped handful of water over his helmeted head.

"Take a look at it now!" he shouted. "We are going to see it again at Rainkin Falls!"

"The boundless joy and energy of youth." Overdulf shook his head. "Save it for the trip ahead. It will not be easy."

Water still running down his armor, Kejen fell in beside the old trapper. Jerik brought up the rear and Kuran and Trif, both archers, were in the middle. From that position, they could rain arrows down on any attacker from behind or in the front. With any luck, such attackers were hypothetical. With a dash through the Forests of Skulka planned, expecting the worst seemed like a wise course of action.

Kejen waved at some loggers floating trees down the river and kept looking ahead for any wagons or traffic coming down the road. He did not see any.

"You won't either." Overdulf said. "I told you before. No one goes in very deep into the mountains. If they do, it's along the river."

"So anything coming down the road here is going to be hostile?" Kejen asked.

Overdulf shook his head. "Still a little early for that. Might see some trappers for a few more miles. If we see any, we will find out what's what and if they have seen anything odd."

"How long to Skulka?"

"A week." Ovedulf predicted.

Kejen looked over his shoulder at Trif, Kuran and Jerik. "I will bet you we can get there in five days."

"Five days?" The tone in Ovedulf's voice suggested Kejen's confidence was seriously misplaced. "A dooklie from Sparent is going to challenge me to a race in the mountains?"

"What is a dooklie?" Kejen guessed it was some sort of insult.

"That is what they call non-mountain people here." Kuran said from a few feet behind them.

"Really?"

Kuran nodded in the affirmative.

Kejen turned his attention back to their guide from Glossak, “Do we or do we not have a wager?"

Overdulf looked up at the mountains, now taking up most of the sky in all directions, then looked down quickly at the map. Definitely a chance to make some easy money. "We have a wager my misguided friend."

Kejen loped forward in a trot and ran on for about twenty yards, Everyone followed at the same pace. Everyone except Overdulf. He stopped and looked at the wide eyed trapper. "If we are going to get there two days early, we need to pick up the pace. Besides, I need the map so get up here."

Ovedulf bit his lip. So much for an easy wager. He tightened the strap on his helmet, pulled his grey beard and plodded on grimly. The Ankers would not be easy to conquer but this lad from Sparent seemed determined to do it. Some people had to find out the hard way.

The road curved to the northwest away from the river. The feeling of isolation began to set in the further it led away from the river. Then without warning, the road stopped. Not only did it end, it simply ceased to exist.

"Welcome to the unknown." a heavily sweating Overdulf announced. Overdulf managed to keep up. Kejen had to admit he was impressed.

"Indeed it is." Kejen pulled his sword out from the scabbard strapped to his back. "Now it is beginning in earnest. Second thoughts, anyone?"

Without waiting for an answer, he plunged into the forest.

Overdulf muttered something that probably was not a compliment and followed Kejen in. Kuran turned so Trif could check the quarrel of arrows strapped to his back. Trif patted his shoulder and turned so Kuran could do the same. Satisfied all was in order, both of the company's archers took a spear handed to them from Jerik and followed Overdulf. Jerik looked around and then behind him. No one was following or preparing an attack from behind. He brought his flat of his ax blade up and tapped his nose guard.

"Here we go." He said and dashed forward.

The armor, weapons and backpacks did not slow them much. Kejen had insisted that they travel light for that very reason. Overdulf, who had been traveling these mountains since before Kejen was even born, agreed wholeheartedly. Kuran, a veteran of dozens of long distance marches, thumped his shield in approval. The quicker they could mover through the mountains, especially through Skulka, the better. Running proved not to be much of a problem even if a lot would prove to be uphill. All were in excellent physical condition, including Overdulf, who had run up and down these mountains his whole life despite the fact he did not exactly look forward to it. Age might have slowed him down a little but it did not stop him.

Kejen was determined to maintain a good pace, which was not always easy running on slopes and gliding between trees. Overdulf did a good job guiding everyone between mountains and through the rugged terrain. The sun started to set and darkness came to the mountains with frightening swiftness. Kejen noticed that particular phenomenon in Glossak itself, so he exhorted his companions to keep running until they could not see any more. And soon it came to that as Kejen nearly ran into a tree--twice.

Overdulf decreed a small fire would be fine. They did need light but no big fires. It was simply too dangerous out here in the unknown to attract any attention

"It might not matter." Jerik was never afraid to voice an opinion. "Look at all the eyes around us in the dark."

"Those are just small animals." Overdulf pointed out. "I would not worry until we near the Forests of Skulka. Lord only knows what is in there!"

"Do you think whatever lives there ventures out of the woods at night?" Kuran asked a very good question.

"I am not sure." Overdulf admitted. "But it would be wise to think in that direction."

Kejen turned around and called out to his brother who was out in the shadows on first watch. "What do you think, Trif?"

Trif gave a simple answer. "Yes."

Kuran looked down the length of his sword blade. "I do know one thing. Once we go into that place, expect a fight."

Kuran, Jerik and Overdulf settled in for a well deserved rest, legs and arms aching a little from running in the thin air and a lot of that was uphill. That would take a little getting used to but they could handle it Kejen thought as he took the spear from Trif. It was his turn to stand watch.

The next three days saw more of the same. A lot of running and more consultations with the map. That was to be expected since they were moving deeper into a place humans generally did not go. They traveled quickly and lightly over the forest floor sheltered by the immense pines and oaks. Only the occasional clink of gear or weaponry betrayed their existence. An elk with a huge rack of antlers watched them as they went by. It had probably never seen a human being before. Neither did the bear that wandered by but it only sniffed at the fast moving group once and continued on its way, obviously not impressed. Jerik found the breath to delve into an apparently endless supply of ribald tales and raunchy jokes. The fact he could keep it up for three days testified to the fact he either had led an interesting life or had an incredible imagination.

At noon on the fifth day out of Glossak, Overdulf looked at the map and shook his head. "I thought your were out of your noggin but it looks like we are almost to Skulka."

"A wager is the last thing on my mind right now." Kejen said, gathering everyone in around him, "We are about a half day away from Skulka. Actually we could be there tonight but I don't think we should go in at night."

Overdulf nodded forcefully, “Most defiantly do not go in at night!"

"Creatures of darkness." Kuran said softly. "Going in at night plays to their advantage. For all we know whatever lives there could be as nocturnal as bats. A daylight run could surprise whatever is there."

"Daylight" Trif echoed. "Maybe those things can see in the dark. We can't."

Jerik's ax blade came down on a piece of wood with a metallic ring. Overdulf started a little but quickly regained his composure. "I like to see what I have to kill." The Sea-Farer said plainly enough.

"I cannot tell you what will happen once we get there." Kejen said, "But I do know we are walking there."

Everyone cheered.

"I would not cheer yet." Kejen admonished everyone. "Once we go into that place, I think we will be doing plenty of running. I might even find myself trailing Overdulf!"

The trapper gave Kejen a mock cuff to the head. "I did a good enough job keeping up with you!" Then Overdulf turned serious. "Run, don't run. The important thing is we get out of there alive."

It was hard to argue with that.

"Sooner begun, sooner done." Kejen said as he began walking.

Knowing the dreaded region was drawing closer with every step had its effect. Talking ceased, ears pricked up and everyone's alertness ratcheted up on its own several notches as the first traces of a progressive uneasiness made itself felt. No one, however, would dare call it fear.

Overdulf led everyone up a mountain slope so that they could get a good view of the surrounding area. They all felt that the advantage to seeing the Forests of Skulka in the distance outweighed the climb upwards.

It was not hard to find. It was plainly visible in the distance, not even trying to hide. It seemed arrogantly sure no one could challenge its domain. Skulka, even from a few miles way, looked like a huge gnarled, dead forest. Even Trif, with his sharp archer's eyes, could not discern a patch of green inside the area. It contrasted sharply with the mountains around. Even a blind man could not miss Skulka, Overdulf muttered.

"He does not have to see it." Jerik said. "You can feel the malignance of the bloody place from here!"

Kejen scanned the horizon and looked across the length and breadth of the place called Skulka. He took note of a few things. The dire looking wood was situated on a plateau about fifty or sixty feet above the ravine floor. The ravine itself looked like some kind of ditch, running across the length of the forest as far as the eye could see "You were right then and you are right now, Overdulf. There is not way around that place."

"I would be happy to be wrong." Overdulf spread his hands. "Very, very happy."

"We need to slide along the edge up along the mountains." Kuran said. "It looks like the shortest route through and whatever is in there cannot outflank or surround us."

Kejen nodded his agreement. "We will camp here tonight. No fire. Tomorrow, we move up to that hill down there. Put some concealment between our approach and whatever is in there watching. Then we go in." He waited a second and then added. "Does anyone else have something to add?"

Kuran got everyone's attention easily enough. "Get some rest and check your weapons. We are going to need them tomorrow."

The day began with the Sun rising between the mountains. It would take another hour for most of the sunlight to reach the Northmarchers and their Sea-Farer friend sitting in a pine forest on the slopes of one of those mountains. They did not mind. The existence and placement of the ravine did not look natural. That argued strongly that whatever lived in the Forests of Skulka possessed some sort of intelligence. An evil, twisted intelligence. Kejen hoped the very darkness of the forest meant whatever dominated Skulka was nocturnal. Waiting for a couple of hours past sunrise also conferred another advantage. The members of the expedition could study the place they had come to a little more in full daylight. Maybe they would not discover anything new. On the other hand, the otherworldly looking forest did not seem disposed to revealing anything.

Overdulf used the time to arrange the climbing gear they would need to make it out of the ravine. Ordinarily, it would not be a good idea to climb down and then out of the ravine but it ran on seemingly forever. Like the area itself, there simply was not other way around it. Armor was strapped on and weapons were checked yet again.

Kejen led the march down off the mountain and toward the small wooded hill he had pointed out the night before. It stood between the ravine and the rest of the mountains. It seemed like a natural place to put a sentry, Kuran pointed out. The five adventurers approached the hill carefully. Trif and Jerik split off to the left as Overdulf and Kuran went right. Kejen climbed up the hill, secure in the knowledge that Trif and Kuran's bows were aimed at a constantly changing point in front of him.

All five met up without incident on the forward slope of the hill facing the Forests of Skulka itself. It was a sight they would not forget. The closer they got, the worse it looked. It seemed as if the Forests of Skulka were all ready waging a psychological war against these people who had come from Glossak. Some of the bared twisted trees reminded Jerik of whale bones he had occasionally seen on the beach in his kingdom. He kept that uncomfortable thought to himself. The most disquieting thing about the whole area was the utter lack of noise. The closer the expedition approached, the quieter it was. Now it was silent. Not a bird flew, not an insect chirped. It was if there was an empty pocket right in the middle of an otherwise lush, green mountain range teeming with life. Kejen walked right up to the edge of the ravine and looked down. Most of the morning mist had burned off, so now he could see to the bottom. All he saw was a dirty looking stream. I am not going to drink out of *that* he thought.

Overdulf drove a couple of spikes into the ground and looked sourly across the ravine. "I wish we could make a rope bridge. Or drop a tree trunk across but it is too far. I don't think we could move a tree trunk that big."

"Can't be helped." Kejen said.

The Glossak trapper dropped the rope ladder down the side of the ravine. Kejen slowly climbed down. Trif and Kuran again took up positions, bows strung and eyes scanning for danger. Jerik looked for danger too though his massive battle ax was not a long distance weapon. Overdulf did not use the ladder. He climbed down the rocks and stood with

Kejen on floor of the ravine.

"I was climbing mountains when you were but a gleam in your father's eye." Overdulf laughed at Kejen's incredulous look. "Besides, I need to know I can climb the sides of this thing. I have to get the ladder after we make it to the other side."

Kejen laughed and patted the mountain climber on the back. "I am feeling better and better as the day goes on. By the way, didn't you mean ' your grandfather's eye?' "

Ovedulf pretended to hit Kejen over the head with his rock hammer, “No respect for your elders." Then he became serious again. "Day is not over yet." Overdulf said grimly and began to climb up the other side of the ravine toward Skulka itself, trailing another rope behind him.

Overdulf peeked over the top of the ledge across fifty feet of cleared space in front of Skulka's front edge. Yes, *cleared* space. It seemed to be designed this way by someone. Or *something*, he sighed. He did not like what that presaged. Nothing good he huffed. Kejen climbed up after him, hand over hand, feet against the escarpment wall. Kejen scrambled past him onto the flat surface and threw himself down before crawling a few feet to make room for the others. One by one, the members of the group crossed over. Kejen finally stood up as everyone joined him. Overdulf was last, climbing back to retrieve the rope ladder.

"Might have been a good idea to keep it as an escape route." Overdulf suggested. "You know, just in case."

Kejen would hear nothing of it. "We are not coming back this way. No retreat. Don't worry, my friend. I will bring you through this!" He winked and waved his sword, pointing it towards the dead looking trees. "Forward!"

Kejen was on the point of the small arrowhead formation, Trif and Kuran to the right and left, Jerik and Overdulf a little more over to the sides. From the air, it probably looked like an arrow about the pierce the side of an enemy. Kejen's hands shook a little, not from nerves but from the adrenaline coursing into his system. He was ready for battle. Trif, never one to show much emotion, scanned the approaching tree line; the point of his arrow lined up and pointed wherever his eyes went. Kuran did the same. Jerik trotted along behind the Demon Division officer, ax at the port arms position. Overdulf carried a spear the same way. Come what may, they were ready to fight.

Kejen scrambled past the bushes and undergrowth between the trees and hopped over some of the more gnarled roots that seemed to want to reach out and trip him. They did not. Nor did they trip anyone else. It was almost as dark as night. Here and there small shafts of sunlight stabbed through but not many. The limbs had grown together for a long time. It was almost like a roof. The most disconcerting thing was the utter silence. No birds, no insects, no sign of anything.

Jerik read everyone's mind. "If there is nothing here, I am not going to complain!" he whispered.

Kuran looked around. He did not know where the name "Skulka" originated but so far it seemed like an appropriate name. Lots of trees, very dire looking and probably some skulls around somewhere.

The first mile into the dreaded woods was uneventful. They heard nothing except their own breathing and the snap of twigs and small bushes they crushed traveling westward punctuated by the occasional scrap of thorns against armor. And there were quite a lot of thorns Kejen thought to himself. Somehow, he had expected that.

The second and third miles went by with nothing making its presence known. The undergrowth grew thicker but nothing seemed to lurk in it. Kejen turned around to look at Ovedulf. The Glossak trapper held five fingers up. Five miles to go. On they went.

The formation tightened up a little as the second tier growth grew even thicker. They also fought to keep the maddening silence from driving them into hysteria.

After fighting another couple of miles through thorns and bushes that seemed to be merging into a wall, Kejen called for a halt to consult the map. There were only three miles to go and the mountainside remained in sight to their left.

Jerik took off his helmet and wiped his sweaty forehead. "Maybe all the stories we heard about this place were just that--stories."

"We can only hope." Kuran said. He was not letting his guard down as long as they were in this horrible looking place.

Trif waved over at Jerik. "If the stories are not true, why does this place look like the way it does and why does it seem nothing lives here?"

Jerik shrugged. "Are you complaining?"

"Not in the least."

Kejen handed the map back to Overdulf. "A bit more than halfway there. So far, so good."

Then the frenzied scream ripped through the air, shattering the eerie serenity. Trif and Kuran reacted instantly, putting their backs up against each other, bows drawn. Overdulf ducked behind a fallen log and Jerik found cover behind a tree. Kejen pointed his sword in the direction from where the scream came from. It was, thankfully, to the rear. Unless it wants to push us toward something else, Kejen thought, and then wished he hadn't.

Something fluttered past Overdulf who would have yelled if Jerik had not clamped a hand over his mouth. "Don't" he whispered. "Or that screaming thing will know where we are."

Overdulf shoved Jerik's hand away. "It all ready knows where we are!" he hissed.

"Let's go." Kejen said. "Maybe we can move out of here before anything else shows up."

Slowly the group went forth, carefully stepping over some more fallen logs and pushing past more of the ubiquitous thorns and brambles. The forest grew still again. A half mile later, they heard the scream again; closer and echoing off of the trees. Even worse, it was joined by two more and the forest began to fill with chittering and the noise of bodies moving in the brush.

"In the bloody middle!" Kuran spat. "I should have known!"

The company moved quicker, trying to put some distance between them and whatever was out there. Soon a curious sort of bleating joined the rising forest crescendo, sort of like a giant bull frog. From the right, there was the sound of crashing trees. There was something *big* over in that direction! To their credit, no one in the small company panicked. Kejen led them on, slowing it down a little as they climbed a small hill. He could not see anything from the small swell of ground but noticed it was easier traveling down the hill. It seemed as if the bushes were thinning out and the spaces between the trees were growing larger.

Kejen stumbled out into a large clearing. Everyone else tumbled in behind him. Kejen blinked a couple of times, trying to adjust to the sunlight that had been missing in the forest. The noise suddenly stopped and the silence returned. The quiet was broken only by the sound of Trif, Kuran Jerik and Overdulf forming a circle on Kejen. The merchant turned adventurer took in the situation trying to make sense of it. A bright open space in the middle of a dark forest in the middle of the Ankers? It bore a horrible resemblance to the open-air gladiator sports Kejen remembered reading about someplace. He always wondered what went through those people's mind. Now, he knew, with startling alacrity.

The forests might have been silent but there was definitely *something* there. A lot of somethings. Watching. Waiting. For what?

Kejen heard a snort from the other side of the clearing. He slowly turned his head and his eyes came to rest on a bull. A bull? Kejen's mind did a mental double-take. That was not something he expected to see here. What would something as ordinary as a bull be doing here in what was supposed to be the final refugee of Faerie? Property of a deranged farmer? The landscape seemed to say that. Come to think of it, Kejen thought, what am *I* doing here?

The bull charged. Dirt flew from it hooves and Kejen could see flecks of foam around it mouth but he could not help but noticed the eyes...burning, crazed and unnatural. It was something right out of Church stories of exorcisms.

"It's possessed!" Overdulf shouted. "Get out of the way!", he added, rather unnecessarily.

The circle disintegrated as the bull rushed by, Northmarcher and Sea-Farer alike scrambling out of the way to avoid getting trampled by the maddened animal and each other. Kejen took a step to the side and swung his broadsword straight at the back of the bulls head. The blow bounced off the flat skull but managed to chip off a good part of the horn. The enraged animal turned with abnormal agility and charged directly for Kejen. Kejen backpedaled and Kuran attacked from the other side, dropping his bow and swinging his broadsword in the perfect arc that sliced through muscle and bone, shattering the bull's shoulder with an audible crunch. Kuran pulled the sword out with a twist of his wrist, compounding the damage further. The blow should have crippled it.

Instead the bull turned and charged again.

"How?!" Jerik wondered and shouted at the same time.

"It's possessed!" Overdulf shouted. "I told you. It’s probably possessed by Satan himself!"

Jerik waved him off with an oath and a gesture that was probably an obscenity. "I do not like this Satan person, whoever he is!" He waved his ax. "Over here! Fight me you oversized side of beef! Fight me!"

Kuran delivered two quick blows with his sword and bounded out of the way. "Only a killing blow will stop it!"

Jerik beat the ground with his ax. "Here! You want to make a fight of it, here I am!" No one was sure if he was taunting the bull or the creatures of Skulka as a whole.

The bull noticed the shouting Jerik and charged yet again. An arrow sprung from the animal's neck as Trif let a shot fly but the bull shrugged it off. Overdulf was right, it was possessed.

Kuran retrieved his bow and shot at the back of the bull's head, trying to hit its brain. Instead, the arrow thudded into the animal's ribs with no effect. The bull's legs churned forward, propelling its mass and deadly horns forward, but Jerik stood his ground, ax raised and ready. This was the way combat was supposed to be--the *Locklannigh* way--in the open and where both adversaries could look each other in the eyes.

All of Jerik's compatriots converged on the charging bull. Kejen ran at an angle, preparing to jump on its neck and drive his sword through its head. Kuran was running up on it from behind to do the same. Even Overdulf ran forward with a wicked looking knife that did duty for a small sword. The Sea-Farer's massive frame did not move out of the path of the horned, two thousand pound runaway force. He raised the ax and had all ready had the blow timed. His feet moved a little, getting ready to move out of the way at the last possible heartbeat. The bull was nearly upon him and for a terrible moment, it seemed as if Jerik would be gored. Jerik took a half step to the right and prepared to bring the ax down---hard He felt something whiz past his ear and he hoped it did not mess up his aim.

An arrow punched through the bull's eye and so far into the brain it almost disappeared. The bull's nose ploughed into the ground, pushing up a small mound of dirt and the forward momentum caused the body to flip over.

Kejen jumped over the fallen bull. "Finest archer in Sparent!!!! He shouted. "Best archer in all the bloody world!!!"

Jerik stood there for a second with the ax raised. Then, he angrily chopped down, severing the bull's head in one powerful stroke. "That was my kill!" he screamed at Trif. "I had him!"

"Claim it with my blessings then." Trif managed to say before the still shouting Kejen lifted up by the waist.

Then the shadow fell.

Overdulf saw something move in the trees. At first he thought his imagination was running away from him but soon sheer terror overwhelmed everything.

` `"God in Heaven!" he managed to shout.

Kuran threw himself forward and leveled Overdulf just a half second before a huge three fingered hand would have crushed his skull.

"Back! Back!" Kejen shouted. He had no intention of fighting this newest attacker so close to the trees where it could have help waiting. All five retreated halfway across the clearing, their semi-circle getting wider.

Eight feet off the ground, the monster's baleful eyes glinted manovelently, its mouth opened to show a couple of rows of sharpened teeth. The grayish skin covered a body with patches of hair, supported by two powerful legs anchored on three toed feet. Ridges ran the length of its cranium, hairless except for some tufts on the back of the head. Kejen's attention, however, was focused on the tree trunk it carried for a club.

Jerik could not believe what he saw. It was a nightmare from his childhood come to life. A story to frighten small children into obedience was here in flesh and blood trying to kill him. It did not exist! But it was here, emerging out of the darkest reaches of mythology, a legend come to life.

"*Frolin!*" He shouted. It's a bloody Frolin!"

"I think that means 'troll' " Trif said to Kuran.

"I don't care what it's called!" Kuran growled. "How do you kill it?"

Whatever the proper name was for it, it roared, deep and terrible, and lumbered forward. Then it turned almost ninety degrees with surprising agility and went straight for Overdulf. The monster's speed caught the Glossak trapper flat footed. With a single, powerful kick, the Frolin hit Overdulf in the stomach and sent him flying ten feet, hitting the ground hard. Moments later, the troll towered over the fallen trapper, club raised and seconds from coming down on him.

The other four adventurers were galvanized into action.

Screaming a mindless war cry, Kejen charged the monster head on. Now the Frolin was surprised. Nothing had ever attacked it before.

Kejen dove under the swung club, rolled up onto his feet and plunged his sword deep into the Frolin's stomach. The Frolin's roar echoed for miles. It threw Trif's aim off a bit as an iron barbed arrow hit it in the side of the neck. Kuran found a rock the size of a fist and hurled it into the side of the monster's head. Then came the huge Warron battle ax hurtling in mid air, end over end, the blade glinting and growing more menacing by the second. It hit the monster with a terrible thud and ringing sound and the blade split bone, burying itself in the monster's right upper chest. Kejen dragged Ovedulf out of the way just as the monster staggered backwards. One of its clawed feet came down on Overdulf's former position.

Jerik slammed into the troll with the full force of a running start. He rained blows down on the fallen monster but the Frolin could absorb a lot of damage and still fight on. A thick three fingered hand hammered Jerik in the chest and knocked him back a few feet. The wounded troll rose up and with its one good hand, pulled the ax out and threw it to the side. Jerik leaned up against a tree, spat out some blood and advanced on the Frolin. The Frolin's right arm was shattered and useless but the left was still strong enough to swing a club. Only it never got the chance. The Sea-Farer closed the distance with frightening speed and drove his shoulder into the Frolin's midsection slamming it into a tree. The tree shuddered and creaked and leaned heavily to one side but it did not fall. The Frolin did. It tried to get up but its Sea-Farer opponent stepped to the side, clasped his hands together and swung them like a pendulum. The blow caught the Frolin under the chin. Its neck snapped with a resounding and sharp crack. The Frolin went limp and hit the ground with a crash. It did not move. The huge Sea-Farer grabbed the fallen troll by its ear, lifted it up and let loose a huge, primal roar that reverberated through the forests.

Those forests then exploded with shrill inhuman screams and the tramp of many, many feet. The land came alive with dozens, maybe hundreds of shadowy, ghastly looking creatures ripping and tearing across the ground at the party from Glossak. Sleek, lean dark forms with long, horrible jaws filled with teeth, heavy, spiked shambling shapes on two legs and four and a couple of definite Frolins were attacking from three directions. Jerik's battle had not lasted long enough for these creatures to finish surrounding them Kejen realized bitterly. Fortunately the way west was still open.

Kuran half carried, half threw the injured Overdulf into the forested other side of the clearing and Jerik, scooping up his ax at a full run, was close behind.

"Go Trif!" Kejen shouted. As leader, he was the last to leave after making sure everyone else was relatively safe. Trif nodded and slipped into the trees to the west. Kejen turned to follow--and was knocked flat on his back. His saw the glint of his sword spinning away. The thing towering over him looked like a huge wolf with massive haunches and oversize jaws. Kejen was not interested in details at the moment. Faster than any prairie rattler ever born, one of Kejen's hands shot up and clamped the surprised werewolf's jaws closed. A knife materialized in the other hand and Kejen plunged it into the side of the creature's head. The Northmarcher managed to roll away from the falling carcass and get on his feet. He spotted this sword a few feet away and ran towards it---and the ravening horde that just engulfed the body of the dead Frolin.

Kejen's hand closed on the hilt of his sword just as a clawed hand closed on the blade. Kejen did not bother to look at the manner of creature trying to seize his sword. He just punched it in the face and the claws retreated with a howl of pain. Running back to the trees, Kejen saw another monstrosity leap into the air at him. It looked like a lizard that walked upright and had oversized claws on the hands and feet. The ramrod straight tail must help it guide its jump, an irrelevant thought flew through Kejen's mind. The scaly attacker collapsed into a heap on the ground in front of him. Kejen saw the bloodslickened arrowhead sticking out of the back of its neck and he knew Trif was somewhere close by. He jumped over the dead animal without breaking stride and ran into the trees.

Trif loosed another arrow and took down still one more of the charging horde as Kejen ran by. Trif turned and followed his brother. Kuran, Overdulf and Jerik were bound to be heading in the same direction.

Those three found themselves fighting a battle with several wolf looking things that looked like the one Kejen had killed earlier. They bounded through the woodlands easily enough and descended upon the three humans. One jumped onto Jerik's back, claws scraping on his armor as it tried to bite through the back of his neck. The Crown Prince drove backwards into a tree and smashed his attacker into the trunk. A growl said it was still on his back and blood flowed down his arms as claws continued to rend flesh. Then he heard a yelp and it slid lifelessly off his back. He turned to see Overdulf pulling a spear out of its back.

"I am glad you did not pin that thing to me!" Jerik said.

"It was a risk I was willing to take!" Overdulf laughed.

Northmarcher and See-Farer continued west through the forest and found their way blocked by two more dead wolves. Kuran was still at work, slaying a third with an underhanded sword swing that nearly decapitated his foe. The Demon Division officer put his foot on the dead monster and pulled his sword out. Jerik could not see a scratch on him.

"You people really are the elite of the elite..." The Sea-Farer said.

Kuran barely heard him. "Have you seen Kejen and Trif?" The black clad officer spoke with urgency. "These things are trying to surround us!" The mountainside the party had tried to keep in sight to the left had vanished with the onset of battle.

At that moment, the two people Kuran spoke of burst out of the brambles and thorns. "Go! Go! Go!" Kejen shouted. "There are a lot of them behind us!"

Overdulf ignored his hurting ribs and took the lead with Jerik as Kuran and Trif send arrows cutting into the seething masses converging on them. Kejen shoved both of them forward and followed.

They could hear their howling pursuers less than twenty feet behind them. The gnashing teeth and claws sounded eager for a kill, to curb hunger with the flesh of those who had dared to invade their inviolate realm

Jerik looked back and saw the demonic forces starting to close the distance. He could also clearly make out movement and sounds to the right and left. The expedition from Glossak was just managing to say ahead of the pincers seeking to crash down on them. The Crown Prince of Warron redoubled his efforts as he felt a sensation he had rarely experienced before--fear. He was on land out of his element fighting an enemy that was not even human. He was not sure if that was good or bad. There would be no panic though. Jerik ignored the stinging branches and thorns, knowing that was nothing compared to what the Frolins, wolf hounds and what-have-you would do to him if they could catch up.

Another Frolin suddenly reared up next to Kuran and swung a piece of a tree it was using for a club. The Northcross solider blocked the blow with his shield. Then he dropped the shattered shield and plunged his sword into the monster's side. The Frolin fell heavily and crashed into the underbrush. Kuran darted away like a black shadow that was at home here in Skulka. Kejen felt something very close as he brought up the rear. He stopped and turned and delivered two quick blows with his sword. The scream and blood splattering in his face said the attack had hit home. The Sparent merchant felt an arrow fly past him and he shouted for Trif to keep running.

"It's not my blood and it's not yours!" Kejen shouted as he pushed his brother forward. "So don't worry about it!

Overdulf led his compatriots past a stream and continued barreling westward. That was the only way out of this madhouse and the creatures who held sway over Skulka had not managed to close the sack on them yet. Ovedulf looked up when he heard a piercing shrill scream from above. He saw another unworldly horror in the trees. Green with sharp claws for climbing and attacking, horns running flat along its head, a long narrow nose and frighteningly human looking hands, it launched itself out of the branches with another blood curdling scream--right at Trif. Unperturbed as usual, the Sparent archer calmly hit it in the face with his bow. It fell and Jerik somehow caught it in his huge hands. He definitely did not want to keep it and with an overhand motion, he hurled it into the forests, its screams echoing.

"That was, I believe, known as a '*Leshy* '" Trif said largely to himself. No one was interested in Faerie entomology at the moment.

Overdulf was the first to burst out of the haunted forest. He was nearly blinded by the sunlight but he was happy to be squinting. They had made it out of Skulka! Kuran and Jerik charged out next and Trif was on their heels. First into danger and last out like any good Northmarcher leader, was Kejen.

That is when it happened. The part of Kejen's mind that was always alert turned him around to look back into the place they left. Kejen barely had time to see what was bearing down on him. In the air dropping down on him was a mountain lion with two huge fangs reaching for him. There was nothing to stop it. The whole group looked in horror and as the latest attacker from Skulka landed on Kejen.

Or rather, Kejen's sword.

It roared high and terrible in pain. Kejen had set his feet and absorbed the impact of an airborne animal weighing at least three hundred pounds. The sword blade erupted in a red mist between the lion's shoulders. Kejen grunted and forced the impaled lion backwards. The blade splintered a tree trunk.

Jerik grimaced a bit when he stepped forward got a good look at the site of an impaled mountain lion pinned to a tree but averted his eyes when he saw some of the monster's internal organs and bodily fluids mingling with tree sap. Even Jerik's sea toughened stomach lurched a little.

"Stop gawking and help me get the sword blade out!" Kejen said impatiently.

Jerik helped him do just that.

Kuran and Trif flanked them ready to shoot anything venturing out of forest. Overdulf trotted up and looked at the lion drop to the ground as Kejen and Jerik successfully pulled the sword out. "I am surprised to see the blade did not break!"

"It was made by someone who knows how to make this right." Kejen answered. "His name is Kascar."

"I don't think I know anyone with that name." Overdulf said.

"You don't want to."

With that, Kejen led his band from Glossak into the greener and much safer forests of the Ankers.

Chapter 7

The only things that followed Kejen and his companions from the Forests of Skulka were the screeching and screaming. The noise carried for miles, much to everyone's irritation. For reasons no one could fathom, the dark side of Faerie could not, or would not, venture out of the confines of their domain of dead trees and thorns.

"Another one of its charming features." Jerik growled. He sat on a rock not a hundred yards away and spat defiantly in Skulka's direction.

The little group put another mountain between themselves and Skulka's denizens just in case. Kejen had the sneaking and persistent suspicion that some of the creatures living in that accursed place might be more inclined to rampage out of their homeland under the cover of darkness. If he had to deal with nighttime marauders, it would be, by God, on ground of his choosing.

Aside from Ovedulf's sore ribs, no one was seriously wounded.

"Don't worry about me." Overdulf growled. "I've been thorough worse. There was this one time; I had to keep a bear from taking the fish I caught...."

There were plenty of cuts and gashes to go around but no one had been bitten in half, ripped to shreds or dragged off into the trees to a fate worse than death.

"How many people can say they have been through the Forests of Skulka?" Jerik shouted to everyone. "To it, yes, but never, ever through it."

"That is because no one has ever lived going through it." Overdulf said. "Are you thinking about becoming the first person to go through that place twice?"

"Not bloody likely!" Jerik laughed.

"What makes you think those things want to see us again?" Kejen joined in

"Not bloody likely!" Kejen and Jerik both shouted at the same time.

After a while, the adrenaline ebbed and the euphoria of winning the battle began to wear off. The pain finally began to make itself felt so camp was made and wounds were dressed and weapons once again tended too.

Night fell and Kuran was returning from taking first watch. Kejen patted his shoulder and took the spear. "Another adventure in the annuals of the Demon Division, eh?"

"Definitely one for the history books." Kuran said. "Good thing we have a historian with us." he pointed at the sleeping Trif. "And one who can shoot too!"

He's always been good with his hands and eyes." Kejen nodded. "He can shoe horses faster than anyone, too."

Kuran laughed softly and tugged his black shirt. "Have you ever thought about wearing this?"

"Me?" Kejen was astonished. "In the Demon Division?"

"You did a good job back there in the woods." Kuran said.

"The plan was to keep the mountains on our flank. We got away from that and were almost surrounded." Kejen recapped. "Not exactly what I call perfectly executed."

"You are much too hard on yourself." Kuran admonished. "Not plan ever survives first contact with the enemy. Still, you accomplished something great."

"Getting through the Forests of Skulka?"

"That." Kuran answered. "and getting all of your soldiers out alive. That does not always happen."

Kejen thought about that for a second and then a question formed in his mind. "Have you ever lost anyone under your command?"

The Sparent merchant saw a brief look of sadness on the Demon Division officer's face. It was there and then it vanished. "Yes, I have."

"How did you feel afterwards?" Kejen asked uncomfortably.

"You console yourself with the fact that your men accomplished what they set out to do." the black clad soldier said. "And that if any of your men did die, they did not do so in vain."

That gave Kejen something to think about on guard that night.

The next morning, the trek northwest continued. The increasingly rockier and forested terrain began to take its toll. Kejen's battered hands felt as if they were growing larger with every painful throb. Jerik's huge shoulders started to droop and Overdulf, though he would not admit his bruised ribs were still sore, was not ready to move at full speed for another day at least. Still, he pressed on. The ever laconic Trif simply rubbed his legs occasionally and stopped every now and again to stretch. Even the indomitable Kuran looked spent.

Kejen consulted the map in his head and confirmed his conclusion with the map Overdulf kept in his back pocket. "Sevonicus is only a day away."

"How do we know this Sevonicus, whoever or whatever he is, is not one of *those* Skulka things?" Jerik asked.

"Because I have talked with the man." Overdulf said. "Weren't you listening back in Glossak?"

"I was listening. Listening closely." Jerik claimed. "But don't ask me if I heard anything."

"Ah, staring at the barmaids." Overdulf theorized.

The Sea-Farer's roguish smile was an answer onto itself.

A full night's rest restored everyone's spirits. Overdulf was mostly recovered from his rib injury and the party was able to move at something close to full speed. The terrain kept them from breaking into the run Kejen wanted but they still made good time. The day passed easily enough as they struggled grimly through an undeclared war with the mountains, most of it inevitably uphill.

"The higher you climb, the heavier your legs feel!" Kejen recited the first law of mountain hiking. "This must be why they say the harder path is seldom trod upon."

"Only there is no path here!" Jerik's voice boomed against the Ankers and scarring a few birds. "Nice to see normal animal life again."

"Nothing from the Forests of Skulka walks here." Trif said.

"We would just kill it anyway." The Sea-Farer said matter-of-factly and continued on his way.

A little after Noon, Kejen and Overdulf climbed the slope of yet another mountain. Kejen shielded his eyes and beheld the sight of the long sought holdings of Sevonicus.

"There it is!" Kejen shouted. He pointed down into the valley at a castle a few miles away. "After this slope, the land levels out and we can be there in a couple, maybe three hours."

"Would it not be great if *HeavenSteel* were there?" Overdulf whispered to Jerik.

The Crown Prince of Warron lightly clapped the Glossak trapper on the back. "Have you had enough adventures for a while?"

Overdulf nodded vigorously. "Enough for the next three lifetimes." He looked at Kejen who was all ready thirty yards ahead, beginning the descent to the valley floor. "That one seems eager for more." As if to underscore his observation, Kejen waved at him to follow.

"I would like a bit more myself." Jerik grinned and ran forward leaving a stunned Overdulf staring after him.

"That castle does not look like it belongs here." Trif commented. "The way it is built, the look of the stone. Seems like it was *placed* here."

"By whom?" Jerik asked

"In these mountains, more like by *what*." Kuran said dryly.

They reached the valley floor easily enough. The abundance of the animal life grew in stark contrast to the area around the Forests of Skulka. That Forest was full of life too but a different kind. It seemed the most dangerous thing here were rabbits. Kuran sternly told everyone to keep their guard up.

The path began where Overdulf's map said it would. "See?" the veteran of many Anker Mountain travels pointed out. "Someone lives here!"

"Does your map tell you where the path leads?" Kuran said to Overdulf.

"Where does one spend most of his time and begin all of his journeys?" Overdulf asked rhetorically.

"Home!" Jerik answered. "It felt like I was back in school for a few seconds."

"How many times were you thrown out?" Kejen asked from up in the front.

Jerik tapped the heraldic symbol of the Kings of Warron, a stylized dragonship on the waves of the Sea, on the right breast of his armor. "They were not going to throw *me* out my dear friend!"

An hour passed and the castle Sevonicus presumably lived in drew closer. Kuran dropped to the rear of the party, motioning Jerik to continue his pace. The Demon Division officer whispered something to the Sea-Farer and then waited about a minute before walking up to Kejen.

"Someone is following us." Kuran said in a low voice.

"Are you sure?" Kejen asked.

Kuran nodded slowly one time.

The path ran up a small swell of ground and turned to the left. "Just beyond the curve." Kuran said. Kejen tapped him unobtrusively on the side in the affirmative.

A minute later, Kuran and Trif slipped off into the trees to the left while Jerik and Overdulf darted to the right. Kejen followed them and found a good sized rock to hide behind.

Then they waited.

And waited.

Whoever was out there was rather patient.

Kejen decided to force the issue. He stepped out into the middle of the path, reached back and drew his sword. The gauntlet was thrown down. Now who, or what, would answer it?

"Expensive bait, Kejen." Jerik said to himself. Kejen was going to draw whoever was there to come into the range of Trif and Kuran's bows. When they were stuck with arrows, Kejen would pin them in place as Jerik and Overdulf charged in from the other flank. Best of all, the party that had fought its way through the Forests of Skulka were uphill from this newest attack.

Only the attack did not come.

The first thing Kejen saw was a piece of white cloth. Slowly, the sword holding it was visible as well as a pair of hands on the hilt.

Human hands! That was a plus Kejen thought but still did not let his guard down. Ever so slowly, taking great pains to show he was no threat, a man a little shorter than Kejen walked into view. Conical helmet with a snug fitting nose bridge and plate mail covering some white oversized shirt. Kejen recognized the manner of armament and dress but he did not see the Eagle of Verrent painted on the breastplate. What he did see was an off-center red "X" intersecting over the left side of the chest. Was that the emblem of Sevonicus? Kejen did not hear Overdulf say anything from his ambush site. That was a good thing for it meant everyone was still vigilant.

Kejen studied the Verrentian a little closely. There was some sort of emblem on his shield, seeming to indicate this man was some sort of noble. What was he doing here in the Ankers though?

The Verrentian was studying Kejen too and undoubtedly he was asking himself the same questions.

After a long minute, he spoke. In the Northmarcher language. "Who are you?"

Kejen understood him despite the heavy accent. "Who am I?" He responded with the handful of Verrentian he knew. "Who are *you?*" The merchant from Sparent waited to see if the man from Verrent would get angry.

Surprisingly, the stranger just smiled. He sheathed his sword into his hip scabbard. Kejen found that irritating. He could not figure out why anyone would not want to strap a sword to their back. All you could do with a hip scabbard is trip yourself.

"I am named Vidron." he introduced himself, staying, obligingly in

Kejen's native language. Maybe Vidron did not get a chance to practice it much. He tapped his shield. "Of the holdings of Stugen!"

"Kejen Densky of Sparent."

Vidron nodded but Kejen pointed beyond him with his sword. "Who is that in the trees?"

Vidron turned and waved to the spot Kejen indicated.

Out shambled a man dressed similar to Jerik, complete with horns sprouting out of his helmet. Instead of an ax though, he carried a sword. And he bore the same strange emblem on his armor as Vidron.

"I am Gorvald!" The large red-haired and oddly clean-shaven Sea-Farer announced in his language. Kejen understood it well enough. Kejen waved his compatriots out into the open.

Vidron seemed astonished when Trif rose up not more than ten feet from him and Kuran slightly behind. Then he looked over and saw Overdulf but his attention was fixed on Jerik.

Jerik and Gorvald locked eyes.

Gorvald was a big man but Jerik was still much larger. Jerik still cradled his ax. He was not completely convinced of the friendliness of these men.

"What kingdom and what clan do you hail from?" Jerik asked, flatly. It sounded particularly vicious in the Warron dialect.

"I serve Sevonicus now." Gorvald answered in the same language and without flinching.

That explains the armor marking Kejen thought to himself, silently following the conversation that seemed to be turning into a confrontation. He quietly readied himself.

"That is not what I meant!" Jerik said taking a step closer. Gorvald drew his sword and suddenly everyone got between both Sea-Farers. It was not unusual for blood feuds among *Locklannigh*
to last for generations. Nor was it unheard of for members of feuding clans or kingdoms to attack one another on sight regardless of where they were.

"What kingdom are you from?" Jerik asked again, the snap of command evident in his voice.

"The Kingdom of Eorick and Warron have no quarrels." Gorvald said. "Even if they did, that means nothing here. I serve Sevonicus now."

"And why is that?" Jerik demanded.

"A man's business is his own." Gorvald shot back.

"Almost sounds like a Northmarcher." Kejen cut in with a laugh.

Jerik laughed too. Then he held his ax out with the point angled to the ground, the Sea-Farer sign for a truce. "Very well Gorvald. Our Kingdoms do not trouble each other."

Gorvald stuck his sword into the ground and took a step forward. The two did not shake hands but rather clasped forearms.

"Checking for knives under the sleeve." Kejen explained to Trif.

"Makes a good bit of sense." Trif said.

"Have you come to see Sevonicus?" Vidron asked after tensions receded.

Overdulf stepped forward. "Indeed we have. We have come a long way. All the way from Glossak and through the Forests of Skulka...."

"Through Skulka?" Vidron's jaw dropped. So did Gorvald's.

"Through" Trif confirmed in Verrentian to make sure Vidron understood correctly.

"Even if Eorick and Warron were feuding, I would have declared it over after hearing that!" Gorvald exclaimed. "You are some men to have done that!"

"Some men who have come to see Sevonicus." Kejen said.

Vidron bowed. "Then we shall take you to see him!"

"Certainly did not come here for the scenery."

The trail became a road, then a paved road and then it widened into something resembling a street. A street that led directly to the castle's front. Two men attired in armor with the same strange markings nodded to the seven as they walked into the brightly lit courtyard. Any reminders of the encounter in the Forests of Skulka were quickly squelched. There was a completely different feel to this place. It was a feeling of...

"Sanctuary." Kuran said.

"I did not hear you." Kejen replied.

"I said this place has a feeling of sanctuary." Kuran said again. "It feels like I have walked into a Church."

"It does." Trif agreed. He looked around at the various people walking about doing whatever it was they did in here. More than a few though stopped to look at the strangers who just walked in with Vidron and Gorvald. They came to a stop in front of a simple looking throne in the shade. In fact, it looked more like an ordinary chair that was just taken care of better than most.

Gorvald went to find Sevonicus while Vidron stood next to Kejen. The Verrentian looked totally at ease. Kejen looked around and half expected several dozen armed guards to be in the shadows just in case but saw none. It was almost like he was walking down any street back in Sparent.

Before long, Gorvald returned with a hooded and cloaked figure. The rust colored clothes looked too big for whoever was approaching. Kejen was pretty sure it was the long sought Sevonicus but he stayed quiet. The person, more than likely Sevonicus, sat down on the chair/throne and pulled back his hood.

He was a wizened looking old man with long white hair running down his back and over his shoulders. Kejen looked into the greenest eyes he had ever seen. What he also saw was that neither he nor any of his comrades were in any danger. This man seemed more like a monk than monarch.

Another man dressed much like Vidron brought out a couple of benches.

"Please, please sit." Sevonicus finally spoke in a lilting, somewhat high pitched voice. "You have come a long way, Vidron tells me. A long way just to see me."

Kejen took off his helmet and had a seat. Trif sat down next to him and Jerik plopped down on the other end. Kuran took a seat on the back bench as Kejen knew he would. The Demon Division officer was still scanning his surroundings. He may have let his guard down a little but not all the way. Ovedulf remained standing and he approached Sevonicus.

"We once met." Overdulf began. "It was a long time ago. I am glad to see you are still in good health."

"Thank you." The wise man returned the compliment. "I see the years have been good to you Overdulf."

"You remember me?" the Glossak trapper was surprised.

"There is very little I forget." Sevonicus smiled. "Who do you bring with you?"

Kejen stood up and began the introductions.

Sevonicus nodded his greetings to each one. "Four Northmarchers and a Sea-Farer from Warron. One of the more interesting groups to ever come through here. What will you have of me?"

Kejen stood up again. "Overdulf tells us you know more about these mountains than anyone, including him."

"I like to think that, yes." Sevonicus said.

"We are looking for something very old. A sword from the time of Faerie or pretty close anyway."

"What is so special about this particular sword?"

Kejen took a deep breath. "It is the sword *HeavenSteel."*

Sevonicus sat upright. Activity suddenly ceased and everyone was looking directly at the man who had come from so far away.

Kejen, never shy around crowds, repeated what he had just said but louder this time. "Legend tells us that Lorac Densky, my great-great sometime grandfather hid *HeavenSteel* here in the Anker Mountains. Where it is hidden is not certain. You know these mountains, their ways, their history and their secrets. We were hoping you could shed light on where it is. Overdulf was hoping you actually had it here." he concluded with a wry grin.

"HeavenSteel..." Sevonicus had a far way look in his eyes. "I have not heard that name in a long time. Not since..." he trailed off, a thought still hanging in the air. "Lorac Densky was your grandfather?"

Kejen answered in the affirmative. Kejen did not like the way this conversation was going either. "'Not since' when?"

Sevonicus looked at Kejen for a few moments. It seemed as if the wise man was gauging the character of the merchant from Sparent standing before him. "I have not heard the name *HeavenSteel* or Densky for at least two centuries."

Kejen stuck a finger in his ear. "Did you just say 'two centuries?? ?' As in two hundred years?"

When Sevonicus merely nodded, Kejen nearly exploded. Only Overdulf did it first.

"What sort of nonsense is this?!" their guide from Glossak shouted. "I did not lead these fine men through that patch of Hades on earth Skulka for you to play games with us!"

Vidron and Gorvald took up positions on both sides of Sevonicus and another man appeared with a sword from behind the throne.

"We mean no harm!" Kejen also shouted. His voice carried easily to every corner of Sevonicus's castle. "But we will not be mocked or trifled with!"

Sevonicus waved down his bodyguards. Then he stood up slowly. "How long have you known me, Overdulf?"

The trapper from Glossak's eyebrows came together as he mentally ran back through the years. Too many years to run back past, he thought. "I first met you when I was about Kejen's age. Then a couple of years after that in Glossak. This is the third---"Overdulf held up three fingers--"time I have spoken to you."

"Has my appearance changed since then?" Sevonicus asked

Overdulf shook his head. "I know you have been around for a long time but not that long."

Sevonicus addressed the whole group. "Do you seek more proof? Very well."

The wise man reached back and pulled the white shock of his hair back off his neck, revealing ears that pointed. Trif, not surprisingly, was the first to figure it out. The pointed ears, the arched brow, slender build those green, green eyes...

"You are an elf." Trif said in the same tone of voice he would use as if he were demonstrating two plus three equaled five.

"An elf?" Kejen could not believe what he was seeing.

"How can that be?" Jerik stood up. "I thought the elves and dwarves and the rest of the little people vanished with the passing of Faerie!"

"We saw a lot of things in the Forests of Skulka that were supposed to be legend too." Kejen pointed out. "Remember those trolls?"

"Those were not little." Jerik said with gritted teeth.

"So what is this place?" Kuran finally spoke.

"I was wondering when you would find your voice." Sevonicus said with a smile. "You have been looking over the castle since you got here. There are no threats here. You are in no danger."

"It is simply in my nature." Kuran explained.

"As it is in my Captain of the Guard here, Coylin." Sevonicus pointed to the man who had emerged from behind the wise man earlier. "Men such as he are extraordinary. As are those who brave the dangers of the Forests of Skulka."

"So what is this place?" Kejen repeated his friend's question. He was not going to be thrown off with flattery.

Sevonicus walked up to Kejen and reached up to put a thin arm around his shoulders. "The Forests of Skulka are a remnant of the worst of Faerie. Here we try to preserve the best of Faerie."

"Who are all these people?" Kejen was now genuinely curious. "Are they elves too?"

Sevonicus shook his head. "No, though they do come from all over. Gorvald and Vidron, whom you have met, are from the Kingdoms of Eorick and Verrent. Coyln here is from Kielstrock. We even have among our hundred a couple of Northmarchers."

"God help you." Kejen laughed.

"Oh, He does." Sevonicus laughed with him. "Elves are still around, Kejen. We have never been numerous and never will be. We have not been as visible since the Ages War."

"Why is that?"

Sevonicus motioned everyone to follow him. "Talk with me as we walk to my study. The time you call Faerie was a wonderful time. But it was doomed to end. The Race of Man rose quickly and dominated this world."

"Why would that change everything?" Jerik asked.

Sevonicus entered his study and sat down. Kejen could not believe the number of books here. Bookcases rose to the ceiling. The room continued to run all the way to a large window a good twenty feet away.

The wise man finally answered the Sea-Farer's question. "Man is capable of creating such beauty but at the same time he is capable of such destruction. Your wars, intercene strife, the dizzying speed at which you spread across the world. It was bound to change everything. For the worst in my opinion."

"If everything in the time of Faerie was good and pure, explain the Forests of Skulka." Trif challenged Sevonicus.

"Some of what lives there was in place even the time of Faerie." Sevonicus said.

"Kejen drove his sword through something that did not look like anything I had seen or heard of in legend." Jerik laughed. "Well, it might be a legend now."

"You remind me of Gorvald" Sevonicus smiled. Then he turned his attention back to Trif. "Sometimes I wonder why Man did not choose the wrong side in the War of the Ages."

"You said it yourself." Trif refused to back down. " 'Man is capable of such beauty and of such destruction' . Dual nature. Neither good nor bad. The Cataclysmic War, what you call the War of the Ages, was a civil war between the good and evil of Faerie. The Rise of Man is a result of the battle that weakened Faerie."

"I am impressed." Sevonicus said. "Straight from what the Church teaches you."

"The Church, for better or for worse, has a dim view of that time period." Trif corrected him. "I do not equate Faerie with Satan because it is simply not the same thing."

"After going through Skulka, I wonder." Kejen said to himself.

"I hope I get a chance to debate you again one day before long, Trif." Sevoincus said. "However I do not believe you came all this way just to debate." He slowly got up and selected a scroll from the many stacked up in a shelf. "Tell me what you know of the sword *HeavenSteel*."

Kejen produced his journal and again explained his research. I am getting better and better at this, he thought. Sevonicus listened and nodded occasionally but did not interrupt. Trif looked around at the books as Jerik and Kuran looked out the window down into the courtyard. They had heard this before.

Before long though, all were gathered around Kejen and Sevonicus.

"That is well researched and reasoned." Sevonicus complemented Kejen. "*HeavenSteel* however is not here."

Overdulf looked down at his feet but Kejen patted his shoulder. "You are tasked with taking us to Rainkin Falls anyway so do not worry about it."

"I am sure it is where you say it is, Kejen." Sevonicus said. "But one never knows."

"I do not follow." Kejen was perplexed.

"If you could figure this out, how do you know someone else did not either?" Sevonicus explained. "Someone else with a darker purpose or use for *HeavenSteel*?"

"We would have heard about that by now." Kejen said. "One way or another."

"True." Sevonicus said. "But I have heard rumors."

"What sort of rumors?"

Sevonicus went on as if he did not hear Kejen. "Have you considered the possibility that Lorac did indeed lose *HeavenSteel* at the Three Day's Battle?"

"If he did, *HeavenSteel* could be anywhere." Kejen surmised. "What are you trying to tell me?"

"In the Northmarch, there is the legend of *HeavenSteel*, the sword that fell from the sky." Sevonicus began. "Many nations have similar tales. I am sure you have heard of the Great Sword of the Emperors of Thenros and there is a mighty kingdom in the East with a legend of a sword given to the ruler. The legend has grown that he who possesses it is invincible."

"Is there some sort of connection?" Kejen asked.

"Let us say Lorac lost the sword fighting in the Three Day's Battle." Sevonicus said. "Who was he fighting against?"

"Great Eastern Invasion." Kejen remembered the history lesson. "Are you telling me that *HeavenSteel* is in the East?

"I am only suggesting the possibility." Sevonicus said. "Or perhaps someone else took it and sold it at a market someplace and *HevenSteel* may be at the side of the Emperor of Thenros."

The East? Other than the invasion two centuries ago, there was no real contact with anything east of the Blieben River. It was rumored that the civilizations there dwarfed anything in the Western world but contacts were few, limited and generally antiquainted. The Saracens living in the deserts along the Southern Sea or maybe Thenros could possibly trade with the East but how would that involve the Northmarch? For all Kejen knew, it could have been a whole different world. Individual adventurers had crossed the Blieben but found the land there a veritable wasteland, mostly scrub brush and infertile. It was a place devoid of interest. There was not a single settlement, Eastern or otherwise, in that part of the world. The nations that lived under the rising sun remained a mystery.

Thenros may have been closer but traveling there was not merely a matter of walking or riding. To get there, one had to sail down the length of the Blieben itself! And would the Emperor of Thenros simply hand over a sword that had been in his family for centuries because some stranger said it belonged to him?

"How much of a possibility?" Kejen felt some sort of misplaced anger growing in him. How would Sevonicus know it the sword was at Rainkin Falls or not? In the East? Preposterous! In Thenros? Insane! Utter madness!

"I do not know." Sevonicus admitted. "I hope I am wrong though. I do hope you find *HeavenSteel.* It was not my intention to place doubt in your mind."

"There is none." Kejen said decisively. "We are committed to going to Rainkin Falls."

Sevonicus nodded in approval. "Please stay the night and feel free to provision yourselves. I wish you nothing but the best. Besides, I would like to debate your brother some more."

Trif's grin was predatory.

Chapter 8

Kejen did not know who won the debate that must have surely lasted most of the night but battle honors looked about even. Neither Sevonicus nor Trif would admit defeat so there was no point in asking. The Torna River flowed a couple of miles past Sevonicus's holdings so it did not take Kejen's little band long to get to a suitable landing. Sevonicus had most graciously supplied a raft complete with a sail. Jerik the Sea-Farer inspected it and lavished sincere praise upon the craft's fine construction.

"Seems a little large for five people." Kejen observed.

"That is because we are going with you!" Gorvald's voice boomed from behind him. Vidron stood beside him, backpack on and sword once again hanging irritatingly from the hip.

"Are you now?" Kejen asked.

"I have charged Vidron and Gorvald with helping you find *HeavenSteel.*" Sevonicus said. "If the sword is at Rainkin Falls, there is no telling what else could be there. A couple of extra hands will be most useful."

"How are you coming back?" Kejen wondered. "The Torna flows *toward* Rainkin Falls and *away* from here."

"When the sword is recovered--" Vidron paused to smile, "--we will sail with you down the Blieben to Glossak. Then we walk through the prairies and enter the mountains south of our home. No trips through the Forests of Skulka mind you!"

"Nice to see you have thought it through." Kejen said. "Any help is welcome."

"Welcome aboard!" Jerik shouted. "It feels good to be back on water again even if it is not the Sea! Tell me, what is the name of this craft?"

"I did not know you gave a barge a name." Kejen said.

Jerik pointed at the small lightning bolt painted on Kejen's helmet. "I proclaim this craft to be named *Thunderbolt*!"

"Very well." Kejen agreed. "*Thunderbolt* it is!"

"It would be a good idea for everyone to take off their armor." Jerik suggested. "You don't want to fall in the water and drown! You do remember what it is like to be on the water don't you Gorvald?"

The red headed Sea-Farer pretended to push Jerik off the barge but the Crown Prince of Warron avoided him. "I still have my sea legs. We will see if you still have yours." he laughed.

Jerik took control of the rudder and directed Kejen who was holding on to the sail. "I told you I would get you on a boat one day, my friend!" He looked around as they shoved off. "Well, maybe a real one some day."

"Four, maybe five days at the most." Overdulf called out from the front. "Certainly better than walking and climbing there! And much better than dealing with monsters in the forest!"

"Watch out for rocks and such!" Jerik admonished. "They may not be monsters but they can rip a boat out from under you!"

The next water logged two days were a blur of white water and avoiding those rocks. Jerik enjoyed himself and would have tried to sail to the other end of the world if he could. The only thing that stopped them was the calm waters of a beautiful blue-green lake. Although it was only mid afternoon, Kejen decided to call a halt for the day to enjoy the lake and the solitude it offered. Besides, they were about halfway to Rainkin Falls.

Jerik bounded into the water, followed by Overdulf, whom the Sea-Farer attempted to drown horse playing. Trif sat across from Kejen on a rock and wrote some more. It was a great time to write, sitting under the clear skies. Kejen left his brother to his own devices and went off to engage Kuran in a friendly wrestling match on the water's edge. Vidron was cooking some trout and smell attracted everyone.

"Is anyone tired of preserved rations?!" The Verrentian called out. "Plenty for everyone but you better hurry!" Kuran used Kejen's temporary distraction to his advantage, got the right leverage and pinned his friend from Sparent into the mud.

"Treachery!" Kejen sputtered

"Is a useful weapon!" Kuran laughed.

It was hard to argue with that but absolutely intolerable when the other fellow was right.

Overdulf sloshed his way out of the lake with his dripping beard and pointed at Kejen. "It is about time that rascal got a taste of his own medicine!"

Kejen crawled through the mud to Ovedulf pretending he was one of those large lizard things Jerik told him about. They lived in the southern part of Masovia. What were they called again? "Alligators" or something like that.

"I still don't believe such things exist." Overdulf said, sitting on a log as Kejen pretended to bite the Glossak trapper's leg. Overdulf had heard the stories too. "Why don't I see any here?"

"They like warm water." Kejen remained him.

"I like any kind of water!" Jerik lumbered up.

"You will get to see a lot of it." Kejen said. "Only a couple of more days until we reach Rainkin Falls!"

A cheer rose and drifted across the lake. Life was good. With luck, they would have *HeavenSteel* in their possession sunrise after next.

Kejen clenched and unclenched his big hands in anticipation.

Two days!

The Torna River curved to the northeast heading for its confluence with the Blieben. The Sun rose to the right and front. At least we are not lost, Kejen chuckled to himself. The sword he sought was drawing closer by the hour.

"Lake and river sailing is nice, aye." Jerik shouted to the world. "But sailing on the Sea is much better!" Jerik steered the craft with the causal expert hand of someone who had spent most of his life on the open sea. He deigned to let his friends help guide a little by pushing off the shallows with poles. "Have any of you been to the Sea?" he asked for the hundredth time.

Kejen took a pole from Trif and grinned at his brother, who also knew what was coming. Gorvald winked at Jerik but remained quiet.

"Imagine that lake multiplied by a thousand! And the serenity is astounding..." And so began a two hour litany about the waves, the wind, large mountain sized things called whales and anything else vaguely nautical. It was a good way to spend a couple of hours as the mighty Kalagda glacier made itself felt long anyone saw it. The dropping temperatures and eerie cracking noises announced its presence before Kejen spotted the massive world of ice ahead.

Since time immemorial, the Kalagda glacier had been here. Within its icy layers, its story unfolded, going back countless thousands, even millions of years, back to its beginnings on a forgotten mountain top. The Kalagda had been here when the great reptiles exercised their mastery over the world and it witnessed their demise as well. When the world froze, it grew with the long winters and halted for the short summers. When the millennia of the short summers ended, the Kalagda retreated sullenly and resentfully, leaving behind kettle lakes and the huge moraine built up over the years. A large hole scooped out long before even the days of Faerie became Lake Peka and from it flowed the mighty Blieben River, a seemingly an eternal feature to those short-sighted beings that currently held sway over the world.

"Keep that ice away from us! Use the pole to do that!" Jerik directed. "Use the pole like a lance, aim for the middle. Push the ice away."

Trif balanced his pole and reached out, gently pushing the piece of drifting ice away as Jerik told him to. Kejen did the same but with considerably more force, causing his pole to bounce off the ice and he almost fell in the water.

"No, no, gently!" Jerik repeated. He used his hands for emphasis. "You can't stab ice! Just push it way. Don't try to kill it! It's ice!"

The barge and its occupants successfully navigated its way around the front of the glacier. Jerik took a couple of seconds to look up at the massive wall of ice. He rubbed his eyes. Where those shapes in the ice? Or just shadows?

Trif followed Jerik's gaze. He handed his pole off of to Overdulf and carefully made his way to the Sea-Farer Crown Prince.

"Locked away in the ice are things from every age." Trif informed his friend. "Plants, animals, all sorts of things."

"Really?" An intrigued Jerik asked. "Any people?"

"Probably." Trif answered. He looked up at the ice. Things from every age he repeated in his mind. I have to come back here one day he thought. If I look long and hard enough, I bet I can find something from the dim twilight of the Beginning itself!

Many adventurous souls had ventured here just to see the mighty glacier. Some had actually crossed it, braving the subzero temperatures and howling winds. Some had fallen victim to it as well, entombed in the ice forever, overcome by hypothermia or the treacherous cracks all along the solid looking surface. Most preferred to sail around it instead. As this group of seven from three different nations utilizing each other's talents and skills to achieve a goal that was greater than even the mighty glacier itself.

A smaller but still formidable piece of ice drifted into view, shattering Jerik's thoughts. Better my thoughts than the barge, his mind screamed.

"Iceberg, starboard!" Jerik shouted. Then he remembered his crew, except for Gorvald, came from landlocked countries. "I mean left! Left!"

Kejen easily pushed the barge away from the oncoming berg, turned and bowed.

"Not bad, not bad." Jerik clapped softly. "Not bad for a landlubber."

Kejen splashed him with some water.

The glacier began to recede in the distance and sound of cracking and crashing ice was replaced by the sound of rushing water. The river was starting to buck and heave. Soon, the poles would be used to fend off rocks, not ice. The Torna was beginning to rush toward the larger Blieben. A few hours later, the roar of the great river filled the ears of everyone on the little craft. One river bend later, the two brothers from Sparent, the Sea-Farers from Warron and Eorick, the Demon Division officer, the Glossak trapper and the soldier from Verrent beheld the world's longest river.

The Blieben cut a corridor through the Ankers, hurtling southward all the way to the Southern Sea, giving life to several nations along the way as well as forming the boundary between West and East. The Blieben River had been there since before the End of the Age War and maybe for a time even before that as the shells and bones found in nearby deeper rock attested. It was worthy of the name Blieben, Verrentian, Vidron proudly told everyone, meaning "to remain."

Jerik and Kejen pulled *Thunderbolt* up onto the bank as Vidron also smugly informed everyone that Rainkin Falls was named after the first person, also Verrentian, to explore that far up the Blieben.

"And get out of pulling the barge up on the riverbank!" Jerik commented sardonically. Vidron propped a foot up on a rock and struck an equally sardonic pose.

"A day, maybe a day and half, march up to Rainkin Falls from here!" Overdulf shouted over the river.

"We will have to leave the barge here." Kejen said. "We cannot pull it upstream against this current."

"Ah, the lad is learning the ways of the mountains." Overdulf said. Kejen was fairly certain it was a compliment.

Trif tied the barge to a tree just in case of rising water and ran off to rejoin his fellow adventurers. The Queen City of the Mountains would be easy to find but it was still a long way to walk.

The party that had left Glossak, fought their way through the Forests of Skulka to Sevonicus's small holdings and sailed down the Torna to its confluence with the Blieben now began what they hoped was the final leg of their quest. Kejen and Overdulf led the way again this time along the shore of the Blieben to the north.

Kejen kept his friends on the west bank of the river. Sometimes it seemed as if he could walk across it easily enough, other times, the Blieben widened so much that it seemed like it was part of the Sea Jerik loved so much..

Weaving between trees on the riverbank, Kejen moved inexorably northward, thankful the ground was flatter on this bank and the footing was not as treacherous as Overdulf first thought it would be.

"Not the first time I was happy to be wrong!" Overdulf smiled.

Along the way, Trif aimed his bow and took down a six point buck drinking at the water's edge. Kuran shook his head. "From that distance! If I had not seen it, I would not have believed it! I should take you to Northcross and instruct the entire Division on archery."

Trif shrugged and began butchering the game. It would be a welcome change from field rations and fish.

The shoreline became rockier that afternoon so climbing and crawling became the order of the day. Overdulf muttered something about claiming victory too soon and not reading the map correctly. Nonetheless, the band was making good progress. Rainkin Falls was drawing closer. There existed the possibility they could reach it that night!

Then one of those unpredictable mountain thunderstorms raced down the river. Kejen extorted his friends to continue moving up the river bank against the elements, helmets lowered against the driving rain and eyes watching the rising river. Screaming insults at the weather, Kejen was determined to reach the Falls by nightfall. Grimly he pulled one foot out of the mud and plunged the other one in. Much to Kejen's irritation, it slowed everyone down.

Nonetheless, they rode out the storm without stopping. Darkness though finally drew the day to a close. "Its not like we could go looking around the Falls in the dark anyway." the ever practical Trif pointed out.

Kejen did not like it but he was forced to agree. "I know, I know." He grumbled. "I just did not want to stop five miles from the Falls."

"Those few miles will go by quickly enough!" Jerik promised from his sleeping bag. "Now get some rest or at least let me get some!"

"Don't forget to come out here in an hour while you are resting!" Gorvald, standing watch, called out from the trees.

Kejen trudged out to Gorvald and took the spear. "It's not like I can sleep anyway so I might as well get started now."

Trif stood on watch in the quiet of an Anker Mountain night. He looked up at the sky and the stars told him it was about four in the morning.

Kejen walked out of the camp up to where his brother was.

"Have you slept at all?" Trif asked.

"Too excited to sleep." Kejen said. "If I had known I was not going to sleep, I would have stood watch all night and saved you the trouble."

"I would have told you to go to sleep." Trif replied.

"I know." Kejen laughed softly. "Are you ready for tomorrow?"

"Later today." Trif corrected.

"Later today." Kejen repeated. "Do you really think *HeavenSteel* it there?"

Trif looked surprised, and almost human, for a second. "You are the last person I would have expected to hear that from."

Kejen just smiled. "It is just so hard to believe we are almost there. A few months ago we were just *talking* about it at the kitchen table. Now here we are. Just a couple of mountain ridges away. It almost feels like a dream."

"Since you have not slept at all, how do you know this is not a dream?" Trif asked what not an unreasonable question was.

Kejen lightly punched Trif's shoulder. "No. You are definitely real." He then looked at Trif for a couple of seconds. "You know, many people back in Sparent did not think you could do something like this. You know, go on this quest."

"They were wrong." Trif said flatly.

"Yes they were." Kejen agreed. "I knew they were wrong all along. You, good sir, have performed most admirably. Of course, I am not surprised."

Kejen hugged his brother and Trif hugged him back. Then Trif told him to get ready to move out to Rainkin Falls. Kejen agreed. He knew better than to try to relieve Trif from his guard post early.

A few minutes later, Trif looked back into the camp. Kejen finally did manage to drift off. Everyone, even someone as hyperactive as Kejen needed some rest. But not a lot. Even from the forest, Trif could see Kejen smiling as he slept...if only for a little while.

Slowly at first, then a bit more with every passing minute, the roar of a huge waterfall could be heard. The morning saw the a couple of miles pass quickly before the Blieben turned abruptly to east, doubled back on itself, then swing west again before settling on a northward course. Walking carefully on the loose rocks and roots that seemed to be in all the wrong places, the travelers slogged through yet another turn. The cry of a hawk sounded off somewhere in the distance, a good sign.

Kejen Denksy turned the corner and beheld the long awaited and spectacular view that was Rainkin Falls. Untold millions of tons of water cascaded over the precipice created a mist reaching out almost half a mile away. Even that this distance, he could feel the cold, clean spray. Kejen had to shout to be heard and his voice was distorted by the din but there was no mistaking the look on his face.

"We found it!" the Sparent merchant shouted. "We found it!"

"About bloody time!" Jerik shouted as he grabbed Kejen by the waist and lifted him up. Kuran pounded Kejen's back as Gorvald and Vidron joined in a pile up. Overdulf sat down on a rock with a big grin on his face. They had finally done it!

Trif viewed his surrounding amid the celebrations. One waterfall ahead and one to his right, facing west. No need to consult a map--though he did anyway just to be sure. "Yes, I believe we have."

Kejen raised both arms and gave a triumphant shout. They were at Rainkin Falls! Now they just had to find *HeavenSteel.* Kejen was not worried though. He could all ready see "nature's stairway", referred to in Lorac's journal. It seemed more like a ledge than a staircase but Kejen was not going to worry about that.

Rainkin Falls was situated in a narrow tree lined valley dominated by the Falls themselves. The Kalagda glacier gave the Blieben its strength but Rainkin Falls was where the river was born. The ledge, "nature's stairway", Lorac described it, was the only way up and out.

Kejen slid out of his backpack and quickly found his journal with all of Lorac's carefully written directions. The company huddled around Kejen as he looked over the writings he almost had memorized. It did not hurt to be sure so close! The depository, according to what was written, was located on the west side of the falls. The side we are on, Kejen happily noted. The ledge was on their side as well.

"Getting better and better!" Jerik observed.

Kejen walked up to the ledge and looked up its length. "We are going to have a great view when we get up there!"

"I hope none of it has broken off." Overdulf said. "It's a possibility after all this time with erosion and such. It was been a couple of centuries, after all."

"Maybe we should have just cut across the mountains from the Torna and approached from behind." Gorvald wondered aloud.

"Too late for that!" Kejen said.

"I have my climbing gear here." Ovedulf assured everyone.

"Hopefully we won't need it."

Kejen read aloud,

"After ascending the ledge northward, one finds the guardian in front of Nature's stairway. Then one enters the old open space. Nearby at this structure, lies HeavenSteel."

"Structure?" Kejen mused. "Could that be the tombs Sevonicus mentioned? What is this guardian he is speaking of?"

"That boulder." Kuran pointed at a large rock at the top of the ledge. It did look as though it were standing guard. It was a very good benchmark. That it was still there after all this time argued against the dangers of erosion, Trif added.

Kejen shouldered his backpack and drew his sword before walking to the base of the ledge. It looked sturdy enough to hold a wagon. Quite a few wagons actually. It also looked man-made. Who had built it and why?

"One at a time!" Kuran shouted with the authority of a Demon Division officer. "Let's not put any more weight on that ledge than we have too!" He was not taking any chances when they were this close to finding *HeavenSteel.*

Kejen pointed up with his sword and shouted "One way to find out!" Kejen took a step forward, then another tentative one and yet another. The rock did not crumble. Kejen walked forward with a slightly exaggerated slouch to keep his backpack from pulling him over backwards into the closely following Trif. Nothing was going to stop him now. Soon Kejen's steps broadened from a slight shuffle waiting fearfully for a collapse to long, confident strides, eager and determined to reach the top and recover the long lost sword *HeavenSteel.*

Jerik was third to charge up the ledge, followed by Kuran and then Vidron. Gorvald was next to last and Overdulf was last to climb, mentally kicking himself for being at the end of the line. It's not that far he thought to himself. Maybe I am just getting old and paranoid.

Standing at the top, Kejen and Trif both spotted something that commanded their attention. Kejen saw the ledge led straight to the opening of what looked like an ancient amphitheater. Was this the "structure" Lorac wrote about? Maybe he could not spell "amphitheater" Kejen laughed to himself.

What Trif saw, however, demanded more attention. Much more

immediate attention. At first he thought it was a hawk but then realized it was much too big. Whatever it was, the unidentified object was winging directly for Overdulf still climbing the ledge. Kuran saw it too and, faster than the eye could follow, sent an arrow at its head.

It pulled up out of its dive and hovered ten feet away from a shocked Overdulf, huge wings beating. It looked like a dragon from the old stories but it was the size of a Frolin. The wings and scorpion-like tail confirmed its identity. Straight out of bedtime stories and campfire tales, the Wyvern had come for them.

The snout split, showing more teeth than anyone wanted to count, and unleashed a deafening, grinding roar that drowned out even the Falls.

The Wyvern rose and dove sharply reaching for the Glossak trapper out on the ledge. Overdulf hugged rock and felt the claws scraped across his armor, unable to find purchase and lift him off.

Trif found some rope and threw it down to Overdulf. He ignored it and bound up the ledge faster than a mountain lion could have.

"This way!" Kejen barked and the company fell back into the open space of the amphitheater. At least they did not have to worry about being knocked off a ledge.

"Here we go again!" Jerik shouted. It felt like the Forests of Skulka all over again.

The Wyvern immediately swooped in and landed and found itself under attack from several directions at once. It had made the mistake of not realizing how many people were here.

Trif and Kuran led their arrows fly, embedding them in the dragons shoulder and jaw. The angry dragon charged after them and Vidron, with Gorvald, attacked from the shadows on its flank. They found the monster's scales deflected their swords. Kejen saw that and attacked from the other side, driving his sword forward like a lance. His weapon plunged into the Wyvern's side. Although it was hurt, the Wyvern was monstrously strong, reacting with a backhand that sent Kejen flying. Kejen was monstrously strong too however. He sprang up and charged the dragon head on. The Wyvern did not breathe fire like dragons of old but it did have another weapon. It arched its tail up and over its head to pin down the charging Northmarcher. Kejen saw it, stopped and knocked it away with his sword. Kuran worked his way around the Wyvern's back and stepped down on its tail. Sturdy Northmarcher boots held it down and off balance. He quickly looked up a pile of rocks to the right before turning his attention back to the enraged reptile.

Jerik had climbed up that pile of rocks at the battle's start and found himself several feet about the fight. He watched Kuran lift his foot off the Wyvern's tail and calmly retreat back towards the ledge putting the monster right where the Sea-Farer Crown Prince wanted it. Jerik leapt off the rocks and crashed down on the unsuspecting Wyvern. The impact drove the monster to the ground but Jerik lost his grip on the ax, whose point he attempted to drive into the Wyvern's head. Instead the weapon spun away into the dirt. Mustering all of its tremendous strength, the Wyvern stood up with Jerik on its back and threw the Sea-Farer into the rocky slope. The bloodied animal charged at the hurt Warronite but never got to him. Kejen and Trif attacked from one side while Vidron stabbed at the base of the beast's neck from the other. Kuran jumped into the Wyvern's midst and out again, leaving the unscaled belly with red gaping streaks. Most importantly, the Demon Division officer had bought Gorvald enough time to drag Jerik out of harm's way. Jerik would hear nothing of it, wrenching himself out of the other Sea-Farer's grip and charging back into the fray. Gorvald grinned, raised his sword and charged in after Jerik, an ancient battle cry from Eorick ringing in everyone's ears.

Overdulf began making the climb Jerik made earlier. "Don't let that thing see me!" he shouted at Trif. Trif nodded and stuck another arrow into the side of the dragon's head. He grunted with irritation. He had been aiming at its eyes.

A blow from the Wyvern's tail sent Kuran spinning but the black clad soldier rolled back on his feet and the dragon's teeth only closed on air. Vidron and Kejen attacked from the rear again and to their surprise, Jerik exploded out of the dust, lashing with his mighty battle ax. He missed the Wyvern's head but the blade sank deep into the monster's shoulder. The Wyvern staggered back, a high pitched scream reverberated off of the rocks and trees.

The Wyvern was not the most intelligent animal but now the fact the battle was lost was beginning to enter its tiny, vicious mind. Its wings spread out and it was ready to take off.

The previously missing Overdulf suddenly landed on the Wyvern's back. Wicked ten inch knife drawn, he dove and stabbed into the Wyvern's spine. The great wings shuddered once and went limp. Overdulf's daring move tilted the battle completely against the Wyvern. It crashed into the ground and Overdulf, like Jerik, flew towards the same rocky spot.

As the Wyvern fell under more blows from the rest of the cohort, Overdulf sat up, unscathed. Overdulf brushed some dirt away from the spot he had landed. Something did not seem right. Wood! Planks! He was at the base of a door. Covered by a few centuries of dirt! When Jerik had been thrown from the Wyvern's back, he had missed hitting the door by about a foot.

Swords and a massive battle ax crashed upon and cut into the Wyvern. Somehow it dragged it torn and tattered form back across the clearing. Mortally wounded, it still fought on despite leaving a massive trail of blood. It tried to lash out with its tail again but Kejen, almost lackadaisically, knocked it away with his sword again. Kejen would have admired its spirit if he had not been involved in a battle to the death with the bloody thing. On the other hand, it was probably more of a vicious desire to simply kill something before it went into the next world he thought.

Kejen had maneuvered the Wyvern back to the ledge that Lorac had named "nature's stairway." The dragon shambled unsteadily and now its back was to the ledge.

Jerik charged running past Kejen and stabbed the failing Wyvern right in the heart with the iron point of the Warron battle ax. Kejen heard bones crack just before the world was drowned out in the deafening bellow of a dragon's death rattle.

Jerik ripped the ax out and ran back, lest the falling Wyvern somehow got its claws onto his person and drag him over the cliff. It would do that if it could, Jerik realized as he inadvertently looked into its hate filled eyes.

The reptilian monstrosity staggered back, bright red froth gurgling from its mouth. The beast stood outlined against the blue afternoon sky for a long moment before finally tumbling over the edge.

"How do you feel?" Kejen asked Jerik after he heard the impact of the dead dragon hitting the water.

"Hurts but I am doing better than that thing!" The Sea-Farer laughed. "I am going to sit down a while."

The rest of their comrades ran up and looked over the ledge. Kejen took off his helmet and wiped off the sweat. He swatted a fly and took a look at the view. Kejen could see a long streak of blood down the side of the cliff where the dragon hit on its fall into the river. Trif pointed and Kejen followed his finger. He could see the dead Wyvern drifting toward the Falls.

"Doesn't look like that thing will bother anyone again." Kuran declared.

"Seems like something that belongs in Skulka." Trif said.

"Certainly does." The Demon Division captain agreed.

"I know one thing." Kejen said. His all encompassing wave included

Lake Preka in the distance and the Elk river flowing northward across the tundra to the polar regions. "This is really a great view!"

"A lot of blood but the cuts are shallow." Jerik summed up all the injuries. "No more fighting today!" Then he bent over. "Oh, my ribs hurt. My back too."

Before Kejen could say anything, Jerik waved him off. "Nothing a little rest won't help." Kejen signaled Trif to come over and attend to Jerik. Regardless of what the Sea-Farer said or threatened, Trif would just ignore him and do what had to be done. Jerik saw Kejen's brother walking over and sat down on the dirt in surrender. Some people you simply could not argue with.

"What possessed you to jump on that thing's back?" Jerik shouted to Overdulf.

"I did the same thing you did!" The trapper shouted back. "Only I did it right!"

Jerik laughed but shot him an obscene gesture nonetheless.

Ovedulf thumped the wooden door with his fist to get Kejen's attention. "What we are looking for must be behind this!"

Kejen jogged over past Kuran putting a field dressing on Gorvald's scalp. For the first time, Kejen had a chance to inspect his surroundings.

It really was some sort of amphitheater. It had been carved out of the mountainside, seats and steps hewn out of the rock and the middle where the battle had been fought was rolled flat. A great stone walled entrance was built as the only way in or out. With a circumference of over a hundred feet, the amphitheater, built by only God knows who, could hold quite a lot of people. The years had taken their toll though as the pockmarked surface of the once smooth stairs testified.

"How old do you think this is?" Kejen asked Overdulf.

"Old." Overdulf answered directly and to the point. "This door is odd however."

"How so?"

"It is made of wood. I noticed when that thing threw me into it." Overdulf rolled his eyes. "Why has the wood not rotted through? I don't know how old this door is but I don't think many people travel this way to use it!"

"Cool dry climate maybe plus covered by earth?" Vidron offered.

"Coated with lacquer of some kind?" Gorvald suggested. He touched the top of his head. "This scar is going to draw notice when it heals."

"Your hair all ready draws notice." Vidron jabbed.

Before Gorvald could throw an insult back, Kejen fell through the door.

"I keep telling you, boy." Overdulf said when the dust had settled. "You don't know your own strength!"

Kejen stood up in the doorway. "I placed both of my hands against the door and pressed them against it to gauge the door's thickness."

"Didn't seem so stout after all." Jerik said.

"Let's go in, shall we?" Kejen invited everyone.

Jerik and Gorvald stood guard outside just in case. From what they had seen in these mountains, attackers tended to come from the rear. Kuran's approval only confirmed they had made the right choice. "Don't worry, Kejen." Jerik told his friend. "We will see the sword when you bring it here."

"I just wanted you to be there when I found it." Kejen explained.

"It would be even better if you found it and were not ambushed on the way out again." Jerik parried.

Kejen nodded and walked into the darkened chamber, followed by Trif and Kuran. Overdulf and Vidron brought up the rear.

"Are these the Elven Tombs Sevonicus spoke of?" Overdulf asked.

"We will know soon enough." Vidron said.

Kejen darted ahead and called everyone over. He directed everyone's attention to an open coffin.

Overdulf's eyes widened like saucers. "You did not open that, did you?"

"That lid weighs more than my horse." Kejen snorted.

"Well you always were the sacrilegious type." Kuran laughed.

"Very funny."

Lying in the coffin was a skeleton in old, decaying and formerly regal robes. "That man does not look very big." Kuran remarked. "About five feet tall maybe?"

"Not a man." Trif said. "Elf."

"Elf?" Vidron repeated. "Are you sure?"

"Look at the fresco paintings on the wall." Trif pointed. "This must be the place Sevonicus was speaking of."

They progressed deeper into the dark, dank musty smelling underworld. The walls were decorated with paintings featuring small framed, slender looking people in the mold of Sevonicus in woodland scenes. Another painting seemed to be that of a great king of the time. Slightly slanted eyes, pointed ears, it did look a little like Sevonicus. The stern eyes of the portrait looked straight at Kejen from out of the past into a future he could not possibly have envisioned.

"What would he say if he knew we were here?" Kejen wondered.

"Probably something like 'get out of here, you grave robbing thieves.' " Overdulf laughed. "It stands to reason someone has had to have come here in the years this has been here."

"True." Kejen said. "But we are not here to steal anything so don't take anything but *HeavenSteel*, Clear?!"

"Clear." Everyone answered.

A few seconds later, Vidron shouted excitedly, "There is a sword here!" He reached it but Kuran quickly clamped a hand down on the Verrentian's wrist.

"Not so quickly!" Kuran said. "It could be rigged with a trap."

"I did not think of that." Vidron said sheepishly.

"Hopefully there is nothing to worry about but why take chances." Kuran echoed everyone's sentiments.

"Besides." Trif interjected. "That is not *HeavenSteel.* Too small."

Kejen drew his sword and held it up for all to see. "About this size, maybe a little bigger. Stay on guard anyway. We do not know what is down here."

The line of tombs stretched into the distance, the end unseen. This was the place the Mountain Elves, Kejen christened them, came to bury their kings and queens. Someplace, someplace here, was *HeavenSteel.*

The underground chamber was linear in construction. No side passages or independent rooms. That was a relief since no one wanted to split up in this place. Overdulf checked the walls for any signs of hidden rooms but found none. In all actuality it reminded Kejen of a large horse stable in that each sarcophagus was separated from the others by three foot high rock dividers. There were no rooms. It was one large sepulcher carved out of the living rock.

After fighting through the horrors of Skulka, painfully walking up and down countless mountains, and battling a Wyvern (or whatever it was called, Kejen thought), it seemed almost criminally ironic that success or failure of the entire enterprise could hinge on a search that seemed no different from looking for a misplaced book. Kejen shoved the thought out of his mind and continued looking.

Some of the sarcophagus lids had to be lifted to see if the weapon buried with its owner was *HeavenSteel.* Kejen had no wish to desecrate any graves but there was often no alternative. The grim work continued. Some of the lids were all ready broken. That led to another fear. What if grave robbers had taken *HeavenSteel?* That sent a chill up Kejen's spine no Wyvern could ever hope to duplicate.

The tombs followed the same pattern. In the center of the "stall" lay the coffin and a painting of the deceased monarch. There was also some writing but it was in a language no human could read.

The further down the chamber they went, the older the artifacts.. Trif estimated the lid he and Kejen were prying off was at least a couple of thousand years old. That would make it older than *HeavenSteel* but Kejen was determined to look over every square inch.

The company continued to work their way done the corridor past reminders of an age past. Surprisingly, the weapons and armor were not rusted. Trif attributed that to the dryness and construction of the chamber. It was meant to last and it was obvious what the builder's interpretation of forever was---forever.

Kejen felt his disappointment grow with each lid removed and searched. It had gotten to the point where it was expected. Trif probably felt worse than Kejen for he could see the bitterness and sadness in his brother's face.

It had become progressively darker as they worked deeper into the heart of the mountain. The roar of Rainkin Falls could be heard through the rock. It seemed to be getting louder even though the slight upward grade suggested they would emerge behind the Falls. Provided there was an exit. A few more minutes passed and Kuran noticed it was becoming brighter. The Demon Division captain drew his sword and went forth to investigate with Overdulf.

Kejen angrily slammed another lid into place when Kuran returned with Overdulf. Neither looked happy. Kejen somehow knew what they were going to say but decided to wait. Maybe there was a miracle in all of this.

"I went ahead to see what was the source of the sunlight." Kuran explained and answered one question at the same time. "There are two large doors there. The doors were concealed with dirt on the outside. We of course are here on the inside."

"You found this out by opening the doors from the inside and having the dirt fall in?" Kejen asked hopefully.

"No." Kuran's blue eyes bored into Kejen's brown ones. "They smashed their way in with a battering ram."

"Who?"

"Grave robbers. First dozen or so coffins were ransacked." Kuran said.

Kejen stood up in alarm. "The grave robbers took *HeavenSteel?"*

"I don't know." Kuran shifted his feet uncomfortably. He lightly pulled Overdulf forward.

"The raiders took off with a lot of things." Overdulf said. "I can not tell you what exactly but I do know it happened less than a day ago."

"What sort of people makes this part of the Ankers their home?!" Kejen demanded. "It seems like a long way to go to rob old tombs no one knew was here!"

"These kind of people." Ovedulf answered, showing Kejen a medallion one of the raiders must have dropped. It was a solid silver-colored disc with the stylized outline of a five clawed hand.

It was the sign of the Argual.

Chapter 9

The Argual?! What were they doing so far south? *Why* were they so far south? The questions Kejen threw at Overdulf came at him from every direction, questions he did not have answers to.

The reasons behind Kejen's consternation were understandable. The Argual was a cult located in the zone above the Ankers but before the rolling tundra, the doorstep to the polar regions. The cult was centered around the worship of something called The Argual, a being whose nature remained a subject of rumor and speculation. The consensus was that The Argual was a demon or supernatural being of some sort. It was clearly not human. The stories were that it emerged out of some tomb at night participating in the bloody rituals the cult was infamous for. Rituals that included human sacrifice. *Living* human sacrifices. If there was anything that met the definition of Satanic, the Cult of The Argual set the standard for it. Fortunately for most of the world, the Argual was not really close to civilization. Unfortunately, the only nations it was close to were the easternmost Sea-Faring Kingdoms. Kejen could see the anger seething from both Jerik and Gorvald. The Arguals had fought some vicious battles with *Locklannigh* and had undoubtedly sacrificed those they caught in the human sacrifices on that accursed alter.

"Blood flowing like rivers off the heretical alter." Jerik described it. Kejen did not doubt a single syllable. The stories he heard were along the same vein. Trif thought it ironic to hear the word "heretical" from Jerik but he kept the thought to himself. "There was a village called Nifleikham out on the fringe of the tundra. The Arguals overran it and took every man, woman and child to their unholy mercies."

"About fifty years ago." Gorvald added. Then he spat on the ground. "That on the Argual."

That was fifty years ago. The cult had not disappeared. If anything, it had become self-sufficient. Many wondered, how could that be? That was where the rumors of cannibalism had started.

"With *HeavenSteel* in their hands..." Vidron gasped. Horror choked off anything else he wanted to say.

"Who knows what they could be capable of." Trif finished.

What to do seemed pretty obvious. They had to catch this group of grave robbers before they returned to that perverted place they called home.

"Overdulf!" Kejen snapped. "Where is the effective boundary of the Argual?"

Overdulf unrolled the map. "The Arguals claim everything north of the mountains as their involitale realm. In reality, they control very little of it outside their temple. I would expect them to have someone at the point the Talon River comes out of the mountains."

"Let's move out to where there is a little light." Trif suggested. They trotted out beyond the shattered gate. The doors hung off their hinges at a crazy angle and the log the Arguals used as a battering ram lay there discarded, thrown to the side after it had served its purpose.

It would soon have another. "We need to sail down the Talon and get them." Jerik picked up the erstwhile battering ram. "Here is one log we can use. It is too far to retrieve *Thunderbolt* and pull her up against the Blieben and let's not forget Rainkin Falls. We need to build another raft!"

"Can we build a raft before sundown?" Kejen asked.

"Yes we can." Jerik said with more determination in his voice then Kejen had ever heard.

"Tell us what to do."

The quest for *HeavenSteel* had become the pursuit of the legendary sword. The chase was on. Little did the Arguals know, but they would be sought after by a most determined, resolute and utterly implacable foe. One willing to hunt them down in the very heart of their realm, a place where Kascar had described so long ago as a place even angels fear to tread.

An hour of sailing before sundown was not much but in a race like this, Kejen was willing to take anything he could get. Their quarry had a big lead. Kejen and Ovedulf took up positions at the front of the newly christened *Swordfish*, poles ready to engage and fend off rocks that would smash the raft.

Gliding across smooth surface of Lake Preka was easy but the Elk River promised to be anything but. Kejen could all ready see some of the rocks and white water rapids waiting for them. With any luck, maybe the Arguals had smashed into one.

"Remember how you handled the ice!" Jerik yelled as *Swordfish* began to buck and heave. "A little lighter touch though. Rock has no give in it!" he managed to add without biting his tongue off. With that, the wild and tumbling ride down the Elk River began. Jerik looked up to the sky and mumbled a prayer to the gods he believed in. He even sent a prayer to

Kejen's God.
With a landlubber crew on a wild river, Jerik was taking no chances.

It seemed Someone was listening. By the end of the day, the party was on the Talon River, bolting past the point of divergence from the larger and burlier Elk. Aside from bouncing off of a few rocks, raft and crew performed admirably. Well, "adequately" was probably a better description, Jerik amended. One look at *Swordfish* and a man from the desert could tell that the craft would never make another voyage. Each scrunching and grinding noise of rocks grating against wood made Jerik's heart skip a few beats. Nonetheless, they were here on the Talon drifting northwest under their own power.

"Talon River." Gorvald said. "Such a lovely name for such a lovely place." A look at the surroundings confirmed that. After a few weeks in the mountains, it seemed strange to be able to see more than a mile of flat land. Not there was much to see. Lichen covered rocks dotted the landscape, occasionally broken by tufts of pale sickly green but hardy saw grass.

"Welcome to the edge of the tundra." Overdulf announced. "Even I have never been here."

Kuran pointed at the occasional hills. "Don't be fooled. There could be more out here than you think, especially the closer we get to the temple of the Argual. Backside of a hill is a good place to attack from."

With the sun starting to set, it was very good advice.

A few minutes later, they pulled up to land---at a former Argual camp.

Overdulf squatted down on the sandy bank and tried to learn what he could in the failing sunlight. A couple of times he had to angrily shoo away his curious comrades lest their footprints mix or cover the Argual ones.

"About eight people." Overdulf announced his findings to Kejen. He pointed out a path for Kejen to follow and showed him something else. "See this?" he asked pointing to a rounded imprint in the sand. "Any idea what this is?"

"Some person with a large posterior?" Kejen laughed.

"Some person with a large bag!" Overdulf corrected. "He dropped it off here as he slept for the night."

Jerik emerged from the weeds. "Pointed prow. Don't worry, I waded over through the water." the Sea-Farer said before Overdulf could tongue lashes him for tromping over anything. "The line in the middle indicates a keel."

"A what?" a perplexed Kejen asked

"That is not important." Jerik said. "What is important is that they are not piloting a mere barge but a real boat. A small one but still a boat."

"Does that mean they are all ready back at their temple?" Kejen was afraid he knew the answer.

"Probably." Jerik mumbled. Kejen felt as though someone had punched him in the jaw.

"If this camp is from last night, then they have a day's lead on us." Overdulf added. "On the other hand, how do we know they left at dawn? They are in their own country."

"Very good point." Kuran agreed, walking up from the other side. He had crossed a few yards into the forest to avoid bothering Overdulf.

Kejen thought for a few moments. "Let's sail west for another day. We may catch them yet. Like Overdulf said, the Arguals do not think anyone will follow them out here. Maybe they are lazing about enjoying the scenery." he concluded with grimace.

"If they are, they are stranger than I thought they were." Overdulf spat. "And on this trip, that is saying something!"

Jerik made some repairs to make sure the barge held together a little longer. The fact he could do it by dark testified to his seamanship. Gorvald, although he had lived with Sevonicus in the heart of the mountains for years, proved he had forgotten nothing from his Sea-side home. Kejen, as usual, brought a measure of enthusiasm to the project but in the end, he was relegated to watching. At least he enjoyed the learning process.

The land grew a little rockier and hillier and the river began to misbehave again but the repairs held. "It gets smoother after a while!" Kejen yelled. "That is what the map says anyway!"

The river wound around a large outcropping and turned sharply to the west. Trif was on the corner of the barge pushing off the bank that came up too quickly. *Swordfish* quickly rounded the corner---and hit an Argual barge head on.

Swordfish landed on top of the Argual barge's front, its weight pushing the rear of that barge up into the air. There was hardly time for surprise to register.

The black boots and loose red clothing with the yellow piping worn by the Argual cult members seemed bright and burning in the sunlight and cloudless sky. One of them began shouting something to the other two but he never finished.

Kejen hopped across and planted a knee in the Argual soldier's groin.

Kejen's sword bit into the red clothed side of another Argual, chopping through the muscles like a side of beef. Ripping the sword out, Kejen immediately engaged this third opponent in less than five seconds. Trif lowered his bow since his brother jumped into his line of fire. Kuran landed on the curled up Argual and put his foot on his prisoner's neck.

The third Argual managed to get his hands on one of the barbed swords the cult favored. He swung at Kejen over handed but the Northmarcher stepped to one side and delivered a ferocious right hook. Blood and teeth sprayed into the air as the Argual staggered back on the edge of their raft, about to fall overboard. Kejen raised his sword and took a step forward to finish the job but Trif saved his brother the trouble, planting an arrow in the center of the enemy's chest.

Kejen watched the stricken Argual fall into the water. he turned around a looked at Trif. "I guess it took a few seconds to put down the pole and get the bow."

"Hold on to something!" Vidron yelled.

The Argual craft took the brunt of the impact but running aground is something no one wants to do with any watercraft. A couple of crates they were hauling floated by but Jerik and Overdulf retrieved them easily enough. Trif hooked a third one with his bow and brought it ashore.

Kuran kept his grip on the captured Argual and threw him roughly on the ground. Slowly the party surrounded him and looked down at the member of the cult they had heard about. He looked human enough albeit in a bit of shock and pain. The clothing he wore looked a little bit like what Sevonicus wore. He did not look ready for combat either. No armor or helmet, just a lowered hood.

Soon an arrogant smirk grew across his face. Kejen felt anger rising in himself. That was because the Argual prisoner was looking directly at him and Kejen knew what he was looking at. A bloody glob of spit flew at Kejen and landed on his shoulder. Kejen backhanded the prisoner upside the head. More blood sprayed the sandy bank.

Jerik grabbed a handful of the Arguals shirt and lifted him up with one arm. He shouted something in a language Kejen had never heard. Apparently, Jerik had learned the Argual tongue from someplace.

"No more sacrifices for you!" is what Jerik yelled. Gorvald punctuated that with a punch to the stomach. The Argual realized now that he was in the custody of two *Locklannigh*. Now he seemed fairly alarmed.

"So what brings you to death's door?" Jerik mocked the captured Argual. "Where you trying to snatch more fodder for your rituals?"

Without waiting for an answer, Jerik began dragging the struggling Argual to a small cliff overlooking the river. Gorvald walked alongside him, occasionally kicking the doomed man.

"Remember the sword, Jerik." Kejen called after him. Jerik nodded in response and continued his tirade/interrogation/beating. Angry Sea-Farers were not gentle. And rarely gentle even when they were not angry. The same could be said about Northmarchers.

Kuran, Overdulf and Vidron were back at the river's edge, looking through the crates. The crates did not look very big but Kejen hoped that was because he was still a few yards from them.

"Rations." Kuran informed Kejen and Trif as they approached. "Overdulf found a diagram of the Temple of the Argual itself. I do not know why these three would have that though."

"Maybe there is a watch post up stream?" Trif asked. "How did we get past it with no one noticing?"

Kuran shrugged his shoulders. "Maybe they were looking the wrong direction. Maybe these three were going to establish the watch post."

"So you do not think these are the men we are looking for?" Kejen once again knew the answer but was again hoping for a miracle.

Kuran just shook his head. Ovedulf answered for him. "We were looking for a party of at least eight. Plus the Arguals we are looking for are going to the temple."

"The rafts look totally shattered." Kejen observed. "And there are probably watch posts further west. They would see us on the river. If we can't catch them in a day..." he trailed off, not sure what to say after that. "Maybe Jerik and Gorvald will.come up with something."

At that moment, everyone's attention was riveted on a scream coming from an airborne Argual, hurdling head first from the cliff, arms flailing wildly, falling toward the rock-filled river. The Argual officer hit the rocks with a sickening thud. An awful silence followed and the body was washed away, leaving a lot of red on the rocks.

"Or maybe not." Kejen said flatly.

Jerik trotted into view. He seemed pleased with himself. "I gave him a taste of his own medicine." Gorvald followed Jerik, shaking his head.

Vidron stepped in front of Jerik. "Did you have to throw him off a cliff?" Then he pointed an accusing finger at Gorvald. "And you did not try to stop him?"

"It was not my decision.." Gorvald began.

"It was mine!" Jerik cut in, angrily. "What would have me do? Let him go?"

"A Prince is supposed to abide by the rule of law and temper it with mercy." Vidron admonished. "Killing an animal is one thing, killing a man---"

"----Is sometimes necessary!" Jerik exploded. "Besides, that was no man, it was an Argual."

"They are human too." Vidron said.

"You have been on your mountain with Sevonicus too long." Jerik stepped forward. "You have forgotten what the outside world is like."

Kejen stepped between the Verrentian and the angry Crown Prince before the exchange could escalate into anything serious. "If we fight, we gain nothing."

"I was not planning on fighting him." Jerik said

"Nor I you." The Verrentian said with a bow. "You are a friend and an ally. We are just having a difference of opinion."

"Very well." Jerik backed up a step as a sort of an apology.

Kejen stepped out of the way as both men grasped the other's hand. "We can wrestle later if you like." Vidron said.

"I never doubted your bravery." Jerik laughed. "Your sanity may be another matter all together!"

Kejen and his company continued to probe along the banks of the Talon in the direction of the Temple of the Argual. All hope of intercepting the Argual grave robbers seemed gone but Kejen appeared determined to charge all the way up to the front gate.

Argual soldiers began to make appearances but only in small groups of three or four. And few of those. Overdulf wondered if most of the cult was at the Temple for some sort of dark ritual to merge the power of *HeavenSteel* with their own. That terrifying thought brought all conversation to a sudden end.

What were they to do? That question swirled through everyone's mind. Recovering a sword was one thing. Preventing the growth of Argual power was another. That was something for an army to do, not a band of adventurers who never expected to be here in the first place. Unfortunately it would take time to get back to the Northmarch or Sea-Faring Kingdoms and muster an army. And only God or Satan knew what the Arguals may have done to strengthen themselves in the meantime! And would an army even march? The Sea-Faring Kingdoms were not under any one ruler. They also tended to fight with each other. If anything could weld them into one army, a war to exterminate the Argual could be it. Once again, there was the time element and the land between the nearest Sea-Faring Kingdom and the Argual was harsh and incapable of providing forage. The Northmarch was not going to send an army up through the Ankers, especially if it meant leaving a hostile and full strength Masovia salivating over an undefended border.

"Wrong time and the wrong place." Jerik lamented

"We need the right tool for the right job." Kejen found himself quoting Kascar yet again. Kejen and six brave, good men did not seem to be the right tool for this task.

Or were they?

"Let me see that diagram again." Kejen said to Overdulf. An interesting thought began to take shape. So interesting, Kejen almost walked into an Argual observation post dug into the back of a hill.

Kejen came around the hill and jumped back into his brother. Fortunately, the scrape of armor went unheard. Luck smiled some more on the party from Glossak. A scant second before Kejen appeared from behind the hill, the Argual sentry turned to listen what his fellow guard comment on what appeared to be pieces of a raft drifting down the river they were overlooking.

Kejen suppressed the urge to attack the post by running over the crest of hill. Instead he directed his friends on a southward loop around the Argual occupied position. Such an attack would serve only to alert the Arguals someone unfriendly was nearby. And for what Kejen was contemplating, utter surprise was vital.

"No one would expect that." Overdulf agreed. Kejen's hopes flew. Then they crashed. "Because it is utter suicide."

Trif kept watch a few yards away while Jerik watched things a few yards away in the other direction. Kejen led the cohort about a mile south away from the Argual temple. He was not risking any voices carrying. This discussion had the potential to become very heated.

Vidron scratched his chin. "It is a bold idea. An attack on the Argual temple is certainly something they would not expect. By all signs, they have absolutely no idea we are here."

"I would not call it an attack." Kejen began. "It is a raid. According to this diagram Overdulf took off one of the dead Arguals, the living quarters are all on the second story. The bottom floor is where *HeavenSteel* would be. One of these 'treasure rooms' I guess you would call them."

"How do you plan to get in there?" Overdulf asked. "The diagram, and from what we have seen without our own eyes, the place is surrounded by a moat with spikes. Big spikes. It's not a big moat but the spikes are. The causeway in the front is the only way in or out. If we somehow slip in the front, how do we get out?"

"I was thinking a quick raid in and dash out but I do not think that is possible." Kejen allowed.

"My point exactly." Overdulf said.

"The temple is surrounded by hills in the back and sides. The front opens up to flat and open land, so a frontal approach seems unlikely." Kejen studied the diagram. "I think we can jump from the hillside onto the roof of that round structure in the back."

"Are you mad?!" Overdulf almost yelled

Trif and Jerik hissed at the trapper from out of the dark. You never could tell how far your voice traveled at night.

"Climb down through the hole, look for *HeavenSteel* and run through the front door." Kuran guessed correctly. "A classic attack from behind!"

Kejen sat back. "Yes. The Arguals could never guess that was coming for a hundred years."

"I think it is a good plan." The Demon Division captain said. "It is audacious, unexpected and you do not need many to pull it off."

"What about the risks?" Overdulf asked.

"There are many, many things that could go wrong." Kuran gave an honest assessment. "Even if this plan works the way we want it too, we may not live through it."

"I for one would like to live through it." Overdulf said. "And speaking of one am I the only one opposing this madness, this insanity?"

Vidron looked to Gorvald to and then Overdulf. "The Argual is more dangerous than you can imagine. If it fuses itself with the power of *HeavenSteel*, who knows what it can do?"

"I may be a simple soldier." Kuran began with a massive understatement. No one wearing the black of the Demon Division could ever be dismissed as a "simple soldier." "But I do know this. Vidron is right. This is no longer just a quest for an old sword. The Argual now is just an isolated cult here in the middle of nowhere. If it is infused with the power of *HeavenSteel*, how long will that remain true? They will march to the Sea-Faring Kingdoms and then through the Ankers right to Glossak. *Your* home Overdulf. Maybe not tomorrow, maybe not for years but one day they *will* come. And it will not stop there. Evil like this never stops. It will just keep growing. Even now, even if it does not have the sword, the Argual seeks ways to increase its power. It may have found a way with *HeavenSteel.* There is no time to get an army to raze this place. Years from now, when the Argual seeks to conquer and destroy, we will regret the moment we had a chance to end it before it grew."

It was a powerful speech.

Overdulf looked up at the sky. It was hard to respond to something like that. What could one say to something like that? The trapper saw in his mind the horrible images of his children and grandchildren doing battle with the red robed Arguals. He felt a hand on his shoulder.

"You have been magnificent on this journey." Kejen said. "You have exceeded my expectations. This does not have to be your fight." He pointed to Vidron and Gorvald as well. "Nor is it yours. I do not expect Kuran, Jerik or even my own brother to charge into the teeth of the Argual if he does not think it necessary. Nor will I force anyone to do so!"

Kejen stood up and spoke as loudly as he dared. "I will swear on oath to God Himself. I free you of any obligations you feel you have to this quest."

Trif stepped forward out of the dark. "Where you go, I go."

"You know where I stand." Kuran declared.

Vidron stood up as well. "I will do my part, whatever it may be."

Gorvald joined him. "Better to fight them here then later when they are stronger."

"I hate Arguals." Jerik approached with a huge smile on his face. Then he patted Gorvald on the back. "Besides, I do not want the Kingdom of Eorick claiming all the credit that should go to Warron!"

Gorvald rolled his eyes. "I will be happy to fight alongside you, Crown Prince." He stuck out his hand and Jerik took it willingly. Not at the wrist or forearm but at the hand.

Jerik shook Vidron's hand as well. "You are the bravest man I have ever met."

The Verrentian nodded and took a step back.

Kejen unsheathed his sword and held the hilt under his chin in a salute. "You honor me more than I deserve."

Overdulf tugged on his grey beard. "Oh well. I am not getting any younger or any more handsome." The rangy trapper from Glossak put on his helmet and tossed a sketchy salute back to the man from Sparent who had brought him here. "Besides, everyone at the tavern says I am too ugly to live forever!

Chapter 10

"Why did you not tell me about this earlier?" Kejen looked at the parchment scroll Vidron had just given to him. "Granted it is a possibility. We did speak of it at your lord's place but what would some Eastern ruler want with *HeavenSteel?*"

"Events rarely move in a straight logical line." Vidron answered. "Humanity rarely acts in a rational manner."

"*That* is very true." Kejen agreed.

"Sevonicus gave this to me to give to you just in case the sword was not at Rainkin Falls. It appears the Arguals may have *HeavenSteel* in their possession but I feel I should give this to you just in case....." Vidron was not sure how to continue. "Well, it is a risky undertaking."

"That, my friend, is an understatement." Kejen said. He motioned the members of the risky undertaking to him. The scroll was Sevonicus's theory, in writing, that the sword could be somewhere in the East.

"Well, that narrows it down now doesn't it?" Jerik said with just a little bit of sarcasm. "In the bleedin' East. That is only about half the world. I am happy to see he is not mentioning Thenros anymore. Personally, I think I would like that better. No one here and anyone we know has ever been over the Blieben." The Sea-Farer pointed angrily in the direction of the Argual temple. "Even those people have never been there. If anything, they have no idea anything exists outside their little world!"

Kejen got to the center of the matter. "The question is," he waved the scroll about, "Does this change anyone's mind about raiding the Argual temple?"

Kuran unsheathed his sword. "What I said last night does not change. We cannot take a chance on having the Arguals unlock the power of the sword. If nothing else, we can confirm it is not here."

"And if it is in the East?" Gorvald asked.

"Then there is not a thing we can do about that." Kuran said. "If the sword is not here then we can take some solace in the fact we did every thing we could."

"Including getting killed." Overdulf added.

"I knew I would have to take that risk when I first put on this uniform." The Demon Division captain stated.

"Don't worry." Overdulf said, rapping his helmet with that wicked knife he carried. "I am still with you."

"Your words do you credit, my friend." Kuran punched Overdulf's shoulder. "I am sure your actions will do you more."

Kejen drew his sword. "I am glad we were up early." Then he smiled wickedly as everyone brought their hands in. "Let's take 'em!"

In the northern latitudes during Spring and Summer, the Sun rises early and sets late. Even in the wee hours of the morning when most are asleep, those who are awake can see as well as they could at Noon. Kejen was going to attack early and make the most out of maximum daylight. He could hear Kascar's warnings about this place drone on in his head.

"I know all ready." Kejen mumbled to himself. "Obviously I am not listening." He tightened his grip on the grapple hook and rope.

Jerik looked over at his friend. "Do I really want to know about this?" he laughed.

"Only intelligent conversation I can find in this place." Kejen chuckled back.

The black clad Kuran took the lead, walking out to the very edge. Edge was right. This part of the hill had been shorn away, dug so that the moat could run around the back of the Temple. Here it was only about ten feet wide, easy enough to jump over. Looking right and left, one could see the moat was not as wide here. A bit further down, they could see the massive arches holding up the causeway. The moat there was much, much deeper.

Trif scanned the back of the Temple, bow drawn and armed, looking for anyone gazing out of a window. Only there were no windows on this part of the Temple. That was encouraging and disturbing all at once. One hand, it seemed to corroborate what the captured diagram said: It was an auditorium. On the other hand, what sort of warped mind would want to sit in the dark all day? The little hole on top of the roof was not there for light.

Gorvald glanced down at the bottom of the moat and saw, twenty feet below, the sharp wooden spikes driven neatly into the ground, each one precisely one foot from its neighbor. I wish we had some sort of clever ruse to get it from the front, he thought. Of course, that was impossible he knew. Still, he was glad he was not the first to jump the moat. Only a lunatic would want to go first. There were quite a few people to meet that description he thought. *Including you*, his mind said, *After all, you are here too!*

Vidron signaled there were no Argual interlopers to the rear and

Kejen waved in acknowledgement. Then he ran about twenty feet directly for the moat, picking up speed and kicking up dust with every step.

Kejen's feet gripped the edge, his knees bent and with one powerful thrust, he was airborne, sailing across the moat. He reached the zenith of the arc well past the half way point before he began to descend. Jerik gave out a low whistle. It was quite an impressive leap. And in full armor!

Kejen landed on the curved, smooth surface feet first. He leaned forward so that his hands landed on the hippodrome too, taking some of the shock of landing off his feet and help balance himself. The landing had been surprisingly quiet. Trif held his fist up in an encouraging salute as Kejen slinked down to the gutter and tied a rope around a stone gargoyle's neck. *Just in case it comes alive* he laughed to himself. After the last few weeks, anything was possible. Kejen threw the rest of the rope to Overdulf, who drove a spear into the ground. Then he tied the rope to the shaft. Now they could cross hand over hand.

Kuran sailed over the moat too, his legs pumping in midair before landing. He had tied his armor down to keep it from making any noise. "You did not think I was going to let you be the only one to jump across, did you?"

Then Jerik impacted into the dome's surface, leaning a bit too forward and knocking the wind out of himself. "Oh, my poor ribs." He rolled over to his back. "I will be fine. Just let me rest a few moments."

Trif jumped over easily enough. "Not too bad." Kejen critiqued. Trif answered in the way of a rare smile and moved to the top to look down the hole there. He found the wind on his face during the jump quite invigorating, something he realized he was savoring. He had just taken another step in understanding his brother.

Vidron and Gorvald jumped over without incident.

"So why did I bother tying the rope to that thing?" Kejen pointed at the gargoyle.

Overdulf's leg appeared over the gutter, followed by his hands gripping the aforementioned gargoyle and then his sweating, bearded face, "Because I am too bloody old to be jumping about like a frog." The old trapper scornfully refused any help in climbing the last few inches and stood with his comrades on top of the Temple of the Argual. "Never in my wildest nightmares did I ever think I would be here!"

Jerik sat up and announced quietly, "All aboard."

Kejen patted his head and moved up to where Trif was. "See anything?"

Trif shook his head. "Very dark."

Kejen dropped onto his stomach and peered into the hole. His eyes could not penetrate the darkness nor make out the vaguest outline of anything in there. He produced a small rock from his pocket and dropped it through the hole. It hit the floor, echoing as a sharp crack. There was nothing to absorb the noise.

He stood up and let Kuran tie a rope around his waist Kejen held his sword point down just in case something was waiting to attack down there. Confident the rope was secure, he walked over to the hold, gave a little hop, and was swallowed up by the darkness.

Kuran's corded arms showed little strain as he carefully and slowly lowered his friend into the unknown, maybe even the jaws of death, he thought uneasily. Kejen felt like a worm on a hook. He did not care for this feeling but at least he could sense the floor rising to meet him. Kejen swung slightly but not too badly. Then his feet abruptly landed on something hard and slanted. It was definitely not the floor. Landing on a floor made a solid sounding noise, not a hollow one. His eyes adjusted to the darkness and Kejen realized he was standing on a huge sarcophagus, at least twenty feet long and at least five wide, made of stone, its lid carved with ornate decorations of animals and symbols of some sort. He also noted, to his unease, there was no dust on it. Kejen produced another rock and tossed it onto the ground to trigger any booby traps. Nothing happened. He untied the rope and gave it a couple of good yanks. It was quickly and quietly yanked up.

The air was not dank or even damp smelling like the elven tombs at Rainkin Falls. The air here, strangely enough, was clean and cool. Now that his eyes were fully adjusted to the darkness, Kejen saw a great stone alter in front of the huge sarcophagus. He shuddered, thinking about how many people had been sacrificed on it, still beating hearts ripped out even as the victims lived. It did not keep him from jumping on it and then to the floor however.

Kuran landed on the casket too. "Another one of these bloody things?" He followed the same route as Kejen, stopping only to squarely spit on the alter. Trif was third, followed by Overdulf. Vidron shook his head, seeing the sarcophagus and Gorvald looked as though he was seriously considering smashing it then and there. Kejen remembered that Sea-Farers had a history with this place whereas Northmarchers did not. It did not matter. Kejen still did not like the Arguals. He could not think of anyone who did.

Jerik was in last and he looked ready to do battle. If anyone hated Arguals more than he, Kejen was not sure if that person had been born yet.

As the gigantic Sea-Farer described in vivid and unvarnished terms what he would do on the Argual alter, Kejen looked at his surroundings. Aside from the huge coffin and the alter, both situated on a raised dais, the dome was empty and strangely clean for a place that saw so much use. Clean other than...

"Look at the blood stains on the alter." Ovedulf breathed. "This is truly an evil place."

Trif looked up at the coffin. He was quite certain that was where The Argual, whatever it was, rested. Kejen and Trif eyes met and both knew instantly the other thought the same thing. Kejen moved quietly to the large wooden doors that were the only way in or out.

Other than the immense size, the doors themselves seemed rather unremarkable. Metal fastenings held them in place and they featured a couple of large ring door handles. Twenty men could walk through easily enough Kejen thought. Or one Argual said a thought he wished he did not have.

Kuran pressed his ear up against the door. Someone was approaching he signaled with his hands.. Sea-Farer ax was cradled, bows drawn and broadswords were readied. The Battle of the Argual was about to begin.

Through the heavy wooden door, a scrape of a boot against the marble floor carried easily enough. Kejen could hear a few snatches of a conversation on the other side. He did not know the Argual language but Kejen guessed what they were talking about easily enough. The guards on the other side of the door were eagerly discussing the end of their early morning shift.

Somehow Jerik divined that the doors were well balanced. Kejen never had a chance to ask though. At the Crown Prince's signal, Gorvald quickly and easily yanked the door open, flooding the dome with whitish sunlight reflecting off of the marble walls, ceiling and floors of the rest of the Temple. Two long Sea-Farer arms clutched a handful of red robe and dragged two surprised Arguals in before they could cry out.

Overdulf dispatched the first, driving his knife between the man's shoulder blades while Jerik rammed the other into the wall with the handle of his ax under the guard's chin. Kuran quickly relieved the man of one of those horribly curved and serrated Argual swords as Gorvald quickly shut the door, remembering at the last minute not to slam it.

Unfortunately for Kejen and his compatriots, the Argual guards were closer to the end of their shift than anyone realized. The relief came up to the door and looked around for the men they were to replace. It was unthinkable anyone would desert this post! Guarding the Most Holy Doors was an honor only a few could aspire to. The guards milled about in confusion for a few seconds. Could the Master have called the other guards in? Hesitantly, they both began to push the door open.

Kejen shoved his sword in the captured Argual's face.

"Tell us where a sword like this is and we will let you live." Jerik translated.

The fires of fanaticism burned in the Argual's eyes along with absolute unreasoning hatred for anything or anyone not of his cult. He was not going to answer and there was no time for an interrogation.

Then the door began to open...

Kejen clamped one of his big hands over the captive's mouth, pulled the man off the wall and shoved him through the open door. The Argual guards reacted immediately to the sudden movement. They drove their swords through the charging shape---their fellow Argual. Kuran's sword came up and over and smashed in the skull of on Argual and Vidron cut down another. Three more Arguals charged into the fray from someplace nearby and the battle was on. Kejen strapped on his shield and charged out into the main hall. Trif and Overdulf followed him as he ran to the room in the northwest corner that the diagram said treasure was held. Jerik, Kuran, Gorvald and Vidron attacked the other Arguals. It looked as thought there was going to be some fighting after all. Not that Jerik minded. He shouted with reckless abandon as he chopped a red robed attacker practically in half.

The Argual Temple, excluding the auditorium, had a square base. The walls and floors were made of white marble, giving the Temple a deceptively clean and antiseptic appetence. From the great stone arches which held the ceiling up, hung several tapestries and decorating the walls were colorful mosaics. It was a place not many could have claimed to have seen. Seen and lived to tell about it.

The rooms on the bottom floor were along the walls. A great hallway ran down the middle of the temple and it was there the cult gathered to meet before its bloody rituals in the dome.

The sound of fighting carried even to the living quarters on the second floor. The sound of tramping feet was not something Kejen wanted to hear. He redoubled his efforts and kicked down the first door he saw.

The clean marble floor in front of the Most Holy Doors was slick with blood. Argual blood for a change. Both Sea-Farers, the elite Demon Division trooper, the Sparent archer and the soldier from Verrent stood their ground against more Arguals. The Arguals did not wear armor, only their red hooded robes, but numbers could make a difference. Kuran was determined to make them pay as his upward sword swing smashed through an Argual arm, severing it. Blood fountained out of the stump as the Argual tried to instinctively put his hand over the fatal wound. The blood seeped out between his fingers in jets as he sank to the floor and slumped over in a pool of blood. Still more Arguals came on.

Kejen charged into the treasure room. And found nothing that looked like a sword. Another swift kick, powered by anger, took a door to another room off its hinges. He bounced inside and still found nothing.

Trif and Overdulf guarded the door but found a dozen Arguals emptying out into the hallway, some armed, some not. They had no idea what was happening. Trif showed them as he cut quickly cut down two with well placed arrows. Then he shouldered his bow, seized the initiative and charged into them with the spear he carried. Ovedulf pulled out a second wicked ten inch knife and followed him into the mass of stumbling Arguals. They fell over themselves trying to escape the madmen stabbing at them. Then they staggered backwards into another group of better prepared soldiers rushing down the corridor. Suddenly Jerik appeared from no where, attacking from behind. His ax cut swathes into the rear of the panicked mass of Arguals. Blood and bone sprayed everywhere. Kuran, Gorvald and Vidron followed Jerik, wading into the gore, stabbing and slashing. Soon all the Arguals in the corridor were dead. But there were a lot more coming.

"Any luck?" Jerik shouted.

The crashing of things thrown against the wall in the nearest treasure room answered the question negatively. Time was running out. Everyone was beginning to consult the escape route they kept in their head.

Kejen crashed out of a room with a look of absolute fury on his face. "One more room over there!" he pointed.

"Make it quick." Trif said calmly as usual.

"We are running out of time." Overdulf stated. "They will regroup and find us soon."

"Too late!" Jerik shouted as at least a couple of dozen Arguals swarmed down the hallway at them. A few slipped on blood and entrails but there were more than enough to smash those who had violated their temple.

Kuran held his sword up. "Charge!!!!" he roared. Instead of waiting for the attack, the adventurers lunged forward. The maneuver caught the numerically superior Arguals by surprise. Trif stabbed viciously with the spear, and Kuran used his sword to devastating effect every time he swung it. Overdulf picked up an Argual sword its owner would never need and put it to good use. Gorvald and Vidron killed many, many more but the numbers seemed to keep growing.

The Arguals were driven back a few feet but they did not break. These were not weak willed conscripts. They were true believers, fanatical and willing to die for the safety of the Cult and the Great One slumbering in the dome. Most of all, they were entrusted to serve and defend the High Priest, who happened to be down on this level at this inopportune moment. The Arguals pressed the advantage of their numbers and pushed back.

The Argual counterattack drove the adventurers back and it began to take a toll. Armor, something Arguals lacked, deflected many a blow but not all. Near misses, harmless from any other sword, still cut and slashed as the serrated edges of Argual weapons performed the task for which they were grimly made.

"Into that hallway!" Kuran shouted. "The narrow one!"

The raiders found themselves with barely enough room to stand shoulder to shoulder but they understood why Kuran ordered them here. Not only were the rooms Kejen was ransacking nearby, the Arguals could not outflank them here.

One group of Arguals ran through the living quarters above the battle seeking to use the stairs at the front of the Temple to keep the raiders from escaping out the front doors. Another twenty or so were sent through the treasure rooms to flank the attackers.

Trif, Overdulf and the two brave men in the service of Sevonicus fought their way toward the main doors. They were now the front of the attack. Once there, the party could escape across the causeway. They heard the tramping feet above their head and fought even harder to avoid being cut off. But the resistance they faced was increasing. Kuran and Jerik held back the Arguals with their shields but they were simply too many. They were losing ground in the fight for their lives. Jerik shouted and cut down more Arguals but he was absorbing damage as well. He felt blood dripping from his arms and legs, his shield was next to useless. Kuran's shield was still holding and he fought on like a machine. Jerik and Kuran were now the rear

The walls themselves were protecting the flanks but sooner or later Argual numbers would crush them flat. And Kuran could hear Arguals in the treasure rooms.....They were going to burst through a door any moment now and be in among them!

Only those Arguals made the mistake of attacking an ill tempered Northmarcher in a room of sharp objects. Kejen knocked over everything and found not a sign of *HeavenSteel.* This was a room full of Argual weaponry. Several cult members burst through the door howling like rabid wolves, intent on attacking the Northmarchers and their Sea-Farer allies from still another direction. The first three died before they realized someone else was in the room. Kejen stabbed wildly, screaming like he was possessed. The Arguals could not see who or what was in the room and they fled backwards, falling over each other. Kejen used a pike to wedge a door shut and charged out into the bloodslickened hallway.

Kejen stepped in between the Sea-Farer Crown Prince and the Demon Division officer and nearly decapitated an Argual trying squeeze between them. Kuran and Jerik instinctively knew Kejen had not found *HeavenSteel.* None of that mattered as they found themselves fighting for their lives.

The main doors drew closer. There seemed to be more Arguals on Jerik and Kejen's side than directly in front. Vidron took charge and pushed forward into the Arguals with his shield, Trif guarded his right and Gorvald did the same on the left. The Verrentian knew time was running out, The door on the stairs was going to open any second now and God knew how many Arguals would come out and cut off the way to the front. Vidron charged forward and landed on the stairs. Overdulf took his place and prayed he was swift enough.

He was. Vidron jumped up the stairs three at a time, killing a couple of red clothed attackers along the way. He wedged the door shut with an Argual sword and began to descend the staircase. But several Arguals were running up the stairs toward him.

Vidron had the advantage of a higher position. And he used it. He drove his attackers back down the staircase but the door he had wedge shut was beginning to buckle. It was not going to last much longer.

Kejen smashed an Argual up against the wall with his shield and stabbed underneath. The stricken man screamed and Kejen threw him into the rest of the seething crimson mass. Then he slipped on blood or entrails and crashed to the floor. Several Arguals tried to pull him into their midst. Kejen bit the one hand that was closest and sprung up again---just as Jerik's ax came down on one robed arm. He ventured a glance backward. The front doors were drawing closer. And for some inexplicable reason, they were still open! Kejen hoped the Argual memory lapse would continue.

Trif tried to reach the staircase with the trapped Vidron on it. The Verrentian killed one attacker and Trif was able to hit the other with a discarded boot. How did that get there?

The Argual soldier was distracted enough to allow Vidron to get through his defenses and another died in defense of the cult.

The door behind him exploded. The heavy door fell down the steps. Vidron tried to block it with his shield but it caught him off balance. The Verrentian crashed down the stairs but Trif was able to drag him back. Vidron immediately charged back up the stairs to fight, blood streaming from his head. Too many! Trif's mind screamed. Too many!

Ovedulf took an overhand shot that hit him right on the helmet. The trapper went down but Gorvald managed to pull him up. Then there was the sound of something heavy hitting metal and then the Sea-Farer in the service of Sevonicus was down. Overdulf stood over him and slashed away at the Arguals, shouting at Gorvald to get up and fight.

Gorvald did not move.

The cleft helmet said he would never fight again.

That was all Overdulf could spare for the fallen Sea-Farer. He was doing all he could to stay alive himself. The prospects of that were not looking particularly bright at the moment.

Kejen, Jerik and Kuran locked shields and heaved the ravenous Arguals back a few feet. "Keep pushing for the doors!" he yelled just as an Argual ax sent a piece of his shield spinning. Kejen smashed the skull of his opponent with that same disintegrating shield.

Vidron stood like an immobile rock on the staircase behind his shield. A few Arguals were jumping the railing but they were landing in front of Trif and Overdulf and not behind or among Kejen, Jerik and Kuran.

Jerik's back foot touched the staircase. Vidron shouted his warning and put his back up against the Sea-Farer's. Jerik shifted his shield and crushed yet another Argual running down the stairs.

Vidron took up his place next to Overdulf. "Where is Gorvald?" he shouted.

"Dead!" Overdulf shouted in way of a eulogy.

An angry Vidron found new strength and slashed away at the Arguals with even more abandon. The doors drew a little closer. "I shall avenge you!" he shouted with terrible fury. Arguals fell with each stroke of the massive Verrentian broadsword.

The tip of one of those accursed swords raked across the outside of Kejen's arm and another skidded down the side of Trif's leg. Most of the blows were turned aside but attrition would soon start to take an effect.

Overdulf and Trif both lost their shields at the same time. Every time

Overdulf swung, he let his guard down and he paid when an Argual sword lodged itself between armor plates, cutting into his shoulder. The Argual wrenched the sword out and an enraged Overdulf stabbed straight ahead, ignoring the blows ringing off of his helmet.

Kejen saw from the corner of one eye, a man in a flowing yellow robe, shouting orders from the staircase Vidron had fought from so well. His craggy eyebrows and cruel facial features were emphasized by his shaved head. Kejen knew that was the High Priest himself. He wished he had something to throw at the yellow robed heretic.

The High Priest's hand dropped and even more Arguals charged down the hallway. There was not enough room for all of them but the High Priest was not taking any chances. He was throwing every cult member he could find into battle. The rank and file surged on as commanded, sometimes crushing those who fell over their dead comrades, all thoughts washed away in a flood of pious bloodlust.

The weight of the fresh Arguals pushing up against those all ready fighting slammed into Kejen, Jerik and Kuran full force. Incredibly, they held the line. And then, despite the mounting weight, they heaved the first attack, ripped and bloody, back into the faces of faces of the Arguals behind. The narrow hallways gave the two Northmarchers and Warronite Crown Prince a few seconds to steel themselves before the next onslaught. Trif, Overdulf and Vidron continued to advance against increasing resistance, moving slowly toward the front doors. They stabbed and slashed without aiming, the enemy was so massed together. Every blow could not help but land, drawing blood and smashing bones. The screams of pain could be heard above the screams of hate, but nothing could stop the angry Arguals and they continued to rush forward to attack.

The second and third echelons slammed forward into Kejen's line. The Arguals threw the fallen forward to stop the broadswords and that terrible *Locklannigh* ax. The two Northmarchers and their Sea-Farer ally held for a second but the inevitable finally happened. Like water bursting through a dam, the Arguals shattered Kejen's line.

At the same time, Overdulf, Trif and Vidron were knocked asunder and the hallway filled with wild, desperate fighting. It raged so heated that Arguals could not tell, or care, if they tore into friend or foe.

Jerik fought his way through a side door and he spotted Kejen fighting in a rising crimson tide. He shouted "Warron!!!" and began clearing a pathway with each vicious swing of the massive ax oblivious to the damage he was absorbing from the Arguals trying to swarm him under.

Kejen and Trif found themselves standing back to back, weapons ripping and tearing into the human obstructions between their position and Jerik. The huge Sea-Farer reached with one long arm and indignantly pulled Kejen by the nose out of immediate danger. Trif somehow hung on to his brother's shoulder and landed inside the doorway.

The Arguals were right behind him.

Jerik stood in the doorway and hammered away at his attackers with his shield. He could not hold the mob back and they bulled their way in. The Sea-Farer took a step back and Kejen knocked over a ceiling high stand of swords and brought it down on the first half dozen Arguals in the doorway. Trif unstrapped his bow and fired a few shots point blank into the Arguals climbing over the fallen stand. It felt good to use the weapon you knew best, if only for a little while. Trif strapped his bow back over his shoulder, picked up an Argual sword and followed his brother out through another door leading into one more as yet unstained hallway. Arguals, followed by more Arguals, screeched in maddened pursuit.

While both Densky brothers and Jerik hacked and slashed their way across the Temple, Kuran found himself in a most inevitable position--cut off and in the middle of a sea of bloodthirsty Arguals.

The Demon Division soldier shrank back behind his shield for a single second before exploding forward in a swirling maelstrom meting out death. Without Kejen or Jerik on his side, he could attack without hitting anyone but Arguals.

Two Arguals lay dying with open throats before they knew what hit them. Three more dropped in rapid succession as Kuran spun into them, dropping his shield and cutting into the enemy with a broadsword in one hand and a knife in the other. His elbow landed on the side of another Argual head and Kuran took the sword of the pair of nerveless hands and drove it into the chest of still another cultist right up to the hilt. The black clad Northmarcher soldier ducked under another wildly swung sword, picked up his own weapon and nearly chopped another attacker practically in half. Kuran found himself *advancing* against superior numbers as Arguals began to break and run from this black clothed demon. He actually ran past a couple of retreating Arguals, darting toward the open doors like a streak of armored lightening.

A huge, burly Argual towered over Jerik for a second, blocking any advance toward the front. Then a knife sprang from the side of the man's neck and Kuran bounded over him and into those behind him before the body hit the floor. Jerik followed him into the new horde and Kejen and Trif charged on. Vidron and Overdulf were still missing.

Their guide from Glossak was pinned against a wall but he was determined that if he were to die today, it would be fighting and not on that accursed alter. He grabbed one Argual by the throat and smashed his head into a wall but one of their swords sliced across his upper left leg, burning as if someone had poured salt in it. Ovedulf's tumbled over, pulling down yet another attacker with him.

Vidron lashed out, trying to disregard his accumulating injuries, hitting two more Arguals but they just kept coming. His left arm no longer wanted to respond to his commands and the shield seemed to become heavier and heavier. The Verrentian soldier had no idea where his comrades were or if they still lived. Kejen is a crafty one, Vidron thought to himself, he will find a way out. Another sword hit him in the side and he did his best to block out the spreading pain and strike back. Another Argual died. Somehow Vidron knew it was coming.

At least I will have died well, he thought.

Two Argual swords came in on overhead swings. He fended off the first but the second smashed into Vidron between the neck and shoulder. Suddenly a third and fourth sword impacted, glancing off of his conical helmet and smashing into his damaged side. Then the number of blows increased and Vidron disappeared under a horde of Arguals.

On the other side of the Temple, The Arguals assembled some bowmen. They launched a barrage of arrows and darts in the direction of charging Kuran. But most of the projectiles hit other Arguals. The High Priest was willing to pay that price to destroy the attackers. A second wave cut into the struggling mass as it surged within a few yards of the front doors. One of those accursed darts hit Jerik in the inner elbow and his arm felt as though it were on fire. Kejen quickly yanked it out as he felt a dart bounce off his helmet and shoulder armor. Jerik yelped some thanks and hacked away at more Arguals. Their numbers finally appeared to be thinning. The only Arguals near Kuran were dead and he lunged into yet another knot. There were about thirty. Mostly unarmed. And they surrounded none other than the High Priest himself.

With a renewed howl of hatred, Kejen charged after the redoubtable Kuran, Trif and Jerik in tow. Now their bloodlust and fury was greater than that of the Arguals. The entourage began to disintegrate, their will to fight starting to waver. Where was the Great One? Why would He not join in the fight?

More pursuing Argual swordsmen arrived from the rear but they were too late. The desecrators were in among the High Priest! The fighting spilled out through the long sought front doors. The bowmen on the second story unleashed another hail of arrows and darts.

A slave girl jumped at Kejen, trying to claw his eyes out but he cut her down ruthlessly with the broadsword and bashed the last cringing sycophantic escort out of the way. The High Priest, so proud and arrogant earlier, screamed in terror when Kejen came up to him face to bloodied, contorted, angry face. He turned to run but ran into Jerik's massive chest and bounced backwards---impaling himself on Kejen's sword.

"He would have made a nice hostage." Jerik admonished but Kejen did not hear him as his attention was focused on the onrushing Arguals that represented the last of the fighting men in the cult. It probably would not have mattered anyway, Jerik thought.

Trif heard a grunt and saw his brother lift the dead High Priest up over his head and threw the corpse. The Arguals stopped and stared at the body rolling toward them as if it were anathema. They could not believe the High Priest was dead. Some retreated back down the corridor but most, angered beyond rational thinking (a difficult concept for an Argual cultist in the first place...) surged forward.

At least it bought the raiders a little time. Trif alertly saw the rope that was tied the outside of the door. While Kejen and Jerik locked what was left of their shields and slowly backed out the front door onto the base of the causeway, Trif pulled the other door shut. Or most of the way, considering a few dead Arguals blocked the door's path.

"Where is Kuran?" Trif shouted. "He was just here!"

Neither Kejen nor Jerik had time to answer. The last Argual attackers were almost upon them.

Inside the Temple, not far from the doors, a couple of exhausted Argual soldiers stood bent over with their hands on their knees. It had been a brutal fight and they had seen quite enough. A third Argual picked through the human wreckage littering the floor, partially submerged, ankle deep in some places, in blood, all ready turning dark.

The Argual soldier walked past the base of the stairs where the Verrentian had fought so valiantly. He also knew one of the Sea-Farers had fallen somewhere nearby. The raiders had fought well and fought hard.

There just were not enough of them. Now where was the third one, he wondered. That one's armor was different and so was the helmet.

The searching Argual found him, still and unmoving, atop two dead Arguals with their guts spilled out. The smell was nauseating. He was about to make sure this attacker was really dead when in mid-kick he looked up at the noise of renewed fighting.

Ovedulf grabbed his leg and shoved a barbed sword through the Argual's kneecap. The red robed soldier fell back, screaming. His two companions ran as a bloodied and battered but still very much alive Overdulf rose up and bashed his screaming adversary in the face with his helmet. The Arguals fighting at the door had their backs to him but the trapper from Glossak ran straight for the stained glass window next to the door.

Arguals now fired arrows and darts out the window at two Northmarchers and their Sea-Farer comrade out on the base of the causeway. Trif retreated to what he correctly guessed were gears and controls for the causeway. In seconds, he figured out the causeway could be made to collapse. A second later, he knew how to make that happen.

Kejen and Jerik jumped from the door, holding up what was left of their shields to ward off more arrows, to Trif's position easily enough. The Arguals did not seem too eager to pursue them when it was much easier to fire out the windows at them. Word of the High Priest's death was beginning to spread too.

The small guard house offered some cover but Kejen was not sure how long that would last. Someone in there might take charge and lead an assault to push the adventurers over the edge into the gorge. On the other hand, maybe no one wanted to die for a High Priest who was obviously not immortal.

Kejen angrily ground his teeth. *HeavenSteel* was not here. It had never been here! Now Vidron and Gorvald were dead. Kuran and Overdulf were missing and he feared the worst.

Kejen happened to be looking straight at the stained glass window when Overdulf crashed through it head first. The lanky trapper curled into a ball before hitting the ground and rolled toward Kejen's redoubt. The barrage of arrows and darts stopped for a couple of seconds as a quite a few Arguals blinked in surprise. Trif looked up and saw one Argual with a look of disbelief on his face. Then Trif shot him through the throat with an arrow. The dead Argual fell and crashed right in front of the guardhouse.

"I'm cut and bleeding enough!" Overdulf shouted. "So what is a little glass? Besides, the helmet caught the impact."

"Have you seen Kuran?" Jerik shouted back.

Overdulf shook his head negatively. "I haven't seen anyone until now!"

Trif waved for everyone's attention. "See this lever? It is what will cause the bridge to fall." He tied a rope around it. "If we can get out of bow range or close to it, we can yank on this rope and the down goes the bridge. They can't follow us then."

"Can we make it across the bridge before it falls?" Kejen asked. "It is at least fifty yards to the other side."

"Closer to forty." The archer corrected.

"Across one at a time." Kejen said. "I am the best runner here so I will be the last. What I need to do is yank on this rope and run."

"You will do no such thing." Jerik protested.

Then Kuran burst into view, bowling over a couple of Arguals. The grimace on his face told of the great pain he was in and his black clothes were shredded and very, very dark with blood. Kejen and Jerik reached out, grabbed him and nearly threw the Demon Division soldier into Trif.

"God in Heaven!" Overdulf exclaimed at the blood. "How much of that is yours?"

"Some but most is theirs!" Kuran ground out. The intensity in his eyes made Overdulf look away. There was not doubt Kuran considered himself still in the thick of battle.

The hail of arrows and darts had not lessened. Now it grew as more rained down on them. Kejen felt another bounce off his helmet and ignored the one that grazed his forearm. Kuran pointed at the lever with the rope tied to it, then to the bridge and Trif nodded.

"Jerik and Overdulf. You two run first." Kejen said.

"I am not leaving you behind, Kejen!" Jerik yelled.

What a bad time for the Sea-Farer sense of honor rear its head. "You are not abandoning anyone!" Kejen yelled back. "If we all run together, it's a target the archers up there can not miss!"

Jerik shook his head. "Even you cannot run that far that bloody fast!"

"Looks like we will find out soon enough!"

Jerik reached forward and growled in his friend's dirt streaked and bloodied face. "Then swear on that God of yours that you will run across that bridge when you pull on that lever!"

Kejen looked at his friend in disbelief. "Now you want to discuss religion? They are going to charge any moment!"

Jerik was not budging an inch. "Swear on the Cross or God or whatever it is you do!"

"Fine!" Kejen screamed. "I swear it. Now go!"

Kuran reached over and quietly curled the rope around his fist as Kejen and Jerik argued.

"I am going most of the way. Break your oath and you better hope your God gets to you before I do." Jerik warned.

"GO!"

The *Locklannigh* Crown Prince and the Glossak trapper bolted across the bridge. That caught the Arguals off guard and only a couple of darts broke ineffectually against the stone bridge. At least two from those who set out from Glossak will make it out alive, Kejen thought.

"Kuran and Trif." Kejen said. "You two are next."

"I should stay with you and run last." Kuran said.

"Don't be ridiculous." Kejen spat.

"I am pulling rank on you after all, Lieutenant." The Demon Division captain laughed. "I also have the rope, so I will run with you."

"Has everyone gone insane?"

"No militia officer will ever boast he can outrun anyone from the Demon Division." Kuran chuckled. "Go on Trif. We will be with you shortly."

"Please tell me you are still sane, Trif." Kejen pleaded with more than a little sarcasm.

Trif hugged his brother and shook hands with Kuran. "See you over there!" he said.

"Go!"

Trif sped down the bridge too, easily outdistancing any arrows or those accursed darts. The volume of that seemed to be slacking off. That meant either Arguals were deserting or massing for a final charge at the guardhouse. Since this was the only way in or out, Kejen suspected they would be up to their armpits in Arguals soon.

Kuran stood up a little unsteadily. "Ready?"

The merchant turned officer got up. "On three."

Kuran nodded and began counting off. "One."

Then the rising shouts behind them said the Arguals were coming.

"Go, go, go!!!"

Kejen took off running. He heard Kuran's footsteps but did not look back. He was concentrating on gaining the other side of the bridge before if fell out from underneath him.

In seconds, Kejen was on the other side. He was expecting Kuran to come thundering in next to him.

Trif and Jerik both pointed. "He just bloody stopped and turned around!" Jerik almost screamed in a voice much higher pitched than it had been in years.

Kejen turned around in shock. His mind was screaming wildly.... *WHY*?

Many, many Arguals fell with the bridge and uncounted numbers swarmed the guardhouse at breakneck speed. They could see Kuran standing in front of them for a second before he was engulfed in a tide of crimson.

With both legs damaged beyond an extended run, Kuran had made his monumental decision in the middle of Kejen and Jerik's argument. In order for all to live, he chose, on his own free will, to make the supreme sacrifice. They may not have found *HeavenSteel* but the cult of the Argual was destroyed. That counted for more than a hundred faerie swords as far as Kuran was concerned. Now with the bridge fallen, the victory over the Argual was sealed.

Kuran yanked on the lever with all of his remaining strength. The grating stone, clanking chains and falling bridge told him his task was complete

The screams of the Arguals on the bridge turned to cries of dismay as the bridge collapsed...with them on it. The Arguals on the bridge tried vainly to turn around but their collective weight only hastened their doom.

From the other side of the chasm, the four remaining members of the band from Glossak helplessly watched the rest of the scene unfold.

A red tide of Arguals swept over Kuran, who killed two more before he was submerged. He was still determined to take more down however. The fierce determination and iron will that served him well in the Demon Division served him well here too. Kuran exploded out of the roiling mob, helmetless, blonde hair bloodied, broadsword skewering still another Argual. The bridge groaned and began to fall over, slowly at first and then it started to tip over picking up frightening speed It collapsed into the gorge, drowning out the noise of Kuran's final battle. The massive dust cloud obscured the sight of the horde sweeping over the edge in a mass suicide. The prophecy had come true. The End was here. Kuran fell over the ledge with them, dragging one more Argual into the afterworld, stabbing and slashing all the way down, fighting all the way to the very end.

Chapter 11

Kejen, Trif, Jerik and Overdulf stood unbelieving amid the dust rising out of the gorge. Their minds took in the scene, spun it in several directions and tried to reinterpret what they were seeing. Try as hard as they might, the situation stubbornly refused to change. Gorvald and Vidron were dead, Kuran was gone, the great stone causeway lay stuttered in the chasm below and the surviving Arguals were diving into oblivion as if they were lemmings. Most painful of all was the realization that *HeavenSteel* had never been here in the first place.

Suddenly Kejen felt as if someone had yanked the ground out from under him. He hit the ground and hit it hard. Kejen felt a warm trickle of blood in his mouth and he realized he had bit his tongue. All he could here was a deep rumbling from the very bowels of the earth itself. Rocks and dirt rolled past and Kejen felt himself start to slide forward. He looked at Trif but could not hear what he was saying. Reading his lips, it looked like he was shouting something like *earthquake!*

Jerik and Ovedulf backed away from the new ledge that had appeared in front of them. "Is this your God doing this?" the Sea-Farer shouted at Overdulf.

Trif threw himself at the lip of the crevice and called for Kejen. Through the chaos he saw his brother fighting doggedly up the slope. Trif stuck his bow down into the mess so Kejen could see it. Jerik got on his stomach and using his longer arms and a commandeered tree branch, reached down as well.

Kejen wiped the grit from his eyes, reached up and found the tree branch. At the same moment, the ground under Jerik began to give way ad the Sea-Farer found himself about to slide down. The slippage abruptly stopped and then reversed itself as Trif grabbed a hold of Jerik's ankles and pulled back with a grunt. Overdulf emerged out of the dusk and helped drag Jerik and Kejen back to something resembling stable *terra firma.*

All four lay there panting for a few seconds before Kejen stood up on his knees and instinctively looked back over his shoulders. The quake only lasted a few seconds but the damage it wrought was catastrophic.

The Temple of the Argual was in ruins. The roof of the hippodrome had collapsed and the one of the Temple's walls fell in, taking more of the roof with it. I wonder what happened to that sarcophagus, Kejen wondered. Pitiful cries of wounded and crushed Arguals drifted across the dusty landscape but no one was in a charitable mood. There was also the sound of something large moving in the ruins.

"I think I saw some flapping wings!" Overdulf gasped. He pointed at the wreckage but no one could see anything definitive in the dust.

"Great." Kejen spat. "Another bloody Wyvern!" All four backed behind a small stand of rocks hoping for the best but ready for the worst.

No screeching flying monster rose from the smashed building however. After a long couple of minutes, everyone dared to breathe again. "Must have been seeing things." Overdulf mumbled.

"The plateau on which the Temple rests looks about to crumble." Trif observed.

"Good." Kejen growled. "That will kill anything left in there. Anything we can do to help push it over?"

"No." Trif said. "No one is ever coming back here again."

"Certainly not I." Kejen declared. "What a waste. What bleedin' waste!" He hit his own thigh in frustration one, two, three times. Then he muttered something Trif could not quite hear and was probably blasphemous. "The sword was never here and the Argual was going to be destroyed by an earthquake anyway!"

Jerik took a step forward and pushed his face into Kejen's. "There is no way you could have known! How do you know if someone we killed in there would have survived the quake and then resurrected all of this, this..." The Sea-Farer tried to find the word that best summed up his contempt of the Argual and anything associated with it.

"Depravity." Trif offered.

"Sickness!" Jerik finally found what he wanted.

Kejen was angry. Kejen wanted nothing more than to lash out at something but there was nothing to focus that anger on. He knew Jerik was right but emotionally, the wounds caused by the deaths of Gorvald and Vidron were still raw. The loss of Kuran was like pouring salt on it.

Jerik took a couple of steps back to give his friend a little space. Kejen gave a half wave in acknowledgment and then his eyes again found their way back to the ruined cult.

"I liked 'depravity' better." Overdulf whispered to Trif.

"This is not his first language." Trif whispered back.

Kejen stared stonily at the destruction of the Argual. If he could, he would destroy it a hundred times over and a few more times just to be sure. Intellectually, he understood that the loss of only three men to end the cult (and potential threat years from now) was certainly better than fighting a full scale war but it still did nothing to end his pain. Kejen knew there was a risk of having someone under his command die. He had known that for a long time. Embracing that in the abstract was much different then actually having it happen though. Perhaps what hurt the most was the realization that the quest had failed.

"I was so sure." Kejen hung his head.

Trif walked up and threw his arms around his brother. "We have to leave this place. There is nothing more we can do here."

Kejen let go after a few seconds. "A few minutes more."

Trif nodded his understanding and sat down on the dirt. "I will be here when you return." He could all ready see a few tears on Kejen's dust streaked face. Everyone mourned in their own way. Trif would too. Only a bit later.

Kejen walked for about thirty yards or so and ducked behind a boulder and a cluster of rocks. He was not about to cry where everyone could see him.

Overdulf walked up to Jerik. "He is a strong lad. He will be fine. Only needs a few minutes to get his wits about him again."

"I know." Jerik agreed. "I know."

The trapper and guide shook the map. "We cannot go back down the Talon River."

"Why not?"

"This cult is like a snake. We have cut off the head but the rest of the body has not died yet. There are bound to be watch posts and patrols on the outer fringes who do not know what has happened here. Or maybe when they stop getting messages or supplies, they will drift back here to learn what has happened." Overdulf's lanky body seemed to convulse for a second. It showed the depths of his disgust with the Arguals. "And I do not think we are in any condition for a big fight right now."

"Very true." Jerik replied wearily. "What is the route you are thinking about?"

"East along the edge of the foothills where it meets the tundra." Overdulf said. "In the direction of the Twin Mountain."

It seemed like a good idea to Jerik. "Then cut through the Ankers to Lake Preka and sail down the Blieben back to Glossak?"

"Exactly!" Overdulf thunked the Sea-Farer's shoulder. Jerik tried not to grimace. "If we had some horses we continue east and skirt around the mountains all together."

"Horses?" Now Jerik's grimace was plain for all to see. Why would you *not* want to just sail down the river?"

"Because the Talon, and the Elk for that matter, have strong currents that flow in the wrong direction. We would have to walk to Lake Preka and a lot of that, in case you have forgotten, tends to be uphill."

"So riding around the side of the mountains would not take as long?"

"Ah, you can read a map!" Overdulf beamed.

Overdulf diplomatically let Jerik proclaim it was something all needed to be consulted on. Besides, it was time to rest and let injuries, physical and otherwise, heal.

The four were camping in a narrow, easily defensible ravine not far from where the Temple of the Argual used to stand in arrogant splendor. Now it was a pile of rubble. Kejen stood on watch that night. He occasionally looked to the west, half hoping to see Kuran somehow stagger out of the darkness but he knew it was not going to happen.

"Not in this world." He mumbled to himself and looked over to the east instead.

Trif came out to relieve him. Nothing even remotely dangerous had appeared in the day following the collapse of the cult but this was not the sort of place to take chances. "How are you feeling today?"

"Better than yesterday." Kejen answered. "I remember something Kuran told me after we made it through the Forests of Skulka."

"What was that?"

"I asked if he had ever lost anyone under his command. He said he had. Then I asked how he felt afterwards. Kuran said that 'you console yourself with the fact that your men accomplished what they set out to do. And that if any of your men die, then they did not do so in vain.' "Kejen quoted his lost friend. "Only we did not accomplish what we set out to do."

"No, we did something greater." Trif rebuffed his brother. "We destroyed that cult. Kuran did not die in vain. Neither did Vidron or Gorvald. No one will ever be stretched out on that alter again and have their still beating heart ripped out! Kuran, Gorvald and Vidron sacrificed themselves to save a great many lives of people they will never meet. That counts more than a hundred *HeavenSteels*."

"I just wish I knew there was an earthquake coming." Kejen was wistfully.

"How do you know that was not God himself making sure the job you started was not finished?" Trif asked.

"You never have been the theological type." Kejen commented.

"It does not mean I do not believe." Trif had a little peasant stubbornness in him too. "I may not flaunt it as others may but I do believe." He crossed himself to emphasize the point. Then he made another. "Everyone dies, Kejen. Everyone. Mother and Father, Grandfather one day. Jerik and Overdulf. I will one day and so will you. Kuran was fortunate enough, if you want to call it that, to die well."

"That he did." Kejen said. "He sacrificed himself when he realized he could go no further. He did what he did so we could live. And probably kill a few more Arguals." he added.

Trif put a hand on his brother's shoulder. "So let us earn what he gave us."

Kejen slept well that night. Jerik saw the smile on his sleeping friends face. Kejen had made peace with what happened. The Sea-Farer looked furtively at Trif in the distance. The Crown Prince of Warron looked thoughtfully up at the stars for a minute or two. Kejen's brother had his own way of working miracles. It was like that story about the one the Christians called Jesus. But not quite, Jerik thought before his snores filled the night. Trif could bring a charging Argual down from fifty feet without even thinking about it.

The maniacal glint was back in his eyes. "The Twin Mountains is where we go next!" Kejen almost shouted, early the next morning. Very, very early Jerik thought with a bit of barely repressed rage.

"There could still be an intact Argual watch post or garrison there." Ovedulf stated. "Why do we want to go anywhere near it?"

The Twin Mountains rose several hundred feet over the tundra. Only a few miles of open country separated them from the Anker Mountain chain itself. One could see them for miles. Kejen could and pointed his sword at it. "Why do we want to go there, you ask? You yourself told us why a couple of days ago."

"I did?"

"Yes" Kejen jumped up on lichen covered rock. "You said if we could get some horses, we could ride around the east end of the Ankers."

"True." a confused Ovedulf answered.

"Look at the surrounding land." Kejen invited everyone. "It's flat. How do you think the Arguals get there?"

Jerik snapped his fingers. "Steal some horses!"

"If there are any Arguals there." Overdulf felt compelled to say. "What if there are none?"

"Then start thinking of a name for another raft." Kejen said. "Until then, the Twin Mountains are not getting any closer." He hefted his backpack and marched east. Trif fell in beside him and then Jerik bounded up and followed. Overdulf sat on the ground with his legs curled under him for a few seconds more. Then he looked up to the sky, rolled his eyes and slowly got up. After this trip, he vowed he would never leave Glossak again. Even if God Himself commanded it! And if that did happen, even He was going to find Overdulf a tough sell.

The land was bleak in all directions. Other than the occasional gnarled shrub and dwarf tree, nothing grew in this gardener's nightmare. Things did live here though. Kejen saw plenty of birds and Overdulf saw what he called "shambling beasts with curved tusks" away in the distance.

"Are they coming toward us?" Kejen asked.

"No." Ovedulf said. "I don't see anything coming towards us from Twin Mountain either. Not that that is a bad thing. Any revenge minded Arguals running around will be south of us."

The four pressed on, soon passing under the shadow of the Twin Mountains. They found a trail leading from the Mountain but it did not as if it had been used in the last few days. Overdulf got down on his hands and knees and looked hard. He confirmed no one had ridden here for a while.

"But they did ride?" Kejen phrased what was a hope as a question.

Ovedulf nodded.

The Sun was staring to drop so camp was made. If there was any Argual traffic on this trail, it would not gallop by in the dark of night. Morning however, was replete with possibilities.

Before the Sun had risen, Trif hid behind a rock, his bow trained on a spot on the trail. Kejen and Overdulf ducked out of sight and Jerik found a place to watch in the other direction just in case something or someone did approach from out of the west.

Before long, hoof beats could be heard. From the east, in the direction of the hypothetical Argual watch post. But it sounded like more than one horseman! Kejen's ears, long around horses, told him two riders were heading toward their position. Then he saw them. Red robes with the hoods up and those wicked serrated swords strapped to the saddle. Arguals!

Faster than the eye could follow, Trif rose up and fired an arrow into the chest of one Argual. He fell out of the saddle before he knew what was happening. The second barely had a moment to realize that he was in the middle of an ambush. There was nothing he could do except lean down along the neck of the horse and present a smaller target. Trif had a second arrow winging toward him in under two seconds. It smacked into the

Argual's upper back. He convulsed and instinctively tried to reach around his own back to yank it out. All he accomplished was unhorsing himself.

Kejen grabbed the reins of one horse and Overdulf had already secured the other. Trif ran up to the face down Argual and planted a foot on the back of his head. He was not going to let this Argual up and give him a chance to attack anyone.

Kejen called for Jerik and the big Sea-Farer was there almost instantly. "One is still alive, eh? Let's see what he knows."

Jerik flipped the Argual rider over on his back and put a foot on his throat. Trif hovered over him a second with the bow drawn to let him know an archer was watching him before retreating to let Jerik do his work.

Jerik shouted at his prisoner in the Argual tongue. Kejen still wondered where his friend had learned it. He reminded himself to ask before he forgot. The last time he wanted to find out, he found himself in the middle of a fight to the death in a corridor full of red robed madmen trying to rip him to pieces.

Kejen did not expect Jerik to take too much time with the prisoner but what surprised him was the sudden change in the tone in Jerik's voice. Instead of an interrogation, it seemed to become an almost normal conversation. He even took his foot off the Argual's throat.

Kejen walked up to both of them. "What is going on?". At least Jerik did not let the captured Argual sit up. This was still an odd turn of events to say the least.

"This gets stranger and stranger." Jerik mumbled.

"How so?" Kejen was confused.

"He made me give him a promise."

"What?!"

"There are more horses in the watch post up ahead and to the right." Jerik answered the first of many questions Kejen had. That was not the first thing Kejen wanted to know but it was what had brought them to the Twin Mountains. "He told me some interesting things....some strange things. He said he would tell me everything I wanted to know if I gave him an honorable death."

"What sort of things?"

"I have to keep my promise first." Jerik said.

"Kill him now. I don't care." Kejen shrugged. "Would you like me to do it?"

Jerik shook his head and told the Argual something. The Argual cultist got on his hands and knees. Kejen took a couple steps back to watch this confusing drama.

Trif walked up to Kejen. "I think Jerik is going to behead him."

"Dead is dead." Kejen was indifferent to the shape and form of Argual fates as long as they led to the same place.

The Argual captive nodded and stuck his neck out. Jerik's ax came down with a thud and the Argual's head rolled off the trail. The body swayed for a second and then toppled over, blood squirting from the severed arteries in the neck. Kejen looked at the pool of blood spreading out from under the body for a few seconds before turning his attention back to Jerik.

"What else did he say?"

Jerik leaned on his ax. "Did you know, somewhere in the deepest part of Argual...ah....beliefs, there is a prophecy of a 'golden haired man' coming to destroy the cult?"

" 'Golden haired man?' Kejen asked.

"A 'golden haired man who moves like a panther' is what our headless friend here said." Jerik continued.

That fit the description of one person they all knew. "Kuran?"

"Also referred to as the Creature of the Night." Jerik continued. "It had been foretold that he could come to destroy the Argual. The first rider came to tell this fellow that and both were returning to see it for themselves."

Blond hair, black clothes, black armor...."My God!" Kejen exclaimed. "They saw Kuran and thought it was Armageddon...well, to them anyway."

"I say that is what happened, wouldn't you?" Jerik almost laughed. "Only good Argual is a dead one." He concluded with kicking the beheaded Argual.

"When this trip is over, I am never leaving Glossak again." Overdulf stated definitively. "This just keeps getting stranger."

"Stay on guard in that watch post." Kejen returned to the business at hand. "There could be anything waiting for us in there. Anything at all."

Kejen pressed on toward the watchtower that was beginning to rise up little by little against the clear blue skies. Even from here, it looked abandoned. If Kejen was expecting to see a thin line of ravening Arguals ready to tear apart any trespassers, he was sorely disappointed. All that remained of anything vaguely Argual here were discarded robes and swords strewn carelessly about on the tundra, left there to rust. Four horses were left in the stable bringing the total in the party's possession to six.

"Now we don't have to carry so much ourselves!" Jerik deduced gleefully. The Sea-Farer was willing to endure horseback riding if it took time off the journey home. "We can really make good time now!"

Kejen, Trif and Overdulf readily agreed after their anger over finding horses abandoned and unfed had worn off. Even a deranged Northmarcher would never treat a horse like this! If Kejen needed another reason to hate Arguals, this would do. Nevertheless, he had plenty of reasons to hate Arguals as things stood.

Overdulf picked through what was left of the watchtower supplies, keeping what the group would need and tossing what was useless into the center of the stable. One useful thing he found was a fairly detailed map of the Ankers as far south of Rainkin Falls. He elected to keep that for himself and took a keener interest in the map detailing the country further east. It showed the fords and narrow spots of the Elk River as it flowed out the mountains. He was most gratified to see nothing indicating an Argual presence was there.

"I have been there before." Overdulf said to Kejen. "But it always helps to have a few reminders just in case something changed."

"Nothing near running water is apt to stay the same." Kejen's finger landed on the Elk River. "Have you ever followed it that far east?"

"Not that far east." Overdulf answered. "I will leave that to someone else to do!"

"A week after we make it back to Glossak, you will set out for that very spot!" Kejen predicted. "You are not the lay about sort."

"Two weeks." Jerik laughed. "He will take some time to loiter about in that tavern he likes and chase the lasses about a bit until his wife clouts him on the head!"

Overdulf held up his hands in mock despair. "Oh Lord, what have I done to deserve such a fate." Then the lanky resident of Glossak laughed. "You are probably right. I might be getting a little long in the tooth for this sort of nonsense but I am not that bloody old and babbling with senility!"

"You're right!" Jerik clapped his hands. "You are not too old yet! The babbling bit however..."

Overdulf reached down on the stable floor, found something unpleasant and threw it at Jerik. "And my aim is still pretty good too!"

The journey east across the tundra and above the mountains continued. The goal was the Elk River. It was not as powerful as the Blieben but it was still formidable. Unlike the Blieben, one could walk along the banks with a horse. Or most of the way. Some parts of the river contracted into a watery string flowing through a rocky needle. As if he was reading his mind, Overdulf showed Kejen the map again. At least they would know where the rough spots were.

The closer they moved toward the Elk, the greener the landscape became. Rock and tundra gradually gave way to grass and trees and before long, all four adventurers found themselves walking through a small grove of birch. Kejen had the distinct feeling that fortune was smiling on them again. A light rain began to fall and with the northern slopes of the Ankers draped in mist, the Elk River flowed into view. It was a good place to camp and everyone looked forward to the salmon Overdulf promised lived there.

Knee deep in the water, standing strongly against the current and outlined in the early morning sun were Overdulf and Kejen. The Glossak trapper was teaching his eager pupil the fine points of spear fishing. The five fish cooking over the fire testified to Overdulf's prowess. Kejen's skinned knuckles testified both to his amateur status and boundless enthusiasm. The two large fish he held up in each hand also showcased a rather hardnosed determination.

"Sometimes, he really does scare me." Jerik yawned and rolled back into his sleeping bag. The Crown Prince of Warron never was nor claimed to be a morning person.

The trip alongside the Elk River proved rather uneventful. There were a couple of tight areas but Overdulf found ways around them. Sometimes they followed their guide into the mountains and sometimes they waded through the river itself but they never stopped. A few days later the river tumbled out of the mountains and continued its way into unexplored country. Overdulf glanced achingly in the direction the river flowed. Every line in his body shouted he wanted to see where it led.

"If you want to follow it, feel free to do so." Kejen said. "You have held up your end of the bargain and much more. I could not have asked for a better guide or a more resourceful fighter! As for us, we are turning south into the open country."

"I will go with you." Overdulf said. "I promised to bring you back to Glossak and I will." Before Kejen could say anything more, Overdulf continued. "Besides, I need to remind my children who I am. They had better not be disobeying their mother is all I have to say!"

Kejen did not want to be the child drawing that ire. That is probably why I have always been such a good runner he laughed to himself.

The wind blew across the steppe, whistling in their ears. After so long in the Ankers, the open steppe country seemed even more spacious. Trif and Kejen could not help but compare this unfamiliar place with Sparent. They looked out across the vast emptiness that both had missed. For two people growing up in Sparent, it had a friendly quality to it. Jerik followed the ripples moving across the prairie grass like the waves on his beloved Sea. To mountain folk like Overdulf, it seemed disconcerting. There was no need to look for landmarks. All they needed to do was move along the base of the mountains and follow it to the Blieben.

Kejen shielded his eyes and looked eastward at the approaching storm clouds. They looked dark and threatening. The clouds were also moving fast. The thunderstorm would be upon them soon. Anyone living on the prairies knew how fast these storms traveled. What Kejen did not know was as bad as that storm would be, the one behind it was much worse.

Much worse.

Chapter 12

The thunderstorm struck in the late afternoon, bringing with it high winds and rain that drove like daggers. Kejen was sure he saw a few pellets of ice too. A streak of lightening hitting something nearby made everyone's hair stand on end and not just from the static electricity. Instead of struggling for a few drenched, mud clogged miles, Kejen, with experience unique to plains dwellers, camped on the backside of a small knoll. The water might have been inescapable but at least they were able to block out the worst of the wind. Even better, if there was any flash flooding, they could mount the hill top and ride it out.

Unless God decided it was time for another Noah's Flood.

"No danger of landslides out here!" Kejen nudged Overdulf.

"That takes an immense load off of my mind." Overdulf sardonically answered. He was about to say more but another peal of lightening sounded terribly close. The rain continued to come down in bucketloads and Nature continued her spectacular display of raw power. Overdulf kept watch even though he knew no one could see anything out there. Anyone out there would have to be out of his mind. Anyone out there would probably drown.

Jerik could sleep through anything and proved it yet again. Kejen and Trif joined him mainly because there was nothing else to do. Overdulf shook his soaked beard. He could swear it easily held a couple of gallons. Another lightening bolt ripped the across the sky and utterly obliterated something beyond his line of sight. It was oddly comforting. If lightening like that hits me, I would never know it, he thought.

"Might as well sleep after all" the veteran mountain traveler said around a yawn. There was not a thing he could do about the weather except endure it.

Kejen and his cohort stayed camped the next day. The mud would not allow travel. Other than to check on the horses, everyone stayed in the tents. Kejen and Trif, experts in prairie mud, assured Jerik and Overdulf that tomorrow would be different.

"I notice you said 'different', not 'better' ". Jerik said, possibly in jest.

The land behaved as Kejen and Trif promised it would. The ground was dry and the cracks so characteristic of the plains reappeared, thirstily hoping for more rain in the doldrums between deluges. Kejen led his charges southward across the tanning steppes and through the rapidly diminishing humidity.

The miles passed under foot quickly, the pace picking up with seemingly no effort at all. It was much easier crossing the plains unmolested than fighting up and down mountains. Trif commented that Jerik's horsemanship was indeed getting better. The Sea-Farer had not fallen from his mount yet. Jerik's skill with horses was not good enough to chase Trif however.

The party had long gotten in the habit on not sleeping with a fire. Out on the steppes, one could see a long, long way. Someone else out on the open country was sleeping with a fire though. Kejen was the first to spot it through the predawn darkness.

"Due south about a couple miles." Trif gauged the distance. "I cannot imagine who it could be. Most do not go any further east than the Spielwald."

"Most do not." Kejen agreed "But there have been caravans, great long caravans that have been to the kingdoms of the East."

Trif was not convinced. Then he proceeded to dismantle Kejen's hypothesis piece by piece. "Only one fire. Means two, maybe three people. Too small for an expedition going that far. Any caravans going to the East? Very rare and we would have heard about that back in Sparent." Brutal and effective.

"Trif's right." Jerik said. "Too small to be a caravan or even part of a caravan. You live on one of the main trading routes. Talk of anything going to the East would make the rounds quickly."

Overdulf looked at his map. "Unless they are going to Spielwald but who would want to do that?"

The Spielwald was a large forest east of the Blieben. The area around it was steppe or wasteland so it was not a place anyone had seriously considering settling. The only people who would live there Kejen thought might be outlaws but living in the Spielwald seemed more punishment than what anything a person's home country could deal out. Including execution. It was better to die and get it over with than live out your days in the Spielwald and surrounding wasteland.

Kejen rummaged through a saddlebag and found a rag that might have once been white. He took Trif's spear and stuck it on the point. "We should go see who it is before they come to us."

Trif agreed wholeheartedly. It was better to have the initiative when dealing with unknown strangers in the middle of nowhere.

All four horsemen, of varying skill, rode in a spread out line at a leisurely canter. There was no sense in startling the strangers out here on the prairies with them. Kejen hoped they were not the easily excitable type. He was making an effort not to look aggressive. Maybe I should have taken off my helmet and armor he thought. Never mind, I do not know who they are or what they are doing out here. This situation was the perfect example of the old saying of planning for the worst while hoping for the best.

If he had known of the strangers earlier, Kejen would have swung around and rode out of the Sun. That way, in case the unknown persons proved to be hostile, they could not aim with the Sun in their eyes. As it was, Kejen led his comrades southward and the sun rose to their left. At least the wind was blowing against Kejen which was an advantage. The unknowns would not hear them as well.

About a half mile away, Kejen was able to discern some details. There were two individuals attending to the horses and a third mounted and keeping watch but looking in the wrong direction. Two others were off in the distance riding southeast about to disappear over the horizon. The horses themselves looked a little strange. They seemed like ponies but much more muscular looking. The riders looked short and compact as well. Their broad shoulders reminded everyone of Trif, suggesting they were archers. The armor looked different too. Not different in the Verrentian or Nyhissian sense but different in a way Kejen had never seen.

The mounted one either heard the party's approach or happened to look in the right direction. He gave a quick shout and his two companions looked up quickly. The sentry spurred his horse in the direction of Kejen, pulled out a curved sword on the hoof and charged.

At that moment, Kejen remembered his cavalry sword was back at home hanging from a peg in the wall. His broadsword would have to do right now. Overdulf and Trif veered to different sides as Kejen charged at the oncoming attacker head on. Jerik rode somewhat behind Kejen but he was determined to aid his friend.

Both men charged toward each other, a direct attack that was now a collision course. The distance between them rapidly evaporated, the anticipation of impact evident in their bracing forms. The wind rushed through their ears and hair. The world for them had shrunk to this small patch of ground.

It was not the sound of clashing swords echoing over the prairies but rather the sound of a rider hitting the ground. The attacker swung first and Kejen ducked under the curved blade. Instead of stabbing straight into his opponent's heart, Kejen's muscular arm shot out and he clotheslined him instead. The surprised man was ripped out of his saddle. The stirrups gave way and he found himself falling backward into the hard packed down prairie. He tried to rise but Jerik vaulted out of his horse and smashed him back into the dirt with a vicious forearm to the back of the head.

Overdulf rode after Jerik's panicked horse and retrieved it. Kejen saw that Jerik was going to ensure the forcibly dismounted man was going nowhere. Trif stood over the two other strangers, both of them sporting an arrow sticking out of their chest and back respectively.

"Both of them were reaching for a bow." Trif explained.

"I don't blame you." Kejen said. "You saw that one attack me for no reason! What is wrong with these people?"

Without waiting for his brother to answer, Kejen turned and angrily stalked back to Jerik. He was going to get some answers and get them this very moment. Attack when you are under a white flag? Kejen was going to get the answer to that personally and his erstwhile opponent was not going to enjoy the process.

Jerik sat up in the dirt. "I think I broke his neck."

Kejen walked up to the fallen man, wound up his leg and delivered a powerful kick anyway. Jerik flinched a little when he heard a rib crack. The Sea-Farer realized he may have done the man a favor with that tackle.

"No need to worry about it." Kejen said. "What do you think we would have done afterwards? Now, who are these people?"

Jerik slowly rolled the fallen horseman over. Up close, Kejen saw how different the armor really was. The Northmarcher kicked the rounded helmet away. It was about as different from the crested one he wore as anything could be. Kejen reached down and pulled the corpse up by its jerkin and dropped it roughly. They were clearly people of the steppes and lived around horses. A lot like Northmarchers actually.

"Only we do not attack people for the sport of it." Kejen growled at his own thoughts.

Jerik was not sure who Kejen was talking to but he could feel the anger radiating off of his Northmarcher friend. He would not have been surprised to find it cooler a few steps away.

Trif pointed with his bow. "This man was an Easterner."

"*Was* is right." Kejen spat. Did you say *Easterner*?" Kejen took a closer look. As usual, Trif was right. Round face, broad nose, golden and tanned skin, black hair.

"Looks a little like the *Skraelings* up around the polar regions." Jerik commented. "Only I have never heard of them attacking anyone unprovoked."

"Different nation or tribe." Kejen said. "What is a bloody Easterner doing here?"

"We are beyond the Blieben." Trif shrugged. "According to the map, we are in the East."

Kejen laughed. "Not that far in, my dear Trif! This is a mere sliver." He kicked the dead Easterner again. "This individual came from much further away."

"Where ever it is, they make good bows." Trif said. He held up one he stripped from a dead adversary. "Look at how this constructed. Looks like horn and sinew. The draw weight on this is more than one mine." Trif drew on the captured weapon. Kejen could see his brother grit his teeth just a little. "And the range is greater than ours."

"Does not do any archer any good if we can kill them before they can use their weapons." Kejen remarked.

"In the hands of someone skilled and with time to use them though..." Trif trailed off.

Overdulf rode up, holding the reins of his horse in one hand and the reins of two other horses in the other. "Do you know how far I had to ride to get your horse?!" he shouted at Jerik. "And one of our pack horses ran off in the other direction!"

"But one horse stayed in place." Jerik bowed, performing a rather fair imitation of Kejen. He reached over and patted the aforementioned horse on the nose. "Such a well behaved beast. You must see the good in all situations my dear Overdulf." The Sea-Farer concluded his impersonation.

"You have the accent all wrong." Kejen critiqued.

"He most definitely does." Overdulf said. "While I was galloping all over God's creation gathering horses, I found the tracks coming from up out of the southeast. Five sets of tracks. Tracks from these people. The other two are long gone."

"Southeast." Kejen turned and looked in that direction. "What do you think that means?"

Ovedulf took off his helmet and ran his hand through his hair. "These must have been scouts of some kind. They are in uniform, more or less, riding together and attacked us on sight."

"A fat lot of good that did them." Jerik guffawed.

Overdulf's smile made him look like one of those "shark" fish things Jerik often told Kejen and Trif about. Wolves that lived in the water. For a second, Overdulf looked like one of his barbarian ancestors. The barbarian always lurked just below the surface of any Northmarcher. "One attacked so the others could either ride away or follow his lead."

"They were acting in concert." Trif completed the thought. "Soldiers."

Overdulf turned in the saddle and looked in the direction from which the tracks originated. "There is an army out there. Question is, who does it belong to and where is it going?"

"You and Jerik should ride to the frontier and tell everyone you see. Then go to Northcross and tell them. Maybe even the King himself." Kejen said. "Trif and I are the best riders here. We can ride southeast for a couple of days and see if that army is heading this way."

Jerik bounded up despite wearing all of his armor. "No. We started out from Glossak together, we will end this journey there together!" He cut Kejen off before he could say anything. "If we ride south a couple of days, we will see if there is anything to worry about. For all we know, maybe someone in the East is just out exploring."

"I am telling you there is an army out there." Overdulf said.

Kejen climbed up in his saddle and weighed the options. What if there was an army out there? Was it going to go to the Blieben and stop? What if it did not? Maybe it was going to turn and go elsewhere. No matter from what angle he looked at it, it was Kejen's responsibility to find out.

"We have to find out. Learn where it is going first of all. Anything else we could learn would be helpful." Kejen looked at Overdulf. "You were tasked to take us to Rainkin Falls. You have done much more than I could have asked. If the King still gave out patents of nobility, I would demand he give you three at least!" Overdulf looked down at the ground, uncomfortable with the praise. "I ask you to do one more thing, my friend. Raise the alarm! All along the frontier! Then go to Northcross and tell the King himself if you have to."

The expression on Overdulf's face said that was the last thing he wanted to do.

"This is no time to be shy." Kejen leaned forward. "If this does turn out to be another Great Eastern Invasion, we will need every possible moment to prepare for it."

"Very well." Overdulf said sourly. "I understand your reasoning. I just did not want to leave something undone in midstream."

"You are doing no such thing!" Kejen exclaimed. "We were on our way back to Glossak anyway. Now, something much greater has reared its head. Your obligation is no longer to us but to your country."

Overdulf nodded and rode forward a couple of steps. He clasped Kejen's hand. "It has been an honor and a privilege. Try to remember you are supposed to observe, not try to fight that whole army yourself!"

"I will." Kejen promised.

"See you in Glossak one day before long, Sea-Farer." Overdulf shook Jerik's hand. "You know where to find me."

"That I do!" Jerik laughed. "You are one person I know I never have to clasp wrists with. Well, maybe when a pretty barmaid is involved but only then!"

Overdulf gave him an ironic smile and a playful tug on the Sea-Farer's beard before turning to Trif.

"I have a one more thing for you to do Overdulf." Trif said first. He handed their guide from Glossak a small leather journal. "Give this to the first Demon Division soldier you see. Or the King himself if you must. It is a written record of everything we have done."

Overdulf looked awed. "That I certainly shall! Everyone should know of what Kuran did. Vidron and Gorvald too. Now they will!"

"I wrote two copies of everything." Trif waved a second journal for all to see. "I may end up writing some more."

"Hopefully not." Overdulf said. He saluted his companions, turned and rode off to the west. Toward the Blieben. Toward the Northmarch. Toward home.

"We have a little more work to do." Kejen said even before Overdulf disappeared past the horizon. That spoke volumes of the gravity of the developing situation. "We will ride south a couple of days and see what there is to see."

"We have plenty of rations." Trif said. "Maybe we should ride for three days to be sure."

"Not a bad idea." Jerik voiced his approval.

"Three days then." Kejen said. "Only three of us so don't expect to get that much sleep."

"Whole army out here with us perhaps. Too nervous to sleep." Jerik barked.

"It will not be a problem." Trif said.

"I know." Kejen smiled at his brother. "I suspect you will be writing a copy of your back-up journal."

The trip south passed slowly. The scenery crawled by seemingly slower. Kejen, Trif and Jerik wound their way past a couple of small hills, found a small stream and followed it. Any scouting patrols would certainly gravitate to it somewhere along its length. Still, they found no sign of anything. It seemed as if they had the whole world to themselves. The open spaces reminded Kejen of home. He surprised himself thinking how much he actually wanted to return. Even without triumphantly hoisting *HeavenSteel* up for all to see, he and Trif would still have an amazing tale that would resonate for a long time to come. If only it had not come with such a high price, Kejen sadly reflected. Kuran was a good man and a good friend. Surely he was in Heaven with God all ready. Kejen had not known Vidron and Gorvald for all that long but they too seemed to fit in the extraordinary mold of Kuran. Kejen sent a quick prayer for their souls as well. Surely God would look after them. He also promised himself to somehow send Sevonicus a message about the gallant sacrifice of two of his best men.

"I find it odd we have not encountered any patrols or signs of an army." Trif said that night. "I am certain we have not missed them. We have followed their tracks in reverse and when those vanished, we continued southeast."

"Very true." Jerik rocked back and forth. "We should have seen *something*. On the other hand, maybe this nothing is something. Maybe there is no army out here."

"So where did those scouts come from?" Trif asked.

"A man and a woman fell in love." Jerik chuckled. Trif frowned in disapproval. Jerik sighed. "Maybe they were three individuals of hostile disposition on their own."

"Maybe they were deserters." Trif theorized. "That would account for the uniforms. But why desert to the middle of no where?"

"They did seem a bit too far away to be scouting for an army." Jerik said. "An army we should have seen some sign of."

Trif stood up and walked out into the night. "My turn for watch. Kejen has been listening to us all night. Maybe he will find something we missed."

"I doubt it." Kejen handed the spear to his brother. "We just cannot seem to find the answers."

"I hope the answer does not find us." Jerik said.

The second day on the southward journey was as uneventful as the first. "All we have to do is turn to the left and the Blieben will be there before you know it." Jerik said hopefully.

"Maybe the commander of that army is saying the same thing." Kejen answered.

"Are you still confident we will find some sign of the phantom army out here?" Jerik inquired.

"Not as confident as I was yesterday." Kejen admitted. "I am beginning to think we should turn around. Perhaps we missed it and it is north of us."

"That is a possibility." Trif said. "Here is another for you to consider. If those scouts are steppe people like we are, perhaps they scout at considerably longer distances from the main army."

Jerik put his head in his hands. "I really wish you had not said that."

"If we have not seen anything by nightfall tomorrow, we will ride to the Blieben and back to the Northmarch." Kejen promised. He was tempted to begin the return trip home this very moment but tomorrow would be the third day. Jerik beamed and even Trif nodded approval. If they did not find anything tomorrow, there was nothing to find.

Midmorning on the third day of their own scouting mission found Kejen, Trif and Jerik in high spirits. They crossed into a small series of hills and found no one there planning an ambush. Jerik was laughing and rowdy and actually improving his horsemanship. He was able to make turns without risking a fall out of the saddle.

"I am glad to see you finally learned what stirrups are for!" Kejen laughed.

"Ah there are many, many uses for stirrups my friends!" Jerik laughed back. "And a few are for horses!"

Kejen almost fell off of his horse laughing and Trif just shook his head. Jerik did see a smile on his face though. The Sea-Farer took this opportunity to dive into another hair raising tale of lusty wenches and dozens of hijinks.

"You don't speak to your mother with that mouth, do you?" Trif said to Jerik after yet another raucous anecdote.

"Who do you think told him that story?" Kejen asked.

"You wound me, sir!" Jerik pretended to slump in the saddle.

"Your riding skills *have* improved!" Kejen complimented his earthy friend. "I remember not too long ago you were too nervous to even think about doing that in the saddle!"

"I was thinking of becoming a lancer!" Jerik announced. "Hand me that spear and I will show you."

Trif obligingly handed Jerik the spear, riding a bit closer to Jerik's horse than he would if he were another Northmarcher. The Sea-Farer still was not a proper horseman. Jerik took the spear and nodded his thanks, still looking at the back of his mount's head.

Jerik balanced the spear and charged up the side of a small hill. Kejen and Trif followed him. "Not too bad." Kejen said as they mounted the final hill---and looked out over the largest army the world had ever seen.

"Oh my God." Kejen had the presence of mind not to yell. Suddenly he was very glad Overdulf had ridden for the frontiers three days ago. Jerik for once was speechless and Trif had fervently hoped the last three days that he was wrong. As usual, he was not.

Huge squares of men and horses stretched endlessly to the eastern horizon. Kejen had the feeling the tail was somewhere beyond that. Carts and banner moved along with the mass of milling humanity. Clouds of dust gave the still rising Sun a blood red look to it. The army moved westward and it moved with a purpose. A purpose that seemed to radiate from it with frightening intensity. Armies existed for one purpose and one purpose only.

"You don't take an army that big this far just to show the bloody flag." Jerik finally said. "It's heading straight for the Blieben River." He looked at the map. "Straight for Nyhissia."

"I think they have more than just Nyhissia in mind." Kejen muttered.

"We need to get off this hill before someone down there sees us." Trif said quickly. "Now."

The three slinked down the hill and began trotting west. Somehow Kejen, Trif and Jerik had negotiated their way past the sentries and pickets without realizing they had done it. Now they had to do it again before galloping away at full speed. Overdulf's three day head start seemed wiser with every passing moment.

Kejen thought about the small clash that led to this side trip southward. The more he thought about it, the harder the same realization stuck in his mind. It was more than a mere chance skirmish. It was the first battle of a major war.

Chapter 13

The largest army in Khaizani history marched resolutely toward the setting Sun, studied from a distance by a small group from nations the soldiers of Khaizan might well fight fairly soon. Those onlookers were struck with disbelief.

Rank after rank of mounted warriors, clad in beautiful and lacquered armor, recurve bow shouldered, cantered through the immense clouds of dust, some visible, others menacing specter like shadows. Assembled in *tumens*, huge black squares of thousands moved forward, horse hooves scrunching and shuffling, pounding the land flat amid the jingle of countless harnesses and stirrups. More frightening than the display of raw physical power was the aura of discipline and barely controlled savagery. Most disheartening of all, from an enemy's view, was the confidence that exuded from these men. Theirs was the mightiest army in the world and they knew it. All of these factors combined had struck terror into the hearts of their enemies for years. Even those not yet encountered.

The splendidly aligned rows passed below the awed Northmarcher brothers and their *Locklannigh* comrade, their numbers seemingly endless, their state of training obviously superb. The army moved in rhythm like some horrible organism that lived to crush and kill. The scene hung over the potential enemies in a pall thicker than the all of the dust obscuring the sun. Ever since the Great Khan united the tribes of Khaizan, the Imperial Army had moved from conquest to conquest, the appetite of the rank and file, the *orluks* and *noyons* and above all, the current Khan himself, for greater glory and power completely insatiable.

When the Sui Chen emperor returned from his failed Western venture two centuries earlier, he was struck down by a Khaizani vassal with a strange and wondrous talisman brought from the ferocious Three Days Battle. Towering above the fallen Emperor, brandishing his new prize, the now Great Khan prematurely proclaimed the establishment of the Khaizani Empire. It took thirty years of savage fighting to unify the fiercely independent Khaizani tribes but once his countrymen had been welded into a cohesive unit, they were unstoppable. When Khaizani brawn was integrated with accumulated knowledge of their former Sui Chen overlords, the Khanate became an invincible juggernaut.

In the two centuries since its birth, the Imperial Army had never lost a battle. And the mysterious sword had been at the side of every Khan in every battle. The legend that he who held the sword grew with each inevitable victory. It was as much a birthright of the Khans as the Imperial Scepter and the Mandate of the Gods.

Absorbing the Sui Chen was just the beginning of the Khaizani avalanche. One by one, then in groups, the nations of the East fell in rapid, bloody succession, pushing the unconquered and fleeing against the Ocean of Great Peace. Totally misnamed in the Khaizani mind, it proved a most useful ally in the Urga campaign, pinning the enemy in one place for a slaughter. The ocean also provided a convenient means of disposal. It was said sharks still tried to come on land years later to beg the Khaizani for food.

The Khaizani tide rolled forward, a nation on horseback whose fearsome archers made the noonday sky as dark as night. Those who valiantly tried to resist fell, their fields trampled, cities razed and rivers turned red for days on end. Then the Khan would take his revenge, watering the conquered soil with the blood of its sons and daughters. That only slacked the Khaizani thirst for power, glory and wealth long enough until the Khan ventured out again, hungrily looking at the next neighbors, each nervously wondering who among them would be next. For all of their wisdom, they never knew was the gifts and bribes sent to stave off the growing Empire only served to whet the Khan's ravenous hunger. That and providing a little time before dying in a hail of arrows and iron shod hooves.

There were few kingdoms in the East not under the Khaizani boot. Plans were in place to destroy them one by one piecemeal. That suited the Khan well. Idleness, aside from defeat, posed the greatest threat the Empire. The Khaizani predilection for constant war and greed of ever more power was typical of an empire that could win wars but not govern. Instead of harnessing the productive powers of the conquered, the Khaizani drained them. If Khaizani imperial growth were ever stopped, its own characteristics and tendencies would turn inward and the Empire would rip itself to pieces. Khaizan bore a striking resemblance to the sharks the Khan was so fond of. The Empire had to keep moving to survive.

Little of this weighed on the Khan's mind however. He was leading his army on its greatest campaign. Four leviathan columns marched westward, justly feeling it was the mightiest force the world had ever seen, the greatest danger posed to it only by itself.

"There are so many!" Kejen and Trif said at the same time. Jerik would have laughed but he too was thinking the same thing. This was a huge army. With an equally huge objective he thought as well. Stuck on horseback suddenly did not seem such a major inconvience. "You do not think they are going to turn south, do you?"

"Let's ride and discuss what to do at the same time." Kejen said. "If we stay up here, someone down there is going to notice and invite themselves into our little conversation."

Kejen, Trif and Jerik rode carefully on a northwest vector between the hills. They were not sure if there were flanking guards or sentries about. If there were not, that in itself said the army a few hills over was in a hurry.

"Something that big does not need a bloody security." Kejen answered his own question.

"If they turn south, Overdulf is raising the alarm for a threat that is not coming." Jerik said.

"They are moving west and will continue to do so." Trif concluded. "There is nothing between here and the Blieben worth fighting for. To come this far and turn to attack something to the south is a waste of time. And that army has a lot of cavalry. Nothing but forest further south on this side of the Blieben. Lots of steppe country on our side of the river."

"I for one do not fancy merely following them into Northcross." Kejen concurred.

"Maybe they just want to fight Nyhissia."

Kejen was not amused. "If there is one thing Northmarchers have learned from fighting those Masovian idiots so many times is that you are stronger with your neighbors than without them."

Jerik thought about that for a few seconds. "Very true. Besides, you would not send an army that big halfway around the world just to fight one country. They mean to ride all the way to the Sea."

"And through anyone who tries to stop them." Kejen added.

"It will take every country west of the Blieben to stop that army." Trif said. "We could very well find Masovians fighting alongside us."

"Heaven forbid." Kejen groaned. He saw Trif's point but still did not like it. "If we fight separately, we will hang together."

Trif nodded gravely. He was no more fond of the Masovians as the next Northmarcher. It would not have bothered him to see Regalwood fall into the Sea. Well, maybe after this crisis was resolved. At the moment, help would be welcome from anyone.

"You two need to ride full speed and do it now." Jerik said.

Kejen turned in the saddle and looked at his Sea-Farer friend. "You are coming with us. Then we can get you on your way back home."

Jerik stared at his friend angrily. "You know I am not the horseman you and your brother are. I would only slow you down and as Trif said, there is a lot of cavalry out there."

"I refuse to leave you here to die." Kejen replied, voice rising dangerously. "Especially in a war that is not yours!"

Trif made frantic shushing motions.

"Did you not hear your brother?" Jerik whispered. "'If we fight separately, we will hang together.' This is *my* war too. Besides, who said anything about dying?"

"Are we supposed to ride back to the Northmarch without you? Are *you* planning on fighting that whole army yourself?"

Jerik almost laughed. Almost but not quite. Trif's warning glance saw to that. "No, no silly. But not a bad idea." Kejen looked at him as though his Sea-Farer friend lost his mind. With Jerik, it was a distinct possibility. "If I die fighting, I live with the gods forever but I am in no hurry to do that, I assure you."

"I am happy to see you are thinking more than a few minutes ahead." was Kejen's rather sardonic answer.

"You need someone to trail this army." Jerik explained. "You need someone to watch these people. If they do indeed go south, I can see it and tell everyone when I cross the river. If they continue west---"

"They will." Trif cut in.

"---I can watch and learn where they are specifically going." Jerik continued. "Then you can attack without waiting along the whole river. And who knows what else I can uncover. You learn a lot from just watching. Maybe even find a weakness."

"There is some cleverness under all that hair." Kejen stroked his chin. It was a pretty good plan.

"Back in Warron, it is called 'being a fly on the wall.' "

"You are a very big fly, my friend." Kejen laughed softly.

Jerik pulled his ax out of a holster on his saddle. "A fly that can bite too! Now, go defend your homeland! We will meet again."

In this world or the next the Sea-Farer amended silently.

Kejen must have been thinking along the same lines but he too kept that to himself. "Learn what you can. Be sure to live so you can pass it on."

"That is a good thing to remember." Jerik said dryly. "I am so glad you reminded me."

Outside the Khan's yurt under a star filled sky, the *orloks, noyons* and generals awaited their lord's appearance patiently and with just a hint of fear. The Khan was a man who executed those who displeased him quickly and without remorse. Thankfully, nothing had gone wrong on the march west from the Khaizani domains...Or rather the previous Khaizani domain. As the Khan was fond of saying, every step to the west increased the size of the Empire. The fact that it was infertile wasteland or marginal steppes being *de facto* annexed seemed to have little effect on the Khan as he scanned the map updated constantly to fit his vanity concerning borders. For all practical purposes, everything east of the Blieben River was his---*his!* To do with as he pleased. To raze, to build, to lavish on, to ignore, anything he wanted. Where the Khaizani not the ones truly blessed by the One Who Ruled The Sky?

Soon everything west of the great river would be his too. The round eyed fools living there would be his greatest allies in bringing themselves under the control of the Khanate. Fighting among themselves in petty disputes while desperately trying to hold ramshackle countries that should not exist in the first place, the Khan laughed contemptuously. The concept of a nation without expansionist endeavors was beyond him. If the army and its generals were not preoccupied far from their homeland, what would keep them from plotting, or even worse, acting against their masters? It was the Khan's father who had laid the groundwork for this, the Khanate's grandest conquest. It was he who ordered the kidnapping of a selected few Saracen merchants and personally handled the interrogations. The Khan and his minions were persuasive men. Extremely persuasive. He even granted them the honor of a bloodless execution: wrapped in blankets and trampled to death. It also precluded any chance of word of this monumental undertaking reaching ears it was not intended for.

The next stage was a wave of spies, again mainly Saracens but a few Westerners who love of gold was paramount. From them, the Khaizani would collect information on all the nations on the other side of the world, especially its fighting spirit and state of its military. The Khan ordered that the spies come from nations south of the Centola River. He was taking no chances.

As their knowledge grew, the future Khan and his father poured over the history of the failed Sui Chen invasion two centuries earlier, identifying the mistakes made by their predecessors and former overlords.

At the same time, they began the Herculean task of assembling and training the largest army of all time. Drawn from every corner of the Empire, the Khan was ensuring no one would stand a chance against any part of it.

Shortly after the army was ready, the Khan died.

A couple of provinces revolted the new Khan was a better general than even his father. He crushed the rebels ruthlessly and made horrific examples of the few that were allowed to survive for that very purpose.

The Khan smiled. He enjoyed galloping across the steppe, the wind rushing through his hair and his soldiers at his back. He enjoyed watching his enemies beg for mercy they knew they would not get. Why should they? What would they do if the roles were reversed? The young Khan had proved his worth in the field and now that huge army so laboriously gathered together enthusiastically rallied around him. All thirty of his years had been spent in the Khanate's service and no man was more dedicated to its, and his, aggrandizement.

After sending for the mysterious sword he and his ancestors had carried from conquest to conquest, the march west began. What grander fashion could one begin a reign? And it had the advantage of placing many plotters who coveted the throne in the field under his direct command.

The generals had been kept waiting long enough. The Khan stepped outside of his yurt, the flap held open by one of his guards. The assembled officers stood up and bowed respectively. The Khan ignored them and strode across the open space and into another, larger tent. He did not even look to see if anyone followed. He knew they would.

This tent sheltered a large table with a map laid out, rocks holding the corners down from those treacherous drafts that occasionally came in through the tent flaps.

After a brief look at the crowd of impassive faces, the Khan began his recitation of the overall strategic plan. "The Blieben, "his tongue fought with the foreign sounding words, "is only three or four days away. You have been told of the character of the people we will fight as well as those of our allies."

Allies?

The Khan smiled. Little surprises like this kept his commanders off balance. The Khaizani definition of "ally" generally meant someone who had surrendered without a fight. Anything that contributed to the perception of the Khanate's invincibility and all powerfulness kept the rank and file in awe of the Khan. That in turn kept any ambitious general's mind on what it was supposed to be on.

"All four of our armies will attack directly west of the river, ripping into the nation called Nyhissia." His fist came down on the map with a thud. "Any one of our armies is more than a match for one of theirs. Against our combined strength, Nyhissia will be destroyed. In the West, they send all of their men to decide the war in one battle in one place." The Khan said contemptuously.

The assembled generals laughed in derision. The Khan let them. This once. After all, they were ridiculing the enemy. The Khaizani had perfected the art of destroying their enemies in vast strategic maneuvers on country-wide scales with multi-directional attacks. "They will come straight ahead like an arrow. Make them pay for their ignorance. The honor of the destruction of Kronkus goes to the Middle North Army. I hear the kinglet there has several fine daughters."

The generals grinned. The rank and file would like that.

The Khan wondered if he should issue an order reserving them for himself. War excited him more than a mere woman could. "The Greater South Army will force the Kazmin Pass. The strange route of the Pergus River provides a good place to crush most of the nation of Verrent. Imagine their surprise when they see one great Khaizani army to their east and another great one suddenly appears to their south!"

"They will wail like women!" one general shouted.

"Indeed they will!" The Khan agreed. He memorized the man's face. He had better perform well. "Then the Greater South Army feints for Clutzen and then continues west. The Verrentian capital is for the Middle South Army to seize. The army they do not see the army that was coming straight for them across lower Nyhissia."

The Khan pointed at the commanders of the Middle Armies. They obediently stood. "After the capitals of Nyhissia and Verrent have fallen, do not take any time out to plunder. Leave the siege equipment if you must but you continue west. Anyone who disobeys orders will be punished by me. *Personally*. Do you understand?"

Both men gulped and answered the only way they could. In the affirmative. Not only would they be punished but their families would pay for any perceived transgression.

"Now the general of the Greater North Army has the most difficult task of them all. Tell me what that is, General."

The general of the Greater North Army stood, bowed and said, "The mission of the Greater North Army is to cross the Prania River and invade the nation called the Northmarch, my Khan."

"And what historical role did the Northmarch play in the last war?"

"It was their intervention in the Three Day's Battle that turned the tide of the war, my Khan." said the general, his name Yuan, the Khan remembered. He was a skillful general. And skillful generals became successful generals with loyal armies. He would need to be watched, the Khan made a mental note to himself.

"Correct." The Khan said, much to the man's relief. "Except..."

With that word, everyone's blood turned to ice. General Yuan began visibly sweating. "There has been a change of plans. You see, General, " The Khan walked up to the clearly nervous officer, "For a little gold, a chance to destroy their longtime enemy and a couple of other promises I do not intend to keep, courtesy of a skillful emissary, the Northmarch is our ally."

The assembled generals nodded. The Khan was not only a master of things military but his prowess extended to the realm of the diplomatic as well.

"When you cross the Prania River, you are to join up with the Northmarchers and use their country as a route west to descend on that land calling itself an empire, Masovia. The Greater North and Greater South Armies will converge with the Middle Armies on the town of Tornsat"

The Khan brought both of his hands together in a loud clap. "It is there the West will meet its doom. The greatest envelopment in history!"

The generals and their staff officers were almost too stunned to cheer. It was an audacious and wondrous plan. A plan only the warriors of Khaizan could accomplish. It promised more than mere glory. This was a chance at immortality!

"After that, it is a matter of mere riding to the Western Ocean." The Khan concluded. His heartbeat and breathing were elevated. The Khan lusted for battle. He wanted it and wanted it now. "Any questions."

The Greater North Army general stood up and bowed. "My Khan, where am I to meet our Northmarcher 'allies'?" He heaped more scorn on the word that it could hold.

"In a place called..." The Khan deigned to show the general on the map. "...Sparent."

West of the main army, ten Khaizani scouts rode out into the great emptiness to begin a grueling day long patrol, looking for potential ambushes and spies. The area south of the Speilwald was cut up with ravines, gullies and coulees. The scouts did not expect to find any opposition but it was good practice. As the sun rose ever higher, the patrol rode to the north and turned slowly to the left. The ten scouts spread out, knowing that they would converge on a point an hour west. It was a chance to iron out any glaring deficiencies. Soon, one of these rides would be on enemy soil.

An hour later, the scout leader nodded approvingly to the men under his command. They were all here, where they were supposed to be. The scout commander covered his eyes and looked into the setting sun. No one had gotten lost and there were no enemies to be found. Not yet at any rate. He did not hear the hoof beats until they were upon him. Suddenly he was bent over from a sharp kick into his kidney.

Kejen sat down in the saddle and pressed himself against the horse's neck. That way he was a smaller target. Trif rode next to him doing the same.

Trif turned in the saddle, fired an arrow and ducked a low branch as he and his brother rode down into a ravine. He managed a quick look over his shoulder. There was ten Khaizani when he and his brother rode up on them. Now there were nine. Trif allowed himself a wicked smile and rode on. There was no time to celebrate. The Khaizani were good riders too.

With the sun in their eyes, the Khaizani bows and their fearsome archery could not come into play. It did not matter for the rolling terrain sprinkled with many turns and small hills to hide behind was not the ideal place for archery practice. Instead, the Eastern horsemen drew their swords and pressed on seeking to run their quarry down.

Kejen and Trif found themselves directing their horses to jump over fallen logs and chaparral. The Khaizani, like Northmarchers, were people who grew up around horses. They were keeping up easily enough. The problem was that night was approaching fast. Up to a few minutes ago, this patrol was convinced that there were no other people anywhere near here. Now, they were not so sure. For all they knew, there could be a battalion hiding in this gully. It was their duty to find out.

The Khaizani began to steadily close the gap. Kejen saw that and tried to coax more speed out of his mount. He could hear his ride's breathing become more ragged. The best way out of a situation that you are losing your grip on is to do something unexpected, Kascar once told Kejen. Now seemed like a good time to see if it held true.

Kejen rounded a hill, unexpectedly cut across Trif's path and charged up the hillside. Trif nearly collided with his brother but reacted expertly and made sudden turn, scaling the latest obstacle without losing momentum.

The pursuing Khaizani overshot the point where Kejen and Trif began their ascent but quickly changed direction and rode up after them. The two Northmarchers tore through a line of bushes, flat against the horses back, hugging the muscular neck to avoid getting ripped out of the saddle. They burst out of the shrub line and rode across open ground.

"We have to end this soon!" Kejen yelled to his brother.

And almost went over the edge of a precipice that yawned out in front of them. Kejen yanked on his reins so hard, he pulled the horse's head around.

It was not really a cliff but it was too steep to really be called a hillside. Whatever the cartographers wanted to call it, Kejen called it a problem. Trif looked at some of the afternoon shadows, did a couple of mental calculations and arrived at the approximate angle of the slope.

"Too steep." Trif summed it up. The only math Kejen was interested in at the moment revolved around the number of Khaizani who exploded out of the same bush line. A quick glance to the right and left showed a run in either direction was futile since the Khaizani would have the inside angle on the brothers. Charging into them did not seem particularly wise so that left one option.

"Fortune favors the bold!!!" Kejen shouted.

Even Trif's unflappability was pushed to the limits as he watched Kejen drive his stirrups into the horse's side and vault over the edge.

"Hail Mary, full of Grace..." Trif prayed as he followed Kejen and embarked upon the wildest ride of his life.

Only the agility of a natural horseman would allow someone to even contemplate in theory such a move. It has been often remarked that there is a thin line between bravery and stupidity. Kejen found himself not only riding on the thin edge of lunacy but considerably beyond it. Sky, earth and vegetation all melded into a green and brown kaleidoscope rushing by with occasional blue and white. Spittle flew from the horse's mouth and the lather on the flanks merged with Kejen's sweat, all left in the torn air swirling behind them. Kejen hung on the saddle pommel with one hand and the other arm trailed behind him as a sort of rudder. The whole world seemed to be in slow motion, Kejen thought to himself as he shouted in exhilaration. It seemed as if a greater force was somehow guiding the horses feet, skillfully avoiding rocks and roots that could trip it up.

Trif felt like he was in a dream that he could not wake up from. Everything rushed by very slowly, in exquisite detail. His horse somehow knew exactly where to put its feet, as if Someone else was guiding it all thirty feet of the slope. To his surprise, he found he was enjoying it! The normally reserved Trif shouted with wild joy too.

The Khaizani scout leader did not realize how steep the slope was. He bravely leapt over it without breaking stride and found himself fatally airborne. The horse panicked and flipped over in mid air, legs wildly askew. Tightly strapped, its rider could not fall out of the saddle. The first part of the Khaizani horse to hit the sloped ground was the back of its neck. The scout leader felt one great white shock rocket through his being and he would never again fear the Khan's wrath. The horse sustained a concussion on impact but it rolled, twisting its neck and breaking it with a coldly clear snap, following its master into the next world. Another Khaizani almost made the same mistake but was fortunate enough to jump out of the saddle before his horse took a fatal fall down the same path. His mount crashed down the hillside, neighing wildly until its brains were smashed out on a rock, red turning white. The rider got up clutching his shoulder and shouted at the other soldiers to shoot arrows at the two escaping Northmarchers.

Kejen successfully rode to the ravine floor with suffering nothing more that scratches on his face from exploding through a thorn bush. Trif was there next to him, still gripping the pommel of his saddle with both white knuckled hands. Without looking behind them, Kejen and Trif rode into the trees and into the open land beyond, leaving the frustrated Khaizani behind.

Jerik remained hidden in the hillsides north of the passing Khaizani army. He spent his time making futile attempts to approximate its strength and soon settled on the obvious answer: *A lot.* The Sea-Farer Crown Prince had spent the entire day in one spot and the army continued by. There seemed to be no end to them. Jerik was not sure where he would go next. He was running out of hills to hide among. The forbidding openness of the steppes was in full view from his position. It seemed more and more apparent that he would have to emerge in the Khaizani wake and then ride northwest. And when could he do that, the Sea-Farer wondered for the hundredth time, watching the armored horde snake across the plains.

That night, Jerik emerged from his hiding place and stretched. He was doing no one any good staying here. The Sea-Farer poured some water out of his canteen over his face to wash off some of the dust. If nothing else, by staying behind, he ensured that Kejen and Trif could ride unencumbered and at full speed back to the Northmarch. Looking eastward, Jerik, for the first time, did not see campfires, draft animals pulling siege engines or countless mounted archers. This, finally, was the tail of the Khaizani snake! Jerik had spent enough time watching his opposition over the last few days to get a feel for their cycles and how they positioned the watch. The more he thought about it, the more the idea of breaking into the camp appealed to him. What was the purpose behind such a move?

Because I am *Locklannigh* and I do not like waiting! Jerik growled, took off his helmet and any chance of its distinctive outline giving him away. Like an oversized panther, he crept closer to the encampment, staying close to the ground. Finding the gap between the sentries and pickets was easy. The Khaizani were disciplined soldiers but they were not expecting to see another human being this far out in the wastelands below the Spieldwald. The Khaizani were, though Jerik would argue otherwise, susceptible to human folly.

Between the picket lines and the camp itself, Jerik forced himself to slow his progress. It was his experience that this was the area where infiltrators made mistakes. Quite often, traffic and messages between the camp and guards crossed through here without any pattern. Jerik could dispatch an errand boy easily enough but someone was waiting for that message and if it did not arrive in a timely manner, others would be sent out to find out why. More activity, more eyes looking around, more chances to discover a Sea-Farer in a Khaizani camp.

Jerik's wisdom was rewarded. Out of the dark marched four armored infantrymen in a line. Probably relief for their comrades, Jerik thought. Then he noticed they were marching toward the bush he was hiding under. The Crown Prince of Warron did his best to imitate a turtle and pull himself under the plant life. He knew not to make sudden movements. The soldiers could not see him in the dark but the human eye would immediately register movement. Jerik pulled his hand slowly, ever so slowly back over the cool dirt. The Khan's soldiers were almost on top of him. Jerik froze. His heartbeat sounded like a drum in his ears. How can they not hear that?! The only part of his body exposed was his hand. He prayed to his gods none of them were looking at their feet like a lot of people did when they walked. At the last second Jerik cursed himself for not covering his hands in dirt. That probably would not have mattered. Camouflaged or not, human hands have a distinctive shape that stick out in places they are not supposed to be.

Jerik gritted his teeth as one of those boots landed right on top of his hand. Then it was gone. Jerik did not unclench his teeth. He knew there was another man behind the first. Fortunately, that boot missed his bruised hand all together.

Jerik remained motionless for a few more minutes before crawling out from cover and toward the yurts. Soon he stood up and walked, with a Khaizani bootprint on his hand, confidently toward the first tent he saw. No one could tell who he was in the dark unless they were next to him. At this late hour, it was unlikely anyone was just walking around. Furthermore, the guards were too far out to see anything and were looking the wrong way.

Jerik stopped out side the flaps and listened intently. He did not hear any tell-tale signs of breathing. Earlier in the day, he watched this tent and pegged as a storage place for supplies. Jerik grinned at his good fortune. Food and casks of water. Granted it was Khaizani food but water was still water. The Sea-Farer filled up his canteens. He was inspecting the food, most of it some kind of dried noodles and drier meat when the flaps opened suddenly and a wizened old man stepped in.

Jerik tried to become part of the tent wall but there was no mistaking a giant Sea-Farer the size of three Khaizani standing in the middle of a supply tent.

The old man's eye's widened almost twice their size. He turned to run but one of Jerik's hands grabbed a hold of the back of his shirt collar and the Sea-Farer threw the supply officer into the center of the tent. Then the massive ax came down. And hit only dirt.

The supply officer rolled up onto his feet and assumed a combat stance. Jerik lunged forward and caught a foot to the side of his head. The old man was using some sort of fighting style that turned his hands and feet into weapons! The supply officer tried to run past Jerik but the now angry Crown Prince collared him around the neck with a massive forearm. The Khaizani soldier grabbed it and somehow Jerik found himself in front of the old man, flat on his back. The little man jumped over the now infuriated Jerik trying desperately to reach the tent opening. Jerik reached up and took a vice like hold on one leg and again heaved his opponent into the open space in the tent center. This time Jerik brought a solid crate of something heavy down on the Khaizani head to make sure he stayed down. Jerik looked around, hoping no one heard anything. Sound carried further at night. No one may have heard the struggle but someone was going to notice a dead supply officer Jerik thought as pool of blood spread under his fallen opponents head. The Sea-Fare quickly walked out of the tent and back toward the bushes he was hiding under earlier. He did not waste time trying to hide the body. Someone had to have heard that. And human bodies had a lot of blood in them. Sooner or later, the blood would draw notice no matter where he dumped the supply officer. Hopefully they would think it was mere robbery but Jerik was not interested enough to stay and find out. Into the dark he vanished.

"They escaped?!" The Khan roared. "You chased them through an unfamiliar area, lost your commander, and you do not know who they are?!"

The man with the bandaged shoulder and arm winced in the face of the Khan's shouting. The sharp shoulder pain was forgotten in light of an execution that seemed likely. The tale of the encounter in the gullies made its way up the chain of command quickly and the unfortunate scout found himself quaking in front of the Khan.

"But my Khan---"

One of the bodyguards hit the scout in the side of the head, adding another bruise to his list of injuries. One did not speak to the Khan unless bidden.

The Khan was too busy berating his staff officers to notice the offence. "Send two *jagun* thought that place to find those people! Tear it apart! Use what you need to seal off the area! Do it now!"

One officer bowed and ran out of the yurt. The Khan's anger landed on the general in charge of gathering intelligence. "You told me that Westerners never cross that river and if they did, it was never this far to the east."

The general felt his bowels turn to water. He gulped and began to stammer out something but the Khan would hear nothing of it. "I want no excuses or weak explanations." The Khan jabbed his fingers at the hapless man's eyes. "Another mistake of this magnitude and you will pay for it with your life! Like this miserable scout!"

The scout fell to his knees and begged the Khan for his life. Had he not charged in bravely and risked his life to capture the spies, he sobbed hysterically. All for the glory of Khaizan! The Khan was not moved nor did he give an indication he had even heard. The Lord of Khaizan was looking at the map with other officers. Two guards seized the offending scout and dragged him out of the tent. A few minutes later they returned. The scout did not.

The Khaizani armies split into halves at dawn and proceeded around the gullies Jerik hid in like water around a boulder in a stream. By mid-day the maneuver was easily completed and the march westward resumed. The Khan observed from the saddle and even smiled. The army was indeed well trained and ready! By the end of the day, forward patrols would be reaching the Blieben. The penultimate moment of Khaizani glory was approaching!

Taking shelter in one of those gullies, feeling distinctly uncomfortable with Khaizani all around him, pressed up against a tree was Jerik. More disturbing were the Khaizani here in the gullies riding around looking for *him*. What Jerik did not know was that the soldiers were tiring of the hunt. They wanted to get on with the war that was certain to break out in the next couple of days. The *jagun* commander in charge of this part of the search confided in his colleague that he believed no one was here. False trails, broken limbs and pressed down shrubbery were in abundance but with the invasion ready to be unleashed, did it matter if a couple of lost riders were here? Nonetheless, it was the Khan's will. The *jagun* commander still pressed on with prosecuting his frustrating orders.

Jerik was pleasantly surprised the Khaizani did not find his horse during his infiltration into the camp. Then he embarked on a dangerous nighttime ride from the hills to this region of gullies to find himself in the same situation. He growled in frustration. Once again he had to wait for the entire Khaizani army to pass. Looking around, he saw plenty of rabbits. No danger of starvation. Rabbit could be a bit monotonous but Jerik did not wish to find out what was doled out in the Khan's prison camps. That is, if the Khaizani even took prisoners.

Jerik looked out from his shelter at the marching army. It seemed as though it was now moving faster. They were eager to close with and destroy the enemy. The Khaizani could move and move quickly. It was frightening how well ordered this force was. It was not just an army, it had the air of a force of nature about it.

The sun had half set when Jerik charged out into the steppe country, his horse galloping at full speed, directly into the sunset. In a few hours, he would angle a bit to the northwest so his path would not be too predictable. With night reigning supreme on the eastern horizon, the Khaizani, if any were around, would not even think to look for a reluctantly horse bound Sea-Farer cutting across the army's wake. Only Jerik did not take into account the rear detachments that guarded lines of communication stretching halfway around the world back to Khaizan itself. A few hours after beginning his westward bolt across the plains, Jerik spotted just such a detachment, whose members also saw him.

Jerik stood up in the saddle, nearly fell out, and waved, shouting an incomprehensible greeting with the hope the Khaizani thought he was one of their own. Instead, it spurred them into action. At least he had a lead on them, Jerik thought. Then an arrow shot past him. The range on Khaizani bows was something to behold. Jerik cursed in his own language and violently zig zagged, almost panicking the horse, so that the archers could not draw a bead on him. The whole plan had gone horribly wrong.

Actually, the timing could not have been better. Jerik's horse was better rested than those of his pursuers. Unbeknownst to the Sea-Farer Crown Prince, the patrol chasing after him had been on the move for nearly twenty-four hours. Now minutes before being relieved, Jerik materialized from thin air. And there would be no help from the relief, still too far away to know see or hear what was happening. All Jerik knew was he wanted to be out of range of those arrows.

The chase went on for a couple of hours. Jerik realized there were no Khaizani to the northwest. He was not sure why nor did he spend much time thinking about it. There was quite enough to worry about at this moment. The deadly game of tag across the plains continued. The loser could find himself dead. As if to accentuate the point, another arrow flew past Jerik, who began another series of violent maneuvers and added an obscene gesture for good measure. It was unlikely the Khaizani knew what it meant but Jerik did not care. Most of his hesitant backward glances reveled nothing but shaky glances of darkness and the same ten pursuing shapes. Other than the steady pounding of hooves and wind whistling through his ears punctuated by fear he could practically taste, the chase, ironically, was uneventful. Jerik could not hear the Khaizani's horses ragged breathing and groans betraying weariness. Jerik was more concerned with his own horse's ragged breathing and slowing pace. His mind raced frantically trying to recall what Kejen and Trif did to encourage their failing mounts. Jerik took another worried glance back and to his horror. saw the Khaizani were closing the gap. An arrow bounced off his shoulder armor and another flew by past his head.

"Faster, curse you!" Jerik yelled into his horse's ear. "Faster! Those buggers will turn you into soup!"

The horse was at the end of its strength. Its spirit was starting to flag but Jerik could not afford that right now. He felt his ax strapped securely to the saddle. The time to need it might be at hand. What good was it against a bow though? Hopefully the gods would welcome him as a friend.

Miraculously, the Blieben River came into view, glittering like a silver thread in the darkened distance. Jerik pulled his ax out of its makeshift carrying case and held it up over his head, letting loose a whoop of joy. The river drew closer. He was almost there. Less than fifty yards!

Then his horse died in a hail of arrows.

Jerik flew off his mount, hit the ground and rolled. His helmet was stuck in the ground, almost comically with one horn in the dirt and the mighty battle ax was nearby. Jerik yanked his helmet out of the ground, grabbed his ax and ran for the water. The mounted Khaizani were moving at full speed however. Jerik stopped and turned as an arrow flew through the space in front of him. Jerik lashed out and unseated a rider who did not see him in the dark. More arrows flew about but suddenly the Khaizani were not sure where Jerik was. Jerik was not sure where they were either but he knew where the river was.

An arrow smacked into his upper leg. It burned like fire but the Khaizani archer who fired the shot died when one his compatriots mistook him for the enemy they had been pursuing. Pure adrenaline propelled Jerik forward and he dove into the cool water head first. He only hoped his armor did not pull him under and drown him.

It was pulling him under. What a choice, Jerik thought bitterly. Shot by arrows or drown. He angrily rejected both. His feet found the muddy bottom and somehow managed to break the water's surface. Jerik took a quick breath and ducked into the river again. He knew he was heading toward the right bank at least. The gods had guided him to the shallows too!

My God or yours? Jerik heard Kejen's voice shout at him from somewhere in his memory. Jerik would take aid even from whatever the bleedin' Khaizani believed in right now.

The armor held him under the water and Jerik mustered enough strength to crawl stroke a couple of times. His knee struck a rock and Jerik breached the water like a whale before diving under again. He was determined not be punctured by Khaizani arrows so close to safety. Whether or not the Khan's horsemen were going to continue the chase across the river did not enter Jerik's mind until a couple of horse legs suddenly plunged loudly into the water in front of him. Another pair appeared on his other side and Jerik felt someone seize him by the back of his neck and pull him to the surface. The Warron Sea-Farer was so surprised he was not able to even throw a punch.

He did not need to. Jerik looked into the face of a man with a saucer shaped, wide brimmed armored helmet. The odd way of wearing what looked like red and gold tapestry over his armor confirmed that Jerik's rescuer was a Nyhissian soldier.

Not that he needed rescuing, Jerik maintained. Nonetheless, after swallowing a mouthful of the Blieben River, he wheezed his thanks and allowed himself to be guided out of the water and onto the riverbank.

Jerik pointed east across the shallows but the Nyhissians could not understand what he was saying. He did not speak their language either. Nor did it matter. The Khaizani on the other side vanished back into the east.

One Nyhissian shoved a wooden block into Jerik's mouth and as the Crown Prince wondered if that was some odd Nyhissian custom, the man yanked the arrow out. Jerik spit the wood block into the nearby Blieben.

The Nyhissian laughed and quickly dressed the wound. It did not seem too bad. The soldier who had pulled Jerik out of the river handed the Sea-Farer a canteen. Jerik accepted it gratefully and pointed to himself. "Jerik."

The Nyhissian nodded and thumped his chest. "Eridoc."

"I like the end on your name." Jerik laughed and upended the canteen.

It was not water. It felt warm trickling down his throat and then it hit his stomach like thunder. Best of all, the pain of the arrow wound began to fade away.

Jerik held the canteen up in a salute to his new friends. "This'll wake you up in the morning, that's for sure!"

Then he emptied the rest in one swallow.

Chapter 14

Fleston, reigning King for the Northmarch, sat uneasily on his throne, leaning forward, hand on his chin. The bags under his eyes testified to the long night of planning that preceded this meeting with his advisors. Between the torrid debate that was certain to follow and the war unleashed against the West, Fleston looked older than his twenty-eight years. He would have not been surprised to find grey speckling his dark hair by the end of this day.

Then came a matter that was certain to grey Fleston's hair prematurely. The necessity of selecting a regent to hold the throne while Fleston led the army into battle. A regency that could become permanent, the King reminded himself. His two young sons where the heir to the throne at eight and five, respectively, There was no realistic hope they could shoulder the burden of the monarchy. If the King were to die in the upcoming war, the Northmarch could find itself with the same succession crisis it nearly faced fifty years ago when Maridon nearly drowned in the Blieben, saved by a one Leworl Densky. He was on some strange quest up in the Ankers, a strange quest recently undertaken by his grandsons. History had a strange way of repeating itself at the worst possible moment.

The only person who could undertake the burden of leadership at the moment was Fleston's queen, Aurora. The King smiled to himself. Her eyes really did sparkle like the aurora borealis she was born under. Unfortunately, he was not sure the quiet young lady from that village in the west would be able to run things while Fleston was at war. The King would not admit it but he was seriously considering naming his uncle regent. Uncle Konem had a fierce strength of will. At seventy though, Fleston was not entirely at ease with putting him on the throne. Konem's son, Angklis, was a good man but he seemed to lack the command presence of a King. If anything, Konem seemed a better choice.

No. Aurora would have to rule and she would have to learn quickly. There was no other way around that. The King had made his decision.

Fleston reached down and picked up a small bar of gold sitting next to his throne. From the finest coffers of Khaizan, selected by the Khan himself to give to a man of great stature, the mealy mouthed emissary said.

"How much blood went into making this?" Fleston tossed it contemptuously to the side. King Fleston was not a man who could be bought. An honest man with the uncanny ability to see through appearances and look at real people, Fleston was adored by his people. And why not? Was he as much a Northmarcher as they? Were they not as much a Northmarcher as he? Sycophants and power-worshippers were not welcome at the Northmarcher King's court. The Palace Guards had a genuine, personal loyalty to their King. Fleston took the values of his deceased father to heart not only through words but in deeds as well. The fact that Fleston, a man of irreproachable integrity, was about to pull off one of the greatest feats of diplomatic duplicity of all time seemed almost incredible. In the arrogant tone of the Khaizani emissary, the King saw both a danger and a splendid opportunity

Anyone who would crassly attempt to bribe, yes, *bribe* the King of the Northmarch five minutes into an audience could not possibly be capable of respect. Fleston thought back to that back a few months ago when those people from the East patronized him here in this very throne room. Then strongly insisting on an extended private audience! In the middle of the night they came. Like thieves! Fleston was not surprised. What they said could not stand the light of day. That is why he moved the audience to Sparent. To see how the arrogant foreigners would react and just in case the Easterners had something more sinister in mind. They pouted and came anyway, then made their obscene demands disguised as an alliance.

Phrases like "uniting the world, ushering in an era of peace for all under the benevolent rule of the Khan.", "...the Khan sincerely hopes you accept his offer to act as his Western viceroy" and "You, King Fleston, whom the Khan holds with the greatest respect..." grated in the King's mind. Quaint, personal touches. And dangling in front of him the chance to finally rid the Northmarch of the Masovian danger! Now that was like trying to bait a fish! The Khan did indeed have skillful diplomats. It also belied the unfortunate fact that Khaizan knew more about the Northmarch than the other around. Fleston knew soon he would learn more about the Khanate than he ever wanted to. The fact Khaizan could mount a campaign of conquest from the other side of the world made the danger posed by the imperialists down in Regalwood pale in comparison. The Khanate's obvious strength and vastness allowed the Khan to assume he was the one dealing from a position of strength. It was, unfortunately, a realistic assessment. It also led to a perhaps fatal overconfidence. After all, the Northmarch was quite strong too! Fleston's hand came down on the armrest with that thought.

The King could not be bought but there were others that possibly could. That was what the Commander of the Palace Guards had said to his King. Repeatedly. There was nothing more dangerous than the enemy within. Fleston sighed. He knew exactly who he was talking about.

Taetin.

The fair haired landowner, with immense holdings east of the capital, often behaved as though he was the king of his own country. He claimed he could trace his ancestry back centuries to the original nobility of the Northmarch. He probably could, Fleston admitted. Probably back to Baron Melas! The mere thought of that traitors name was enough to bring an uncharacteristic scowl to the King's face. Seven centuries earlier, Baron Melas tried to lead his fellow nobles in a bid to remove the King by force and take the throne for himself. And he nearly succeeded! The resulting nine year war, called the Noble's Revolt, devastated the country from one end to the other. Some of the nobles however, remembered their loyalty was to King and country. They rallied around their rightful lord, never deserting him even when everything looked worse, and cast down Melas. When the terrible struggle finally ended, the loyal nobles removed their own patents of nobility so that no Northmarcher could ever pay homage to anyone but the King of the Northmarch.

Taetin, it was reported, thought otherwise. There was no need to rely on reports though. Taetin was quite outspoken in his sentiments. In that respect, he seemed like a typical Northmarcher. He felt the practice of nobility patents should be resumed. Starting with himself. Now he sounded like a bloody Masovian! A man with such power so close to the capital needed to be watched in peacetime. People like that lusted for more. Now with a war on the horizon, would a man with such ambition actually act on it?

A war with a foreign power was bad enough without having to worry about the possibility of a traitor so close to home. Fleston's personality was that which inspired loyalty but some people simply had their own agenda. The Palace Guards existed because of such people.

"When is the meeting with my military council again?" Fleston asked on the omnipresent Palace Guards.

"In three hours, my lord." The Guard cradled the heavy spear with the massive point with muscular ease. He was ready to move when the King moved and follow him wherever he went.

"Wake in two and a half hours if I am not all ready up." The King yawned and vanished down one of the castle halls he had grown up in. Two Palace Guards followed him effortlessly. In happier times of peace, Fleston would occasionally try to outrun his Guards down the passageways and hide. Later, the upset Guards would berate him but Fleston would just laugh. He was after all, the King of the Northmarch. A rather easy going King but a King nonetheless!

What seemed to be half a second later, the rather easy going King of the Northmarch had murder on his mind when he was gently shaken awake. "Has it been two and a half hours all ready?"

He looked up at a man dressed in black standing next to one of the Palace Guards. "Your military council is assembled and waiting, my lord." Roeth, Commander of the Demon Division, said.

Fleston sat up. He felt remarkably refreshed though he would have gladly welcomed another hour of blessed sleep. Fleston bounded up and quickly walked down the hall. He was immediately flanked by Roeth and Perlis, the Commander of the Palace Guards. Down three flights of steps the King scurried with his guards in tow. Soon he was back in the throne room, where someone had brought in a large table and a chalkboard with innumerable scrawling on it. It looked as though his generals had all ready been planning for a couple of hours.

"Not bad for one of the boys in the pretty shirts." Roeth whispered to his friend Perlis. "You're not even breathing heavy."

The Palace Guard commander grinned and lightly punched his black clad comrade. He tugged on the sleeve of his green, black and gold shirt, the Northmarcher national colors, sticking out from under his armor. "I made that little jaunt in full armor. I should hope you are not breathing heavy!"

Roeth patted his friend on the back. The Demon Division and the Palace Guards always had a friendly rivalry. Perlis was a former Demon Division member himself. So where many other Guards.

The generals were so into their planning and arguing that they did not notice the King for a few seconds. Tignall did and brusquely called everyone to attention.

Fleston quickly motioned for them to sit down. "No time for that. Planning is much more important. This is not a Christmas pageant after all!" The King quickly scanned the room. making sure everyone who was supposed to be here was indeed here. He looked around until he found the person he sought.

Queen Aurora sat quietly on her throne surrounded by four Palace Guards. The slender dark haired Queen smiled at the sight of her husband and refrained from jumping up and running to him. The King smiled in return and waved her over. The Queen's movements were graceful and wholly out of place in a council of war. No "woman's work" arguments today, Fleston thought. As his potential successor, she had every right to be here.

Fleston's commanders would royally serve the monarchy regardless of who it was but Aurora, naturally shy to begin with, tended to be somewhat intimidated around crowds. Bringing her up to the front helped immensely.

The Commander of the Northmarcher Army was a large, well over six foot man with fearsome dark eyes and hair from some mountain village in the north. Eltsen Tignall began his military career some thirty years ago as a volunteer infantryman of the lowest rank. He was a man who knew the Army inside and out and from every possible angle. His deputy commander was a big man too but he had fair hair and the most piercing blue eyes anyone in the room Fleston ever saw. Piern was an exceptional commander as well, a formidable man who dedicated his life to the defense of his nation.

Another blonde man, Wilnef, headed up the northern armies. He informed Tignall that everything not needed to maintain basic civil order was camped here outside the capital and awaiting his commands. The southern command, headquartered in Sparent of all places, was led by Dreklin, a short, muscular man. Most of his forces were also here in Northcross, he reported. However, there were still some brigades not fully assembled and not here yet.

"I am ordering the marchout tomorrow." Tignall's deep rumbling voice filled the room. "Send messengers to those not here and have them join us enroute east." Tignall was fully confident the Northmarcher penchant for improvisation would serve the nation well yet again. Dreklin nodded and whispered to a younger officer. The man left the room in a sprint. Fleston was sure there would be riders outbound within five minutes.

The western part of the country was shepherded over by Arnles. The tall red haired general had the awesome responsibility of guarding the volatile Masovian border, earning the western command the reputation of being the most dangerous. Now that dubious "honor" belonged to the general in charge of the east, Kergis. It would be a miracle if his sandy hair had not gone completely grey by the end of the week. It was his broad shoulders that would bear the brunt of the fighting. That was if Masovia did not try to attack from behind without fully understanding what was really happening. With Masovia, that was always a distinct possibility.

The King and Queen sat down at the head of the table and the debate opened with Tignall unrolling a map of the Northmarcher-Masovian border.

"My lord." Tignall rumbled. "Do the emissaries you send to Masovia bring back any different news?"

The King frowned and shook his head. "The Masovians are as obstinate and hostile as always. They are not looking at the entire map."

"I believe they mean to move against us." Tignall said. "But they will not be able to for some time. Their large scale raids into Rhenia have a good part of their army preoccupied."

"Perhaps they will awaken to the real danger by then." Fleston was hopeful but realistic. "Or maybe they will just attack to the east into Verrent again."

"Keinsen would be easier." Tignall tried to read the Masovian mind, never an easy task. "Verrentians will be occupied on the other side of the country. Do you think the Khaizani have spoken to the Masovians?"

"If they did, there would be a lot more Masovian soldiers to the north or east." Fleston reasoned.

"True enough." Tignall agreed. "Arnles, what can you spare from the west?"

As commander of the regions furthest from the threatened eastern flank, Arnles's forces would take the longest to get anywhere. They were expected to be reinforcements after the war began. And he had an unstable border to guard as well. "Anything you command, sir. I do feel though that I will have to have half of my command to guard against the Masovians."

"You will have to make due with a third." Tignall said flatly. "What the Khaizani do will probably determine the course Masovia takes."

"As you command, General." Arnles did not look happy with the decision but he understood the logic. "Nonetheless, I do have a plan in case the Masovians do come over the border. Something more than a mere holding action."

"And what is that?" Tignall put his hand on the border.

"Attack down the Plikon in the direction of the viper's nest itself, Regalwood!" Arnles announced. "The best defense is sometimes a good offense."

"Indeed it is!" Tignall seemed genuinely happy. "I like that plan. You will not be able to take their city but you will get them to react to you and pull away from our side of the border."

Arnles rolled up his map and the commanding general of the

Northmarcher Army unrolled another. This one was of northern Nyhissia.

"Is this were we meet our friends from Khaizan?" Fleston inquired.

"Or in Sparent as you told the Khan." Tignall answered.

"We need to confront them far from our borders." The Queen said quietly. She may have spoken quietly but what she said reverberated throughout the room. The assembled generals smiled in varying degrees. It was good to see the Queen has some strategic sense, however rudimentary.

"Very good, my dear!" Fleston said encouragingly. He turned his attention back to his highest ranking general. "Have you decided where in Nyhissia?"

Tignall looked over to Kergis and deferred to the commander of the eastern armies. Kergis stood up and spoke to the King. "Yes, my lord, we have." He spoke with great conviction. "I have been to that part of the country many times and many, many of my soldiers have too. It is a place we are familiar with. It is the city of Lamptra."

"Why Lamptra?"

Kergis began his briefing. "Northern Nyhissia is basically one long plain, an extension of ours. Outside of the city is a rather tall hill. From that lone hill, one can see any army approaching for miles. And you can use the city to hide an army until we unleash it. If it comes to that, of course."

Fleston nodded and looked down at his hands. It was a good plan. Part of him hoped against hope that it would have to be used but the Khaizani did not seem the enlightened type nor were they going to be scared off. The problem though was he did not know what the maniacs in Masovia would do.

"Are our actions in the east going to be determined by what Masovia does?" Fleston said aloud to himself. "This is like the fable of the chicken trapped between the hungry fox and the farmer going to market."

A long second passed.

The King jumped up out of his chair and brought an angry fist down on the table. "We are not helpless, scared chickens! We are Northmarchers!!!"

The generals stood up and shouted in approval. Even the Palace Guards shouted and slammed the end of their pikes into the floor.

"We will NOT abandon our Nihyssian and Verrentian allies with whom we have stood with for so long!" Fleston declared forcefully. "To do so only help the Khaizani put chains on our wrists. If Masovia attacks in this most dire hour, than God help them when we deal with them!"

When the furor finally subsided, Tignall stood up. "My King, it has always been my honor to serve you as it was your father. Let me say, I have never been more proud of you or to be your general than at this very moment."

More cheering rocked the throne room.

The King of the Northmarch issued his orders. "We march out tomorrow at dawn. Any soldiers or formations not here will join us as we march to Lamptra. If the Khaizani want to taste Northmarcher steel they will. And they will find out that it bites and bites hard!"

The citizens of Northcross were awakened the next morning before dawn by undulating cheering and sounds of sword pommels striking against shield bosses. The King had given the same speech to the Army as he had the generals the day before. The soldier's confidence in the King was higher than ever. Come what may, the Northmarcher Army was determined not only to fight but to win!

An hour later, that Army marched down the cobblestone streets of Northcross, horse shoes and boots striking the ground in rough cadence with the whirl of bagpipes and drums as the cheers of the people cascaded down on the troops. Harnesses jingled, armor clanked, also hanging in the air was, though few would admit it, fear in the hearts of all assembled. Husbands and sons marched eastward to war. A few combative wives and daughters tried to join too. It was not unheard of in the outlying communities near Masovia for some women in the militia. They may have been turned back here but one would imagine that some of them would find a chance to kill some of the enemy somewhere, somehow.

Strength and resolved bolstered, the Army's readiness was as high a state as it could be. Other formations had arrived during the night and still others waited patiently along the road leading out of the city, ready to add their strength and numbers to the growing train of military might. All three of Sparent's brigades were ready to charge into the fray.

Fleston led the Army's march, mounted on a black charger, clad in the traditional manner of a Northmarcher soldier- armored in body and shoulder plate mail, an open-faced and crested helmet rather than his usual simple iron crown, a broadsword strapped to his back, shin and forearm guards, all designed for protection while ensuring the mobility a cavalry trooper needed. Flanking the King, in full armor, Tignall and Kergis cantered next to their sovereign lord, their faces stony masks of determination, prepared to go to any length defend the Motherland. Beside them were two other soldiers, holding aloft the triangular black, green and gold flag of the Northmarch, fluttering proudly against the clear skies. The other soldier carried Fleston's personal banner, a white unicorn on a field of green, the symbol of purity and strength with the fertile fields that brought forth life.

Behind them marched twenty-five Palace Guards, armored and fierce looking, ready to protect the King and ride into battle if the occasion called for it. They were not only mere bodyguards. They were soldiers.

Many in the crowd saw a few soldiers with black shirts sticking out from under black armor. Only a few though. Most, if not all, of the shadowy Demon Division were speeding away to the potential war zones. Their barracks were practically deserted, watched over by their brother-in-arms, the Palace Guards.

The Church was represented as well. Ten priests in their brown robes, walked in a line across the street. Father Michael was one of them, holding the Cross as a standard, evoking the Will of God, asking that He lend his strength to the coming struggle.

Then came the Army, ten columns wide and countless deep. Armed, ready and willing to fight and defeat those threatening the Motherland. The crunch of gravel and stone beneath thousands of feet moving in unison, united in purpose and spirit. It was a sound much more terrifying to an enemy than any amount of screeching and shouting.

Infantry, archers and above all, cavalry, marched down the causeway leading east out of the city, past the reviewing stand occupied by the Queen, regent until the King's return, and Generals Wilnef and Piern, Northcross's defenders until ordered otherwise. From *me*, Fleston prayed silently, not some Khaizani overlord. Arnles and Dreklin had departed last night, extending their hopes for success but needing to return to their posts to guard against any Masovian incursions.

Rank after rank passed by the reviewing stand. Fleston felt a slight heart tug as he passed by Aurora, wondering if he would ever see her again. He forcibly shifted his thoughts back to the war and riveted his eyes to the southeast.

The infantry tromped past the Queen, swords up in salute. The archers rode by and then the cavalry lances up in a mass salute, a solid wall of iron points on which the defense of the Motherland rested. Mounted infantry rode by next, swords held up under the chin. The blades gleamed sharply, honed for their sacred duty.

On it went. Brigade after brigade. The Army made its way out onto the sultry plains, battle standards flying, bright vivid slashes of color against the crystal blue skies and tan steppes, straight into the rising Sun.

The army finally disappeared over the horizon. Slowly, the citizens of the capital began to go about their business. They did so in muted, occasional bewilderment. The crisis had unfolded with such speed that many were unable to believe it was happening until actually seeing the Army march off to do battle with an enemy no one even knew existed. This strange, unpredictable world just took another bizarre twist and went about its way, leaving everyone, some with tears in their eyes, trying to catch up.

Kejen and Trif thundered into Sparent like a pair of horse riding demons, scattering pedestrians and creating the general havoc that had been missing in the last few weeks. Unfortunately, the war drawing inevitably closer had replaced it. The two brothers made a bee line for the Castle and found Leworl and Gaking in an emotional reunion. Then Reri appeared and tears really started flowing.

"Have all the brigades been mobilized?" Kejen asked before anyone could ask about the Ankers and *HeavenSteel*. "I saw only young boys and old men in the streets."

"Not too old to skin your backside!" a familiar voice growled.

Kejen turned and saw Kascar. He was not sure but he thought he saw a little mistiness in the misanthrope's eyes. Then he noticed Kascar was in full armor.

"Just in case the Masovians start to feel a little cagey." Kascar explained and thumped his armored chest. "I guess they must have forgotten the beating I gave them last time."

For the first time, Kejen saw his father was wearing a bit of armor too. "I am helping handle the supplies." Gaking said. Then he lifted a spear. "But I can still stab a couple of those Masovians if the country wants me too."

Leworl shrugged his shoulders. "I can bring the gate down on a couple of their heads if need be."

"With the Army on the march, we need to go join them." Trif said. "They were probably a little to the north of us."

"But you just got here!" Reri protested.

"You need to rest." Gaking said in a tone of voice that loudly declared that there were no protests allowed in this matter. "Galloping around all over the map and now off to this horrid war."

Before Kejen could say anything, Leworl cut him off. "You must rest for one day. You can easily catch up to the Army. Besides, you have to tell us about your adventure!"

Kejen looked down at his feet. "We did not find *HeavenSteel."*

"But other things happened?" Leworl asked.

"Yes." Kejen answered. "Not all of it was...pleasant."

"Have some food." Reri commanded with the authority even Tignall could not command.

"And then tell us what happened." Kascar added. "Everything...even what you called 'unpleasant.' " Kascar was still Kascar and he was not afraid to face anything.

An hour later, dozens of people were gathered around the entrance of the Castle of Sparent. Kejen and Trif moved back into the center of the Castle's courtyard to allow more people to come in and listen.

Kascar found some parchment and ink and sat down at the table he set up. He brought a Bible and Kejen put his hand on it to convince any nonbelievers. After a few minutes, Kejen began to recite the tale of his and his brother's quest to find *HeavenSteel.*

Kejen told his growing audience, deferring to Trif for occasional clarifications, of the trip to Northcross and then Glossak. Then he spoke of ascending into the Ankers and the foray into the Forests of Skulka. The crowd gasped as one and even Kascar looked stunned, looking down at the Bible to make sure Kejen's hand had not strayed. Kejen described the Wyvern battle and the crushing disappointment of not finding *HeavenSteel.* He did not speak much of Sevonicus and said nothing but praise of Gorvald and Vidron. Kuran, he said, was nothing short of magnificent. Kejen explained that by telling all how they thought the sword had been taken to the Argual. Now the crowd was truly horrified. Kejen choked up a little but pressed on nonetheless when he spoke of the fall of Vidron and Gorvald and the sacrifice of the gallant Kuran valiantly sacrificing himself to save his comrades and destroy the evil cult.

At that point, Leworl took over recording duties as Kascar, armorer turned calligrapher, began asking questions at a rapid fire pace, forgetting to record the answers. Leworl laughed and rubbed Kascar's head. The town metal worker looked annoyed as usual.

Kejen described what he saw and knew of the Khaizani. They were a tough, resourceful and powerful foe everyone agreed. But they had made the mistake of underestimating Northmarchers, Kejen shouted. Some of the Khan's soldiers had all ready found out the hard way! Kejen's resiliency was truly incredible.

When he finally finished his tale, Kejen was nearly flattened by a deluge of shouted questions and queries. An hour later, Gaking and Kascar, with some help from the few soldiers still stationed at the Castle, finally herded everyone out. Almost everyone.

Kejen saw General Dreklin standing in front of him.

"Quite an adventure!" The general said. "I could use a couple of stout fellows like you two here just in case the Masovians do jump the border."

Kejen nodded. "Is the danger from them that great, sir?"

"They are what they are." The general summed it up. "You have earned the right to tell me where you think you will do the most good. Here or out east?"

"The greater danger is from the East." Kejen gave his opinion. "Furthermore, the men I trained with are headed that way. I cannot, in good conscience, stay here waiting for something that could happen when I know they will definitely be charging into harm's way."

"Spoken like a true officer!" Dreklin praised. "Your men will need you. Your country will need you. What does your brother over there think?"

"I will do more good in the East." Trif replied.

"Very well." Dreklin said. "Your orders are to rest tonight. You can catch up to the Army tomorrow easily enough. I will also have some dispatches for you to deliver. I need every single man I can keep here."

Kejen saluted and took his leave. Trif however walked up to the general.

Trif handed his superior officer a leather bound journal. "I have made three copies. This one I would like for you to send to Northcross to the Demon Division. For Kuran."

"That will be done." Dreklin promised.

"One more thing, sir." Trif was not finished quite yet. "I expect them to read the part about Kuran to the entire assembled Division and to the King himself when the war is over. Kuran deserves no less."

Dreklin blinked in surprise. He looked to Kejen with a smile. "You brother is giving *me* orders! You must have bones made of iron! The Khaizani will be sorry they ever looked west."

Trif saluted and walked with Kejen back to their home. It would be good to sleep in his bunk if only for a night. There was a war to be won.

Dreklin had a lot to do but he took a few seconds to watch the brothers walk away. After the horrors of Skulka and the Argual, what sort of terror could a mere general wreak? Could the black terror of the Khaizani even shake them? Northmarcher soldiers could fight those of the Khan well enough, Dreklin was convinced of that. If Kejen and Trif were any indication of what Khaizan faced, the Khan would be best advised to turn home. The general thoughts went back twenty years ago to the Masovian War he fought in. The best way to win a war was not to get into one but sometimes you did not have a choice. Dear God, what would this one be like?

It took two days of hard riding but Kejen and Trif finally caught up with the main army a day west of the Prania River. It was not hard to find the Army. One merely had to follow the huge swath of foot and hoof prints cutting across the prairies. Soon they spotted a thin black line on the horizon that rapidly grew in thickness. The sound of armored men and horses grew louder by the minute. The outlying pickets picked up the Army's two newest members and escorted them to their respective units.

"For a few days, I thought I would have to lead these ruffians into battle!" a relieved Crinklin laughed as Kejen was swamped by the platoon. "I managed to keep them from putting another officer here. I knew you would come back!"

Kejen shouted his thanks as his men lifted him up on their shields. The whole scene held up the army's march for a few minutes until Kergis himself came over to see what was happening. The general smiled though. The army's morale was high.

And the army marched on.

A day later, the Northmarchers executed an army-sized turn to the south and the Prania River would soon come into view. Kergis spent the day riding up and down the length of his army, dealing with the problems that always seem to crop up with armies on the move.

"He is a good man." The King said of the general in charge of this army. "Always moving, tries to deal with problems before they show up. Deals with them efficiently when they do."

Tignall nodded. "An outstanding officer."

"Ah, Kergis." Fleston said as the general rode. "The very man the Commander and I were talking about."

"I hope you were saying good things about me." Kergis laughed.

"If I were not, you would not be here." Tignall said evenly. He was not a man to waste time with pleasantries. "What was the problem back there?"

Kergis showed no offense. He had known Tignall for nearly a quarter of a century. "Just checking the spacing between a couple of brigades."

"We need to review the overall plan." Tignall informed his subordinate.

Kergis pulled the right map from the many cases on his saddle. "Basically it is the same as we discussed back in Northcross. We confront the Khaizani at Lamptra. Should it come to blows, we hit them and hit them hard."

Tignall actually grinned at that.

"If we do not manage to kill every one of the mangy nits, we can fall back to the Prania, our side of course, and pull them after us." Kergis said.

"That move will relieve pressure on the Nyhissians and disrupt the Khaizani plans." Tignall explained to the King. "The problem is what the Masovians will do."

"What do the dispatches say?" Fleston asked.

Tignall held up a couple. "I have some coming in two and three times a day. The Masovians have increased patrols on the border but they are staying on their side." Then he frowned. "It may still be too early to tell."

Fleston looked exasperated. "We have told them about the threat. We have told them what is coming. What can they be thinking?"

"Dreklin has told me that he is ready for them just in case." Tignall read another dispatch. "He has pulled every man he can find into his army. Anyone who can walk it seems."

"I hope they remain bored." The King said. "I am afraid however we will not be. The Khaizani did not send their armies this far to return with nothing to show for it. Do we know what is going on south of the Prania?"

"I have sent scouts across the river, my lord." Tignall said. "It is not that I do not trust our allies but sometimes even allies do not tell you everything, especially when it comes to bad news."

"Very true, very true." The King said. "Sometimes though, you need to hear the bad news."

Tignall turned to look over his shoulder. The dust the Northmarchers were throwing into the air could not be missed. "Soon, people in Khaizan will be hearing a lot of very bad news."

Tignall's smile reminded Fleston of a wolf.

A couple of days later, just before Sunset, the Northmarcher Army arrived on the banks of the Prania River. It flowed slowly northeast before taking a sharp turn to the southeast merging with the mighty Blieben. The steppe on the other side of the watery boundary, looking very much like the soil on which the King stood. At first glance, it would be hard to believe that it was another country with its own history, language and culture. A friendly besieged country called Nyhissia. A land where many soldiers would fight and die and never leave. The King hoped most of them would be Khaizani.

The Northmarchers camped on their side of the river. No commander with something more than water in his skull would camp with a river to his back. The Northmarchers were greeted in the failing sunlight by a delegation of desperate looking Nyhissians. That did not seem to bode well. The Nyhissian messenger began to bow to the King but Fleston, never one to stand on ceremony, sat the man down on a stool gently but firmly.

The news was as the King feared.

The Khaizani massed across the Blieben waiting a day to make sure all was in order but the invasion was all ready underway. Operatives and specially trained teams of men were active, seizing portages, shallow parts of the river, bridges and sowing general confusion and terror. The next hours saw the full might of the Khan's army unleashed on Nyhissia. The Khaizani moved faster than anyone could have possibly anticipated. Only about half of the Nyhissian Royal Army had been mobilized when the coursing eastern hordes were sighted on the road to the capital of Kronkus, practically on the outskirts, almost within sight of where the King of Nyhissia slept! The Nyhissian Army bravely sallied forth but to no avail.

"We charged them and the air above us turned black with arrows!" The shaken messenger said. "Most of our soldiers were unable to close with the Easterners. Those who did fought well. The Khaizani had a fight on their hands but our knights could not make a difference. They were slaughtered!"

"We need to devise a way to get in close enough to render their archers useless." Tignall quickly saw an important point.

"Sir" the messenger cut in. "The range on their bows is much greater than you can imagine! After our charge was shredded, SHREDDED, I tell you, they ambled forward and shot down the survivors with almost no effort. The final Khaizani charge finished off the rest."

"You...were there, weren't you?" Fleston asked.

The Nyhissian took another gulp from a metal cup someone handed him. Fleston was sure it was not water. "Yes, my lord. The King's oldest son fell. Some of our soldiers fought their way out of the iron ring of Khaizani...he held back that final charge as long as he could..."

Tignall had no time for emotions. "Is Kronkus still holding out against the Khaizani?"

"The King and his other son lead the defense of our capital." Another Nyhissian said. Without an interpreter. "The Khaizani have the city under siege. Siege towers, battering rams, everything but Kronkus is a city built with that in mind."

"How long can it hold out?" The King of the Northmarch asked. "And what is your name?"

"Major Eridoc, my lord." He said. "Kronkus can hold out for a long time. Her walls are thick and well manned. They were built two centuries ago just for this occasion. My ancestors knew the Easterners would return one day."

"But they cannot hold forever." Kergis breathed. "But long enough for us to hit the Khaizani from the side!"

The Nyhissian officer looked at the Northmarcher general and leaned forward. "The Khaizani Army has broken up *by design* into four smaller armies."

"Four?" The Northmarchers were taken aback. Controlling two prongs was difficult enough. Four was incomprehensible.

"Yes, four." The Nyhissian liaison confirmed. "One besieges Kronkus, and another continues to attack west. A third has turned south and one is riding in this direction towards us."

"The army moving in our direction." Tignall asked. "How far north has it come?"

"The Khaizani are in Lamptra." The major said. Fleston could feel his generals deflate. "But not in force."

"How much of a grip do they have on the area?" Tignall asked quickly.

"Only a small garrison." Hope suddenly returned. "It was a cavalry detachment scouting ahead. They left a few men behind and rode off to the southwest."

Tignall turned and said something to a man in black armor. The King stepped in and heard what the two men had to say. He nodded and turned his attention back to the Nyhissians.

"I know you are anxious to fight for your kingdom but please feel free to rest and provision yourself." Fleston said. "When you do go, tell your King, we ride with him!"

The meeting broke up and its contents were disseminated among the Northmarcher soldiery. That night, Fleston walked around quietly among his soldiers. He did this at night so no one would recognize him easily. The scheme worked for a little while. Soon, the King found himself surrounded by cheering men and a few of the bolder ones slapping him on the back. One of them pressed a flask of something strong smelling into his hand. The King tried to find the owner but he was lost in the crowd. The Palace Guards finally managed to get the men to quiet down and soon they gathered around.

The King stood up and cleared his throat. "I wanted you to know how very proud I am of you!" The ragged chorus of cheers cut him off but soon the officers and noncoms quieted their troops. "You mobilized quickly, formed up ranks and here you are. I am impressed! More are still coming, catching up to us and finding a place. It is a credit to you!" The applause and cheers echoed across the plains. "And your officers!" There were some good-natured groans.

Even Tignall, a man who did not where his emotions on his sleeve, laughed. Around his fellow soldiers, he tended to be a bit more relaxed.

"The Khaizani are a tough, resourceful, vicious enemy. This will not be an easy war. They will be difficult to beat but they are not invincible. They are not ten feet tall. They may fancy themselves world beaters but this time, they are on *our* side of the world!" The cheers and applause were thunderous. "They fight because someone ordered them too or else their families will be enslaved. I look at free men fighting to keep their families free!" The King felt it was time to conclude. "I look out across this field at you and I know one thing. After we are through with them, the Khaizani will never look in the direction of the setting Sun without tears in their eyes!"

This time, the noncoms and officers did not try to stop the ground shaking din. They were part of it.

Fleston managed to make it back to his tent. He and his generals still had some work to do. Northmarcher scouts were returning along with a few more Nyhissians. They brought back additional information to fill in the details and to confirm Eridoc's recounting of recent events. Most importantly, the scouts returned with the best possible sign of good fortune. Every single one of them had returned.

Trif sought out his brother, walking from campfire to campfire, methodically following the brigade standards until he found what he was looking for. The fires reflected off of armor and weapons, giving everything an otherworldly look. It was difficult to see who was who until you practically went up into someone's face. Kejen characteristic loudness and unique profile made Tirf's work a little easier.

Kejen was sitting on his haunches, knees drawn up and glowering at Gusaric over a chess board.

"Any last minute regrets or wishes to change the past before we cross the river?"

"All ready talked to my guardian angel." Kejen snickered.

"Too late now." Gusaric added. He moved a pawn and looked up at Trif. "I heard you did quite well up in the Ankers."

"I was surrounded by good men." Trif deflected the praise he was never comfortable with.

"We are very proud of you back in Sparent." Gusaric said as Kejen killed the pawn he moved. No one would ever look at Trif the same way again. Gusaric moved his bishop, threatening Kejen's rook. "So give me the opinion of someone who has actually seen the Khaizani Army."

"They ride on horseback and shoot off the back of their horses, like we do." Trif said. He watched Kejen maneuver his rook out of trouble. He was trying to bait Gusaric's bishop Trif saw. "Our archery is as good as theirs, but their bows have a longer range. I would venture to guess they fight well dismounted as well."

"That is what I expected. Looks like the mounted infantry will stay mostly mounted." Gusaric hypothesized.

It was a strange moment in a strange place. What did you say to your friend before going into battle. How much you enjoyed his company? The three friends simply went about their
chess match and talking until word was passed that it was time to go to sleep.

Kejen stood up and hugged his brother.

"No unnecessary heroics." Trif thumped Kejen's shoulder. "We have seen enough adventure for about three lifetimes. No need to end it prematurely."

"Crush the attackers and head home." Kejen said. "Does not look like we would have gotten a lot of trading in anyway this summer."

"Certainly not." Trif answered. "May good health and happiness follow you. It certainly does when I am with you." Trif disappeared into the dark and picked his way through the camp back to the archer unit he was part of.

"Good hunting." Kejen said after him.

Flifern, a large rawboned captain, cantered around on a horse with a lantern making sure all but those on watch were going to sleep. "You too,

Kejen!" he called. "If anyone needs rest, its you, galloping around all over God's creation!!"

"In due time, Captain, after I tuck my men in." Kejen smiled.

"Do it soon!"

Kejen acknowledged and waved his troops back into the platoon area. Regardless of anyone's good intentions, Kejen would see to the men first.

Surprisingly, everyone was quiet, thoughtful and calm. Even the youthful Leron and the usually hyperactive Svaric. The calm before the storm, Kejen thought as he drifted off. Tomorrow they could cross the Prania into Nyhissia.

Eridoc walked among the Northmarchers soldiers. He wanted to cross the Prania and continue fighting the invaders who had attacked his country. He wanted to do more than just fight however. He wanted to kill the Khaizani attackers. In great numbers. The Nyhissian army may have been shattered but it was still lived! As long as the King reigned in Kronkus, Nyhissia still lived. Nyhissia just needed some time to pull itself together and strike back at the Khaizani. And their Northmarcher allies were going to help Nyhissia do just that.

He walked past a Northmarcher lieutenant who was unrolling a sleeping bag. Eridoc nodded in approval noting that all of his men were asleep first. Then the young officer turned around and looked Eridoc in the eyes.

"Pleasant night." the lieutenant said. In accented but understandable Nyhissian.

Eridoc touched the brim of his saucer like helmet and tipped it slightly. "And a pleasant night to you as well."

"You will sleep well and safe tonight." The Northmarcher promised. Eridoc politely kept himself from staring at the man's large nose. "You are among friends here. This is the Northmarcher Army and this is as far as those heretics are coming."

Eridoc clapped and smiled. Then he moved on. Had this confident man actually *seen* what Khaizan was capable of? The Nyhissian major wondered if anything could stop the Khaizani. He did know one thing. He would rather die fighting the Khaizani than live as a slave under them.

The King, Tignall and Kergis finished yet another strategy meeting. This time they were focused on a map of Lamptra. More information and even sketches of the area had arrived. There was even a report about the story of two brothers who had been in the Eastern border country and saw the Khaizani Army on the march. Impressive drill and army wide movements they reported. One of them made sure to tell the messenger that he had the impression that despite the armed might of the Khaizani, the rank and file seemed to follow orders to the letter. If their plans were disrupted, they would have trouble reacting. Attack and kill the leaders, he said. Tignall made sure that got out to his soldiers.

The three stepped outside the tent and relished the warm spring air. It was hard to believe they would have been knee or hip deep in snow a few short months ago.

"What I like most about the steppes is that on a clear day, you can see forever." Fleston said.

"And on a cloudy day, about half of forever." Kergis added.

Tignall was quiet for a moment. "I would like to see all the way to Khaizan, march to it and burn the Khan's palace down around him."

Chapter 15

Two shadows moved furtively between the trees in front of the small fortress guarding the northern approaches of the city of Lamptra. There was no further movement for a few minutes as the men made sure they had not been seen. Satisfied that their concealment had not been compromised, the two figures began their work with a quick study of the structure that had brought them here.

Slowly, one, then the other, drew their bows at took aim at the two Khaizani guards at the portal. Many have said that death comes as a hooded apparition or a blinding light but on this moonless night, it came for two soldiers of the Khan with a soft twang and a louder thud when the arrows slammed into their chests and threw them against the wall.

Suddenly, utter confusion reigned as the unexpected descended out of the night. The fighting was to the southwest! Not here, far from anything! Who was attacking? Were the people of Lamptra rising up against the Khan? Grapple hooks loudly clattered along the battlements. More shadowy forms materialized and rushed through the gates as about half the Khaizani garrison ran up the stairs to engage an enemy on the roof who was not there. The other half never stood a chance.

The Khaizani officer in charge stumbled out of his quarters and was nearly cut in have by a barely seen adversary swinging a broadsword. The Khaizani struck back, hitting his attacker before retreating back to his room and slamming the door. More and more enemies were appearing from nowhere!

The enterprising officer shoved his bed against the door, knowing he could not fight off ten men at once in the open. With luck, his men would rally and know he was here. When they had won back control of the fortress, the reprisals would begin.

Luck was not with him however. The door leapt off its hinges with an explosive roar and the bewildered Khaizani was hit by the bed he used as a barricade. Sword arm broken and head pounding, the Khaizani soldier searched frantically for his sword, lost in the blast. The mob he expected to pour through the door did not come.

The dust settled and the Khaizani looked up at a figure standing on top of a shattered desk, bow aimed at his eyes, it seemed. The Eastern prisoner's mouth fell open in disbelief.

It was not the populace of Lamptra that had risen against Khaizan. The man's black shirt, pants, boots and armor gave a clear indication of that. The crested helmet, with its overhanging nose guard and slim cheek pieces, provided the conclusion the dazed Khaizani was coming to. The Fortress of Lamptra had been taken from the soldiers of the Khan by the Demon Division of the Northmarcher Army.

Derzis laughed at the look of shock on his prisoner's face and hopped off the desk, landing in front of him. "Take this person and tie him up. I do not want him running off!"

Two other Division troopers grabbed the Khaizani none too gently. There were still some holdouts in the fortress so the job was not quite finished. Derzis ran back outside the portal with his bow trained on the path leading out of the forest to the castle. There had been a Khaizani post up that path and Derzis listened for hoof beats.

Instead a jubilant Northmarcher in black ran out into the open with his thumbs up. That was Sirklin. The rope he put up between the trees on the path must have worked like he said it would. Derzis smiled and walked back into the courtyard.

"Still a couple who won't give up." a soldier reported. "One in the tower in the southeast corner. Another in the guardhouse."

"Kriesen!" Derzis called. "Take the guardhouse, I will handle the tower."

"Yes, Captain." Kriesen said. He handed Derzis a sack he dropped off running into the fortress. "You might need this."

"Indeed." Derzis said. "Hard to believe what a trapper in Glossak can invent in a tavern. A powder like this looks harmless enough..."

Kriesen laughed and ran off toward the guardhouse. He had work to do. So did Derzis.

At the guardhouse, the Northmarchers broke through the door and were confronted by a solitary Khaizani archer who fired into the mass of black clad soldiers. He dropped one with a shot from his horn bow. The man shouted in agony, clutching his leg. The Khaizani's joy was short-lived as Kriesen charged up the stairs with a pike. He dodged the bow swung at his head and with a well aimed powerful thrust, the pike shattered the thin Khaizani archer armor and ripped through the shoulder. The Khaizani soldier howled and the Demon Division soldier shook the pike with the man still on it, causing him to shriek louder. Another thrust embedded the pike into the wall and the wounded servant of the Khan was left hanging in agony, impaled through the shoulder.

"Just desserts." Kriesen spat. "Leave him there. That is what he gets for shooting my cousin in the leg."

Seconds later, there was an explosion out in the courtyard accompanied by a bright light. The Nyhissian citizenry of Lamptra had been awakened by the fighting and was fearfully wondering what was exactly going on. The sight of one of the fortress towers slowly falling over to the inside was bewildering to say the least.

The Demon Division soldiers scrambled out of the path of the falling brick structure. It seemed to gain velocity before smashing into the dirt courtyard. A couple of troopers swore they heard the Khaizani holdout in there screaming just before the tower became one with the earth. Derzis peered through the dust and saw a bright red and white, pulpy mass with a couple of discernible bones. He correctly deduced that the protoplasm splattered among the broken bricks was one an archer in the service of Khaizan.

"Not anymore." he muttered.

The rest of the Khaizani prisoners had been brought out, tied together. Even in the dark of night, the surprise on their faces was evident. One kept staring through the open doorway at a fellow and still very much alive Khaizani soldier hanging from a pike on an impaled shoulder. Derzis could read his thoughts. What sort of people are we fighting?

"The wrong bloody sort." Derzis answered. He did not think the archer could understand him but the tone seemed to get the point across.

A couple of other prisoners, officers by the look of them Derzis guessed, seemed to be trying to explain something. They seemed totally befuddled by the attack. The Khaizani appeared to think this was all some sort of mistake. Derzis was not surprised. He knew the story of the prewar diplomacy.

"It went as planned, more or less." Kriesen reported. "We have twenty-three prisoners to play with. Caught them still sleeping, snoring quite contented until we showed up!"

"Casualties?"

"Two killed and five wounded." Kriesen informed his commander with just a hint of sadness. "Six of the enemy died and fourteen are wounded in addition to those we caught. We have mounted patrols sweeping through the town looking for any stragglers but none have turned up. I do not think they ventured far from the fortress here."

"I would not think so."

"Also have some Nyhissian cavalry who showed up at the last minute according to Sirklin. Many of them live here so they know where to look." Kriesen concluded.

"How is your cousin?" Derzis asked.

"He will be fine." Kriesen waved off the difficulty. "Tough bugger from Lans."

"Yes they are." The captain from Dunrovin chuckled. Derzis walked out through the gate, grinning. The ironic thing was that the plan to take this fortress had been drawn up by a Palace Guard. Life was strange.

The townspeople of Lamptra began to slowly piece together what had happened. It explained the black clad horsemen galloping up and down the streets. The fortress emptied out a few days ago, its garrison riding forth to do battle with the Eastern invaders. The following day, a force of nearly three hundred Khaizani rode into Lamptra and despite the best efforts of dozen or so soldiers there, seized the fortress. Obviously, something had gone dreadfully wrong in the east. Rumors flew that the King's son had fallen in battle and the capital was under siege. Most of the Khaizani had ridden westward to continue the invasion, in turn, leaving a small garrison. Now the black, gold and green Northmarcher flag fluttered in the wind, letting the people of Lamptra know their town was free again, courtesy of their northern neighbors. It was no longer "privileged to become forever part of the Khan's domain". That was what one townsman told Derzis the Khaizani read out in some proclamation. Somehow, Derzis hated them more now than ever.

"I want to hurt them." Derzis said in accented Nyhissian. "Not just badly but up close and personal."

"And I as well." The Nyhissian civilian said---In the Northmarcher language. The man looked around and then pointed to the north. "Are there more coming?"

Derzis nodded. "Yes there are. If you are looking for someplace safe, get behind me. A whole army is coming and this is as far as those Easterners are going to go."

That army was not far away. In fact, it was almost in sight of Lamptra. Soon, the dust clouds could be seen from the town's center. Kejen looked around and wondered if they could see the approach at this very moment.

Kejen's platoon was wedged in between two others. To the right were Gusaric and his regulars. The regulars and militia generally traded good natured insults and shouting matches but there was none of that as of late. The Motherland was in danger and the regulars came over to check on the militia and give pointers and advice. War was not something to be taken lightly. The militia troops realized that quickly. They were all comrades in arms. On the left was the cavalry company's other platoon. It was led by someone named Perhan. Kejen cantered over to meet him. It seemed like a pretty good idea to know who was guarding your flank.

"Are you the one I have heard so much about?" Perhan asked. Perhan's dark eyes suggested that much of what he heard had been blown out of proportion.

"Depends on what you have heard!" Kejen laughed.

"I heard a lot of things." Perhan said. "But are they true?"

Anger flared in Kejen's eyes for a second. Losing a good friend and two good men was not something to be dismissed lightly. On the other hand, he was not going to get into a fight with someone on his own side before a battle. "I would swear on a Bible in front of you if you like." Kejen said. "And if you still question me after that, I will tell you what you can do with your opinion."

Perhan's black eyes widened for a second. Then he laughed. "What you tell me is true then, I have no doubt. What I wonder about is if others have added or subtracted from it."

That seemed fair.

"I have a sure proven way of knowing what you tell me is true." Perhan continued.

"What is that?"

Perhan leaned in close. "I have not seen or heard of you strutting around boasting about it. You only speak of it when someone asks you."

Kejen found himself nodding in agreement without realizing it. Perhan might have been a bit on the cynical side but he was a keen observer of human nature. Good and bad.

"Great deeds are glorious and wondrous but they come with a price, often in blood." Perhan confirmed Kejen's thoughts.

"I do not like to talk about some of the things that happened." Kejen said.

"But to tell the whole story, you will have to." Perhan replied. "Or perhaps write it down. Your tale deserves to live forever."

"My brother wrote it all down!" Kejen beamed. "I helped a little."

"Does he speak of the Ankers?" Perhan asked.

Gusaric rode over and entered the conversation. "Trif does not say much to anyone about anything."

"Sometimes the calmest parts of the river have the strongest currents." Perhen said with the conviction of someone living next to a river.

Kejen's family was named after a river. "True. I found that out in the mountains. Trif did some things no one would have thought he could do."

"I hope he does that again." Gusaric said.

Perhen reached out and shook Kejen's hand. "I am very glad to have you on my side, Kejen. For what it is worth, I wish you had found that sword."

"I do too, Perhen, I really do." Kejen said. "Then the whole quest might have actually been worth it. Maybe."

Kejen refocused his thoughts. He had made his peace with what happened. He would probably find himself having to still deal with it in one form or another in the years to come. But not now. Kejen Densky had a war to fight.

Yuan, who had the honor of *Noyon* of the Greater Northern Army, had enjoyed a good war so far. The first battle had gone as the Khan said it would. The Nyhissians had charged straight into the teeth of the Khaizani. The Nyhissians were brave. And what good did it do them? Now they were almost defeated. He calculated that at least half of the Nyhissian army was destroyed and about a third of the country that gave birth to it was occupied. There was almost no resistance in the occupied areas. The people living there were still in utter shock and disbelief at the sight and size of the army riding through. Kronkus was under siege from the Middle Armies. True, the capital's defenses were massive and greater than originally believed but no city could withstand a siege of the magnitude Khaizan had laid on. The Khan's siege engines and the men who ran them were the finest in the world! The Greater South Army was about to take the Kazmin Pass and invade Verrent. The Verrentians were sending their armies eastward. As the Khan said, they would be utterly befuddled to find that they too were invaded! The forward scouts of his own army had secured Lamptra and soon Yuan would cross the Prania and ride on to meet with his Northmarcher allies. Yuan's smirk could probably been seen from Khaizan. "Allies" indeed. The Khan's divide and conquer approach was masterful. Pit one set of brawling barbarian Westerners against another! It was a much more successful approach than that of the Sui Chen a couple of centuries earlier. The irony of his own ancestry escaped the general at the moment. He had his army to worry about.

A small *jagun* encountered the fortresses garrison south of the city. Again, brave but foolish. They should have stayed behind the walls. Of course, they would have succeeded only in staving off defeat a little longer but it perhaps the Khan would have simply accepted their surrender and sent them on their way. Or maybe they would have fought to the death. Either way, it was better than getting cut down in the open like game. Lamptra was occupied with little problem. The Khan intervened and ordered the *jagun* commander west instead of north to look for any intact Nyhissian formations hiding in the as yet unconquered west part of the country. Now Yuan would have to operate for a little while without his forward scouts. He did not like it but what could you do when the Khan ordered otherwise? Nonetheless, his new orders where to halt at Lamptra until he got his scouts back so there might have been a little sense to this. Night was falling and Lamptra remained out of reach today and probably tomorrow soon Khaizan's armies would ride through it northward. It was as inevitable as the sun rising tomorrow. The general decided to dispatch a messenger so that the idle scouts could better utilize their time getting some supplies ready for his army. He thought better of that and ordered that two be sent. That was the number of runners you sent through hostile territory. Granted he did not expect much trouble between here and Lamptra, especially with the remnants of the Nyhissian army trapped in Kronkus, but Khaizan did not become a world's greatest empire by doing things by halves. Two messengers!

That same day, the Northmarcher Army entered the town of Lamptra to the cheers of the flower-throwing populace. For as long as anyone could remember, Nyhissia and the Northmarch had stood together against all enemies. Together they fought, gladly helping a lending hand and sadly, their children's blood, so that all could live free. Both nation's soldiers (and quite often, those of Verrent!)fought side by side against Masovia many times and even once before against Eastern invaders much like these. And they would again. The Nyhissians may have been a little wary of their northern neighbors, who seemed to be a little closer to their barbarian roots than most, but the liberation of Lamptra would draw them closer still. Personally, Kejen preferred Sea-Farers for company.

Tignall stood in the shadows watching tears flow freely. He wondered how much blood would soon follow. It was much too early to celebrate.

The Demon Division disappeared into thin air with the rising of the sun, hurrying off elsewhere to do other nefarious things. The town walls were hurriedly garrisoned by some Nyhissian soldiers and a few armed citizens scraped together into an understrength company. Again, Northmarcher scouts sallied forth in all directions to pinpoint the exact location of the Khaizani and the King, keeping a low profile, conferred with Kergis and Tignall.

The Greater North Army moved through the early morning fog like a knife though silk. Its speed was picking up across the uncontested plains as the army drew closer to Lamptra. General Yuan was worried. Where were those messengers he sent to the town last night? Did the Nyhissians have some sort of ambush set up? The power and speed of the Khaizani armies had wreaked unprecedented havoc so he thought it was unlikely they could reform themselves and strike back. As far as he knew, there was no nation other than Khaizan capable of such a concerted effort. He ordered the army to pick up its pace. They were too close to send scouts now. The best way to handle this problem was to arrive in overwhelming force before the Nyhissians were ready to spring any traps. The Khan had stressed the importance of arriving on time or even earlier to the rendezvous with the Northmarchers. It was necessary to impress the barbarians, the Khan said, with the appearance that nothing could stop or even delay Khaizan.

If I had it my way, Yuan said to himself, I would ride right over Northcross instead of disgracing myself and pretending the Northmarchers were allies just to use their country as a corridor to strike other barbarians. Deep down, Yuan knew the Khan's plan was a better one but the idea of dealing with inferiors as equals grated on his imperial soul. Even if it were merely a deception. He knew many, many others thought the same. Perhaps there is a chance in all of this to improve his fortune by acquiring a throne of his own once the war was over, the general thought slyly. Now that would provide for some pleasant dreams.

The general took his place at the head of the ranks with renewed vigor and the Khaizani accelerated to the man and horse killing pace that had won them the largest empire the world had ever seen.

Just south of Lamptra is a man made feature simply known as The Trench. Almost a mile long, the Trench was dug in the course of the Ages War as a defensive line. Who fought there and over what had long been forgotten but the evidence of the long vanished warriors struggle remained. Originally eight feet deep, time and the elements rounded the edges. widened the width and raised the original depth by at least a yard with sediment. The Trench was now a gentle, sloped descent followed by a swan curve up to the more level plains. A linear dent on a grassy table top extending interminably in all directions. And it was perfect for Derzis's purposes a few centuries later.

Aside from a couple of messengers easily dispatched by the Division's ambush master Sirklin, there had been no sign of the Khaizani. The Khaizani Army quickly galloped into view on its own however. Its speed and disposition were noted. They were coming straight for Lamptra without even slowing down. That told Tignall the Khaizani still thought the town was securely in their hands. In taking Lamptra, the Northmarchers inadvertently blinded their Khaizani opponents.

Trif was the third archer in the rank marching up Lamptra Hill, where lookouts were posted for any sign of the approaching enemy everyone knew would soon be here. It began the same story known to soldiers in any time. The worst part of any battle was waiting for it to begin. Mouths were dry, stomachs felt queasy and the soldiers were sweating profusely and not totally from the summer heat.

Trif finished digging a trench and looked south to compare his handiwork to the greater Trench out on the prairies. He also saw ever so perceptible dust clouds out on the horizon in that direction.

Kejen and his horse fidgeted from the inactivity, almost begging for the release battle promised. Gusaric was a model of almost Trif-like calmness and Perhen looked down the ranks of his platoon for anything amiss. The soldiers under their command equally restless but ready. The training and conditioning had come down to this. Even at this late hour, it was hard to believe that they were actually going into battle soon.

"I wish we were out on the plains." Gusaric said. "Not cooped up in here. What is this place anyway?"

"Indoor market." Kejen answered. "I have been here at least a half dozen times." He took off his helmet and spat on the floor. "I never thought I would fight a war here."

Trif inspected his work on the forward slope one final time and then looked south once again. The dust clouds were certainly closer. He knew the source of those clouds and somehow that seemed to defile the otherwise cloudless, crystal blue skies.

The lookout on the hill crest now judged what he saw to be close enough to constitute a threat. His one word shout galvanized everyone into action.

"Khaizani!!!

Chapter 16

The Khaizani Greater Northern Army galloped toward Lamptra oblivious to the beehive of activity its approach was causing. Battles have begun in many ways throughout history. Often patrol clashes draw in large forces. Other times armies have been attacked crossing rivers or on the march in towns and villages. The Battle of Lamptra began with a greeting.

The Khaizani army slowed as it approached Lamptra. Yuan could see an army assembled before the city walls but even at this distance he could see the banners were not Nyhissian. Some distance before it, was a solitary soldier on horseback coolly apprising the thousands of men riding towards him.

The general shielded his eyes from the noon Sun. The man on horseback appeared to be an embassy of some kind. A Northmarcher embassy, he realized. What was this man doing here? Could these people not follow simple instructions?

It suddenly became very clear to the Khaizani general. These greedy barbarians had jumped the mark and invaded Nyhissia when it was clearly defeated so that Fleston could demonstrate how "valuable" and eager an "ally" he was. Probably an excuse to exact a bit more gold. The general promised himself he would skin the Khaizani scout who left this rabble in charge of Lamptra. No Khaizani worthy of the name wanted to sit on garrison duty while the promise of battle beckoned but orders were orders!

On Yuan's command, his troops slowed to a halt and thousands of eyes caught a glimpse of one of the Khan's esteemed allies, a soldier in the service of the appointed postwar Western Viceroy of Khaizan.

Yuan saw the same thing his soldiers did. A man on horseback in dirty, dust streaked black armor and a poking out, a shirt that might have been black once but was now closer to brown from living in the dirt for a week.

The army at his back looked much different than the Nyhissians the general had fought so far. These men looked confident and somehow more vicious than those the Khaizani had cut down in front of Kronkus to begin the war. Yuan grudgingly admitted they seemed rather well trained. He also found himself wishing they were not so close.

Derzis surveyed the ranks about twenty feet before him, quickly locating the man he was looking for. He was not hard to find. The Khaizani general's arrogant demeanor certainly helped.

Yuan waited for an irritating moment and then summoned an interpreter. "Let us see what he wants." He commanded his horse to take a couple of steps forward.

Derzis raised his spear in a salute. Yuan returned the gesture smartly in the Khaizani manner. He was not bowing before any barbarian.

The Demon Division captain cleared his throat and made a quick mental review of what he was supposed to say. He could only imagine the anecdotes that would follow from this for years to come.

"We, the willing and enthusiastic allies of Khaizan welcome you and your brave army. I present to the Khan the city of Lamptra!"

Derzis did not wait for the translator to catch up. That was part of the plan. "As a token of our gratitude, My King offers you this gift!" Derzis's horse cantered forward. "This spear, handed down to him from his father and his father before that!"

The Khaizani general's mind reacted with unabashed revulsion at the prospect of having these barbarians this close to begin with. Having one even closer was going to bring on something akin to hysteria. There were other more tangible things he did not like about this impromptu ceremony that sent red flags flying in his mind. Like the speed and angle in which the Northmarcher was suddenly riding at him and the way the spear was suddenly reversed. The spear Derzis found in the guardhouse the night before flew straight for the general's head.

Yuan moved at the last second and the man behind him screamed, pierced through the neck by a spear that had the hawk of Khaizan on its shaft. Yuan, and the rest of the Khaizani army, stood in mute shock for a second either watching the stricken officer fall out of the saddle or Derzis disappear over the lip of The Trench.

The Yuan exploded with white hot rage and ripped his sword out of the scabbard. His very soul screamed for vengeance against this duplicity.

The Khaizani army surged forward, following its general, flowing into the Trench, and immediately received a few dozen nasty surprises. Several Khaizani riders and horses ended up impaled on spears driven into the ground at an angle. They screamed out their hatred and agony at the treacherous enemy who planted this forest of spear points as blood seeped down the wooden shaft and mixed with the dirt of the Trench. Simultaneously, bear traps seeded all around the Trench snapped shut on slender horse legs. Meant to hold bears in place, the traps had a devastating effect on the Khaizani horses, as Yuan fell from his magnificent mount now on stubs crashing down on the far slope, neighing wildly from pain more excruciating than it had ever known, hot blood pumping from the legs like hoses.

The first Khaizani to gain the far edge of the Trench were cut to pieces by a volley of arrows from the charging Northmarchers. Blood, entrails and bodies spun back into the faces of Khaizani rushing forward to do battle. The second row met the same fate as the first though it got a little further. With many in the first ranks caught in traps, others back into the Trench, filling with blood and death, and no attempt made at flanking the oncoming Northmarchers, the attack was in danger of fatally stalling. Before the Northmarchers could exploit this advantage, the Khaizani horse archers made their presence known.

They archers behind the heavy cavalry fired their wicked arrows, just clearing the heads of their comrades clawing their way out of the Trench. The screams of pain and crumpling riders, some with their horses, announced the devastating effect on the first rank of Northmarchers. Derzis turned around just in time to have one of those arrows tear though his shoulder, splitting the bones apart.

The first rank of Northmarchers may have been decimated but the Khaizani, to their horror, realized the army as a whole was too close for them bring their archers to bear.

The Khaizani cleared the Trench and continued forward with shocking speed. The Northmarcher horse archers fired again over their men and this time a row of Khaizani heavy shock Calvary fell, lances, spears and cudgels reaching vainly for the throats of enemies they could not reach. The Khaizani archers could claim credibly they were the best in the world but they could not release a withering counter fire with other Khaizani in the way. Then Khaizani archers started falling out of their saddle. Northmarcher archers were on Lamptra Hill too, using the hill top to maximum advantage. The Khan's archers fired up at the hill while riding but the shafts fell short, piercing only topsoil not flesh.

The Khaizani army reconstituted itself in midgallop and traversed the distance between the Trench and the closing Northmarcher army with astonishing speed. Even without the support of the dreaded archers, the shock power of this army was evident. Viewed from the commanding heights of Lamptra Hill, the Khaizani charge was a numbing phenomenon. The Khaizani spread out over the steppes like an enormous bloodstain from a mortal wound, pumped into the invaded country by the heart of a mighty empire.

Tignall and Kergis used the little time allotted to them to make last minute adjustments, checking the cavalry hidden behind the hill and in the city. If all went well, the cavalry would turn the Khaizani flank.

Yuan crawled out from under his horse, which had served him well as a shield. The stench of death in the heat and the flies that rose out of the Trench was familiar enough to the veteran general but the sight of the trampled carnage crushed into coagulating pulp by thousands of hooves made him want to vomit. He snagged a riderless horse and rode toward the fighting, stifling the urge to retch at the sight of one of those horrible spears reaching up triumphantly into the sky, encrusted with dried blood and pieces of flesh hanging off of it like obscene pennants. The war had just taken a definite turn for the worst.

Fleston stood on the city wall and the King shuddered when he saw Derzis riding slumped forward, a red hand holding onto an arrow protruding out of his shoulder. A couple of other Northmarchers in black took charge of their wounded leader and the gatekeepers hurriedly closed the massive wood doors.

The speed of the Khaizani that had destroyed so many enemies in the past was now used against them. The concealed cavalry units charged out from behind the hill the second Tignall signaled them to. What few Khaizani arrows that rose out from behind the shock troops overshot most of the new force of Northmarchers or bounced harmlessly off armor. There was simply no time for the archers to fire as a whole as they came under attack from Northmarcher archers on the hill.

Thirty feet. Twenty feet. Ten feet.

With shouts and screams, the two armies slammed into each other, lances lowered, the impact of armor and bone shook the earth for miles in all directions.

Men on both sides fell in scores as Khaizani and Northmarcher ripped and tore at each other in a paradox of hate and glee. The follow-on ranks slammed into the battle with even more velocity. The original line of contact shuddered but refused to move, piling up in dead and wounded.

"My God!" Fleston exclaimed. "They are not moving!"

General Yuan ran the emotional gamut from elation to fear.

At last! A real enemy worth fighting! The general wanted to shout aloud, his earlier contemptuous assessment forgotten. A true test for the world's most powerful army!

Yet the Northmarchers were not breaking apart. The barbarians were withstanding the attack of the world's mightiest army and fighting it toe to toe!

The Northmarcher right flank anchored itself on Lamptra Hill while the center thinned out from both casualties and attempts by Northmarcher and Khaizani to outflank each other. Soon, the infantry from both armies waded through the battlefield to come to grips with each other. Fleston, looking on from the city walls, involuntarily flinched at the impact.

Howling, the Khaizani swordsmen threw themselves at the prickly, hedgerow that was a checkerboard formation of pikes. With a muffled crunch, swords and lances ripping into flesh and metal, the Northmarchers staggered back but the line held and with a tremendous heave, the Khaizani were thrown back. Shattered and pilfered forms fell back into the faces of the next charging row. A few Khaizani hung transfixed on the pikes as some Northmarchers tried to shake them off. Instantly, the Khaizani were upon the Northmarchers again, giving the enemy no time to regroup, violently hammering at the center to crack and splinter it. The line convulsed wildly but some segments looked about to give way but it held, barely holding the Khaizani flood back.

The hill came under its first attack as several hundred dismounted Khaizani charged up the side, swords drawn, under the cover of the archers on the plains. Most of the arrows bounced harmlessly off of the bunkers or armor but it provided a little cover for their climbing comrades.

With one deft motion, the Northmarcher bowmen drew their bows and sent their arrows cutting into the massed infantry. Go for the leaders, Trif shouted to the men on both side of him. Go for the leaders! Trif selected a target, aimed and dropped a Khaizani officer at the head of his troops. He was a great believer in leading by example.

The Khaizani were stopped in their tracks, looking to fallen leaders for guidance. Although Trif did not know it, he bore responsibility for stalling the Khaizani for the man he cut down was the *jajun* commander.

The Northmarcher commander on the hilltop was alive and well and he saw an opportunity. "Fire at will!!" he bellowed. The entire Khaizani front row toppled over to a man, arrows sprouting from their bodies. The rest began to flee downhill to their original starting position. The Northmarcher bows hummed a second time and more Khaizani bodies rolled down the hill, bouncing over the rocks.

One huge Khaizani, towering over his fellow soldiers by a head, turned around and went completely berserk. Shouting "Khaizan!!!" he charged back up the hill on his own, swinging a large, curved sword wildly. Three arrows sprang from his body. staggering but not stopping him. Gallantly, he groped his way forward, exhorting his comrades on with a hoarse shout before his midsection was pierced with two more arrows. Then another hit him in the throat. The berserker stood defiantly against the clear blue sky, blood trickling from the corner of his mouth, before finally falling over, a brave Khaizani soldier perishing for his Khan and Empire on a hillside in a distant, foreign land. Trif admired the man's courage, even if he was an enemy. Trif did not hesitate to put the fatal shaft through his throat either. Some people were simply too dangerous to keep around.

The Khaizani took their large friend's example and sacrifice to heart. With a roar of exultation, they charged up the hill again, the battle cries of two centuries of imperial glory filling the air. The every bow in the Khaizani army trained itself on the Northmarcher bunkers and unleashed a barrage that made a plague of locusts pale in comparison.

The Northmarchers fired back, many climbing out of bunkers and trenches despite the manmade hail to get better shots. Some were hit, some were not.

Through sheer force of will, the Khaizani infantry bravely advanced, absorbing appalling losses. It seemed as if the Khaizani had deemed everything depended on reaching the hillcrest, so much that life itself meant nothing.

Trif launched more and more arrows into the advancing human wall that was looming larger by the second. He had stopped aiming since the target was so huge. And it showed no signs of stopping.

Trif and the man sharing the sheltered trench with him, Durgan, scrambled out to their position before the Khaizani engulfed it. They ran for the next series of trenches, dodging the arrows falling from the sky like rain and running between the shafts of previous ones sticking out of the ground like malicious asparagus.

A scream of pain rising above the din told Trif that at least one arrow had found a target. Durgan went down with an arrow skewering his lower left leg and another thudded into his shoulder. Trif was sure the second arrow was sticking only armor but Durgan was helpless and immobile in the face of the oncoming Khaizani. Trif grabbed Durgan by the collar and dragged the wounded man screaming up the hill, trailing blood.

Earas, the platoon commander, felt his blood turn to ice. Trif, burdened by his wounded companion, was going to be overrun. The officer stood up on a firing step, ignored an arrow that bounced off his helmet and shouted "Trif! Down!"

Trif hugged the ground and heard the whistle of winged shafts pass overhead and strike their living targets. That was all the time he needed, half pushing, half throwing Durgan into the trench before diving in himself.

The rate of arrows plummeting out of the sky dropped off sharply, heralding the immediate Khaizani ground assault.

Suddenly, they were on the lip of the trench and in seconds, the forward positions were inundated with battle-crazed, bloodthirsty Khaizani infantry. The battle now degenerated into a hand to hand brawl with swords, knives, fists and shovels. Men grabbed at each other's hands, hair or anything else, rolling around in the blood and gore collecting in the bottom of the trench. Trif seized a sword from a Khaizani falling into the ditch and drove it into another of the Khan's soldiers up to the hilt, leaving it there.

A scream next to Trif became a gurgle as his commanding officer clutched his bloody face and sank slowly before three Khaizani rushing past him. Past him and straight for Trif, who had all ready seen a good bit of close combat in the last few weeks in the Forests of Skulka and the Argual.

Trif met them head on, slashing one in the throat with his knife so viciously that he could not pull it out, losing it in the fountaining crimson. Undaunted, Trif pulled out a second knife and stabbed the second attacker in the stomach just as he planted a boot in the other Khaizani's rib. Then the expired Khaizani fell forward into Trif, who fell backward and found himself pinned under the man he just killed. The other Khaizani shrugged off the kick and towered over Trif, blotting out the sun, cudgel raised for the kill. His leer became a look of surprise, then disbelief as the man's weapon slowly slid from his nerveless fingers. After a brief and ineffectual attempt to stave off the inevitable, the Khaizani's eyes glazed over and he fell forward

"Great." Trif groaned, shoving him off. "More weight."

The knife sticking out of the back of the Khaizani's neck and Durgan's grinning face told the story.

"I guess we're even now." Durgan croaked. "And that knife is yours by the way."

Trif retrieved his knife and leaned up against the trench's dirt wall. The sickening quiltwork of dead and wounded made it impossible to tell friend from foe. Durgan closed his eyes and wished it would all go away but Trif knew what would not happen.

Some distance from the base of Lamptra Hill, General Yuan watched the battle, gauging its progress and trying to stay one step ahead of the Northmarchers. The cavalry and infantry battle still raged back and forth on equal terms. And he hoped it would stay that way for the key the battle had become the hill.

From atop the city walls, King Fleston and his general of the army made the same observation.

"I know what they want to do!" Tignall pointed at the hill. "It's the perfect place to use our reserves, block them and strike at the same time!"

"Go do it!" Fleston said excitedly. He found himself talking to his guards. Tignall had all ready run down the stairs and jumped on a horse. With Kergis in the middle of the fighting, Tignall was going to oversee and lead the attack himself.

Despite heavy losses, the Khaizani made considerable progress, breaking past the first line of defenses in some parts. With less space to defend further up the hill, the attack was beginning to bog down.

Yuan hurled more men up the hill to break through the stubborn defenders once and all.

Trif and Durgan found three others from their unit and finished clearing the Khaizani out their position. Happily, one of them was Earas, who had some difficulty talking since an arrow had shot through his cheek.

Fighting still raged to the right of them and Northmarchers to their left were shooting up the hill at the Khaizani who had broken though. They started shooting down hill again and Trif saw why. Another Khaizani force was making an ascent to push the flagging attack to the top of the hill.

The fresh Khaizani saw their chance to go down in history as the victors of Lamptra evaporate when Northmarcher foot soldiers swarmed over the top of the hill and tore into their surprised and tired Khaizani foes. The Khaizani held for a second, wavered and broke, retreating back through the trenches downhill. The Northmarchers, with the advantage of attacking from higher ground, coursed after them, ripping into the second force and driving it back.

Namsos shook Tignall's shoulder and pointed at the blue flag signaling his unit to attack.

"Ignore it." Tignall said.

The Khaizani horse archers were about to fire en masse into the Northmarcher infantry surging downhill. No one thought to watch the archer's flanks. No one in the Khan's service at any rate.

Tignall raised his sword and bellowed "For the Motherland!!!"

The Sparent Brigade charged, a huge wedge of iron that thundered directly into the neglected Khaizani flank lances lowered.

Kejen charged into the melee with an almost reckless abandon. He and his men chaffed at not being in the battle's start but now here they were. Adrenaline rushed through Kejen in gallons. He felt completely hyperaware of everything and everyone around him. He felt ten feet tall and ready to fight all the way to Khaizan before nightfall.

The brigades smashed into the archer's full force. Khaizani foot soldiers who were not trampled to death were sent flying. Lances and broadswords carved a swath through the lightly armored Khaizani archers, most of which could not use their bows at such close range. A few did and some riders and horses went down screaming.

Kejen galloped straight into a surprised Khaizani archer and drove his lance squarely into the man's chest. He felt the momentary resistance of the human body before it gave way to the steel shod lance point that ripped the man's upper body, exploding out of his back, a red spray hanging in the air.

The Khaizani left flank was in danger of being turned and the Khan's men on the hill were about to be cut off.

Gusaric clipped the side of an enemy archer and then kicked the wounded man out of the saddle, leading his platoon deeper into the crumbling Khaizani flank. Out of the corner of his eye, Kejen saw on his other side, Pehren's men were slashing just as hard, their leader helmetless and hair flying as Khaizani archers all around him died.

The Brigade's charge had pushed the Khaizani back but soon Yuan directed more heavy cavalry into the fray. The Sparent Brigade's advance came to a sudden halt.

The sun began to fall and afternoon shadows lengthened. The battle along the Northmarcher left and center still raged on but neither side could gain a clear advantage. A draw, Yuan knew, favored the Northmarchers. He began cobbling together damaged units into one massive shock force. What it lacked in cohesiveness, it would more than make up for in sheer striking power. It was a classic Khaizani way of solving problems. The General vowed to break the stubborn Northmarcher right flank before nightfall.

Kejen's battalion drove the Khaizani back almost away from the hill but not quite far enough. As the battle raged into late afternoon, his battalion was pulled from the line, replaced by another. Kejen had the feeling they would be used for some scheme of Tignall's before long. He looked at his men, seeing most of the familiar faces. Leron's was blustery red from the fighting and the heat but he was more than ready to go on. Kejen knew that for a fact, remembering the youngster smashing down two foes at once with a strength he did not know he had. Crinklin looked stoic and dour in contrast to the usual smirk. Bolshin carved another mark into his saddle and he even saw Flifern checking his bloody sword for any chips or notches on the blade. Svaric was no where to be seen and Kejen feared the worst.

The battle went on.

General Yuan was all over the battlefield, shouting orders and encouragement. He did not want the Northmarchers noticing him lingering around their right flank too much. His men and officers had fought hard and fought well in the best tradition of Khaizani arms. The problem was that the barbarians on the other side were fighting well too. They learned from the Nyhissian mistakes and unscrupulously gotten in too close for the Khan's archers to shred them. And then came dreadfully close to decapitating the Greater Northern Army before the battle no one expected had even started! Yuan took that personally. This was an unconventional enemy that had to be beaten into submission. And he was going to use the force he was gathering together as a club to do just that.

Yuan gave the order. An officer smartly saluted and the word went out to the ranks. The Khaizani unexpectedly fell back and the Northmarcher cavalry, howling, charged after them. Right into a trap. The dreaded Khaizani horse archers finally made their presence known. The hailstorm of arrows stung the charging Northmarchers and nearly half a regiment felt the teeth of Khaizani archery. Suddenly, the Northmarchers were falling back!

Yuan's hoarded shock force crashed into the weakened line holding the connecting the hill that anchored the Northmarcher right flank. They were rewarded with a breakthrough. The Northmarchers fell away like pieces of a dike giving way before a flood. The Khaizani charged into the gap to exploit the break and finally cut off Lamptra Hill. Yuan looked up to the sky, thanking the gods he believed. The Khan's men poured through the growing hole.

Khaizani infantry charged up the hill again, this time determined to put paid to the Northmarcher archers who had hurt them time and time again.

The Khaizani cry of victory sounded.

Then it was abruptly overwhelmed by a thunderous collision.

Tignall, moving with inhuman speed, had Demon Division spotters tracking through Yuan every step of the battle. He noted the force gathering out of archery range on his right flank and deduced what the Khaizani general had up his sleeve. The general in charge of the whole Northmarcher Army hurled the entire Sparent Brigade, elements of two others, at least a hundred Demon Division soldiers and even armed Nyhissian townspeople right off the city walls straight into the face of the Khaizani shock force. If nothing else, he could swamp it through sheer numbers.

Back on the hill the town was named for, the Khaizani cheered and clambered upwards, beating swords against shields. Meanwhile, the Northmarchers were determined to rid themselves of these incessant hill charges once and for all. They volley fired at the Easterners again and again, ripping great holes in their line. The Khaizani reformed and kept coming. The whole day their attacks had smashed and broken themselves against Northmarcher defenses like waves against some immobile rock. This time, their grim determination was carrying them forward in spite of the losses.

The Northmarcher archers stayed just out of Khaizani reach, abandoning the first row of trenches that the Khan's men had nearly breached earlier. A Khaizani infantryman stepped into the trench and felt his foot sink in some sort of foul smelling black oil. He wrinkled his nose and continued on. A second later, he saw a volley of flaming arrows and suddenly, too late, realized what it was. Could it be-----?

Explosions rocked the hill and great walls of flame rose up to the sky. Many Khaizani found themselves on the wrong side of the flames. Many more were burning to death. The ragged volley of Northmarcher arrows said the screams of those in the fires unnerved even men who had been in battle the whole day. The Khaizani fleeing downhill were noticeably fewer than the number that began the final charge.

Kejen yelled in mindless, borderline demonic fury swinging his sword and connecting with some unlucky Khaizani's shoulder. Smashing and rending flesh and bone with each blow, feeling the shock of impact rocked down to his heels and his stirrups strain to keep him in the saddle, Kejen fought on, knowing his brother was up on Lamptra Hill. That easily trumped exhaustion. This attack had to succeed to keep the hill from being cut off and the rest of the army outflanked. So far it was working. Kejen was on the front edge and he was advancing, ripping and tearing into the invaders before him. His lance had long since shattered but his sword was filling in well enough. The Khaizani were driven back. A few of them noticed the large nosed barbarian was the heart of the attack. The weary Northmarchers took heart and inspiration, driving their tiring bodies past the limits, swords and lances lifting and falling and jabbing and thrusting mechanically.

The soldiers of the Khan finally made their stand. Screaming, Kejen charged into them. The Khaizani tried to pull Kejen off his horse, to kill him and destroy the driving force behind the assault. Many tried, all failed, and most died. Kejen slid from anger to nearly berserker fury, turning everything around him into a death filled wasteland, shredding Khaizani and nearly hitting a couple of Northmarchers scrambling to get out of the way of this madman determined to cut the whole Khaizani army in half by himself.

The Khaizani held and Kejen came close to doing himself in, standing in the saddle to kick one of the invaders while swinging his sword at another. Luckily, Gusaric caught him and pushed his friend back into the saddle.

Yuan picked up a discarded arrow and angrily threw it. The attack had come so close! If anything, it may have succeeded but somehow these *barbarians* collected themselves and threw it back! How? How could this have happened?! It went against everything he had ever known. It was impossible! He looked around for answers but there were none to be found. His staff officers had the same far away look in their eyes. It did not matter. He was in command here. And it was his responsibility to issue orders no Khaizani had ever heard. Numbly, he did.

Tignall could not believe his eyes. The Khaizani were starting to pull back away from the town! Tignall's gambit not only blunted the Khaizani attempt turn the Northmarcher flank, but the attack stopped it cold. And to think, his original intention was to hold the line long enough to evacuate hill overlooking Lamptra! Night was falling and the Khaizani, for the first time in their history, had been stopped.

Smoke wafted across Lamptra Hill. So did the smell of burning flesh. It smelled oddly enough like pork. Trif felt his mouth water. Disgusted, he spit on the ground. No amount of water could wash that feeling out. It would be a while before he ate roasted pork again no matter how loud his stomach rumbled.

Lamptra was free for another day.

Chapter 17

The Khan first turned pale, then red when the news of the Battle of Lamptra reached him. He knew something had gone terribly wrong when a frightened looking runner, literally shaking with fear, stood waiting to be noticed. A mere minute before, another messenger had arrived with the happy report that the Kazmin Pass had been seized with little difficulty. The Verrentians were sending their army east and now were confused, wondering what was happening in the southern part of the country.

Up until this moment, the war had progressed impressively on schedule. Kronkus here in front of him was under siege and would fall. The Khan knew that would be a while yet but when the city fell, so would the rest of Nyhissia. Nothing could withstand the will of Khaizan for long. The Middle Armies were about to cross the Verrentian frontier and, of course, the Greater Southern Army had accomplished its most difficult objective.

Now this!

Treachery! The Khan's mind screamed in outrage. The messenger now was wishing he could just sink into the ground and disappear. The Khan angrily threw his cup of *kurmiss* at the messenger and shouted for his advisors. The runner slinked away, grateful that his sovereign lord had forgotten he existed. It was probably the only reason he was still alive. The Khan returned to his maps and waited for his advisors to arrive. The news had undoubtedly reached them by now.

The Khan's generals and advisors scrambled in, almost falling over each other, obeying their ruler's summons. The Khan turned his back to them and leisurely moved some markers about on the map, deliberately keeping the nervous men waiting. The Khan's guards stared at them, watching for any untoward movement. Desperate men did desperate things. At this moment, a Khaizani soldier at Lamptra was safer than these officers. For what seemed an eternity, silence, eerie and diabolical, pervaded.

"Quang Tzi!" The Khan called for his general in charge of intelligence on foreign nations.

The general took a step forward, his fright plainly evident. "Yes, my Khan." His posture was upright and chest was out. He did not know what would come next but he would face it like a man.

The Khan kept his back to the general. "What happened at Lamptra?"

"My Khan, the Northmarcher barbarians---"

"Betrayed us!" The Khan spun and shouted in the hapless man's face. "Like you said they would not!"

"But Yuan---"

"Do not blame others for your failings!" The Khan cut him off. He stared into the general's eyes. He could see some of the man's resolve start to crumble. Pathetic. A sycophant in the court, working his way into this position with nothing but insincere praise. The Khan's father kept this pitiful excuse of a man who was a fortune teller, not a student of military affairs and master of psychology.

And you kept him. a small voice in his mind said. *Now how many of your soldiers lie dead at Lamptra because you kept him?*

Quang Tzi stared into the flat, bottomless black eyes that promised no mercy. Now he knew what doomed fishermen felt when they saw the great white shark coming for them in the Ocean of Great Peace. Instinctively, Quang Tzi knew he would never step into that cool, sea-green water again.

"Is your deputy here?" The Khan asked flatly.

Quang Tzi nodded and gave what was likely the last order of his life. Quang Tzi's deputy stepped forward smartly. The Khan's look told him he had better do a much better job than his predecessor.

Much better.

The Khan's guards gruffly yanked the offending intelligence officer forward. "To your knees!" The Khan commanded. "And bow!"

Quang Tzi obeyed without hesitation.

The Khan pulled out his Birthright Sword, which was definitely not Khaizani in origin. The sharp edges gleamed brightly, almost sparkling. The blade was large but not curved in the manner of the Khan's people. The cross hilt hinted of Western ancestry but the sword had an aura about it that bespoke of a forging and craftsmanship beyond that of mere mortals. This was the sword of the Khans of Khaizan, the mightiest rulers in the world.

This sword was second in importance only to the Imperial Scepter. This, in fact, was the very sword used by the original Great Khan to strike down his Sui Chen overlord after bringing it back from the failed Western venture two centuries ago.

One meaty chop and the deputy became the senior, turning white in the process. Blood spurted from the stalk that used to be a neck. The Khan handed his sword to a servant who wiped the blood off of it and carefully handed the sword back to his liege. Very, very carefully. He felt the bodyguard's eyes on his every move. A few more entered the Khan's yurt during the proceeding and they quietly took up positions behind each general and advisor.

"At least I gave him a painless death." the Khan said to his literally captive and now extremely attentive audience. In the traditions of the Khanate, an honorable death, other than in battle, involved no bloodshed as the executed was wrapped up in a blanket and trampled to death. A dishonorable man leading a sniveling life deserved to have his blood mix with the dirt and forever remain part of the conquered soil. "Do not disappoint me further."

"Yes, my Khan!" The assembled men shouted as one.

Good, the Khan thought. Executions did wonders for refocusing . "I have new plans for the northern barbarians." The Khan began barking out new orders. "Immediately reinforce the Greater Northern Army by sending the Middle North Army here to merge with it. Everything that is not needed to continue the siege of Kronkus that is."

Another general raised his hand. "My Khan, who is in command in the North?"

"Yuan will remain in command." The Khan decreed. "He fought well in a battle that he never expected. That was not his fault."

The general bowed and stood at attention.

"Dispatch a runner to General Nugyen of the Greater South Army and General Boigati of the Middle South Army. Their missions do not change. Boigati to pin the Verrentians in place and Nugyen to attack their flank." The Khan sent more runners out, turning words into action.

"Lamptra was not a defeat." The Khan declared. "It was a work of treachery and is only a setback. Let no one, even barbarians like the Northmarchers, think for a second, they can thwart Khaizan!"

The officers, generals and advisors cheered. Even the errand boys were moving with inspiration. "We will destroy the Northmarchers and raze their capital to the ground, killing everyone and everything we find there!

Looting is allowed but there will be no fighting among our soldiers. One more good blow and we will settle our score with them."

The men in the service of the Khan ran to do their master's bidding. They were ready to take the fight to the enemy again. This time, they would make sure it was settled for good.

"One more thing." The Khan said to a scribe who was writing a dispatch to the Greater North Army. "Fleston is mine. I want him alive. For him I have plans."

Yuan woke up bleary eyed and hating the sun for shining in his face so brightly. Even *that* seemed against him in this accursed land! It had been a long, loud and sleepless night, punctuated with around the clock Northmarcher raids.

Khaizani pickets and sentries were swallowed up by the night. The raiders attacked, slashed and disappeared before Yuan's forces could strike back. Occasionally, the Khaizani would land blows but more often than not, they lashed out and hit nothing.

Counter raid squads galloped out into the darkness and saw only glimpses of black shirted Northmarchers like the ones at the Trench the day before. And again, they left traps and sprang ambushes. The Northmarchers laid a strong claim to the night. Somehow, a few had broken into the camp, wreaked a lot of havoc and vanished. Only a few but the effects of the pinprick raid were magnified by the Khan's soldiers themselves. One raider was seen by several Khaizani and the stories spread, leading to the impression there was a black shirted Northmarcher hiding in every nook and cranny waiting for a chance to slit someone's throat. The name "night demons" stuck to them in a way Khaizani patrols could not. And they were quite adroit at this night fighting business, Yuan shuddered, remembering a couple of hamstrung horses only a couple of tents from his. It reminded everyone on both sides why humanity in general feared the night.

Before dawn, the raids finally abated and the Khaizani readied themselves for a possible Northmarcher debouching out of Lamptra. The barbarians had the initiative, curse them! Yuan was waiting for them though.

Only they were not there.

The night guards and watch on the city walls were absent. The Khaizani general found that to be quite unusual for a city with an armed enemy outside.

Around midmorning, Yuan sent a few men forward to the city gate under a white flag. Slowly the gate opened, just enough to allow one man through. An unarmed man, a Nyhissian citizen, guardedly came forward, hands out to emphasize the fact he was without a weapon. The Khaizani forced him to walk all the way outside of bow range of Lamptra's walls. Yuan was not about to take another chance with Northmarcher trickery.

"That is close enough." Yuan said. Someone who could speak the Nyhissian language was next to the general. "Where are the Northmarchers?" the general demanded through his translator.

"They all left last night. Went to the north." the man said.

A Khaizani cavalry officer gave him a rough shove. "That is a general you are addressing! Bow to him as if you were before the Khan himself. Bow until you eat dirt!"

The Nyhissian townsman got down on one knee. A look up at the glaring general convinced him maybe two knees were better. Yuan wanted him to put his forehead on the ground but there were other things to worry about right now. Like the location of the Northmarcher army.

"We will have plenty of time to instruct them later." Yuan told his officers. He turned to his translator. "Tell this person that he and his are now the subjects of the Khanate of Khaizan." The general waited a moment as the translator informed the Khan's newest subject of that fact. "Now tell him that a general safe conduct will apply to his town as long as no one raises a hand against us. If only *one* is rash enough to do that, we will destroy the town and sow salt in the soil." The look on the townsman's face said the message had gotten through loud and clear. "Ask him again if there are any Northmarchers hiding in the town. If we find one, everyone in there will die, starting with his family."

"Mercy, my lord!" The man stammered when that was translated. He seemed to be showing more respect now. His hands were together. "The Northmarchers left last night, my lord! They have left!"

"Tell him to get out of my way."

An hour later, the Khaizani Army, for the second time, entered Lamptra. This time in force. The citizenry stayed indoors and did not resist the Khaizani barging into their homes looking for any Northmarchers staying behind to torment them further. The searches turned up nothing but signs the Northmarchers had indeed left in a hurry.

"The raids last night were to cover the retreat north." Yuan said. One of his officers grimaced at the word "retreat" as any Khaizani would. The Northmarchers did not retreat. They merely left. The officer kept that thought to himself however. He liked his head right were it was.

Yuan scaled Lamptra Hill, looked around and sighed. This piece of commanding terrain was in his hands by default. Repeated charges up these blood soaked slopes had yielded nothing but death and failure. His attention was drawn to the north where dust clouds announced were the Northmarchers were. The Khaizani might be able to catch them but Yuan knew his army was in no condition to fight so soon.

Time and time again, the Northmarchers not only held the Khaizani charge but pushed it back! Who could have foreseen that? Now the Khan was coming here himself. The dispatches did not seem to indicate the Khan was angry at Yuan but what could one do? There was no where for the general to run. Yuan did not know how much time he had left in this world but he was determined that if the end of his life was arriving with the Khan, he would face it as bravely as he had everything else in his life.

The Northmarcher Army rode back toward the Prania River, morale higher than some of the wispy clouds in the clear blue skies over the steppes. But there was some grumbling in the ranks. Did they not stop the all powerful Khaizani dead in their tracks? As a matter of fact, they *pushed* the Easterners back and away from Lamptra! So, why retreat to the Prania?

This was not a retreat, Kejen explained to his men. This was part of the plan! Northmarcher soldiers were good, tough, brave men but Kejen knew most, if not all, were not destined to wear general's stars.

The Northmarch was the greatest threat to the Khan's scheme of conquest. Why else would Khaizan have attempted eliminate Northmarcher opposition through a false alliance? Now, the Khaizani forces were drawn northward to fight a war they never anticipated. This would relieve the pressure on Nyhissia and Verrent while spreading out the Khaizani armies. Somewhere, the rope would break.

The King, Tignall and Kergis held yet another horseback conference. It was not a problem. Northmarchers rode and lived on horseback almost as much as the Khaizani. Both nations had more in common than anyone on either side cared to admit.

"We do not seek to subjugate and conquer our neighbors." Fleston spat in the dust. Out here in the dirt and filth of the field, one would have thought the King was just another sweating soldier. A soldier that had the full attention of the Commander of the Northmarcher Army.

They will seek to cross the Prania on a wide front or at several points at once." Tignall predicted. "We will not be able to stop them there."

The King immediately voiced his opposition. "I do not care for the idea of allowing the Khaizani to invade the Homeland unopposed!"

"Nor do I, my lord." Tignall said. "But trying to defend the length of the Prania is what the Khaizani expect and hope we do. Since they can cross at almost any point, a point we cannot determine, it could all easily turn into an envelopment. The same sort of thing that happened to the Nyhissians."

"How are the Nyhissians?" The King asked.

"They are holding on." Tignall answered. "It has come down to Kronkus for them. The city remains under siege but King Kenderick still commands. The Khaizani have very good siege engines. The Nyhissians have good defenses."

"Is all of their siege equipment there?" Kergis asked.

"Yes it is." Tignall smiled.

"We may never understand how badly we caught them by surprise!" Kergis laughed.

"We have some idea!" Tignall ventured a rare chuckle and a rarer joke. "I bet their Khan needs new undergarments!" Then he turned serious again. "The Khaizani have crossed the Verrentian frontier west of Kronkus but they do still seem to be advancing towards Clutzen. Not as fast though. They may stop and assume a defensive position if we are still drawing a good part of their whole army north. They seem to there to keep the Verrentians from interfering with the siege of Kronkus. Another Khaizani army is in southern Verrent."

"Another army?" Kergis was appalled.

"This is a powerful enemy." Tignall stated the obvious. "I wish the Verrentians had guarded the Kazmin Pass more heavily."

"We have to worry about our part of the map." The King interjected. "How are the troops?" he asked Kergis.

"They seem a little miffed about pulling away from Lamptra but they are not afraid of the Khaizani!" the general said. "Not reckless or arrogant but they know they can fight them."

"Good." Fleston said. "Are the Masovians behaving?"

"At this moment?" Tignall growled. He never had or would trust the imperialists who made Regalwood their home. They had done their best to kill him in the last war. "Dreklin reports no major activity on their side of the border but he is still keeping his guard up."

A rider handed Kergis some parchment and the general quickly read it. Then he frowned. "The Khaizani have reinforced their army here in the north considerably. And the Khan has assumed command personally."

"That is what I thought he would do." Fleston said. "Back to our situation." The King commanded.

"I think we should get to the other side of the Prania and wait for them in the Holmin." Kergis ventured.

"I agree." Tignall said.

"Why do you think that?" Fleston asked.

"The Khaizani have two options after crossing the Prania." The Commander said. "Go west across the steppes is one or come into the Holmin after us. If they try to go west, they do so with an armed enemy on their rear. Don't forget Arnles has an army at Northcross too. We can crush the Khaizani between us. They must know this."

"With the Khan taking command and their army reinforced, there has been a shift of priorities." Fleston said. "The new objective, I fear, is Northcross itself."

"Do the Khaizani believe themselves to be so powerful as to fight off two armies at once?" Kergis was shocked.

"They probably do." Tignall gave his opinion. "The Khan, based on what we know about him, will regard Lamptra as simply a stroke of bad luck, a fluke."

"Then he is going to die." Kergis said plainly. "And he is going to take his army with him. Straight into Hades I hope. Let him bother the Devil and leave us alone."

Tignall looked directly at his subordinate. "The Khan will fail and die here, I promise you." Something dangerous glinted in Tignall's eyes. Kergis had seen that before. When he had that look, something was indeed going to die.

"We are going to dare him to come into the Holmin after us." The King explained. "The Khaizani aura of invincibility has been damaged. They need to erase that with a victory and an overwhelming one at that. They fight best out on the steppes but how will they do in the hills, gullies and forests of the Holmin?"

"We know the ground there better than the Khaizani ever could!" Kergis exclaimed. "Many of my men were born there! They know every rock, bush and worm there by its first name."

"They come in after us there, they will have nothing when they make it out the other side." Tignall said grimly. "If they make it out at all."

"But how do you know the Khan will come in after us?" Kergis asked.

Tignall had an answer. "After Lamptra, the Khan needs to quell doubts eating away at the mind of his army and generals. We dare him to come in after us. Do you think he can afford to back away from our challenge? To restore their superiority, they have to beat us at our own game at a place of our choosing."

"The Holmin it is then." Kergis said with a savage smile.

Back in Lamptra, the Khan arrived at the head of his army, entering the city that was once again part of his realm. His presence here boosted the morale of the battered soldiers here. With the Khan here to lead them, how can anything stand against Khaizan?

Lamptra was the only place the Khaizani had actually been fought to a stand-still so the Khan moved quickly to squelch any rumors that were turning the Northmarchers into ten foot man-eating monsters. Lamptra was a battle the Khaizani were not expecting. They would be ready for the next. The Khan would see to that personally. And he wanted to preside over the destruction of Northcross.

General Yuan approached the Khan and prostrated himself.

"Arise General." The Khan said. "Be seated."

Yuan did as he was told, knowing that behind the smiling teeth was the iron of a sword that could take his head with but a single command.

"The man responsible for Lamptra has paid for that mistake with his life." The Khan informed Yuan. "You are to be commended. You and your men fought well in a battle that was not supposed to happen. Now Lamptra is ours."

At a very high cost, Yuan amended silently.

The Khan did not wait, or even slow down, for an acknowledgment. "Now for our men who fell here, we are going to invade and destroy the Northmarch. Have the army ready to ride in one hour. We are going to trap the vermin against the Prania River and destroy them!"

Less than an hour later, the Khaizani army, now swollen with reinforcements, rode due north. The Khan had single-handedly restored his army's confidence and sense of purpose. The treacherous enemy would pay. Oh, how they would pay!

The army divided itself into three prongs, moving toward the Prania River. The central column would engage and pin the Northmarchers in place, the Khan said, and the other prongs would converge and overwhelm the enemy flanks and crush them. Simple, direct and to the point.

Yuan rode with the Khan in the central column. He was more than a little uneasy. Unlike the fresh soldiers and eager officers the Khan had brought with him, the General was the only one of the ruling circle here to have actually fought the Northmarchers. The barbarians not only knew to avoid the full thrust of the Khaizani horse archers but they had actually done it! They seemed to know more about the Khaizani and how they operated than the other way around. The Khan still brushed off the whole Lamptra experience as simply bad fortune. He seemed to be making the same mistake Yuan had in underestimating the enemy.

The Khan gave the order that unleashed a wave of scouts to scour the ground between here and the Prania. The Khaizani were not going in blind this time. At least that was one mistake the Khan was not going to make.

The Northmarchers were well ahead of the Khaizani, drawing them further and further away from their original plan. Splashing across the Prania, back into the Motherland and up into the Holmin would keep the Khaizani at arms length. In their infuriated state, hopefully the Easterners would follow them straight into this region of broken, rough terrain. The Holmin was a place that offered little maneuvering room but plenty of places to hide and ambush. To an invading army, it promised only misery and death. The Khaizani army will melt here like ice in Spring, Kejen thought.

For what seemed the thousandth time that morning, the Khan looked at the map. The Prania River was drawing near and there was not a sign of the Northmarchers. There were signs of an army passing by but no sign of the army itself. Scouts to the east and west reported no attempts at any flanking maneuvers. But the enemy was not to be found to the front either. Were the Northmarchers going to try to hold the river on their side? That worked to the Khaizani advantage too. Simply locate the Northmarchers, cross the water somewhere else and still pin them against the river and crush them.

General Yuan had been a soldier his whole life. He had long ago mastered the art of thinking one step ahead. What he saw on the map bothered him more and more as the Prania River drew closer. The General rode up to the Khan, waited to be noticed and showed his ruler what he saw on the map. *Behind* the river.

"It is a hilly, almost mountainous region, my Khan."

"We will trap them before they can hide in there." The Khan said. "Surely they are not going to let us cross into their country without a fight."

"With all due respect, my Khan." Yuan proceeded carefully. "They do not think the same way we do. They do not think sensibly like we

Khaizani."

"That can be a nuisance at times." The Khan allowed. "We must endeavor to trap them."

"Why not let them go into this..." Yuan sounded out the foreign words..."Holmin place. We can turn to the northwest and gallop straight to Northcross."

"Surely you are not suggesting we leave an intact army to attack us from behind, General?" The Khan inquired acidly.

In things military, Yuan, like most generals, was more decisive regardless of whom he was dealing with. "We move faster than the Northmarchers. They will arrive in Northcross just in time to bury their families." He concluded with a pointy tooth grin. He also knew which levers of the Khan's personality to pull. "And if they do somehow catch up, they still have to come to us."

"What you say is sound, General." The Khan gave out rare praise. "It is a very good plan. You will find, however, that the problem of Northcross will take care of itself."

"I do not understand, my Khan."

"It is not necessary to understand what I say, General." The Khan said in supreme confidence. "It is only necessary you do as I say."

"Of course, my Khan."

At the Khan's personal order, a small handpicked group of men detached itself from the army and rode northwest, entrusted with a mission that could win the war in one decisive move.

These soldiers were from the Khan's elite, a unit wearing black much like the Demon Division, called the "Crouching Dragons.". It was the original Great Khan's first army. Ten thousand strong as a whole, the formation was raised to its elite status a century earlier. Not just anyone could wear the stylized silver dragon on the sleeves. Each Crouching Dragon represented the embodiment of the Khaizani ideal. Smart, resourceful, able to operate far, far from home and possessing a fanatical devotion to the Khan and the Khanate, the Crouching Dragons were not just the elite of the Khaizani military but of Khaizan itself. They had privileges no one other than the Khan could dream of. Ordinary Khaizani soldiers, other than generals, followed their orders. And the generals took their "suggestions" seriously. In return, the Khan demanded absolute, unquestioning loyalty. And he got it. Crouching Dragons had died rather than fail in their high risk missions. The elite of the elite of Khaizan had played many roles in decisive moments, breaking the backs of many potential rivals to Khaizan and washing them away in waves of blood. Now, they sought to do in the West what they had done so many times in the East.

Bakhu looked over the four men under his command. He was selected to undertake this mission since he had actually been to Northcross before and inside Fleston's castle. Months before, The Khan sent him across the Blieben in Winter as his emissary to the Northmarchers. Bakhu wanted to laugh aloud when he remembered Fleston's incredulous look when instead on a Nhyissian trade delegation, five men from the East came forth instead. Now grim determination was his look.

How could anyone have feigned acceptance so convincingly? Especially a King? Lamptra had shown what lurked in the darkest reaches of the Western mentality, Bakhu thought, conveniently forgetting the betrayal in store for the Northmarchers after the Khaizani had marched to the Sea.

Up until this point, Bakhu and his fellow Dragons had been fighting bravely against the Nyhissians and engaging in long distance raids stretching into Verrent. There was supposed to be no need for the Crouching Dragons against the Northmarchers. Again, Lamptra had changed all of that.

Bakhu and his men crossed into the Northmarch under the cover of night and rode northwest along the axis Yuan earlier had proposed for the whole army to follow. They would ride at night and hide during the day. Secrecy was essential. Secrecy was vital.

The plan was simple as it was audacious and daring, a basic repetition of the event that led to the creation of the Khaizani Empire. Killing the leader of the enemy except instead of the quarry being a Sui Chen emperor, this time it would be the Queen of the Northmarch.

Fleston was definitely with his army. Like the Khan, he left a regent behind in his stead. But the Khan had left his brother on the Imperial Throne whereas Fleston only had his Queen. If the plan worked, Fleston's will to fight would die with his Queen and the Northmarch would be doomed. The thought that such a move could backfire and enrage the Northmarchers further did not occur to him. The idea of killing an unarmed woman did not bother Bakhu either. He would do what the Khan ordered him to do. And the Khan was always right. If you wanted to hurt someone, hurt someone they love.

The jaws of the Khaizani army closed frustratingly on thin air. Revitalized under the personal watch of the Khan, the Greater North Army surged across the steppe, looking for its Northmarcher opponent. With the Khaizani rapidly approaching the Prania River, the Khan ordered the flanking columns to converge and converge quickly. The Northmarchers could not have possibly crossed a river that big with an entire army!

Only they did. And according to the scouts, they did almost two days ago. The Northmarcher Army did not move as fast as the Khaizani but they did move quicker than their Nyhissian or Verrentian allies.

The Khan looked up into the rocky and forested hills on the other side, the Northmarcher side, of the Prania. Then he looked to the west. Although he could not see that far, he knew the plains continued in that direction. Yuan's plan made a lot of sense. Good sense. But was it wise to leave a wily enemy like this at your back? An enemy that moved faster than you originally believed.

The First Lord of Khaizan turned around in his saddle and looked out at his army. He smiled inwardly and nodded. With such a vast and powerful force, how can victory not be inevitable? He compared that sight with the land across the river. The land he sought to conquer. A wild, unruly land that was mocking the Khaizani. The Khan knew the Northmarchers were there, probably watching him at this very moment. They were mocking him. There was something mocking about those hills and tree and cliffs shrouded in the morning mist. A serene confidence it could withstand any attacker, weather any storm, regardless of how hard the wind blew.

Behold the East wind, the Khan replied in thought.

There was some commotion at the water's edge. The Khan rode down with his bodyguards to see what the problem was. After all, it could hold up the army's advance.

Gagged and tied to a spear driven into the ground was a Khaizani soldier. He looked scared and shaken yet unharmed as water lapped around his lower body. Seeing one of his soldiers on the receiving end of such disgraceful treatment was more than enough cause for raw anger but the Khan was staring at the sign some Northmarcher had hung around the man's neck.

The Khan barked for his translator and demanded to know what the sign read since it was in the illegible scrawling the barbarians used.

The man cleared his throat and read it word for word. " 'Death awaits you here. Turn back while you are able. ' "

The Khan snorted contemptuously. "Such acts are for the superstitious and cowardly, not rulers of the world, warriors of Khaizan!"

His show of bravado was enough to wash way most of the fears creeping into the minds of the rank and file, but there remained a residual doubt. In particular, with the men who had fought at Lamptra. The Northmarchers had fought the Khaizani to a standstill and forced the Khan to come here himself with reinforcements. Now the enemy had boldly snatched a soldier and dumped him in front of the army like this. If the Northmarchers were this bold, could they do worse things?

The same question gnawed at the Khan though his impassive face betrayed nothing. He noted angrily how many soldiers were looking into the hills with worried faces as they crossed the river. Victory was the best way to stop any spreading doubts.

The yak tailed standards of the Khaizani crossed into the Holmin unmolested but not unwatched.

Jerik sat the front of his wagon and watched two Northmarcher lancers ride by shouting and yelling, green pennants fluttering from their lances, cutting through the prairie grass like shark fins in the Sea he loved so much.

"No place for us *Locklannigh*" Jerik commented.

"A bit late for that now." Olsen reminded his liege. "How's the leg doing? No sign of infection."

It still twinged but it held up Jerik's weight, which was what is was supposed to do. "It is fine. That Eridoc fellow did a good job bandaging up my leg. I hope he is well. Those Khaizani certainly looked like formidable foes."

"The, what are they called again? Khaizani. They are only men. They bleed and feel pain and die just like us. We just need to kill a lot of them." Olsen swished the reins again. " I am not sure what good fifty of us are going to do in this kind of war. But I am sure our Northmarcher friends will find some place for us."

"I am sure they will!" Jerik laughed. "Sooner or later, we could be facing these Khaizani in Warron. Better to do all we can to make sure that day does not come."

"Do you think that rider you sent had reached Warron yet?" Olsen asked.

"Not yet." Jerik said. "It is a long way. We will have quite a story to tell everyone when we return."

"In addition to the story you all ready have!" Olsen exclaimed. "The audience will stretch back to Traiklef. With a few doubters too I'll wager."

"Bugger them." Jerik snorted. "If they want, let them go to the Forests of Skulka. Tell them not to forget to write a will first."

As Jerik predicted, the first Northmarcher military contingent they encountered did find a use for fifty Sea-Farers. The brigade out of Glossak, the Second Brigade, the red two on the black and gold shield on the sleeve proudly proclaimed, was marching resolutely southward.

"A small part of our brigade is supposed to hold a hill on the northern part of the Holmin." The brigade commander, a tall blonde man named Reydis, told Jerik. Tall compared to most. Jerik was still towered over him by half a head.

"And this hill we are supposed to be on is called 'The Devil's Cradle' ?" Jerik asked. "What sort of name is that?"

"What do you expect from a Sea-Farer?" a familiar voice rang out from the Northmarcher ranks.

"Overdulf?" Jerik could not believe his ears.

"So your hearing is not too damaged after all!" Overdulf rode up. "I made great time coming back and got to spend about three bloody hours at home!"

"Ride in the Sea-Farers wagon if you want." Reydis interrupted. "We are going to Dunrovin and its not getting any closer. Besides, you know where the hill is and those wagons are not going to keep up with us."

"Many thanks for the encouraging words." Jerik bowed sardonically. Reydis was too busy to notice or care. His brigade was on the march.

Jerik helped Overdulf into the wagon and both retreated into the back. The Glossak trapper now soldier made himself comfortable before delving into the mission before them.

"Take off that armor and make yourself truly comfortable!" Jerik all but commanded.

Ovedulf shook his head but did deign to take off the helmet. "No, I have been wearing it since we left Glossak for Skulka so why worry now?"

"Good point." Jerik said as he turned the tap on a cask. "Have you heard from Kejen and Trif?"

Overdulf gratefully accepted the offered mug. "I know they did get back to Sparent."

"I also heard you Northmarchers gave the Khaizani a good whipping!" Olsen yelled from the front.

"Place called Lamptra." Ovedulf said. "A ferocious battle I heard. Surprised them and stopped them in their tracks!" He wiped some ale off his beard and looked at Jerik. "The Sparent Brigade played a pretty big role."

Jerik's eyes widened. "Really? Do you think Kejen and Trif were there?"

Overdulf snorted and motioned for a refill. "What do you think? Kejen tried to take on the whole Argual, remember?"

"Lot of archers in this fight." Jerik said. "Do you think Trif is well?"

"Trif is no prairie flower. He can take care of himself." Overdulf said. "You know that. If anything, he may be more dangerous than his brother. You are never sure what that one is thinking. We could sure use someone like Kuran right now."

"I have a feeling the black shirts have been busy." Jerik observed.

"Indeed they have." Overdulf agreed. "They have done a lot of damage to the invaders. Sooner or later, they will strike something vital."

"What do you know about this 'Devil's outhouse' place?"

" 'Devil's Cradle' " Overdulf corrected with a mock blow to the side of Jerik's head. "It's a couple of hills with a saddle between them. North peak is higher than the south one. From the top, you can see everything in the surrounding area, down into the gullies and ravines. You can see out past Dunrovin and about that far in all directions."

"Why is this hill so important?"

"We have pulled the Khaizani into the Holmin with us." Overdulf updated his friend. "It is about a half step removed from a mountain range. Hit and run attacks on them all day and night. With any luck, we can erode them piecemeal. Maybe even crush them in there."

"From the hill, they can see where the ambushers are?" Jerik said. "Or at least it helps."

Ovedulf nodded. "Exactly. If they even make it that far."

"You saw that army." Jerik said. "Don't underestimate them. That is the mistake they made with you at Lamptra."

"I know better than that!" Overdulf laughed. "I am hoping that I don't have to fight in a battle with them. I have had quite enough thank you. On the other hand, anyone trying to take the place will fight more with the thorns this big..." he showed the Crown Prince a space about three inches between his thumb and forefinger, "...and some serious steepness."

"How many of us are going to be there?"

"A mighty hundred and fifty." Overdulf answered. "With you, two hundred."

"A hundred and fifty?" Jerik nearly yelled. "What about the rest of your brigade?"

"At Dunrovin just in case the Khaizani do make it through." Overdulf said. "If they do, there will be fewer of them, I will tell you that!"

Ovedulf continued. "If they take the Devil's Cradle, they can see out onto the plains and know our strength or get a good idea of it. If they do get out of the Holmin, they will find an army waiting for them."

"That is what makes the hill so important." Jerik said. "Is Dunrovin the only place they can come out?"

"Either Dunrovin or Busselmir." Overdulf said. "Armies waiting at both."

"Dividing your forces?" Jerik asked. "I do not like that. There has to be a way to channel the Khaizani one way or the other. Have your generals the same insight."

"I am sure they are." Overdulf assured his Sea-Farer friend. "No such hill near Busselmir. Having the Devil's Cradle would be a great advantage. Why else do you think we going to be there?"

"For a parade?" Jerik laughed.

"Tignall, the Commander of the whole Army, is pretty crafty. So is the King."

Jerik patted his friend's shoulder. *"All* of you Northmarcher buggers are crafty!"

General Yuan staggered wearily into his yurt and threw off his bloody, dust streaked armor, frustration seething from every pore. It had started again. Incessant raids, mostly at night but by day as well. After a week, he still found the nights were still the worst.

The Khaizani crossing of the Prania River and initial advance into the Holmin was strangely unopposed. That lulled the some Khaizani into complacency. A few even arrogantly presumed the Northmarchers disintegrated and ran in the face of the now bolstered army. Predictably, those were the ones who had not fought at Lamptra. Events were now proving them wrong.

The day spent crossing the river was quiet. Then the night erupted into a calliope of screams, thundering hooves and arrows flying from out of the dark. Again, horses bolted panicked and Khaizani soldiers chased shadows. The Khan ordered his army to continue advancing. Day or night, it was harder to hit a moving target.

The enemy that was allegedly retreating struck back time and time again. The attacks were constant. They never let up. They came from all directions at all times, fierce and withering. Many in the Northmarcher army called this area home and they knew the land well. They led the assaults masterfully, drawing blood with every blow.

The Khaizani continued to advance, harried and hammered at every turn, Northmarchers swarming all about them, stealthful shadowy forms just out of reach, ripping and slashing at the flanks. The Khaizani army at first floundered like a trapped moose in an Anker Mountain snowdrift, ripped and torn from marauding wolves. The wolves here though were plate mail and had crested helmets, riding on horseback or running on foot, bleeding the enemy with every attack. Formations were ravaged as the Northmarchers picked off the stragglers.

The Khaizani lashed out at their tormentors, sometimes landing blows too. Pursuing raiders in a foreign land at night, many Khaizani often ended up in dead ends or caught in fatal, vicious ambushes.

Unrelenting and intensely purposeful, the night attacks had no rhyme or reason to them. Northmarcher raiders were chased in maddening circles, seemingly disappearing and then reappearing in the rear to wreak more havoc. They seemed to be everywhere yet nowhere. Khaizani frustration grew and the soldiers of the Khan lashed out at anything that looked vaguely human. At one point, two Khaizani squads collided with each other and attacked, thinking the other was the hated enemy.

The Khan slipped back from the front of the column, dodging a couple of arrows he swore were meant for him. He found the rear no safer.

The Northmarchers felt their share of frustration too. They were determined to destroy the Khaizani army here in the Holmin. But Khaizan did not raise cowards and weaklings as warriors. Reflecting their impressive training and discipline, the Khaizani reasserted control among themselves and continued to advance.

The sun rose and a Demon Division trooper watched from behind a tree as Khaizani rear guard disappeared to the north. Roeth took off his helmet and spat on the ground. The objective was to shatter the Khaizani here in the Holmin and hopefully there would not be a battle on the other side. Now it looked as if there would be one. The Khaizani shrugged off the damage and moved on.

In the dark of that was after Midnight before dawn, while the Greater

Northern Army was still fighting its way through the Holmin, Bakhu and his comrades were ready to make their move against Northcross. The previous night, they had galloped across the steppes at breakneck speed and by day, the small unit took shelter off an abandoned path in the forest. There, the four Khaizani soldiers under Bakhu's command saw their commander approach a house and return with some supplies. Somewhere, somehow, Bakhu had made a friend here in this large, grand house east of the Northmarcher capital.

"Is she pretty?" one of Bakhu's men asked slyly.

"Get back to the business at hand." Bakhu said gruffly but not quite as harshly as he would with an ordinary soldier. After all, he had ridden with these men for years. Bakhu's comrade smiled to himself and remained on watch. He afforded himself a couple of looks at the rich fields surrounding their hiding place. Maybe after the war, the Khan, in his gratitude, would allow him to farm this rich and promising land.

Night fell and the lights of the city began to dim, flicker and disappear. The hour was almost here.

Bakhu silently climbed a tree and looked into Northcross, studying the street layout and looking for any guards. Their pattern was easy to predict. The elite officer signaled to his men and they set off with the Royal Castle of Northcross in their sights. His knife glinted in the moonlight. He studied its sharpness and honed the blade a little more with a sharpening stone. A delicate instrument to slash a fair, graceful neck. Bakhu quickly sheathed it and jumped on his horse. The five Khaizani troopers rode across the small stretch of plain in front of the Northmarcher capital city.

Some sixth sense suddenly tingled in Bakhu's mind. He drew to a sudden halt and quickly turned in the saddle, looking into the dark forests for something that was not there. Better safe than sorry. Satisfied there were not unfriendly eyes there, the mission continued. Even if there were, it was better to risk failure than to return without trying. Execution by his own Khan was not what he aspired to.

After stopping briefly to wrap their horses' hooves in cloth, the Khaizani silently cantered down the cobblestone streets, eyes fixed on the huge solid block shape of the Castle growing with each step. Somewhere beyond the Castle in the distant darkness on a hilltop stood the city's namesake, the huge iron cross standing guard over the city like a guardian.

Will your God protect you now, Northmarchers? Bakhu noticed a long time ago lightening struck things with no regard to the shaman's prayers. Why did holy men look to the sky for the gods? Bakhu wondered about that. No one could live there without falling. Even birds had to come to the ground sometime and no one had ever seen the gods walking among men.

Bakhu's active mind returned to his mission. He concentrated on the Castle, gauging its defenses, replaying the Castle's interior in his mind, remembering it from the time he was an emissary.

The closer the Khaizani got to the Castle, the warier Bakhu became. Where were the roving patrols he saw earlier? Maybe they were in the war far from here? After all, how could mere barbarians read the mind of the mighty Khan!

The Khaizani entered the city's Centre Park and found places to hide. Bakhu watched the two Northmarcher soldiers with the green, black and gold stripes on their armor at the front gate. "Palace Guards" they were called. Many of them former members of those black clothed demons giving the main Khaizani army trouble. Bakhu realized what he was wearing and wished he had not. Northmarcher Crouching Dragons? He did not like what that implied. Unthinkable! They were too far away for Bakhu to try lip reading. He could speak the language well enough but he would not trust trying to guess what they were saying without actually hearing any part of the conversation. With a salute that was less than crisp, the officer and enlisted man seemed to be carrying on a conversation with less than formal decorum. Whatever the officer said, it required the enlisted man's presence inside. And no one came forth to take the absent man's place!

The gate would not remain unguarded for long! It seemed to smell of a trap but it also seemed too obvious. There was no going back. The war could be over in less than an hour!

Leaving one man in the park, Bakhu and his three men started forward, crouching behind a line of shrubbery pointed at the Castle like an arrow at the heart of a target. They froze when one of the horses back in the park neighed. It carried. Very far. Bakhu glared back at the trees before continuing on. He did not see the man he left back there so at least he was hidden well.

Slowly, the Khaizani made their way forward, waiting for some sort of shout or even a hail of arrows. None came. Then the Khaizani soldier broke into an all out run, swords drawn and arrows notched.

Bakhu ripped open the guardhouse door and his sword cut only air. "You there." Bakhu told one of his archers. "Stay here and keep the escape route open."

Bakhu darted down the corridor and up a staircase he remembered from his previous trip here. His two remaining men, one with a bow and another with a sword, followed him, their footfalls quieter than a cat.

The Khaizani archer posted at the guardhouse leaned forward and looked into the Castle interior. He thought he heard the two soldiers from earlier walking back to the entrance. The archer began to draw his bow. Immediately a blinding white light materialized from the back of his head, courtesy of some blunt object.

Futilely, he tried to stand up and order his numbed fingers to retain a grip on the arrow while his bleary eyes tried to focus. Another blow sent him reeling and he never remembered hitting the floor.

"He is going to have a serious headache when he comes too." One Palace Guard said, cradling a club. He looked out to the park and saw another Palace Guard dragging a limp form out of the bushes by the feet. That one was trailing blood on the cobblestones. That was one Khaizani that would never leave Northcross. He looked down at the other. Odds were not looking too good for this one either.

Bakhu and his two men raced thorough the Great Hall, past tapestries and stone statues. He knew the royal bedchambers had to be in one of two places. Get to the first one. If that was not where Queen slept, then it was the other place. Speed was his best defense.

A day begins and a life ends Bakhu chortled. Then he shoved the thought out of his mind but then another embedded itself tantalizingly into his conscience. A live royal hostage is much more valuable than a dead one! Not only would *that* wreak havoc on the Northmarcher King but it would serve Bakhu well as a tool for a greater reward!

Bakhu ran down the hallway and shouted the long practiced phrase with the best Northmarcher accent he could muster. "My Queen! My Queen! There are attackers in the Castle!!!"

Bakhu lowered his shoulder, ready to knock open the doors ahead of him. Somehow he knew that this was the royal bedchamber. The door opened itself instead and the Khaizani elite trooper stopped in his tracks, staring at the business end of three Palace Guard pikes. Then he heard a sound above him. He did not know of the walkway above this hallway. Why would someone build that here? Now, he knew. At least a dozen Palace Guard archers had their bows trained on him and his men. Bakhu heard some more boots shuffling behind him.

Perlis, Commander of the Palace Guards, was one of the men with the pikes. "I know you understand me." he said slowly. "You are trapped in a hallway. There is no way out. Surrender and you will see your home again."

Bakhu could understand the situation quite well. Surrender and be tortured to death by these barbarians or be tortured to death by the Khan when his ever victorious army finally arrived. It did not take long for him to make his choice.

"Khaizan!!!" The elite Khaizani officer shouted as he lunged forward. Five arrows punched into his neck and exposed lower back. Bakhu convulsed once and fell after a step, dying loyal to his Khan until the very end. The death Bakhu prophesized turned out to be his own.

The two remaining Khaizani looked at the spreading pool of blood under their fallen leader. The Crouching Dragons were to prefer death to capture but that concept was easier to embrace in the abstract than to face in reality.

"Drop your weapons!" Roeth shouted

The Khaizani started at the sound, hesitated and took an unthinking step forward. Suddenly the hallway was filled with arrows. Perlis and his two men advanced forward and stabbed the fallen Khaizani to make sure they were fallen.

Perlis looked down at the fallen enemy. "They were brave, I have to give them that. If nothing else, at least you know they were the enemy." The Palace Guard Commander's demeanor suddenly, frightfully changed. "Bring him in here now! This very moment!"

Two Palace Guards appeared from a door behind Perlis. One was holding a rope tied to the neck of a bloodied blonde man who was having some trouble walking. The other Guard held a spear to his back to make sure he continued making the effort.

"Why hello your Lordship!" Perlis cackled. He did not even waste the effort of a mock bow on this man. If there was one thing in the world any Palace Guard hated, it was a traitor. "I am sorry we could not find accommodations suitable befitting your status on such a short notice."

The hate on Taetin's face was plain to see. Perlis did not care. A backhand across Taetin's face only confirmed the point.

Perlis yanked the rope and pulled the traitor forward. Taetin tried to resist but could find nothing to grip on the smooth wall. Perlis grabbed him by the hair and shoved him to the ground.

"Look at what your handiwork has wrought!" The Commander of the Palace Guards pointed at the dead Khaizani. "They should have never been near the Palace. Why are they here? Why are you here?"

"Why are we all here?" Taetin replied with more than a necessary dose of sarcasm. He was an arrogant one indeed. "Philosophers and monks have been asking that for centuries."

Perlis punched him in the jaw.

Another Palace Guard peeled the prisoner off the wall. "Answer the question and maybe the King will show mercy when he returns. Victorious, mind you."

Ruan, another one of Perlis's men stepped forward. "We found some interesting things out about our friend Taetin here."

"Do enlighten us." Perlis said, never taking his eyes off of Taetin. Desperate men did desperate things. "Unless Taetin wants to tell us himself."

Ruan waited for a few seconds and Taetin, of course, ventured nothing. "Well, first thing, his name is not Taetin. It's Torsovo."

"I see." Perlis grabbed Taetin/Torsovo's ear and lifted him up on his toes. "More than a coincidence he pushed Masovian ideas around." His tone of voice proclaimed loudly Perlis did not believe in coincidences. The Palace Guard Commander released the Masovian operative's ear. "Tell us everything. Everything right now and I promise to be your voice of mercy when the King returns."

Torsovo looked Perlis in the eyes and replied in clear accentless Northmarcher. "Your mother buggers goats."

Perlis tossed the rope up and over the balcony rail and pulled down with all of his weight. Torsovo struggled frantically but his feet were all ready off the ground. His hands instinctively went to his neck trying to get his fingers under the rope cutting into his throat but it was too no avail. One of Perlis's men helped his commander pull the rope down.

"Count slowly to one hundred before you let him down." Perlis left the task to man helping him. "You over there. Take over if his arms start to tighten."

Torsovo was still swinging and struggling as Perlis addressed the Palace Guard who had apprehended Taetin in the act of treason. "I am glad to see you restrained yourself and brought him in here instead of just his head."

The white-faced Guard managed to pry his eyes off of the now fading Torsovo. "Yes, sir. Your orders were to watch his house but not to move in unless enemy soldiers approached. How did you know he was in league with the Khaizani?"

"He seemed a little too chummy with the dead chap on the floor when he showed up here in early Spring." Perlis jerked a thumb at the deceased and punctured Bakhu. "More than just a little curious to merely meet someone from the East. Combine that with his rather obvious ambitions...."

That seemed to answer itself.

"We are still looking through some of the correspondence we found." The Palace Guard who was tasked with stalking Torsovo said to Perlis. "It seems he was also in contact with someone named Beafalo."

"Sounds Masovian too." Perlis grunted. A spy pretending to be a traitor. Perlis was not sure which was worse. The Commander of the Palace Guards could feel his teeth grind. "Good work, Ruan."

One more thing, sir." Ruan had one more question. "How long were you going to have us stay out there?"

The answer seemed fairly obvious to Perlis. "Until the end of the war if necessary."

Torsovo's clearly expired body hit the floor with a thump. Perlis spit on it for good measure. He looked up at one of his men on the walkway. "You say we did capture one Khaizani at the gate?"

The man nodded. "Yes we did. Knocked him out. They were not going to surrender. Probably been told we are going to eat them or something like that."

Perlis shook his head. "No, they don't look all that tasty."

The great thrust to cripple the Northmarch in one single savage thrust had failed.

GLOSSAK
BUSSELMIR
DUNROVIN
HOLMIN
DEVIL'S CRADLE
LAMPTRA
KRONKUS

Chapter 18

The news of the attempted assassination of his Queen reached King Fleston later that day by way of an exhausted rider and horse ridden near death.

"The Queen is well, my lord." The rider gulped in deep breathes. He waved off the water. "My horse first!" he said as any true Northmarcher would. Then he finally accepted water from Kergis and quaffed it. "She is well. Never in the Castle, behind the North Cross when it happened." The messenger was not aware he was spitting water on the King.

Fleston did not care. "She is well though!"

"Yes my King! Unscratched!" The rider said, finally able to stand up.

"And they call us *barbarians* ?!" Fleston shouted. He plucked his sword hanging off the wall. "I will kill the man who gave that order. I will challenge the Khan to fight me man to man!"

Tignall stood in his way. "No, my lordship. Do no such thing. That is only anger speaking."

Fleston glared at the man commanding his armies. For a second, Kergis thought Fleston was going to go through him but the King managed to see reason. Besides, Kergis was confident that Tignall could pin the King down easily enough long enough for the fit of temper to pass. The Commander of the Northmarcher Army had built his muscles up as a child working in rock quarries. Five decades later, the muscles looked to have lost little, if any, of their strength.

"If the Khan would use that sort of treachery to try to kill the Queen, do you really think he would not do the same to you out in the open?" Tignall said evenly. "We cannot afford to lose you."

The King threw his sword on the table. "I know, I know. I just want to kill that...." he tried to find a word to express his outrage, "...that, " The King gave up and his fist rocked the table.

"Destroy his army and the Khan dies with it." Kergis said.

The King just nodded and helped Tignall straighten up the map. "Let us destroy that army."

"We will not destroy them in the Holmin." Tignall said. "But they only have two ways out of there. The Khaizani will emerge out at either Busselmir or Dunrovin."

Kergis looked over at Tignall. "I will say Dunrovin."

Fleston's temper had cooled off. "Why Dunrovin? Busselmir is closer. They must know there is an army waiting for them when they come out. In their mind, fight the battle as close to Northcross as they can."

Tignall pointed at Dunrovin on the map. "The Khaizani know they will have a fight on their hands regardless of where they come out. True. This large hill called the Devil's Cradle, gives them a good view of Dunrovin. They can gauge our strength and plan a little instead of going in blind. The Khaizani do not want to refight Lamptra."

Fleston looked at the map trying to think, God forbid, like a Khaizani general. "What if they try to pretend they are going to Dunrovin but emerge out at Busselmir?"

"They will have us on their back." Tignall said. "The Khaizani may think they can race to Northcross ahead of us but what happens when they get there? Arnles is waiting for them and the Khaizani siege equipment is far away at Kronkus. They have to fight us in order to go anywhere."

"A solid argument." The King admitted.

"The Khaizani cannot fool us nor will they try." Kergis added. "We are in the Holmin with them. Taking the Devil's Cradle helps them in a battle at Dunrovin. The Khaizani cannot sneak up on it and we cannot send a whole army in after them."

"Then Dunrovin it is." Fleston said. "I was rather hoping they would fall apart in the Holmin."

"It would have made our lives much easier." Kergis agreed. "But it is as God wills it."

Fleston did not take the royal prerogative of taking the last word. There was nothing else to say and a lot to do.

The city of Glossak's contribution to this war thinned out as various groups peeled off to meet with the main army at Dunrovin while others went into the Holmin to help grind down the enemy just a bit more. Another smaller force, including Jerik's Sea-Farers and Overdulf, scaled the Devil's Cradle, looking for the person in charge of the men all ready occupying it.

A soldier, probably a big farm boy in peacetime, was hauling rocks to a catapult. Jerik and Overdulf lent a hand and found the man they were looking for.

"I am Lif, Captain of the Dunrovin militia." A tall, red haired Northmarcher held out his hand. "Do you understand what I am saying?"

"Probably better after five ales or so." Jerik answered back in Lif's birth language. "My men and I are at your disposal."

"Very good." Lif said. He seemed ready to jump and run down the hill and back up again. Lif shouted at some men servicing a catapult and then brought his attention back to Jerik. "We will need all the help we can get. The Khaizani are going to want this hill. They will want it badly."

"And we are going to make sure they don't get it." Jerik grinned. He held up his fist. "They don't want to get too close!"

Before Lif could answer, he was cut off by a loud sounding "thwack" and Jerik found himself looking at a head sized rock flying into some ravine in the Holmin below.

Lif motioned for Jerik and Overdulf to follow and he ran over to the catapult. "We have been heaving rocks all about this morning, recording angles and distances and such!" Then he dashed off to another catapult a few yards away. "Step lively, you two!"

"He does move about, eh?" Jerik said to Overdulf.

"I thought my running days were over and then I ended up with you and Kejen in the Ankers. Now I am still running around." Overdulf muttered. "At least it is not uphill for days at a time!"

Another rock flew into the Holmin. Lif patted the man at the lever on the head and ran off to still another catapult. He pointed out into the broken terrain. "Where do you want this rock to go? Be quick about it!"

Jerik pointed at a small hill in the distance before he even stopped.

"That one it is!" Lif said to the catapult crew. "On second thought, drop a rock on that swell of ground to the left. Make it a challenge!"

Immediately, three soldiers wedged a log under the catapult frame and lifted, using the log to move their machine into position. Then they dropped the log and scrambled out of the way as another rock sailed into the crystal blue skies. Jerik and Overdulf's eyes followed its arc until it disappeared into the trees. The sound of cracking tree limbs and a soft thud announced the rock landed where Lif said it would. On target.

"Small ones for practice." Lif explained. "And we have more than just rocks. They tell me you, Overdulf, are responsible for that. Explosive powders and ways to make pitch burn even hotter!"

"Before I was a trapper, I worked the mines for a while as a boy." Overdulf said. "In the mountains, you learn a lot about the earth and what makes it up."

Jerik looked over at his friend from Glossak. He did not know that about Overdulf. "So you decided you would rather walk over the mountains then under them."

Overdulf nodded. "I did not want to walk stooped over all day and forget what the Sun looked like."

"Nor have one of the mountains fall on you." Jerik laughed. "I bet that had something to do with it!"

Lif interjected himself into the conversation. "You two and the rest of the Sea-Farers are going to be on the forward slope to keep the Khaizani off the hill as we drop rocks and other, ah, things on them."

"That we will!" Jerik promised. "This hill is the last thing a lot of those invaders will see!"

"Gordno is the man you want to see." Lif then ran off to inflict himself on someone else.

"Sluggish, isn't he?" Jerik said dryly.

The man named Gordno was shoveling dirt onto some rocks in a trench. "Some nasty surprises for our friends if they stick their nose here. Are you the Sea-Farer Lif told me about?"

Jerik reached down and helped Gordno out of the trench. "He does get around, does he not?"

Gordno laughed and brushed off his hand on his all ready dirty pants. His dark hair looked darker from the dirt that was undoubtedly in it. His even darker eyes seemed to suck in the sunlight all around him. Although he was clean-shaven like most people (most non-Sea-Farers, Jerik thought, Overdulf an exception of course), his labors today made it seem as if he had an earthen beard. "I have known Lif since we were this tall." He held his hand about a foot off the ground. "He has the energy of three men. Lif gets more done before noon than most do all day. And half the next day! He is a good man to have here."

"Where do you want us?" Jerik asked.

Gordno walked over to a part of the hill that no one was on. After meeting Lif, walking seemed more like a treat. Whereas Lif was slight and quick moving, Gordno was stocky and moved with heavier feet. Jerik knew from experience though, people like that could move faster then you thought. He just seemed to be saving his strength for the Khaizani.

"This is the smoothest part of the Devil's Cradle." Gordno said.

"Right here on the saddle between the north and south peaks." Jerik looked down the slope and saw there were people working here after all. Gordno looked over the area and nodded. "Hidden traps will not stop them but it will slow them down!"

"I will take all the help I can get." Jerik agreed.

"A wise man." Gordno chuckled. He turned his attention to Overdulf. "I am going to be here on the hilltop with a reserve to go where trouble might spring. You are going to be my runner."

"Just my luck." Overdulf said. "More running."

Lif was in command of the Devil's Cradle. On the other side of the country, another red-haired Northmarcher soldier studied the Masovian border. Not on a map but rather the border itself. Arnles stood next to one of the large stones that divided the land between the Northmarch and Masovia. One side was proudly painted in stripes of black, gold and green. The other sported more gaudy red, gold and blue. A line of stones marched on endlessly into the distance. Most countries put them a mile apart. Here, they were a hundred yards apart. The Masovians could not use the excuse they had crossed the border by accident. Arnles was not worried about any "accidental" crossings unless they involved a whole army. With what happened at the Royal Castle at Northcross, Arnles began to think maybe a solid wall would be a better option. Were the Masovians cooperating with Khaizan? Perlis wrote in his dispatch that the answer to that question was "no." Torsovo, hopefully roasting in Hades at this moment, saw an opportunity. Was it for him or Masovia was another question. A question that was not going to be answered. Perlis had ended that threat and in doing so perhaps avoided a future pitfall. Torsovo was there, complete with a base of sorts, to do the same thing the Khaizani were attempting in the event of a future war between the Northmarch and Masovia. Arnles was worried and that set of events did not help. With his kingdom fully embroiled in a war with Khaizan, the ever dangerous Masovian border was not as well defended as it usually was. The Masovians stayed scrupulously on their side. Arnles knew they were simply trying to determine why the Northmarchers suddenly stripped the border. They might have thought at first it was some sort of trap. With most of his forces under the command of Kergis in the east fighting the Khaizani, Arnles fervently hoped the Masovians would not take the bait that was not there! By all indications, they too knew about the Eastern invasion. Perhaps they also saw the danger. It would take quite a leap of imagination for a Masovian, Arnles snorted, but it seemed to have happened. How ironic, the general thought, the Northmarch was defending Masovia from attack! That opened the door to another danger though. Once the Khaizani were defeated, would Masovia attack while Northmarcher forces were on the other side of the country? Like any good Northmarcher, Arnles refused to consider the possibility of a Khaizani victory. Whatever happened, he would deal with it, whatever it was. Ever since he had been in the Army, Arnles had prepared to fight and defeat Masovia in battle. In a day full of ironies, he contemplated one more. His greatest victory over the Masovians would be not having to fight them.

Day faded into night and all across the world, eyes focused on the top half of the map. Word of the Khaizani invasion had spread as far north as Warron where a worried King feared for his Crown Prince son and as far as the kingdoms and empires on the shores of the Southern Sea. In Asrine, the Church looked nervously northeast while frantically looking through Biblical passages for guidance, deliverance or confirmation that the end of the world had indeed arrived as promised in Revelations. The rulers of Masovia sat worried on their throne. A great opportunity had arrived to hurt their hated Northmarcher rivals but the danger from the East seemed much, much worse. Some factions in the court even urged reconciliation, temporary of course, with Northcross to fight the greater foe. In the end, they opted for waiting events out. Surely, Masovia was vast enough and powerful enough to defeat horseman from the other side of the world. The other faction stayed quiet, not wanting to be crucified upside down for pointing out that course of action would ensure Regalwood would find itself under Khaizani heels. It was very odd for anyone in Regalwood to wish the Northmarchers luck. Even the Thenrosian Empire was hearing rumors of strange happenings and a great war in the distant north. It seemed too far from imperial borders to be threat but Khaizan was not letting mere distance deter it. The Emperor looked out of a window facing north and shuddered.

Two architects of the Emperor's worries looked over the map in a yurt in the middle of the Holmin. Even here in the Khan's inner sanctum, the sounds of Northmarcher raiders penetrated. The Khan and the man commanding the Greater Northern Army saw the same thing on paper but somehow they ended up with different opinions. The Khan ruled so his was the one that mattered. Still, he gave the General the courtesy of explaining his plans. After all, General Yuan would have to carry them out.

"Yes, General." The Khan began, "There are only two ways out of this nightmare of hills and hidden vallies. A nothing village called Busselmir and another collection of mud huts called Dunrovin."

Yuan smiled at that. In spite of all that had happened, the Khan's contempt for his Northmarcher enemy remained. Through his iron will, the Khaizani Army had fought its way through the Holmin and would emerge out on the steppes intact. He fought the barbarians at their own game on their own ground. Yuan was not sure how much strength the Khaizani army had lost in the grinding campaign of attrition but it pride, toughness and resolution was still in one piece. The army's morale was still high. They wanted to come to grips with the enemy. Enough of these fleabites, Fleston, come out and fight like a man! He shouted those words the other night at the hills and his soldier cheered! They were ready to fight. So was he. All Yuan wanted to do was to know what direction to ride in.

The Khan could see Yuan lusted for battle. The setback at Lamptra and this annoying hill climbing had only served to spur the Khaizani on further. The soldiers of Khaizan wanted the enemy to show his face.

"If we come out at Busselmir, we do so blind." The Khan said. "Just like Lamptra. Unlike that place, here we have to run reconnaissance with our whole army. You lose whole scout troops here. Near Dunrovin however, is this hill." The Khan looked closely at the foreign name. "Devil's Cradle" did not translate well into Khaizani so he gave it a name. "The Twin Hills. It is isolated from any Northmarcher army waiting at Dunrovin. When we take this hill, we can see what is waiting for us. What is your opinion, General?"

It was a good rule of thumb to carefully think about what you were going to say in front to the Khan. In military matters, you could stretch the rules of decorum somewhat. Still, Yuan looked at the map, buying some time to assemble what he wanted to say.

"I think the Northmarchers can see it would be most advantageous for us to come out at Dunrovin too, my Khan."

"Are you telling me it is better to march blind into this Busselmir place like you did at Lamptra?" The Khan inquired with a bit of anger creeping into his voice.

"Yes, my Khan."

The Khan folded his arms over his chest and stared at his general. "Tell me where I am wrong, sirrah." The Khan's omnipresent bodyguards looked more menacing than usual today in their lacquered armor. The wide neckguards of their helmets reminded the general of a cobra's hooded neck. Yuan did the only thing a general could do when insulted by the Khan. Ignore it. He pressed on.

"We have been fighting their fight, my Khan." Yuan said. He was not a coward. No Khaizani was. Khan or no Khan, Yuan's loyalty was to Khaizan. Soldiers came and went, so did Khans but the Khanate lived forever. The future of that survival depended on victory and victory alone. "They caught us off guard, with treachery at Lamptra and we have fought them here in the Holmin."

"I am aware of that." The Khan said. He seemed ready to turn his human bloodhounds loose on his general any second now. The armor that looked like it was made of large square scales shined a bit closer. Yuan stood up straighter. His armor looked as strong as theirs too!

"We have not been able to fight effectively, fight the Khaizani way!" Yuan said. "If we can do that, we will beat them."

"And how do we do that?" Yuan did not like how that sounded but now did not care. It was oddly liberating.

"We attack the Twin Hills with a small force to make them think we are committing to Dunrovin but attack with our main force at Busselmir!" Yuan said, conviction growing with every word.

The Khan looked at the map and traced the routes to both villages with his finger. It stopped at the Devil's Cradle. It moved to Busselmir. Then it moved back to Dunrovin. And stopped. Yuan felt his spirits sink. At least his sword was ready to come out of the sheath. With luck he can take both of these battle-shy virgins called bodyguards.

"If we march out of this place at Dunrovin, they will move up and again be too close for us to use the full force of our horse archers." Yuan used his last ditch argument.

The Khan's hand came up slowly. To Yuan's carefully concealed surprise, the bodyguards took a step back. He could swear he heard them growl in frustration.

"What you say makes a great deal of sense." The Khan said. Yuan began to hope again. "However...." Yuan knew what was coming next. At least he did not have to face the specter of execution. What followed might have been worse however. "We will smash the barbarians at Dunrovin. They wait for us there and we must crush them at their own game!"

"My Khan!" Yuan exclaimed. The bodyguard's armor creaked as they shifted their stances and even the Khan's eyes rounded a bit at the general's tone of voice. "We have beaten them at their own game here in the Holmin! They tried to shake us to pieces and failed!"

The Khan stood up. "Do not use that tone of voice with me!"

General Yuan flinched. It was not fear of his Khan that made him do so. It was something much deadlier. Fear of defeat. A few weeks ago, Yuan knew Khaizan was stronger than any nation in the world. Now, he only thought it was. In fighting the Northmarchers, the Khaizani could not rely on mere brutish strength. They needed to use everything at their disposal. The Khan evidently thought otherwise.

"I am Khan!" Yuan's sovereign lord shouted. "I command here. I command you! Is that clear, General?"

"Yes, my Khan." Yuan said softly.

"Is that clear?" The Khan shouted again in a tone that said he had better not repeat himself.

"Yes, my Khan!" The General said forcefully.

The General remained in a ramrod straight posture as the Khan walked up to him. Yuan did not shiver. His spine was made of metal too. He kept his uneasiness hidden as well. It was not that easy to do when the Khan started speaking nose to nose. It was not just his presence but an aura. An aura of barely restrained fury, the sort of raw energy that drove the army forward in the face of countless blood-draining raids. The sort of almost elemental drive that did not seem human.

"I am the Khan." he said slowly between clenched teeth. "I will say something one more time. It is of the utmost importance that we show these barbarians that whatever they try will be futile. It does not matter what they try or how they try or even where. Our power must be seen as overwhelming."

The Khan turned his back. "Dismissed."

Yuan left the yurt, walked a bit and then stopped to look up at the sky. Could the Khaizani win at Dunrovin? He was sure they could but it was riskier and harder than his plan. The fact it was harder and riskier said a lot about the enemy they were fighting. For the first time, the General realized that Khaizan could very well lose this war. And why? Because the Khan refused to follow a plan that was not his. Yuan shook his head. Sometimes it did not matter who had better archers or cavalry or better generals. Vanity could be a destructive weapon too.

The Khan grunted and clenched his fists. How dare one of his generals tell him he was wrong?! This accursed land was wearing the polish off even the Khaizani Army. Still, Yuan was a good general and he seemed quite popular with the army. Sacking him or even arranging an accident now would not be a good idea. He issued an order to one of his functionaries. The General would have someone watching him. Just in case he had some delusion that he was more indispensable to Khaizan than even its Khan. He picked up the Birthright Sword for the first time in a while. The Khan was not thinking about taking Yuan's head with it. Lately, he had become increasingly uneasy holding this sword. He was not sure why but it seemed as if the sword itself loathed being in his hands. It was a feeling he had never had until he crossed the Blieben River. The sword's clearly Western origin did little to put the Khan's mind at ease.

Another bodyguard brought in General Hortai. After the man finished his prostrations, the Khan regarded him for a few seconds. He was Yuan's second in command. He was an able officer, a little younger but whatever he lacked in experience had been made up at Lamptra and in the Holmin.

"What will the situation be after Dunrovin?" The Khan asked.

"There is nothing between us and Northcross, my Khan." Hortai said. "We may have to swing a bit to the north to avoid any Northmarcher formations in the Holmin."

"Very well." The Khan agreed. "Do you think we should attack at Busselmir or Dunrovin?"

"We will attack and destroy the barbarians at the place you command us to, my Khan." Hortai said.

The Khan knew he had found the man to replace Yuan when the time came. "I see great things in store for you, General. I want you to be as familiar with the plans for Dunrovin as General Yuan is. The Northmarchers have shown a tendency to try to decapitate our army. If the cursed barbarians somehow get to General Yuan, you will have to lead. I know you will do well."

"Yes, my Khan!" The General's posture was straighter than a pine tree.

The Khan dismissed him and returned his attention to the map. After Dunrovin, the path to Northcross was open. Then the Khaizani would have to settle in for winter quarters, the Khan frowned. After Lamptra, the bruising Holmin campaign and what promised to be another big battle in the next few days, even the Khaizani Army would have to stop to rest and regroup. And they would need reinforcements. Guerilla attacks were certain to be coming out of the Ankers not only in winter but for years to come. At least one of those raids would provide cover for Yuan's demise, he grinned. All of this would come to pass if the Khaizani won at Dunrovin.

Then the Khan shuddered. He just used the word *if*! IF the Khaizani won?! He angrily kicked a crate. This war was turning out to be more than anyone had bargained for.

Two Demon Division soldiers panted as they ran up the north slope of the Devil's Cradle. Their black armor was scarred and the shirts looked more brown than black from ground in dirt and white from salt left from sweat but their dirty faces said a different story.

"We have hurt them!" One shouted to Lif.

"So you came all the way up here to tell me?" he asked.

Both of Fleston's Demons laughed. "That and to tell you they are here. Not as may as there once were but enough."

"That was what I thought" Lif said with a mischievous grin. "We are ready for them. When this is over we can build another hill made up of dead Khaizani!"

Both Demon Division soldiers clapped. They helped themselves to some water and disappeared into the trees to the north. Whether they were going to whittle down the number of Khaizani a bit more for Lif or gathering together at Dunrovin was hard to say. Demon Division soldiers never talked about their missions.

Jerik watched them from a distance. He saw in their fierce loping strides the unbelievable strength and determination of Kuran. What their brother-in-arms had done at the Argual still amazed Jerik. It seemed so long ago. If Kuran had been unleashed on the Khaizani, Jerik was sure this war would have been over a long time ago. Jerik looked over at his men resting and looking down the hill for any interlopers. Sea-Farers were good soldiers too. The Khan's men would find out soon enough. Jerik saw no point in going to Lif. Lif, predictably, ran over to him to share what his comrades in black said.

Jerik grinned and walked up to where the slope began. He held up his ax for those down there to see. I am here! He was declaring.

"Is that a good idea to stand silhouetted like that?" Lif asked.

"The Khaizani arrow supposed to kill me missed back at the Blieben." Jerik snorted. "I want them to come up here and fight me eye to eye."

His Sea-Farers agreed, loudly and in some cases obscenely. It did not take much to get a Sea-Farer to go into battle.

Lif smiled and looked at Jerik's men and then at their leader. He patted Jerik on the shoulder. "I want to kill a lot of them too. I hope you kill a lot of them. Maybe more. That way I do not have to work so much."

Jerik laughed and watched Lif run off to check on something. He was a bit strange but he was ready too. Jerik hoped the Khaizani would not keep them waiting. They moved and moved quickly.

Jerik cradled his ax and stared back down into the trees with an intensity that was truly frightening. Even Olsen would not approach the Crown Prince right this moment.

His leg twinged a little but had healed nicely. No one understood the concept of revenge better than a *Locklannigh.* Don't keep me waiting, Jerik thought. He looked forward to paying back this debt.

Chapter 19

The Khaizani Army marched northward, winding its way between the hills. For the first time since they had entered this trap called the Holmin, the Northmarcher raids that had thinned their ranks and ripped isolated formations to pieces were absent. Noticeably absent. Suspiciously absent.

But they are here, General Yuan said to himself as he looked up into the forested hills. He could feel the eyes upon him. They are definitely here and they are watching us. It was just most of them were assembling at Dunrovin, the General knew. If only the Khaizani Greater Northern Army was big enough to attack both Busselmir and Dunrovin at once he lamented. He knew it was not fair to blame anyone for that. No one, no one in Khaizan at any rate, expected to fight the Northmarchers. The thrust of the great Western conquest was supposed to rip through Nyhissia. Now it all hinged on what happened here.

Kronkus still held. That was not unexpected. In fact, according to the original Khaizani plan, that was expected and a positive development. It drew all of the Nyhissians together in one place. And it pulled Verrentian forces eastward as the Greater South Army suddenly appeared in *their* rear area! The Greater North Army was supposed to be in the middle of Masovia by now if not on the shores of the Great Sea. Lamptra and the Northmarcher treachery committed there changed everything. For the worst. The ongoing siege of Kronkus was now pinning the Khaizani in place.

If his army could win this battle, it was still unlikely this barbarian kingdom could be subdued by the end of summer. The Greater North Army was woefully short of supplies and, soon, reinforcements. Then the General nearly fell off his horse. *If* his army could win this battle? Yuan cursed himself for the doubt creeping into his mind. This war was costing Khaizan dearly in ways no one could have possibly imagined.

Some of those eyes watching the Khaizani were on the summit of the Devil's Cradle. They did not bother to hide themselves. If anything, Lif announced the Northmarcher presence by launching some burning pitch from the large trebuchets at the Khaizani. He was not sure he had the range to reach the invaders but the idea of setting fires around them was irresistible.

Balls of flame crashed into trees not far from the marching army. The

Khaizani did not panic or even show concern Lif knew they had to feel. The burning trees and drifting smoke had to at least make them feel uncomfortable.

Yuan growled deep in this throat. The arrogant barbarians on that hill were going to pay. Khaizani troops were all ready starting to climb that hill to clear if of the vermin occupying it.

Fleston and Tignall saw it at the same time. The huge Northmarcher banner on top of the Devil's Cradle was lowering. That was the signal that the Khaizani Army was concentrated on that part of the Holmin. The small forest fire only added to that confirmation. Whoever commanded that hill must have enjoyed hurling fire about. Or maybe he hated trees. Fleston did not know or care. Tignall was in motion sending runners to and fro. The orders were the same. Every Northmarcher who could walk was to converge here at Dunrovin. The brigades at Busselmir would soon be here and even more would be coming from Northcross the very second Wilnef got the word. The King of the Northmarch was not merely going to fight and defeat the Khaizani Army. He was determined to utterly destroy it.

It was still dark when a couple of Khaizani forward scouts gingerly picked their way up the west side of the Cradle's smaller hill. They were quietly dismantling traps. So were the many other scouts on the hillsides at the moment. This pair approached the berm on the hilltop. Carefully, the two scouts crawled through the thorns and under some tripwires. They reached the top and waited, listening. Northmarchers never slept on guard, another startling similarity they shared with the Khan's men. Based on what the Khaizani knew of Sea-Farers though, they were not habitually early risers.

Slowly, the Khaizani soldier lifted his head over the berm's edge---

---And lost it with a quick, clean, decapitating swing of a Warron battle ax.

"Head's up!" Jerik shouted, beginning his part of this war with a very bad pun. "Men of Warron!!!", the old battle cry rang out very far from home. The Crown Prince of Warren leapt over the beam and charged downhill, flowed by a mob of howling, bearded *Locklannigh.*

"Stop!" Gordno yelled, despite knowing Sea-Farers in full bloodlust were not going to listen to anyone. Gordno's men were all ready moving the catapults. Sea-Farers in full bloodlust probably could not listen to anyone.

The second Khaizani stood up and thrust his sword forward. Jerik dodged it and shoved the stabbing point of his massive ax through the man's throat. The downhill charge continued unabated. Jerik's mind wondered why there did not seem to be that many Khaizani on the hillside.

Sven brought a huge broadsword down on another of the Khan's soldiers and a wild cry escaped from his lips.

Then the Khaizani archers opened up on them.

Jerik barely got his shield up in time as three of those barbed arrows punched through it but stayed stuck in the boss. He heard Sven screamed next to him as two arrows struck, one in the shoulder and another right in the hip. Five of Jerik's other countrymen were not as lucky as the rain of arrows left most of the hillside studded with shafts that punched disturbingly deep into the soil.

"Back! Back!" Jerik roared as a second volley rained down hatefully. Jerik yanked Sven up by his yellow hair, grabbed an arm and dragged him up the hill. The Crown Price saw three more of his men fall and a fourth, in full blinded fury, continue running straight for the Khaizani. Amazingly, the Easterners did not cut him down before he plunged into their treeline screaming like a man possessed. Unfortunately, he did not come out.

Jerik heard a familiar "thuck" notice and saw a rock hurtling into that same treeline. If he could not save his berserker, maybe his Northmarcher allies could avenge him. Jerik practically threw his second-in-command over the berm and crouched behind it as another Khaizani volley rained down.

On the other side of the berm, Overdulf tended to a wounded Sea-Farer who was loudly insisting that the arrow transfixed into his forearm was not worse than any half dozen tavern fights he could name.

Overdulf broke off the arrow and slowly removed the shaft. "Only a half dozen you say? Disgracefully low number for a Sea-Farer!" The man burst out laughing. Probably covering for a scream, Jerik thought. At least he looked ready to fight on.

"It's not deep." Jerik said to Olsen. He handed his friend a bottle of ale. "Drink this."

Olsen spat half of it out when his liege yanked the arrow out of his shoulder. "That hurt worse then when it went in!"

"That is why I am not going to punch you for spitting up on the side of my head!" Jerik laughed. "Now I am going to go after the one in your hip. It is going to hurt so get ready."

"Do it all ready!" Olsen growled.

With a quick jerk, the arrow came out. Olsen yelled accusing Jerik's mother of unnatural desires but seem no worse or wear. It was not a deep wound and it only bounced off the bone.

The Khaizani barrage lifted but Gordno did not take any chances with exposing himself. He crawled over and scowled at Jerik. "I guess you learned your lesson. Do not charge these people head on!"

The big Sea-Farer rolled his eyes and grunted an acknowledgement. He emptied the rest of Olsen's ale, remained crouched behind the berm and threw the bottle at the unseen Khaizani.

"If you left a little in there, you would have had good ballast." Gordno said.

"I should hate to waste good ale on those people!" Jerik countered with the argument to end all arguments.

"Everyone get ready! You know they are coming soon!" Gordno shouted.

Northmarcher archers cheered and soldiers beat on the boss of their shields. Not to be outdone, the Sea-Farers joined in. The prospect of close in fighting seemed more promising than charging into arrows.

The Khaizani did not leave them disappointed.

From the west, east and south, Khaizani arrows hurtled up out of the Holmin. Khaizani dismounted infantry swarmed out of the trees with deadly intent.

Northmarcher bowmen braved the Khaizani hail. Their bows sang and cut apart the first row of attackers. It seemed like Lamptra all over again. Unlike Lamptra, there were plenty of places on the Devil's Cradle to hide. This time, they could advance piecemeal behind whatever shelter nature offered. There was a price to pay for that shelter however. Bear traps lay behind boulders and hung from shrub branches. In other places, the ground gave way from beneath the attackers, who found wooden spikes driving into their feet and lower legs. Screams of pain rose above those of fury. Still they came.

The Northmarchers sent a couple of more volleys into the attackers but it barely slowed them. The Sea-Farers and Northmarcher infantry steeled themselves. A glance in the other direction revealed the northern hill of the Devil's Cradle was under attack too. Lif was going to be very busy.

Gordno's catapults and trebuchets were hurtling rocks and burning pitch into the treeline where the Khaizani had massed their archers. Another difference from Lamptra, he mused. There the Khaizani archers had to divide their attention between Lamptra Hill and avoiding getting hacked to death from Northmarcher cavalry. Here, they could give the Devil's Cradle all of their attention.

The Khaizani pushed past the thorns and traps and charged out into the final thirty cleared feet. The archers on the Cradle turned their full might on the first unfortunate rows that emerged howling from the shrubs. Even in the face of massed archery from point blank range, Khaizani discipline remained superb. They charged uphill with courage, speed and conviction that seemed unreal.

Gordno picked up a sword and ran toward the slope the Khaizani would breech first. Jerik was all ready there, at the head of an iron wedge of *Locklannigh* eager to fight the enemy up close and avenge their fallen comrades.

The rain of Khaizani arrows stopped abruptly and Jerik charged, Northmarchers and Sea-Farers following him together over the edge of the berm.

The massive axes bit into the first Khaizani row all ready savaged by the Northmarcher archers. Blood and bone fragments sprayed over the immediate area as the impact stalled the Khaizani advance.

The Sea-Farers held their ground, punishing their Khaizani opponents in the toe to toe slugfest. *Locklannigh* fell victim to Khaizani swords and cudgels too but the Sea-Farers still held the higher ground. Northmarcher reinforcements cancelled out the follow on Khaizani.

"South slope! South slope collapsing!" Gordno heard someone yell. Catapult and trebuchet crewmen snatched up weapons and ran for the threatened sector. A few of the Northmarchers on the back of the Sea-Farer charge turned and ran to help out the others.

The Khaizani climbed over the row of boulders Gordno set there to shore up the defenses. It slowed the Khaizani but did not stop them. That was all he needed. The crewmen chopped down the enemy that made it over the obstructions. The rest could not climb over and fight at the same time. The venerable south slope had been held.

Jerik found himself locked in single combat against a particularly skilled Khaizani swordsman. The Khaizani forces retreated down the hill a few feet and the Northmarchers and their Sea-Farer allies pulled few feet up.

Jerik and the Khaizani swordsman regarded each other for a few seconds, aware that all were watching them.

"Do not let him fool you into charging!" A bandaged but still very much in the fight Olsen shouted. "Stay uphill!"

Jerik and his opponent carefully slinked forward as both sides cheered their champions. Jerik halted first, not wanting to give up his uphill advantage. The usual circling before a fight did not seem wise in this place.

The Khaizani feinted one way and swung up and over with his curved sword. Jerik blocked it with the handle of his ax and tried, in the same motion, swing and connect with the Khaizani's head. He missed and the Khaizani landed a knee in Jerik's side. Jerik growled and swung his massive blade at his enemy's knees. The Khaizan easily jumped over it and landed a foot right on the Sea-Farer's chest. This soldier of Khaizan had a good sense of balance. After the kick sent Jerik staggering backward, he lunged forward and brought his sword down for the kill.

Jerik had always been a good actor. The kick to the chest had been well aimed and had some force behind it but kicking uphill was always hard. The Crown Prince staggered but did not fall. For some reason, people wanted to end fights with a massive killing blow. The Khaizani were human too. Instead of stabbing directly at a falling opponent, the soldier of the Khan gave into the temptation of putting everything into one blow.

Jerik twisted to one side as the sword brushed by, burying itself into the dirt. One of his large feet came down on the flat of the blade while a massive fist connected with the Khaizani's jaw.

The man spun down the hill, bouncing over the rocks, rolling into his own comrades who finally halted his progress. Jerik picked up his opponent's sword and tossed it in the direction of the Khaizani. Jerik bowed in his direction. He had been a worthy opponent.

The compliment was not returned. Instead, he picked up his sword and shouted something at the Sea-Farer. Jerik was in a combat stance when he heard the familiar rush of several arrows fly past him. The onrushing Khaizani was dropped like a rock. Jerik did not wait around for what he knew was coming next. Khaizani arrows fell from the sky right as he dove over the berm.

"I guess I should thank you!" Jerik yelled at the Northmarchers crouched behind the berms. "I should have known they would try to cut me down like you did him. If we live through this, all of you get a pint on me!"

The Khaizani barrage against the Devil's Cradle soon became a desultory drizzle that did nothing useful except make the Northmarchers and Sea-Farers at the top a little more conscience of where they were walking. The upper peak weathered the morning attack easily enough due to its height but Lif sent word that the main Khaizani army had passed by, its path seeming to be Dunrovin.

Jerik could see into Dunrovin from here. He could also see the Northmarcher army assembling in the village from here too. That would explain why the Khaizani wanted this hill. They wanted to get some idea of what was waiting for them when they finally emerged from the Holmin. You invaded someone else's country, what do you expect to have waiting for you, Jerik silently asked the soldiers of Khaizan.

"Here they come again!". The shout was presaged by another storm of arrows. Screams said some of Gordno's men were caught in the open. Jerik ran with his shield over his head to the berm. Risking catching an arrow in the face, he looked over and saw the Khaizani emerging out of the trees and shrubs and from behind rocks, shouting and waving swords, spears and cudgels. They did not seem as numerous this time around, Jerik thought. The advancing soldiers of Khaizan swallowed up those fallen in the first charge and again Northmarcher bows sang out their fatal notes. Suddenly there were a couple of explosions as flaming pitch ripped into the Khaizani line. Gordno or Lif had figured out the right angle for using the trebuchets. The center of the advance staggered a bit but the wings continued on. Khaizani arrows still fell from the sky keeping heads down.

"South slope again!" a Northmarcher over there yelled. Jerik again held his shield over his head and ran. He heard one of his fellow *Locklannigh* behind him hit the dirt in ominous silence.

"Looks like every one of those people are over here!" Olsen exclaimed. No wonder there were not as many Khaizani charging the west slope. Immolation with burning oil and pitch ensured there would be fewer.

The defenders on the south slopes were going to be overwhelmed. The Khaizani had climbed over the boulders that were the main defenses in sufficient numbers this time.

"Men of Warron!!!" The bearded men with the horned helmets, battle axes and broadswords ripped into the Khaizani sweeping the Northmarcher defenders away. The Warronites pushed them back, crushing some of the Khaizani against the boulders but they stood their ground, striking back at those resisting the will of the Khan. Sea-Farers fell too and the Khaizani stiffened, held and began pushing the Sea-Farers back.

Two Northmarchers locked their shields and a third held his over Gordno as he picked up a rope running along the ground in the direction of the now Khaizani owned boulders. He gave it a good yank. Other Northmarchers did the same with other ropes running in the same direction. The Khan's soldiers surging triumphantly up the hillside saw the boulders start to roll forward.

Jerik, even though he was in the middle of the battle, saw the boulders start to disappear over the edge, one by one. The screams and shouts of the

Khaizani not yet on the top of the Cradle's lower peak said they were not going to reach it

They were facing a charge that could not be stopped.. Unable to turn or get out of the way, the Khaizani did what was only human. They tried to dodge the runaway boulders or even push and divert their path. It was to no avail. The soldiers were massed together too tightly. The boulders smashed into them and rolled on, slowed slightly by the bodies crushed underneath them. Screams were muffled and then cut off. Jerik could swear he heard bones crunch as he watched the rocks acquire a slightly glistening red shine, leaving crushed bones and pulpy mass in their wake.

The Khaizani now alone on the hilltop fought on. They fought well and in the end they died well, torn to pieces by angry Northmarchers and blood crazed Sea-Farers. None could bear the disgrace of becoming prisoners and slaves to barbarians.

"They die hard." Jerik said in the way of a tribute when it was finally over.

"Long as they die." Overdulf muttered as someone bandaged a cut across his cheek. "Every bloody one of them."

Night fell and for once it was not the Northmarchers launching raids in the dark but the Khaizani. They had learned well during their time in the Holmin. Arrows fell out the dark at irregular intervals. Sometimes in great masses the enemies of Khaizan had come to expect over the years. Sometimes they fell in ones and two or a couple of dozen. But there was always arrows falling from the night skies. Fires and watches were set. The Khaizani did not assault the lower peak of the Devil's Cradle but they made sure no one would be well rested in the morning.

"That is when they will come." Gordno predicted. Overdulf nodded as an arrow thudded into the ground. Gordno ordered his catapults to launch some more burning pitch into the night. "It will also help us see what they are up too. Try and discourage anyone sneaking around, trying to pick one or two of us off."

"When is it going to break loose at Dunrovin?" Jerik asked. It seems the longer they wait, the stronger you people will be when the battle finally happens."

"If they do not take the Cradle by tomorrow, the day after." was Gordno's opinion.

"Trying to take both heights at the same time is going to be quite a feat for even them." Jerik said.

Gordno shook his head. "No. They will only come after us."

"Because they can see Dunrovin well enough from here?"

"You will make a good general one day." Overdulf nudged his friend in the ribs. "Maybe the best ever!"

"Lif is sending more of his men over here." Gordno said. "We will make it pretty nasty for them."

"I think they will attack the south slope again." Jerik enjoyed thinking like a general. "The west is too obvious."

"Maybe both at the same time." Gordno added. "The Khaizani made a small attack on the east slope but that seems to only spread them out. Of course, north of us is the saddle between the two peaks so I am not worried about that."

"When it comes to these Khaizani people, you should worry about everything!" Jerik grunted.

"I am." Gordno said. " There is no telling what they are capable of."

Khaizani arrows were falling in bucketloads the next morning even before the sun was up. Clearly reinforcements had arrived and wasted no time making a contribution. Jerik had a foreboding feeling in the pit of his stomach. This day was going to be particularly hellish.

"West side and to the south!" Gordno never claimed to be a fortune teller but he seemed to have an uncanny ability to read Khaizani minds.

"What of the east?" The commander of the lower peak asked.

"Nothing!"

Shrugging off the arrows cutting into them, Northmarchers and Sea-Farers aimed down the slope and froze.

"Shoot!" Gordno shouted.

The archers on the southern slope cut down still another row of Khaizani but Gordno saw no such action from those defending the western approach. "Shoot!" he yelled. "What are you waiting for?"

"Captives!" Overdulf yelled back. "The Khaizani are using hostages as shields!"

Gordno darted over heedless of the blistering barrage coming down on his head. The catapults started heaving more rocks, oil and pitch but it did not seem to make a difference. Lif's trebuchets on the upper peak joined in.

Gordno looked over the edge of Overdulf's redoubt and his blood froze. "What sort of villainy is this?"

Providing protection with their bodies, men, women and children, taken from villages in overrun Nyhissia and here in the Holmin, were roughly shoved ahead of the marching Khaizani. All had a spear pointed at their back or had a soldier holding them to keep them from running.

The Khaizani plan was devilishly brilliant. Human shields on one side as the larger force attacked from the south. Even if the attackers on the weakened southern flank were stopped, those with the hostages would reach the top. Gordno could not believe the nightmare he was in. The worst part of it was that this was no dream. Defending this hill was a death sentence for the hostages. Was this hill worth their deaths? It was just dirt, rocks and a lot of thorns. But it was not just a hill he was defending. He was defending his country. If the Khaizani saw this strategy worked, another hill would fall the same way and so on until there was a Khaizani viceroy in Northcross.

The arrows stopped falling, a clear indication of how close the Khaizani were. The screams, begging and tear filled pleas of the captives, especially the women, was, unfortunately, a better method for determining distance.

"Reinforcements behind the hostages!" Jerik observed.

Gordno knew only one thing could disrupt the Khaizani attack. "Aim!" The nightmares would plague him the rest of his life.

Several Northmarchers crossed themselves. Others stared at their commander in shock. Even the Sea-Farers were unsure what to think. Jerik was happy he was not an archer and he ran back over the southern slope. There was going to be a lot of fighting there soon too.

The Northmarchers selected targets from the approaching crowd held against their will Some looked away after picking a target and some aimed intently, hoping to miss a hostage and hit a Khaizani instead. Overdulf raised his bow. He was hoping his shot would land behind the line and hit someone behind it. Gordno could feel the building rage from the Sea-Farers and Northmarcher dismounted infantry taking up positions behind their archer comrades. Any Khaizani who succeeded in reaching the top was going to die.

"The Khaizani are going to burn in Hell." someone muttered.

"Shoot!" Gordno's voice nearly cracked.

The screams that arose from the direction of the attackers were the most shrill anyone, on the hill or attacking it, had every heard, matched by the cries of dismay from the Khaizani who could not believe what had happened. Westerners were supposed to be too squeamish for this sort of thing.

Many hostages and a few Khaizani died on the hillside, joining those who had fallen before them. After the second volley, most of the hostages were either dead or without an "escort". They hit the ground soiled with the blood of innocents and missed the third set of arrows hurtling inches over their heads.

The now shredded human shields had allowed the Khaizani to advance a considerable distance up the west side of the Cradle without resistance. The confusion and delay caused by Gordno's moral anguish benefited the southern force much the same way. They were about to break over the hilltop again. This time in force.

Enraged Northmarcher infantry and their Sea-Farer comrades attacked the Khaizani breaching the southern wall head on. It was fighting more savage than anything that preceded it. But there simply too many Khaizani. The assault maintained its force and the Westerners were pushed back.

The Khaizani were about to overrun the western defenses too when Overdulf grabbed a handful of the sleeves to the men right and left of him and pulled them out of the way. Gordno and two other men pushed a catapult over the edge of the hill. It crashed and flipped down the slope into the Khaizan. The force of five hundred pounds of wood and metal cut a swath a half dozen soldiers wide but the human tidal wave was halted only momentarily. They absorbed the blow as the catapult disappeared among them and continued uphill.

Northmarchers and the remaining Sea-Farers scrambled away from the edge as the Khaizani poured over it, their numbers seeming unaffected.

Explosions rock the hilltop as Lif's trebuchets dropped flaming balls of oil down on the Khaizani. The burning oil combined with the coppery smell of blood and burning flesh permeated everything. Suddenly Jerik understood what that Hell place Christians cosigned people they did not care for was really like.

Jerik held up his ax and bellowed, "Warron!!!". His men rallied to him and formed a circle. If they were to die here, they would greet the gods together.

The Sea-Farers formed a line two ranks deep and began marching forward. "I see the line of my people stretching back to the Beginning..." the *Locklannigh* began to chant what was known as the Death Song.

Swords clashed and armor crumpled but the Northmarcher line was driven back by the sheer weight of the Khaizani attackers. Several punched through the crumbling Northmarcher line and the formation Gordno commanded started to fall apart.

Everyone heard a mournful hunting horn sound seconds before the remaining *Locklannigh* hit the entire swirling cauldron of maddened and desperate Northmarchers and Khaizani. It was a last desperate charge against hopeless odds. It was the very heart of almost every *Locklannigh* legend ever told. Jerik and the men from Warron were going to write another such tale.

Jerik nearly ran down Overdulf, slashing wildly at Khaizani all around him. The Sea-Farers took wide swinging meaty chops into the Khaizani without even bothering to aim, so massed and numerous they were. The move caught the soldiers of Khaizan by surprise but being Khaizani they recovered quickly. The Warronites forward progress was stopped and the Khan's men began to slowly envelop the recklessly hacking "yellow beards."

The Sea-Farers gave Gordno the time he needed to pull his men back. He made the unpleasant choice of having to abandon the lower peak of the Devil's Cradle. At least we made them pay a high price for it, he thought bitterly.

With a sluggish heave, dozens of Khaizani impacted the bulge Jerik's men created, collapsing it. Jerik continued to flail away wildly, frothy blood flying, smashing in more skulls as they surrounded him. The Crown Prince of Warron staggered under several blows at once. Roaring in fury, Jerik killed two more of the Khan's soldiers, the great ax nearly cutting one in half. It would not be enough. There were simply too many hard and accurate hitting Khaizani. The Sea-Farer prince disappeared under a hail of swords and cudgels.

Overdulf saw a bristling group of infantry romp over the small path leading from the upper peak of the Devil's Cradle. Lif himself held a pike in the front row as they collided with the Khaizani. Overdulf ran behind them as they pushed the Khaizani back a few feet. As he guessed, more trebuchets dropped artillery on the hilltop that was now almost entirely occupied by Khaizani. Gordno's men retreated under Lif's cover. More burning oil raked the enemy forces as Lif now skillfully backpedaled his men. The Khaizani for once did not pursue. They were burned, hurt and utterly exhausted. They were also in no condition or mood to pursue.

Soon Lif rejoined the rest of his men and what was left of Gordno's command on top of the upper peak of the Devil's Cradle. The lower peak was shrouded in fire and smoke and the bodies of soldiers and hostages dotted the slopes. No wonder they call this hill what they do, Overdulf thought. He saw looked around and saw no sign of Jerik. The trapper from Glossak never thought he could ever find people or a place more evil than the Argual. Now he had.

Gordno's eyes were red from smoke, fire and grit. And sadness.

"We saw what they did on the west side of the hill." Lif said. As horrifying as his memory was, he know Gordno had seen it from much closer. "It as an evil thing. I do not think even Masovians could do something like that. No human being could even *think* of doing that!"

"It was the most terrible thing I have ever seen." Gordno said, tears welling up in his eyes. He hung his head and began to sob. "We could have held the hill if they had not done.....*that*!!!"

The former commander of the lower peak burst into tears and cried. No one thought any less of him for it. Still, everyone around him looked away. The anguish was understandable. For someone who had no choice to do what he did, it was unbearable.

The lower peak of the Devil's Cradle belonged to the Khan.

Chapter 20

"Is there no limit to the evil these people are capable of?" Fleston roared. The story of the Khaizani use of hostages as shields spread through the army like wildfire. The King almost thought he would have a mutiny on his hands if he did not order his army to attack that moment. If there was an army that could fight at night, it belonged to the Northmarch. "This war ends here and it ends now!"

Actually he meant in the morning but Tignall was not going to interrupt his King on that minor point. The Khaizani played it smart and marched out of the Holmin in late afternoon. The Northmarcher army moved up several hundred feet too. The Khaizani horse archers would have time for maybe one mass volley. With the Holmin at their backs they had very little room to maneuver. More than a few Demon Division troopers remained hidden in the Khaizani rear to make sure one of the Khan's bright young officers did not try to assemble archers to fire out of the Holmin into the battle. He knew that had to grate on the Khan's nerves. Northmarcher horse archers meanwhile would be able to make full use of their talents. Once again, Khaizan had allowed the Northmarch to pick the battlefield.

The two armies stood in position glowering at each other, seemingly daring the other to make the first move. It was approaching midmorning and neither force had made a move since assembling into attack formations. The previous day, all eyes were focused on the Devil's Cradle, watching lines of soldiers surge up and down. The Northmarcher flag still flew from the upper peak, telling the world who owned it. How long it would stay that way was anyone's guess.

"They focused most of their effort on the lower hill." Kergis recapped. "Is it not strange they are not trying to take the other?"

"It is out of character." Tignall agreed. "But they can see us well enough from the lower hill. The longer they wait, the stronger we become. Wilnef is maybe two days away. They have to attack soon."

"We attack in an hour." Fleston said grimly.

General Yuan remembered the old fable of the warrior trapped between fire and ice. He never thought he would be that warrior. The Khan was unhappy with him but the General was popular with the army. Yuan not only led and held the army together at Lamptra and in the Holmin but struck back at the enemy. Despite all of the reverses and dreadful surprises, here they were in the enemy's country! Victory was still within sight.

A victory here would open the door to Northcross. Yuan was certain the Khan planned for the General's "heroic" death sometime after taking the Northmarcher home city. With opportunity came great risk. Win at Dunrovin and the troops will follow you anywhere Yuan thought. Maybe even to the throne back in Khaizan! The General fought to keep his face impassive and inscrutable. Perhaps it was the Khan who would die a hero. A smile almost broke through. But not quite.

General Yuan contrived to spend the morning away from his Khan, checking the archers, cavalry, foot soldiers. The army of Khaizan cheered the commander of the Greater North Army. Yuan wanted the Northmarchers to hear it. Khaizani morale may have been chipped at Lamptra and in the Holmin but it had not broken. The General also wanted to Khan to hear the army cheering him. Him!

One of the Khan's personal messengers rode up. "The Khan wishes to see you now, General."

Yuan nodded in acknowledgment. "You can speak the Northmarcher language, yes?". He recognized the man as one of the departed and unlamented Quang Tzi's.

"Yes my lord." The man answered. He wondered why Yuan wanted to know. Had he somehow captured some dispatches or correspondence?

"Good. Come with me." Yuan called two soldiers over to him and began to ride out into the narrow strip of steppe separating the two armies.

"General! The Khan wishes to see you now." The messenger reminded Yuan.

Yuan whipped his horse around, positioned his horse with a few mincing steps next to the messenger. "You forget yourself! I am a General and I just gave you an order!"

"Yes my lord." The messenger said meekly.

"Do not worry. I am acting under the Khan's direct orders." Yuan lied. One of the soldiers handed the messenger a white flag. "You hold that up where the barbarians can see it."

Yuan forced the messenger to ride out first with the flag. Then the General and two soldiers followed, riding toward the Northmarchers, who began to jeer and shout things Yuan guessed correctly were not compliments. The way his translator winced confirmed that. Yuan was not a particularly religious or even spiritual man but even he could plainly feel the almost solid wall of hatred the Northmarchers projected. He was not sure if it was by design or not.

The Khan pulled the Birthright Sword halfway out of the scabbard. Over the last few weeks, he had felt increasingly uneasy looking at it. Where was this feeling coming from? Was this splendid weapon somehow causing this feeling? He knew that the Khaizani army was near the place this weapon was forged. Could that have something to do with it? He looked out at the Northmarcher army wondering if they were performing some sort of barbaric black magic.

Then the Khan bolted upright in his saddle. *What was Yuan doing riding out to the enemy?!* If *anyone* knew about Northmarcher treachery, it was Yuan. Had he forgotten what happened at Lamptra? "General Hortai!" The Khan snapped. "Be ready to assume command in case General Yuan falls to treachery." The Khan made it sound as if he had personally ordered Yuan out to meet the barbarians. Yuan was not a stupid man. He had to know of his growing power and popularity. There was only room for one Khan and it would not be Yuan, the Khan vowed. The General would fall one way or another in this battle. Then he could continue loyally serving the Khanate as a martyr. On the other hand, maybe the Northmarchers would take care of the problem for him, the Khan thought.

Kergis shielded his eyes from the Sun. "Is he carrying a banner of truce?"

"Indeed he is." Tignall confirmed. "I do not think they are surrendering though."

"It would make our task easier." Kergis muttered.

"I would rather they all commit suicide." Fleston said sardonically. "That would provide a neat end to this."

"True enough." Tignall said in his usual dour manner. "We should still see what they want."

Kergis, though he wore three stars, was the lowest ranking member of the three, prepared to ride forth. Tignall's large hand landed on his shoulder staying him.

"Remember what we tried at Lamptra?" Tignall reminded his subordinate. "You stay here with the King. I will go see what they want. Besides, I think that is the Khaizani commander himself!"

"What if they do try a Lamptra in reverse?" Kergis asked. "I am ready for whatever they will try!" He was trying to find a polite way to point out that he was at least fifteen years younger than the man in charge of the Northmarcher military.

A rare laugh rumbled from Tignall. "I may have some grey in my beard but I was out galloping around slaying dragons with your father, not your grandfather!"

Kergis looked over to the King, who was having trouble maintaining a straight face.

Tignall continued. "I have prepared you as well as I can for you to succeed me, Kergis. Should something happen to me out there, I expect you will do better than I."

Both generals clasped hands and looked over to their King. "What are your orders, my lord?" Tignall asked.

"You have done very well in this war, Tignall." The King said. "No reason I should jog your elbow now."

Tignall nodded once briskly and proceeded to ride forward. The dozen or so Palace Guards around the King made way and cheered the general of the entire Northmarcher Army. The soldiers of that army cheered even louder as he rode between the ranks. Under his leadership, they had brought what was thought to be the world's mightiest army to its knees. His fearsome visage only heartened the Northmarchers. Tignall looked like an avenging Old Testament prophet ready to mete out blood soaked justice to the evil that was Khaizan. How could they lose with such a man leading them?

Tignall made his way to the front and looked over the small Khaizani delegation. One man was obviously a general with two bodyguards and another man taking great pains to show he was unarmed. Tignall's eyes locked with Yuan and both stared at each other for a few seconds.

Yuan was not sure what to expect. Tignall was about his age and physically imposing even on the horse. His eyes were very, very dark. Almost Khaizani dark. The beard was a bit of a surprise. Northmarchers tended to be clean shaven. The grey streaks in Tignall's beard reminded Yuan of the same streaks in his hair. If the Northmarcher general was mocking his wispy chin beard and small mustache, Yuan did not care. His nation stretched halfway around the world. The Northmarch was a good sized country on its own but it paled in size compare to the Empire of Khaizan.

Tignall appraised the Khaizani general in front of him. It was strange actually seeing the man he had been fighting for weeks this close. Tignall did not care for the arrogance radiating from the man or the way his eyes regarded him. So what? The Khaizani war machine had taken quite a beating at the hands of the Northmarcher Army. The general was a good sized man too and quite formidable. Tignall wondered why he bothered with such sparse facial hair. It seemed easier just to get rid of it.

The commanding general of all the Northmarcher armies reached over to his left and picked one soldier to escort him out to the waiting Khaizani general. Over to the right, his hand landed on the shoulder of Kejen Densky.

The three Northmarchers trotted out to their Khaizani counterparts. The translator remained on his horse and held his white flag on a small tree branch. Yuan's horse trotted up next to him as the bodyguards look up flanking positions. All carefully kept their hands in view. Tignall rode up and halted a sword length away from Yuan. Kejen and his comrade kept an eye on their Khaizani opposite numbers. They did not salute each other.

The Khaizani soldier serving as a translator did not seem to be an officer. That was probably some sort of veiled insult in Khaizani eyes. If so, it presaged the message well.

"This is not a parley!" The translator spat out. In the Northmarcher language. Kejen thought it sounded a little odd. It was not the sing song Khaizani accent though. The syntax seemed a little different. At first he thought it was simply because it was not the man's birth language. Then it occurred to Kejen that is was what the Northmarcher language sounded like a couple of centuries ago. Probably learned it from something written during the first invasion.

Kejen did not know how to turn this new knowledge to his advantage so he continued watching the Khaizani across from him. He did not trust anything these people said. In Northmarcher or any other language.

"I did not say it was." Tignall answered with a good bit of contempt of his own. "Say what you have come to say."

"The General in his infinite wisdom generously invites you and your soldiers to lay down their weapons as to avoid the unnecessary destruction of their kingdom." The translator said with the archaic sounding syntax.

There was a moment of silence.

"Is that it?" Tignall asked, clearly amused.

"Yes, it is." the Khaizani translator replied. "You would be wise to accept the offer."

Tignall ignored the insolent man and directed a piercing stare that he wanted to penetrate directly into Yuan's brain. "No."

There was no need for a translation.

Yuan dismounted and drew his sword from the scabbard on his hip. He pointed the weapon at the Northmarcher general in what could only be a challenge.

Tignall dismounted, sword drawn and pointed it at Yuan.

The unarmed translator realized his services were no longer needed, so he turned and galloped off toward his army. Kejen and the other soldier serving as Tignall's bodyguards stared intently at the Khaizani cavalrymen doing the same for their general.

The two armies erupted into cheers and catcalls as Tignall and Yuan circled warily, feinting with swords and feet, trying to bait the other into a premature move. In the end, they both made their move at the same time.

The clash of steel rang across the prairies as the curved Khaizani blade and Western crosshilt crashed overhead. Yuan parried and thrust but Tignall skillfully blocked the blow. The Khaizani general's foot shot out and hit his Northmarcher opponent in his armored stomach. It knocked Tignall back a step and he immediately retaliated with a swing that missed Yuan by inches. The Khaizani general bounded away with agility that belied his years and advanced again. Both swung again and nearly connected. Yuan's sword brushed past the crest of Tignall's helmet and a piece of armor on his shoulder flew off, ripped away by the Northmarcher blade. Yuan leapt and spun in midair, executing a perfect roundhouse kick but missed his target as Tignall sank to one knee and let the foot pass over harmlessly. The Northmarcher general launched himself into the Khaizani still in mid-air but only managed to glance off his foe.

Somehow, both managed to get on their feet quickly but with the other's army behind them. Then one of the Khaizani bodyguards drew a weapon and his horse took a step forward at Tignall's back.

No one would ever know what the man's true intentions were because Kejen lashed out with his sword and chopped him down in the saddle.

Then everything happened at once.

As if on que, arrows, spears and even a few rocks flew out of the ranks arching over the combatants into the enemy on the other side.

Tignall was distracted by the attempted attack from behind for a second and that was when Yuan struck. The Khaizani general dropped his sword and put Tignall in a headlock. Before Yuan could twist his neck, Tignall drove several powerful punches into the Khaizani's midsection, lifting him with each impact. Yuan fell with shot to the kidneys and then Tignall saw a Khaizani lancer come out of nowhere right for him.

Kejen reached out and grabbed the lance with both hands and almost yanked the attacker out of the saddle. Kejen pulled the weapon toward him and connected with the attacker's temple with this elbow. Then he pushed the dazed man staggering into the path of his comrades. The other

Northmarcher launched himself out of his saddle and into the other Khaizani bodyguard. Both men fell and disappeared into the rising dust.

Tignall was very much alone and between both charging armies. He crouched and readied himself to take at least one of the Khan's men into the afterlife with him.

Suddenly, Gusaric and his cavalry platoon burst into view across the rapidly diminishing space between the two armies. They hurtled across the Khaizani front, lances and swords scything, spilling blood and entrails of man and horse. The Northmarchers did not escape unscathed. The Khaizani ripped and tore at the madmen charging into their midst, knocking at least a half dozen out of the saddle .

"Up here!" Kejen shouted at his commander. Tignall jumped onto his rescuers horse with the speed of someone half his age. Fear is a great motivator. Kejen spun and galloped directly for the phalanx on oncoming Northmarcher lances and spears. He yelled at Perhen to lift his weapon. Tignall ducked as he cleared the forest of lance points. No need to take chances now. The two had thundered past a few ranks when the clash of armor, men and horses nearly deafened them. The shock of what felt like two worlds colliding broke over the ranks like a bolt of lightning. The worst part of it where the screams of pain that shrieked over the sounds of fighting.

The long awaited Battle of Dunrovin had begun.

Chapter 21

Both the Northmarchers and Khaizani moved with exceptional speed, which allowed most of their forces to avoid the full force of the others horse archers. Screams from the rear however indicated that not all had made the run under the arrows successfully.

The sheen of lance points glittered briefly in the midmorning Sun before the clash of arms echoed over the steppes, heard well over the horizon. Swords and lances raked across armor and flesh as harnesses strained and broke. Northmarcher and Khaizani ripped and tore into each other, seeking only to destroy the man in front so that he could get on with trying to kill another.

Kergis led the cavalry charge into the Khaizani right flank, trying to turn it before the battle line set and plow into the ever dangerous horse archers in the rear. He ran over a Khaizani swordsman as his men thundered into the segment of the Khaizani line the general deemed weakest- where the infantry center joined the cavalry wing.

Wei-Lang, a captain in the elite Crouching Dragons, saw the Northmarcher attack coming and ordered his command, despite being outnumbered, to charge. The black clad horsemen with the lightening streak emblazoned on their sleeve met the enemy in midstride with weapons drawn. The Khaizani horse archers charged in right behind the Crouching Dragons and fired over their comrades heads into the attacking Northmarchers with horrific results. Dozens of Northmarcher riders and horses went down screaming, including Kergis's mount, impeded from further progress by a forked barb splitting its skull. For the first time in this war, the horse archers of Khaizan finally fought in the manner that had paved the way to a world spanning empire.

Kergis was thrown from his horse but the damage was minimal zed as the Northmarcher general reacted with agility of a lifelong horseman, positioning his body in midair before hitting the ground and rolling across it. Kergis jumped up to his feet just in time to fend off a Khaizani cudgel aimed for his head. The rider looking disturbingly like a Demon Division soldier but that did not keep Kergis from smashing him in the saddle with his sword. He heard another set of hoof beats coming for him from his back.

Wei-Lang recognized the man on the ground as the one commanding the Northmarcher attack. He charged and brought his sword down hard to smash the man's helmet. Kergis blocked the overhand downswing with his sword but the blow took the weapon out of his hands. The Khaizani cavalryman turned around and charged him again. Kergis picked up a discarded cudgel, blocked the sword swing and pulled the handle back to try to hit the mounted Khaizani officer. The Northmarcher general was not familiar with the weapon and his lack of adroitness showed.

Wei-Lang changed direction and made yet another attack pass. This time, Kergis went straight for the horse, this time using the cudgel as a weapon he was used to, a lance.

With a sharp crack and a high pitched neigh, the blade sank into the horse's throat, squirting hot blood in Kergis's face. Wei-Lang reacted awkwardly, taking a wild swing as his mount fell sideways, shearing off a part of Kergis's feathered crest.

Kergis pulled the blade out of the dead horse. He did not hear the sucking noise it made as it was withdrawn instead looking for Wei-Lang. The helmetless Khaizani charged across the small space screaming. The sword rang off the cudgel, echoing off the armor of the soldiers fighting all around them. Wei-Lang took a low swing but Kergis jumped back, the tip of the blade missing his knees by an inch. The Northmarcher general took a step forward and blocked a blow from the quickly recovering Wei-Lang who let his momentum take him into another spin, adding force to his slash.

The shaft shattered in two and Kergis was befrought a weapon. The Khaizani pressed his advantage, hammering away at his Northmarcher opponent. Kergis knocked away the first swing with his forearm greave and ducked under Wei-Lang's second swing. He came up with his knee, ramming into the Khaizani's groin before grabbing his adversary's hair and propelling Wei-Lang's face into the same knee.

The stunned Khaizani curled up into a ball, trying to absorb the pain. Kergis ended it for him, driving a Khaizani sword into the back of his neck. The general did not take time to reflect on the poetic justice of that. Instead he found a riderless horse and went back into battle.

A blood covered Kejen Densky found himself not far from Kergis, swing wildly at the enemy in all directions, sometimes advancing, sometimes retreating but always fighting. The good news was that none of the blood covering his armor was his. At least he did not think so. The bad news was that the Crouching Dragons had stopped Kergis's attack and now the Northmarchers were starting to be slowly but surely pushed back on this flank.

The horsearchers of Khaizan lashed out again.

Kejen thought he was in the middle of a locust storm as the wicked winged barbs cut into his men with all of their fearsome velocity. Leron and Bolshin's horses went down and Kejen saw the point of a Khaizani arrow explode out of his horse's neck, its barbed tip red and dripping, looped with a piece of spinal tissue.

Kejen's horse was dead before it hit the ground. Kejen pulled his feet out of the stirrups, curled up and rolled off the falling carcass. He almost landed on his feet but was a split second late bringing them down. Kejen hit he ground like a sack of potatoes, heels, posterior, back and head all in that order. Ignoring the pain registering all over his body, Kejen was back on his feet and snagging a horse that was missing a rider. Certainly a lot of those, he thought.

The Northmarcher horse archers loosed their arrows this time, over the Khaizani elite troops and into the enemy horse archers. Kergis turned several units ninety degrees in the last few minutes and on his signal, converged on the Crouching Dragons. With no archers supporting them, even these Dragons could not make anymore headway against the heavier Northmarcher cavalry. They could not pull away either as the enemy swarmed over them. The Northmarchers used their swords and lances with terrifying accuracy cutting apart the Khaizani formation in front of them. What started as a Northmarcher attempt to turn the Khaizani right turned into a Khaizani thrust to turn Kergis's flank finally ended with the destruction of a company of Crouching Dragons. They did not die easily.

The Khaizani were far from beaten however. The loss of one cavalry company in the pursuit of the greater glory of the Khanate was inconsequential. The soldiers of the Khan fought on unaffected.

The Khan watched the battle on the flank and saw what he was looking for. The company of Crouching Dragons had sacrificed themselves to confirm for the Khan what he knew all along. The Northmarcher left flank was the weakest. The Northmarcher commander was a clever one indeed! Using the weaker flank to attack and turn the Khaizani before the battle lines set. What better way to conceal a defensive weakness than to go on the offensive with it? The Khan almost felt bad for having to end to these barbarian's squalid freedom. But not that bad.

The Khan gave a curt order to the rest of the Crouching Dragons held in reserve for just this moment. "Avenge your brothers!!!"

Yearning to strike, the elite black clad riders on black horses thundered across the plains, black silver tipped lances lowered, shining menacingly in the Sun. They were an awesome sight. They truly earned the nickname

"The Thunder of the East." The regular Khaizani soldiery barely had time to get out of the way and five died in the rush, ground under by the hooves of hundreds.

The Crouching Dragons smashed into the Northmarcher left full force. The weaker Northmarcher flank splintered at first contact. The Khaizani, elite and regular forces, mounted and foot, poured through the gap in increasing numbers. The Northmarchers pulled back trying to hold a refused flank. The Khaizani pressure was making that difficult. Tignall and Kergis both rode at break neck speed to the crisis area, leaving the King to manage the rest of the battle. The Khaizani cry of victory echoed across the battlefield.

Following the Dragons on a pivot through the shattered flank, once a solid line of men fighting for their country was now scattered groups trying to survive, rode the dreaded mounted archers. They were the pride of Khaizan! What better place for their Khan to be than next to them as they rode to victory? They would provide a devastating first strike and cover for their comrades when they charged into the enemy's rear. At long last, victory was at hand. The Northmarcher Army, the main obstacle to a Khaizani ride to the Sea, staggered off balance before Khaizan. The treachery of Lamptra and the dark days of the Holmin would finally be paid back in full.

Northmarcher cavalry on the far end of the left flank was pushed aside and into a small forest away from the battle. One of the cavalrymen there was Kejen Densky.

"Where is Greniak?!" Kejen shouted, looking for the cavalry company's commander.

"Bought the farm!" Gusaric shouted back. "Blasted arrow!"

Kejen looked around, surveying the situation. He rode to the treeline. His men were at about half strength and Guasaric and Pehren's men added in brought his entire company up to about half strength too. "Perhen! You take that company over there. Crinklin, you have my platoon and Gusaric takes everyone else!"

Kejen's words were drowned out by the Crouching Dragons thundering by, turning in unison to rush the rear. The Khaizani mounted archers followed in their hoof beats, ready to unleash another storm of arrows. It was a terrifying scene. It was also a splendid opportunity. "We are going to hit those archers from the rear! Watch for my signal!"

Kejen tensed up as the archers made their turn completely unaware of the Northmarchers hiding in the trees. *Do not look here,* he prayed, *please do not look over here! Just a couple of minutes!*

His men arrayed themselves into an attack formation as well as they could in the trees and checked their weapons and armor. Especially the shields. They knew what the full wrath of Khaizani archery was capable of.

Kejen raised his sword above his head.

Kergis was desperately trying to keep the stricken flank together as Tignall organized a counter-attack from the rear. He needed time. Time he was rapidly running out of. The elite Khaizani cavalry hurtled toward the woefully unprepared line, lances lowering. The only thing between Kergis and the disorganized flank was a company of dismounted archers deploying in two ranks.

*Dis*mounting?! The general's mind screamed as he did a double-take. Had they taken complete leave of their senses? The sanity of a few archers was the least of Kergis's concerns at the moment. His eyes were glued on the Crouching Dragons, getting larger by the second.

Trif did what needed to be done when he saw the left flank about to collapse. He managed to convince his commander to give him command of an entire company of archers. It was a major risk but then again, like practically everyone in Sparent knew, Trif was rarely wrong about anything.

The archers in Trif's first command rode into the high grass and dismounted, hiding as the horses panicked and bolted. Nothing is perfect, Trif thought as he jumped off his mount into the grass with his men. The oncoming enemy cavalry may have seen some of Trif's two hundred or so co-conspirators duck under cover but they had no inkling of what was lying in wait for them.

Kejen's arm dropped. "For the Motherland!!!"

The Northmarchers exploded out of the trees, bolting across the steppes right into the back of the Khaizani flanking move. So intent were the Khan's mounted archers on preparing to launch winged death at their foes they never saw the attacking horsemen descend on their rear until it was too late.

The Khaizani bowmen only had time to fire one ragged, ineffectual volley in two directions at once. Kejen's company slammed into the lightly armed archers from behind with the fury and strength of a formation twice their size. Dozens of archers were mown down by the lances and broadswords of the attackers in the first few seconds of the charge. The Khan was shouting out orders and most were drowned out in the chaos breaking out from the unexpected assault from the rear. Nonetheless, the orders to fire into the mixed fighting crowd were heard by enough. More Khaizani than Northmarchers fell but Kejen's men, badly outnumbered, could ill afford the losses. The fighting raged so heatedly it was almost impossible to tell friend from foe. Kejen continued cutting into the enemy forms in front of him, determined to keep doing so until there were no more.

The Crouching Dragons surged forward, eager to close with the main Northmarcher army. Rising out of the prairie grass in two lines with Trif Densky commanding was a company of archers, bows notched and ready.

Northmarcher arrows reached out and bit into the first rank of Crouching Dragons. Horses flipped, rides fell and new screams rose over Dunrovin. Trif commanded the first rank to fire again and it did, killing more of the Khan's elite. The second rank fired on the heels of the first and more of the Crouching Dragons hit the ground. The Crouching Dragon commanding officer spent the last seconds of his life wondering why the horse archers behind him were not saturating the madmen in front of him. Then an arrow shot his life out.

The horse archers had angry sword swinging Northmarchers in among them. And the Khan was here with them! The archers threw themselves in the Northmarchers path towards him. By now, some of the barbarians recognized the First Lord of Khaizan, and they shredded the thinning horse archers to get to him.

Trif's men fired away at a furious rate. His own fingers were bleeding and his shoulders hurt but he kept planting shafts viciously into the Khan's soldiers. He ran up and down the line, shouting encouragement and exhorting his soldiers, pausing only to fire and puncture another Khaizani braincase.

The first Crouching Dragon fell a hundred feet from Trif's checkerboard alignment. Those hit in the second volley were a little closer. The third and fourth set of downrange attacks dropped more Khaizani even closer. The blistering rate of fire ripped into the Dragons unabated as Trif ordered the first rank to fall back. Trif knew he would hurt the Khaizani horsemen badly but not stop them.

Then Trif heard the thundering hooves behind him.

Kergis not only salvaged the left flank but he was attacking! The now-ready left flank, bent at a forty-five degree angle to the solid center began to roll forward. Trif had bought the time Kergis needed. The elite of the Khaizani Army had been stopped in their tracks. By militia archers no less!

Battered, cut but very much alive, Kejen smashed through a bow put up as a woefully inadequate defense and cleft in another Khaizani skull. Keen's oversized company had lost a lot of men but against archers in hand to hand combat, the battered unit still held the upper hand... Instead of dispersing and leaving the North marchers behind, the archers were trying to make a stand. Why were doing something that suicidal?

Then Kejen saw why.

In the middle of the archers was a man in rather gaudy looking armor surrounded by bodyguards. The Northmarchers hacked and slashed though archers ill equipped for this kind of fighting toward the man who was giving orders. That is a general of some kind, Kejen shouted. Get him and the archers are finished!

The Khan was throwing more archers into the Northmarchers path hoping to stop them through exhaustion. It did not work. If anything, it was like throwing raw meat to demons. They were fighting like men possessed. The truth of the matter was that everyone in Kejen's group had lost friends to Khaizani arrows. Now they were among those responsible. And they were going to pay.

The Khan ordered all but two of his bodyguards into the melee that was churning closer. The Khan's men charged in without hesitation, ready to fulfill the purpose they had trained so long for. The Khan pulled out the Birthright Sword. The uneasy feelings it had been causing him over the last few weeks were drowned by the adrenaline flowing into his body, preparing him for a fight for his life.

Kejen cut down another Khaizani archer, of which there were noticeably fewer of now, when a cudgel clanged off his helmet. It gave the merchant from Sparent a ringing headache and a nasty bruise on the side of his head but it did not incapacitate him. It only served to enrage Kejen further as he rammed his sword point first through the Khaizani attacker's neck. Jerking it out nearly severed the Kazan's head from his body but Kejen was all ready moving toward the richly dressed man commanding everything.

The Crouching Dragons, stung badly by Trif, found themselves caroming into a revitalized enemy whose forward momentum was building into an avalanche that had them badly outnumbered. Trig found himself caught between his oncoming countrymen and the still charging Crouching Dragons. The Khaizani elite bravely continued on the collision course.

Trif's archers stopped hitting targets and ran forward, some still firing arrows but most running between the Khaizani horses. Trif was not above self preservation, darting between two of the black horses rushing by, rushing into the killing field of slaughtered Crouching Dragons. The nauseating sickly sweet smell of flesh in the first stages of decay was made worse by the Summer heat. The bright splotches of blood marred the black of uniform, armor and horses but it did not keep Trif and his fellow archers from taking cover behind fleshy and sometimes, still living, cover. Some even took a few shots at the Khaizani archers fighting for their lives against Kejen and his compatriots.

A jarring concussion announced the collision between what was left of the Crouching Dragons and the entire Northmarcher left flank. Kergis got the better of the clash, pushing the Khaizani back in a savage counterattacking gate turn that grinded toward Trif and his men and the diminishing Khaizani horse archers a little beyond them.

The Khaizani still would not shatter. Although most of the dead left in the wake of the Northmarcher attack were Khaizani, their discipline held under the hammer blows. Later some Northmarchers would, grudgingly, admit they found that admirable.

At the present moment however, Trif was trying to burrow under a dead horse as the advancing Northmarchers and retreating Khaizani, fighting every step of the way, swept over his contingent.

Kejen and his soldiers did not see or know of Kergis's strike until they found themselves in the middle of the swirling cauldron of clashing swords and thrusting lances grating against armor or rending flesh.

Another person who caught in the middle of the Northmarcher counterattack was the Khan himself. Five archers gathered themselves in front of the Khan to defend their liege. It was then everyone in eyeshot realized who the "archer commander" really was.

Another archer's service to the Khan was abruptly ended by Kejen's sword. Without stopping, the former merchant charged the Khan's last bodyguards just as all five fired at him. Kejen's horse reared up, forefeet lashing out but three arrows piercing its throat and heart were too much. Kejen just had his second horse shot out from under him. His mount dropped forward and Kejen got out of the saddle before the horse could roll over and pin his leg. The archers forgot about Kejen but a screaming Khaizani foot soldier with a cudgel was running straight for him. Kejen brought his sword up and saw a lancepoint explode out of the man's chest. The cudgel landed on the ground and the only thing that hit Kejen was the man's blood.

Gusaric dropped the lance and pointed with his sword at the Khan's entourage. "Get that man and the war is over!". Everyone who could hear him ran in that direction.

Kejen ran with them but the men on horses got there first. The Khan was bowled over when his bodyguards were practically thrown into him. He leapt out of the saddle and landed on his feet. The Birthright Sword was out and ready for combat. Kejen ran straight for the Khan but he was cut off by two of the last Crouching Dragon lancers. Kejen knocked one lance away with his shield and rammed a fist into the second rider's midsection. The Khaizani rider tried to stay upright but Kejen landed a second punch into the man's solar plexus and ripped him off the saddle. Before he could steal the horse, the other lancer burst back into view riding straight for Kejen. The Northmarcher adventurer dropped down into a crouched two point stance, shield and sword set. The enemy came straight on. And never made it to Kejen.

Perhen smashed into the Khaizani elite soldier from the side and smashed him across the head with a casual flick of his wrist. The Crouching Dragon hit the ground hard and was trampled by the cavalrymen Perhen led. They spun around Kejen and charged on behind the rest of the army. Kejen sat down on a rock and gave Perhen an obscene gesture.

"Really Kejen!" Perhen laughed. "I do not know where you get your reputation, sitting down all the time!"

"I had him." Kejen jerked his head at the dead Khaizani.

"Never had a doubt." Perhen said. "I just did not want you to miss out on the end! Get on his horse and let's finish this!"

Kejen could not have agreed more.

Not that far away, Trif ran between two clashing lancers, spun and fired point blank into the Khaizani one before continuing on to find some way out of the maze of maddened horses and thrusting weapons coming from random directions. A Northmarcher horse crashed to the ground in front of him, pinning its rider under its bulk. Trif pushed his shoulder into the dead horse and pushed up, pulling the wounded man out from under it with his free hand. The archer from Sparent propped the man up against the dead horse.

"Your leg does not seem broken." Trif told the man. Then he tossed him a canteen full of water and some bandages. "Wrap it up to be sure. I have some more Khaizani to kill." Kejen's brother vaulted over the horse to continue his part of the mass pursuit of the Khan.

The destruction of most of the Crouching Dragons pushed the momentum of the battle to the Northmarchers. The refused left flank counterattack was now pushing the Khaizani back and the enemy's flank was beginning to collapse. The rest of the Khaizani and Northmarcher lines had held steady in the course of the battle but Tignall was starting to sense some wavering in his enemy's resolve.

Rumors that the Khan was missing began to spread. General Yuan, wounded in his single combat with the Northmarcher commander as well as an inadvertent kick from a horse, may have been battered but his mind was still sharp. Hortari was a good general but *he* was in command. The Khan may have been missing but the Northmarchers were still about to cave in his right flank.

"Where are the horse archers?" Yuan shouted.

"They went in after the Crouching Dragons attack on the Northmarcher left flank." Hortari answered.

Yuan felt a ball of ice form in his stomach. "We have no more horse archers?"

Before General Hortari could answer, a hail of arrows plunged down out of the sky. They were not Khaizani. Men screamed as they were pierced through. Worst of all, there was no counter volley arching into the sky to punish the attackers. The Northmarcher horsearchers stayed in the rear, raining arrows down all over the battlefield. Just as the Khaizani would do.

Yuan heard screaming from close by. At first he thought it was Hortari but his second in command lay dead with a half dozen arrows in him. His eyes were open and staring at Yuan. Then the General realized the screaming was his.

It's over. The Northmarchers have won. The General thought as he lay on the ground. His inner voice sounded discombobulated and even the pain seemed far away. *At least the Khan will not survive me for long.* For Yuan, it was a pleasant thought.

It was also his last.

Kejen saw the Khan, jumped off the hurting horse and ran after him. He slipped past another Khaizani lancer, who missed the agile Northmarcher and stabbed only dirt.

One last Khaizani bodyguard threw himself into a large nosed Northmarcher barbarian but Kejen shoved his sword through the Khan's final defender.

And got it stuck.

Kejen could feel the blade grate against the bones it was wedged against. He tried to pull it out but the sword just would not budge.

The Khan had no where to run. His bodyguards were dead. His army was defeated. He was trapped out here in the middle of some barbaric backwater Western kingdom with its filthy inhabitants closing in on him from all directions. He was not going to be dragged in front of Fleston to beg for his life before they tortured him to death for their amusement. If he was going to die here, he would die with the Birthright Sword in his hand. A death worthy of a Prince of Khaizan! He would take as many as he could with him. Starting with the man in front of him now!

Kejen's shield broke under the force of two quick blows. His mind dimly noted that the sword that split his shield in half was not a Khaizani sword. It looked very much like a Western one.

With a powerful fear-induced pull, Kejen wrenched his sword free, Khaizani ribs giving way with a sharp crack seconds before the Khan's sword came down on the spot Kejen previously occupied.

The Khan blocked Kejen's counterswing and struck back an overhand chop. Kejen stepped to the side and scored a telling blow against his enemy's side. The Khaizani sovereign was well served by his armor as he fought on unwounded. Kejen blocked the next swipe and felt an inordinate amount of force behind the swing rock him to his heels.

No one could be that strong!

The blades clashed and rang again and Kejen felt as though he had blocked three men at once. And the blade on Kejen's sword bent. Then the thought suddenly materialized in Kejen's mind. It was not the Khan's strength behind the sword. *It was the sword!*

God in Heaven!

Gusaric charged the Khan but the Khaizani first lord swung at the lowered lance and broke it in half. Gusaric's eyes widened as he felt the extraordinary shock travel through his weapon down to his heels and even his horse's hooves, nearly throwing him.

The Khan regained his balance and swung at Kejen again, determined to smite this Northmarcher once and for all. Kejen aimed carefully and hit the Khan in the wrist with his bent sword. The blade broke but it shattered the Khan's wrist. Most importantly, the Khan's nerveless fingers lost their grip on the Birthright Sword.

The Khan and Kejen both had their eyes lock on the falling sword, tracing its path to the ground. It bounced once with a metallic thud. Both men reached for it at the same time.

The Khan kicked the sword away and it skittered in the dirt a few feet. Kejen grabbed the Khan's ankles and upended his Khaizani adversary. The Khan tripped Kejen as he tried to run to the sword and they rolled in the dust trading punches trying to keep the other away from the sword they both had a right to.

The Khan punched his nemesis in the nose and Kejen, angered beyond control, savagely bit the Khan on his nose, rending flesh with his teeth in atavistic glee, drawing blood. The Khan fought on, hitting Kejen in the side of the helmet with a rock. Kejen's vision blurred for a second but it quickly cleared and he punched the Khan in the face. He punched him again and then a third time to keep him down.

Kejen rolled away from the Khan who showed no signs of quitting. The look on the Khan's face betrayed his fear and shock as the Northmarcher rolled to the Birthright Sword. Kejen's hand closed around the hilt of the long sought after sword.

Instantly, Kejen felt vast and powerful energy flow into his veins making every nerve tingle. Then there was a brilliant, blinding flash that caught the attention of everyone for miles. Kejen felt the white raw power of lightening coalesce with his blood.

The outline of Khaizani swooping in a last desperate effort to save their Khan stood for a second against the white light before they were absorbed in a deafening explosion that threw all flat against the ground. Everyone, Khaizani and Northmarcher alike, knew to the bottom of their souls that nothing from this world could stand against that kind of force.

The light vanished as soon as it had appeared. Everything was quiet as Northmarchers and Khaizani alike got up and stood confused and apprehensive. The impromptu cease-fire held as they tried to hold down their fears and figure out what just happened.

Kejen stood unharmed in the middle of a circle of charred, blackened ground extending nearly twenty feet in all directions. The smell of burnt grass permeated the now silent battlefield.

The Khan, his back scorched, lifted himself up, spat the dirt out of his mouth and started running for the Holmin. Slowly, first in ones and twos, then in larger groups and then as a whole, the unexpected happened. The Khaizani army started melting away. It started in the rear but the panic soon found it way to the front of the Khan's army. What started as a trickle rapidly became a flood. A few tried to stand their ground and fight but it was hopeless. Those who chose to stand and fight only died where they stood as the Northmarchers crushed them the same way Khaizan had done to its enemies in the past---using the horsearchers to shoot them down from a distance. The rest of the Khan's soldiers began to run. Many others just threw their weapons down and did what no one from Khaizan had ever done. They surrendered. Not all did though. Some ran to the open steppes of the east but the Northmarchers were not letting them off that easy. The bloody pursuit and subsequent slaughter would last for miles.

Gusaric sat dazed on his rump, patiently waiting for the bright lights swimming in front of his eyes to go away. Aside from a few flashburns, he was in presentable condition. The pungent smell of roasted pork told him the Khaizani fighting for the Khan up until the last minute were not so lucky.

Kejen sat down on the ground and held the sword in his lap. He had a far away look on his face as though he was somehow communicating with the sword in spite of the Khaizani flight around him. Of course, no one was going to approach him. Gusaric felt apprehensive as well about walking up to his friend so he decided to just wait until Kejen came to him.

Kejen could not believe it. He was holding *HeavenSteel!* Sevonicus was right all along. Well, Sevonicus did not know the whole truth but he had suspected it. Kejen's wonderment continued. *HeavenSteel* was not just a sword. The energy racing through it made the sword feel like it was a living thing! And it spoke!

Not in words but a series of fast moving images flew through Kejen's mind. Images of the great original Gaking fighting brigands on the bridge over the Densk near Gaking's Grove. In his mind, Kejen saw Gaking hang the sword on his wall telling everyone to keep it for a time of great need. Kejen saw in his mind Roenik Densky fighting against Transkyan barbarians keeping them away from raiding a village. He saw his ancestor also helping strangers along road on the way back home. Images of Harkon followed as he pledged his allegiance to the embattled King and fought to bring the forces of Baron Melas to heel. He also *felt* Harkon's fear of the sword's power and his forsaking to ever use it again. That was something no one had known about! Next, Kejen saw in his minds eye, Diln, as he lovingly oiled the sword and spoke to God about making the world a better place by destroying the atheistic Masovians. Kejen never doubted Diln was insane but he was struck by the sincerity of his sentiments. After all, *HeavenSteel* was there! Unfortunately, one man could not wipe a country off the map by himself. The warm feeling was replaced by horror as Kejen became a witness to a clearly unbalanced Diln destroying an entire village. Then there was the climatic battle at Limbart. Ties of blood were strong however as Kejen found himself hoping against hope that Diln would defeat the Masovians. Kejen felt almost ill as the imperialists took the sword and tried to spirit away to Regalwood. They recognized its power and wanted to harness it for their dark purposes! Soon a man that looked a lot like his brother Trif came into view. That was Lorac! He rescued *HeavenSteel* to avenge his brother and to keep it from being used for evil. Kejen saw Lorac in the middle of the Three Day's Battle fighting Eastern invaders that looked much like the invaders of this day.

A well aimed cudgel flashed into Kejen's mental view. *HeavenSteel* spun away from Lorac's hands. The whole world became a kaleidoscope and *HeavenSteel* lay under a dead Easterner, thwarting Lorac's frantic search for it well after sundown.

Lorac did lose the sword!

Before Kejen could shout out the truth to the world, a new set of images flooded his mind. Unpleasant images. Images Lorac might have been inadvertently responsible for.

Before Kejen could grieve or curse, the Sui Chen Emperor of centuries past filled his view taking *HeavenSteel* with him to the East. There Kejen could feel the filth of betrayal as the Emperor was struck down by someone he instinctively knew had to be the original Great Khan of Khaizan.

Kejen almost vomited. Lorac had saved *HeavenSteel* from the Masovians only to lose it to Khaizan. His sorrow was replaced by sadness and then almost violent revulsion. The images were horrible. *HeavenSteel* was used for something it was supposed to prevent. Kejen could feel the sword's agony and anguish. Images of hundreds, thousands of people in the East dying at Khaizani hands. The road to empire was paved with skulls. Each scene was worse than the last.

Finally, Kejen saw himself pick up *HeavenSteel* and felt surrounded by soft white light that none could penetrate. There was a feeling Kejen had trouble describing. It felt like....gratitude?

The images faded and soon Kejen looked out over the bloodied ground of Dunrovin. Kejen felt exhausted, physically and emotionally as his shoulders drooped. He wanted to crawl into bed and sleep for a couple of centuries.

Kejen used *HeavenSteel* to stand up. He looked around and smiled when he saw a wary-looking Trif approaching gingerly.

"Is that...um...?" Trif began.

"Yes, it is." Kejen said weakly. "This is *HeavenSteel."*

The few dozen Northmarcher soldiers gathered around not caught up in the bloodlust of running down the fleeing Khaizani crossed themselves. It was a legend come to life!

Then Kejen fell to the ground.

An alarmed Trif ran to him and put his arms around his bloodied and battered brother.

"I am fine!" Kejen assured his brother who did not believe him for a minute. "Just a little tired and hurt. I was just in a battle, you know!"

Kejen sat up on his own and Trif decided to believe him. "Yes, I know. I was in it too."

The Northmarchers gathered around cheered and then started to wander off in several directions.

"Lorac lost *HeavenSteel.*" Kejen said, still sitting on his posterior. "He lost it and could not bear to tell anyone."

"I suspected that after the Argual." Trif joined his brother and sat down next to him. He took off his helmet and dropped it on the ground. Kejen did the same. "It is all over. The Khaizani are defeated. We won."

Trif stared at the sword in Kejen's lap for a long minute. He reached out and touched it. "There is a lot of energy in that blade!"

Kejen nodded numbly. "It was never at Rainkin Falls nor anywhere near the Argual." He turned his head and spat on the ground. "It was never in the West!"

Trif did not say anything.

"We should have listened to Sevonicus!" Kejen said bitterly. "And Kuran would be here with us!"

Now Trif did say something. "We have been through this a hundred times!" he said with an uncharacteristic shout. Even Kejen was surprised. "There was no way to know otherwise." Trif's voice returned to normal. "We were the victims of a hoax from a couple of centuries ago. That is the simple truth."

"So that is the bloody sword you have been chasing all over?" Gusaric appeared. Kejen stood up and showed it to his friend and comrade. "I saw what happened and thought it was Judgment Day."

Kejen helped his brother up. "It was for the Khaizani."

"It certainly was." Gusaric looked over the battlefield. "It certainly was."

"Is there a brigade or some people from Glossak up on the Devil's Cradle?" Kejen asked.

Gusaric looked up at the hill. "I see our flag there, I can tell you that much. Hopefully your Sea-Farer friend came out of it all right. I heard it was a pretty nasty fight on the lower peak."

"Sea-Farers?" Kejen gasped. "That has to be Jerik and his men! We have to go up there and find out if he is all right. Overdulf too if there was anyone from Glossak up there."

"First things first." Trif said in a tone of voice that would not tolerate anything that seemed remotely like an argument. "Let's get you a bit more rest first."

Kejen grumbled but Trif would not back down. "Fine, but just a little food and water and sit down on a proper chair for a few minutes but nothing more!"

Together, the three Northmarchers staggered toward the village of Dunrovin itself. The battle was over even though the rout would continue the rest of the day. The Khanate of Khaizan was finished.

Chapter 22

"Follow me!" Lif shouted from the front rank. He kept his sword strapped to his back and ran with a spear held out like a lance. Jerik's Sea-Farers formed the first three ranks. They were determined to find their Crown Prince and if the worst had indeed happened, avenge him several times over.

The phalanx ran up from out of the saddle of the Devil's Cradle and emerged onto the lower peak easily enough. No arrows hissed at them and no sword swinging Khaizani charged down the path to meet Lif's attack head on. It was strangely quiet and Overdulf was certain any Khaizani on the lower peak had left in the wake of their defeat at Donovan. Life did not seem to be taking any chances however. A surprise attack not preceded by rocks and flaming oil from the trebuchets was what the commander of the Devil's Cradle had prescribed for the day.

Someone was waiting for them at the top. Someone with a bandaged head, bloodied armor and a massive battle ax.

The Sea-Farers broke ranks much to Lif's irritation and mobbed Jerik. The Crown Prince of Warron tried to wave them off but to no avail as his men jumped on him. "Don't do that! No! Stop! I am still hurt you oafs! AWWW! That hurts!"

"Did you take this hilltop back by yourself?" Overdulf shouted to his friend from Warron after his men let him stand up again.

"Yes, all by myself." Jerik boasted.

"I bloody well say you had some help!" shouted a Northmarcher soldier in black armor. A couple of dozen more of his black outfitted comrades loudly agreed.

"How is your shoulder, Derzis?" Lif walked up to the Demon Division captain and shook hands.

"Still hurts a little but not too bad!" Derzis shrugged to show his shoulder was at least functional. "Did you think one Khaizani arrow was going to keep me out of the rest of the war? Especially so close to home?"

"Home?" Overdulf asked. "You live here at the Devil's Cradle?"

Derzis laughed. "No, no. Not here." He jerked a thumb in the direction of Dunrovin. "There! My boys and I have been hunting and fishing in this part of the Holmin since we were lads."

"And bringing maidens here to seduce as well, I will wager!" Jerik shouted.

"Lif maybe but not I." Derzis quipped. Lif looked away, his face turning red.

"No wonder you know all the hiding places around here." Overdulf watched Lif turn redder. "Hiding from outraged fathers!"

"Most of the Khaizani left when they lost the battle." Derzis returned to things military. "They did not get far. My boys were waiting for them." The wolfish grin on his face told Overdulf all he needed to know. "Your large friend was snoring under a pile of dead enemy he killed. Took a nasty bump on the head but at least he is not seeing double anymore."

"The headache is not at bad either." Jerik toasted his health with a bottle of ale some Sea-Farer was carrying into battle.

"Those still here gave up." Derzis continued. "We took the hill here back without getting any of our people hurt. A couple of Khaizani fought. Now they are dead."

"What about the ones you took prisoners?" Overdulf asked though he had a good idea what the answer was.

"What about the women and children they took hostage to take the hill?" Derzis shot back. "Can not bring them back but I made sure the people responsible were not going home."

Ovedulf nodded. He now wanted nothing more than to get away from this place called the Devil's Cradle. Somehow it seemed worse than the Argual.

"What about prisoners at Dunrovin?" Lif asked. He could see columns of captives down on the steppes.

"I guess the King will send them home." Derzis said. "I do not think he wants to be stuck feeding them all winter."

"If this were Warron, I would stick them in the mines." Jerik growled. "Get some use out of them."

"I agree with you there." Then Derzis gave an evil smile. "But imagine the shock in Khaizan when their proud army comes back defeated and disarmed. Bound to lead to some sort of civil war or strife of some kind."

"You Northmarchers are a devious lot." Jerik said with admiration. "Devious indeed."

"Proud army defeated and disarmed." Overdulf echoed. Then he kicked a dead soldier of the Khan. "And smaller. Much smaller."

"I am going home." Jerik announced.

The news of the destruction of the Greater Northern Army took two days to reach the Khaizani armies besieging Kronkus. An hour later the shocking turn of events was being discussed by disbelieving Khaizani officers in front of a large Verrentian army outside of Sudhousen. The following day the Greater Southern Army approaching Clutzen came to a sudden and ragged halt. The Verrentians as well as the Nyshissians clutching on to the far western end of their kingdom looked on as the Khaizani stood uncharacteristically indecisive and confused, not sure of what would happen next. The destruction of Nyhissia and conquest of Verrent remained in their capabilities but what would happen when the Northmarchers rampaged victoriously across the Prania River? The Khan defeated? Impossible!

The sudden lack of messengers from the north argued ominously otherwise. If a messenger did come from the north, he would not be bringing good news a Khaizani general near Kronkus thought. Odds are, he would not even be Khaizani.

There would be no Battle of Sudhousen. Nor would Clutzen be menaced. The Khaizani armies in the south turned to the east and began to pick up speed as they returned home. The following day, the defenders of Kronkus saw the siege engines that had rained death on them for weeks were burning and the iron ring of Khaizani might around the city was disintegrating.

The Nyhissians were in no mood to let the Khaizani go unscathed however. Across the oppressed nation, the Nyhissian people rose up and attacked the Khaizani when they could. There would be some small but sharp, bitter fights before the last Khaizani fled across the Blieben. Many Nyhissians endeavored to make sure there were not many Khaizani left to cross the river.

Eridoc led a hundred men through northeastern Nyhissia seeking to scour his Kingdom of any and all Khaizani remnants. A survivor of the battle in front of Kronkus that saw many of his friends killed, the cavalry major was not in a charitable mood when it came to the Khaizani invaders. The people of Nyhissia were taking to the task of hunting down Khaizani stragglers with a savage glee. The occupation had been brief but hard. It promised to be even worse had Khaizan won. Eridoc wondered if the Nyhissian people reacted this way, what would people in the East, under

Khaizani domination for far longer, would do. The probable answer even made even the battle hardened veteran shiver. Those thoughts were shoved aside as Eridoc spied a lone Khaizani rider in the distance.

The Nyhissians closed the distance quickly.

"He is mine!" Eridoc cried out. He lowered his lance and ran down the fleeing Khaizani loner. The man looked dirty, hurt and was unarmed. Eridoc did not care. He spited the man out of the saddle easily enough. The Nyhissian major ruffled through the pockets of what was once a nice robe. He found what seemed to be some sort of badge of authority.

"Five diamonds and a five fingered lizard of some kind." One of his soldiers observed. "A high ranking officer maybe?"

"A dragon." Eridoc corrected. "Yes some sort of nobility I would imagine." He dropped the badge in his pocket. It felt rather heavy. That should be worth a pretty penny to someone, Eridoc thought.

"You might want to put that pretty trinket someplace were no one can find it." The Nyhissian soldier laughed. "There are not three people within a hundred miles who would not fight you for that!"

Eridoc fixed him with a stare that told the soldier not to even think about that. There was no reason to worry though. Nyhissian soldiers were too disciplined for that sort of behavior. There would be no fighting in the ranks over anything.

Maybe I can get the major to put that up in a game of dice, the soldier thought. After all, no officer he had ever met could roll the dice well enough to hang on to something like that.

Instead of destroying the villages that rose up en masse, the Khaizani continued eastward. The surviving generals had other things in mind besides razing backwater hamlets. With the Khan dead, there was a throne back in Khaizan with only his younger, untested brother on it. It called loudly to them along with power beyond their wildest dreams. Later, History would wonder why the individual Khaizani armies did not come to blows with each other before reaching the Blieben.

King Fleston crossed the Prania into Nyhissia with a small part of the army to keep his promise to the people of Lamptra. Their Northmarcher friends did indeed return to make sure the Khaizani were swept clean of this part of Nyhissia. The Nyhissian people and scattered army detachments had all ready seen to that. Fleston continued to Kronkus to call on King Kenderick of Nyhissia. After a quick ceremony, Fleston wished the courageous Nyhissian people and their brave King (who stayed in Kronkus throughout the Khaizani siege) well and vanished into north from where he came. Even Kings became homesick now and again.

The Sparent Brigade returned home to a tumultuous hero's welcome. Kejen presented *HeavenSteel* to his father and grandfather and they decided that the faerie sword, with or without Church approval, would be taken to Gaking's Grove.

"Where it should have been to begin with!" The Bishop of Sparent loudly proclaimed to the cheering throng. Kejen was pretty sure Father Michael was behind that. Kejen was also pretty sure Father Michael would be pressuring him for a good sized donation around Christmas. At least it was for a good cause, he shrugged.

Jerik and his Sea-Farers thundered into Sparent too. Overdulf came along for the ride and held *HeavenSteel.*

"This is truly wondrous." an entranced Overdulf muttered. "No man could have made this!"

"That is the most amazing thing I have ever seen." Jerik agreed. "It shines like nothing else. If your God made that, maybe I do need to convert!"

The Bishop overheard that and pointed to the Church of Sparent, whose spire could be seen from almost anyplace in the city. Jerik hurriedly disappeared into the crowd.

"If you are looking for him, your Holiness, check the nearest tavern." Overdulf shouted.

"Are your traveling days finished?" Kejen asked with a grin.

Overdulf smiled. "I still have another trip to make. Course I have said that more than a few times." He laughed with Kejen and patted Trif on the shoulder. "The Demon Division boys want me to lead them up to the ruins of the Argual in the Spring. Offered me a lot of gold."

"Did you take their offer?"

"I told them it would cost them the gold and something else." Overdulf answered.

"What?"

"I want to be there in the barracks when they do what Trif wants them to do." Ovedulf replied. "Read out that part about what Kuran did up in that place."

"I have a general's word on that." Trif said. "The Division is going to assemble for it. The King himself will be there."

"Kuran was a good man and a good friend." Kejen said with

uncharacteristic solemness. "Even if he had a chance to do it all over again, knowing what would happen, he would still go into the Argual and destroy it."

"Gorvald and Vidron were extraordinary people too." Trif added. "We need to make sure Sevonicus hears about what happened too."

"Somehow I think he all ready knows." Overdulf said. "I am going there after I leave here. Don't worry. I am not going through the Forests of Skulka. Once is three times too many. And I do not want my children to forget who I am when I walk through the door of my own house!"

The trapper from Glossak clasped hands with Kejen and Trif and took his leave of the two brothers.

"I never realized how tall he really is." Kejen said, watching Overdulf make his way through the crowd. Then his attention was drawn to something else. "Are those two men members of the Palace Guard?" he asked Trif.

"Yes they are." Trif confirmed as if the black, gold and green shirt sleeves sticking out from under the armor did not all ready tell everyone who they were. "They seem to be coming towards us."

"Why?"

"And Kascar is leading them right to us." Trif continued. "That cannot be good."

"Seldom is." Never one to let trouble come to him when he could meet it head on, Kejen walked toward the Guards and their glowering sheppard. Trif quietly followed, somehow suspecting what was going to happen.

"Now you two have done it!" Kascar said with scarcely concealed happiness. It was an emotion one did not associate with Kascar so that in itself was rather alarming.

"Kejen Densky? Trif Densky?" Both brothers answered in the affirmative. Then Kejen noticed the man was not just an ordinary Palace Guard. It was Perlis, the Commander of the Palace Guards! Right here in Sparent! That could only mean one thing.... "The King would like to speak with you."

"Certainly." Kejen said. What else could he say?

Kascar slapped him on the back with a massive hand and nearly knocked Kejen into Perlis. "Don't keep the King waiting, boy!"

Kejen and Trif walked with the Palace Guards as Kascar made himself the head of the little procession, leading it to the Centre Park. Everyone stared at them walking by and soon most of them were following.

Criers were out, announcing King Fleston's presence. Everyone in Sparent dropped what they were doing. This was not something that happened often!

Kejen saw the King of the Northmarch standing on a platform from a distance. It really was Fleston! People filled the park as far as the eye could see and more than a few climbed into the trees for a better look. Rather belatedly, Kejen saw his mother and father standing next to the King along with Leworl. It was amazing. It seemed like some sort of dream.

Kascar mounted the platform first, gave the King a bow and scurried past him to stand next to his friend Gaking. Perlis and the other Palace Guard took their places in the ranks, leaving Kejen and Trif alone to face the King. Both brothers dropped to one knee and bowed.

"Rise, rise!" Fleston said jovially. He had to shout because the crowd began to cheer. He raised his hands for silence. He soon got it though it took a few more minutes here than it would if this were some other Kingdom. Northmarchers were, after all, Northmarchers.

Fleston's voice carried easily enough. "Once a long time ago, your grandfather saved my father up in the Ankers. Then your father fought the Masovians bravely twenty years ago. Now, another generation of your family comes forth to aid your country in its time of peril. Many, many people have told me of your adventures in seeking the sword *HeavenSteel* and your great deeds of valor against the Khaizani. I am sure the name 'Densky' will sow terror throughout the East until Judgment Day! Tignall, the commander of our armies has mentioned you. Everyone in your brigade speaks reverently of you. Even a couple of Nyhissians! And then your friend Kascar sought me out and told me even more about your greatness." Kejen sheepishly shrugged as Kascar clasped his hands together over his head. The self-proclaimed misanthrope did not seem that shy around crowds. And that crowd cheered. The King's voice rang out. "From now on, go forth not only as 'Kejen Densky' but as 'Kejen Densky, Hero of Dunrovin!' "

For once, Kejen was speechless.

Now the crowd noise was deafening.

The King waited for a few minutes until the noise subsided to something he could shout over. "Trif Densky! Quiet man of letters with the heart of a warrior and nerves as strong as iron. The world saw you and your brave archers decimate the enemy's elite. You too shall go forth as a Hero of Dunrovin!"

Trif felt the noise break over him like the waves over the rocks in the

Sea he had never been too. One day, Trif said to himself. One day soon!

The King turned his attention back to Kejen. He raised his hands for silence again. A few minutes later, the King put his hand on Kejen's head. "Your nation may need you again one day, Kejen. I order you to be given the rank of captain. As your King, I also command you to take your place in the regular army."

"Looks like your merchant days are over!" Kascar shouted with something resembling good naturedness. Or as close as he could manage at any rate. Kejen smiled at him. The town armorer had more than made up for that day in front of the Castle.

Kejen dropped to one knee and dipped his head to his King. "It will be as the King wishes."

Fleston took a step over to Trif and regarded him for a few seconds. "Trif, do you realize how truly extraordinary you are?"

Trif looked down and away before finally answering. "I do not know what you are speaking of, my King."

A peal of laughter rocked the Centre Park. After the quest for *HeavenSteel* and the Battle of Dunrovin, Trif had a completely new identity. He may have still been the quiet bookish sort but no one would ever see him that way again.

"Tell me something Trif." The King asked. "Is a military life for you?"

"I cannot say it is, my King." Trif answered. "But I will always be there if my country needs me."

"Very well." The King said. Trif dropped to one knee and Fleston placed his hand on his head. "I order you to be given the rank of lieutenant. I also command you to take your place in the army for one year to pass on your skills in archery. Keep that rank when you return to your comrades in the militia."

Trif pursed his lips. For him, it was an almost violent show of emotion. "It will be as you wish, my King."

Fleston addressed his people again. "My beloved, loyal and brave people! It is time for me to return to Northcross!"

"To see the Queen!" someone shouted.

Fleston smiled. "Yes! After all, even Kings have someone to answer too!"

Laughter rippled through the gathered citizenry.

"Until next time!" King Fleston shouted out. "May good health and happiness follow you wherever you may go!"

"May good health and happiness follow you too!" The people chorused the traditional good-bye.

"To that, let us add 'Peace'." The King concluded.

That got the loudest cheers of all.

Jerik and his Sea-Farers stayed in Sparent a couple of weeks, resting and healing. The attention lavished on them after word of their gallant defense of the Devil's Cradle spread helped speed up their recovery. The Crown Prince found time to return to the battle ground and help in the sad but necessary task of building a communal burial mound for his countrymen who died in the fight. *Locklannaigh* generally floated the deceased out to sea on a burning bier but so far from the Sea, Jerik created a new custom for gallantry on land. He made a sign and wrote in the Warronite script.

Here lie thirty gallant Locklannaigh
who died far from home giving their
lives so that all may live forever free.
The gods will honor *them!*

Trif placed a small sign on the base of the mound with the Northmarcher translation, saluted and left. Then they went back to Sparent. The emotional scars from that brutal battle would take a long time to heal but Jerik was beginning to show signs of returning to his usual boisterous drunken stereotypical Sea-Farer self, even if a bit more thoughtful than he used to be. Jerik's men passed through Sparent and left the same way they had come: With a lot of raucous laughter and loud bawdy tales. Some things simply do not change.

Kejen rode with the wagon train a few feet into the forest bordering Sparent. It was a typical Summer at midday, hot out on the steppes but cooler under the trees. The forest, with the sunlight filtering between the trees, looked more inviting than usual.

Jerik jumped out of the lead wagon and Kejen dismounted at the same time.

"Time to finally begin the long journey home!" Jerik said. "Now what is it you wanted to show me?"

Kejen took him over to three small white crosses overlooking Sparent. Each bore a name of a member of the quest that never saw *HeavenSteel* but kept the faith, unshakable to the point that entering a place as vile as the Argual did deter them. The names of Vidron and Gorvald were written in their native script in black on the white crosses.

"I had a little help on Gorvald's" Kejen said. Jerik looked around and saw Olsen's blond head disappear around a wagon.

"I did not know you could read!" Jerik laughed at his friend.

Standing a little bit apart from the other crosses, as he did in life, was the memorial to Kuran. Kejen's eyes did not well up. There was no point. If anything, Kuran would shout from Heaven to tell Kejen to stop. It was the way he would have wanted it.

"Another soldier to guard the gates of Heaven." Kejen said.

"A very good one." Jerik agreed. "And an even better man and you could not ask for a better friend. Even if I did not know him all that long."

"It says in the Bible someplace that if a man lays his life down for his friend, he will be seated next to God forever." Kejen said. "I do not know the Book or Verse. Ask a priest next time you see one."

"None where I live." Jerik snorted. "It may surprise you but we have a similar saying. 'He who lays his life down for his friends feasts in the halls of the gods forever.' "

"Have you ever considered that God and what you believe may be the same?" Kejen asked yet again. "Just different names."

Jerik shook his head. "No. And I can tell you why."

"I am listening." Kejen said.

"Because any one of my gods can drink your God under the table."

"I am not sure you can call that wisdom but I will think about it." Kejen laughed. "Actually I will have to think about what to call it!"

Jerik answered back in the Warronite dialect. "It is good to speak in my own language again. It is home for the likes of us. This trip was much more than we could have ever expected."

Kejen nodded.

"You will come up to the Sea-Faring Kingdoms in the next year or two!" The Crown Prince of Warron commanded.

"I am service for...to?.. King now" Kejen answered back in broken phrases of Jerik's birth speech.

"Spend some time up there with me and you will speak the language better than I!" Jerik jumped back into the lead wagon, waved and the caravan made its way deeper along the forest road. The wagons' creaking began to diminish into the distance, fading as the *Locklannigh* headed home to what was friendly and familiar.

Even at this distance, Kejen could hear Jerik's voice boom through the trees. "May continued good health and happiness follow you wherever you may go!"

The traditional Northmarcher good-bye sounded strange in the language of Jerik's homeland but the intentions were still the same. Nonetheless, Kejen thought, if my voice is going to echo here in the forests where I was born, it will be bloody well be in my own language.

"May good health and happiness follow you too wherever you may go!"

Dasvidonia

About the Author

Constantinos T. Hasapis (or "Haas" to those who have trouble with Greek names) lives next to Fort Bragg in Fayetteville, one place where his obnoxious Northern accent, barbaric mannerisms and Pittsburgh Steelers gear do not draw as much attention as they would in other parts of the great state of North Carolina. He graduated from The Citadel with one degree in History and another in Political Science at the same time the Soviet Union collapsed. With the war he had trained for since childhood over before it started, Haas avoided a court-martial, briefly played free safety in the Canadian Football League and decided to go into radio rather than prison. When he is not writing books, Haas lifts weights, wonders why every cat in the neighborhood likes to play in his backyard and tromps around in the forests near his home in the wee hours of the morning. Haas is currently a radio disc jockey.

www.ingramcontent.com/pod-product-compliance
Lightning Source LLC
Chambersburg PA
CBHW031105030726
47496CB00002BA/387

* 9 7 8 0 6 1 5 2 1 5 1 7 4 *